Carla Cassidy is an award-winning, *New York Times* bestselling author who has written over 170 books, including 150 for Mills & Boon. She has won the Centennial Award from Romance Writers of America. Most recently she won the 2019 Write Touch Readers Award for her Mills & Boon title *Desperate Strangers*. Carla believes the only thing better than curling up with a good book is sitting down at the computer with a good story to write.

Justine Davis lives on Puget Sound in Washington State, watching big ships and the occasional submarine go by and sharing the neighbourhood with assorted wildlife, including a pair of bald eagles, deer, a bear or two, and a tailless raccoon. In the few hours when she's not planning, plotting or writing her next book, her favourite things are photography, knitting her way through a huge yarn stash and driving her restored 1967 Corvette roadster—top down, of course. Connect with Justine on her website: justinedavis.com; on Twitter.com/justine_d_davis or on Facebook at Facebook.com/justinedaredavis.

Discover more at millsandboon.co.uk

REVENGE ON THE RANCH

CARLA CASSIDY

OPERATION PAYBACK

JUSTINE DAVIS

MILLS & BOON

First Published in Great Britain 2022
by Mills & Boon, an imprint of HarperCollins*Publishers* Ltd
1 London Bridge Street, London, SE1 9GF

www.harpercollins.co.uk

HarperCollins*Publishers*
1st Floor, Watermarque Building,
Ringsend Road, Dublin 4, Ireland

Revenge on the Ranch © 2022 Carla Bracale
Operation Payback © 2022 Janice Davis Smith

ISBN: 978-0-263-30352-0

0722

MIX
Paper from
responsible sources

FSC™ C007454

REVENGE ON THE RANCH

CARLA CASSIDY

Chapter One

Luke King raced silently across the tall prairie grass, grateful that there was very little moonlight tonight. It was just after 2:00 a.m. on a Saturday, and as he headed toward Wayne Bridges's barn, his heart beat rapidly. Every nerve and muscle in his body was taut with tension. Even the cool early-June night air couldn't chill the fire that burned in his gut.

Tonight, he was hoping to find the evidence he needed to put his father's murderer behind bars. A little over two months ago, Big John King had been shot dead in his driveway, sending Luke's entire family into a tailspin of confusion and grief.

Even now, just thinking about his father shot a shaft of deep anguish through him. His grief had turned into a ball of rage that never left his chest, a rage that threatened to consume him all the time.

He believed he knew the identity of the man who had shot his father. John King had been running for mayor of their small town of Coyote Creek, Kansas, at the time of his death. He had been running against two other men—fellow ranchers Wayne Bridges and Joe Daniels.

Everyone believed that Big John would be the next mayor, and Luke believed Wayne wanted his father dead and permanently out of the race. He had a very strong hunch that Wayne had hired one of his ranch hands to pull the trigger.

Luke jumped behind a tree as he got closer to Wayne's barn door. He could now hear the men inside, their boisterous, drunken voices and laughter drifting outside the partially open door. He'd followed them here from the Red Barn, a popular bar in town where they'd begun their drunken escapades.

He believed the actual shooter was Peter Jeffries, a particularly nasty man who was known as a champion sharpshooter and a big drunk.

Luke was betting that one night Peter, in one of his drunken hazes, would confess. He would probably boast to his fellow ranch hands about what he had done. And that's why Luke was here, eavesdropping on the drunken fools inside Wayne's barn. He'd been listening to them every Friday and Saturday night for the past two weeks, hoping to hear a drunken confession that he could take to Lane Caldwell, the chief of police.

He crept closer to the barn door and tried to pick out Peter's voice among all the others. It sounded like there were four or five men inside laughing and talking. The current topic of conversation was the women in town.

"Give me some of that Heather Jacks," one of the men said. "Have you seen the rack on that woman?"

"Oh yeah, I'd like to order her right off the menu at the café," another voice said and laughed raucously.

Heather Jacks was a pretty waitress who worked at the café. Luke had gone out with her a couple of times. She was a nice young woman, but there had been no real sparks between them. Still, it fed his anger to hear the men talk about her like she was nothing more than a piece of meat.

He'd just moved a couple of steps closer when suddenly a big hand clamped down hard on his shoulder. "What have we here?" a deep voice growled.

Luke whirled around to come face-to-face with Sly Baskum, a big, burly man who worked for Wayne. "Hey, guys," he bellowed loudly. "Looks like we've got a spy out here."

Luke backed up as several of the other men exited the barn, their faces silhouetted by the bright barn light behind them. "Well, if it isn't one of those stinking Kings," one of them said.

Luke instantly smelled danger in the air. The men were all liquored up and spoiling for a fight. "Did you lose your way, little boy?" another one of them said and poked Luke in the chest.

"Hey, man, don't touch me," Luke said as his heart beat frantically. Fight-or-flight adrenaline soared through him as the men circled around him.

"Don't touch you? Is that what you said, you little trespasser?" Sly pushed him from the back, causing him to fall into Peter Jeffries, Alan Kauffman and Jeff Tanner.

"Okay, I won't touch you… I'll punch you instead." Alan threw a fist that caught Luke in his stomach. The air whooshed out of Luke, and he heard the other men laugh uproariously.

Luke might have had a chance if the fight had been fair and one-on-one, but it was five against one, and as they began to pummel Luke, all he could do was fight back while at the same time trying to get away.

The punches came faster and faster, hitting him in his stomach and on his face and head. Pain roared through him, making him nauseous. The men all laughed, but their laughter was mean-spirited as they fed off each other's drunken energy.

An uppercut to his chin snapped his head back, and that was followed by a blow to Luke's stomach that sent him to his knees. The men then began to kick him. Why didn't they stop? They'd proved their point. He had been where he shouldn't have been.

He attempted to crawl away, but they followed him, still kicking and punching him. Boots connected over and over again with his ribs. Luke's only desire was to get away from the agonizing pain they were inflicting on him.

Nobody knew he was here…not his older brother, Johnny, or his younger brother, Caleb. Nobody was going to suddenly show up to save him, and if these men didn't stop, they were going to kill him.

He took a hard kick to the side of his head. Pain seared through him as stars danced dizzily in his brain. And then…nothing.

HE AWAKENED SLOWLY, his body screaming with pain. Luke opened his eyes and stared in bewilderment at his surroundings. How had he gotten to the hospital? Why was he in the hospital and why was he hurting so badly?

For a moment his thoughts were completely confused. Had he been in a car accident? Or had he fallen off his horse? What in the hell had happened to him?

He closed his eyes and searched his brain, and then he remembered. He'd been at the Bridges barn, and the ranch hands there had given him one hell of a beating. So, how had he gotten to the hospital? He didn't believe any one of those men had brought him here.

His ribs were killing him, and he had a headache that torched pain through him each time he moved. Those men had really done a number on him.

He was now clad in a god-awful pale blue flowered hospital gowns with an IV running from the back of his hand to a bag on a stand next to his bed. So, how in the hell had he gotten here? The question kept repeating itself in his head.

A sound in his room snapped his eyes back open. It was Carrie Carlson, one of the nurses. "Luke, oh good. You're awake," she said. "How are you feeling?"

"Like a truck ran over me, a very big truck, and it ran over me more than once. How did I get here?" He pushed the button that raised the head of his bed.

"I wasn't here when you were brought in, but it's written in the notes that Jeb Taylor found you on the side of the road just outside your ranch. You were unconscious and had obviously been beaten badly, so he brought you straight here."

Jeb Taylor was the town handyman, but at that time

on a Saturday night, he'd probably been going home from a friend's place. Luke would need to find the tall, bald man and thank him.

"Now, I need to take your vitals," Carrie said and moved closer to the side of his bed. She scanned his forehead with the thermometer, and even that slight touch caused his head to pound unmercifully.

She then wrapped a blood pressure cuff around his arm. As she pumped it up, he gazed at her. He'd seen Carrie around town, but he didn't know her personally, and he definitely hadn't really noticed before just how pretty she was.

Her long, dark hair was pulled back into a low ponytail, and her blue-violet eyes had long, thick, dark eyelashes. When she leaned closer to him, he smelled the scent of her, a fragrance of flowers mingling with mysterious spices. It was a very attractive fragrance.

In another life, in another time, he might have flirted with her. He might have even asked her out on a date. But, in this life and in this time, romance and love were the very last things he had on his mind.

The only thing that ticked him off about last night was he now knew he wouldn't be able to eavesdrop at that barn and on those men anymore. He'd been busted, and there was no way he'd be able to sneak back there to listen to them again.

"I'm happy to give you some good news. I have a little pain relief to give you," she said with a smile. She had a very nice smile.

"I'll take it," Luke replied.

"I'm just going to administer it into your IV. You

should feel some relief fairly quickly." She put the medicine in and then stepped back from the bed. "Is there anything I can do for you, Luke?"

Her gaze was soft, sympathetic, and once again he noticed how pretty she looked in the purple scrubs that turned her eyes more violet than blue.

"No, I'm good," he half growled, hating to be in such a state of weakness in front of anyone else.

"Dr. Reeves will be in to speak to you later."

He half nodded and then closed his eyes. True to what Carrie had said, within minutes he felt a softening of the jagged pain he'd awakened with.

He must have fallen asleep, for he jerked awake once again when he heard somebody entering his room. It was an older woman he didn't know, and she pushed a cart before her.

"How about some breakfast, handsome?" She smiled widely and grabbed a tray from the cart. "You've got scrambled eggs with crispy bacon, some toast and coffee. There's also grape jelly, and cream and sugar if you want it." She set the tray on the table that would slide across the bed.

"Thank you, ma'am," he said, surprised to realize that despite everything hurting, he had an appetite.

"You need anything else, handsome, you just press that little button and ask for Wanda. Wanda, that's me. Everyone here knows Wanda." She grinned at him again. "Now, get to eating while it's all hot."

The moment Wanda left his room, he took the lid off the coffee cup and took a sip, grateful that it was strong and good. He'd just finished cleaning his plate when Chief of Police Lane Caldwell walked into the room along with Luke's older brother, Johnny.

"I hope the other guy looks worse than you, but I'm not sure that's possible," Johnny said and sat in the chair next to the hospital bed. "So, what happened to you?"

Luke frowned. "I guess I got the hell beat out of me."

"Who did this to you, Luke?" Lane asked. He stood at the foot of the bed, a deeply concerned look on his face. Luke knew Lane was in his fifties, but in the last month or so, he seemed to have aged ten years. Apparently, the unsolved murder of Big John King, along with other cases he had, weighed heavily on him.

"How did you two even know I was here?" Luke asked curiously.

"Dr. Holloway called me when you were brought in late last night. He wouldn't allow me to speak to you then. I'm the one who called Johnny this morning to let him know you were here," Lane explained. "Now, want to tell me who did this to you, Luke?"

Luke winced as he changed positions in the bed. "It doesn't really matter who did it."

Johnny leaned forward in his chair. "Luke, it does matter. Whoever did this to you should face some criminal charges."

Luke laughed, instantly regretting it as his ribs protested with a searing pain. "Since when do we press charges for a fistfight around here? Besides, what happened was my own fault, and I take full responsibility for it. Lane, all I need from you is to find my father's murderer."

Luke hadn't really told Lane too much concerning his suspicions about Peter Jeffries. He didn't want Peter to be warned that he was under suspicion. Otherwise, Luke might not be able to get the evidence he needed.

"Are you sure you don't want to tell me who did this to you?" Lane asked with concern.

"I'm positive," Luke replied firmly.

"Okay, then I guess I'll just get out of here," Lane said.

"Now, tell me what really happened," Johnny said the moment Lane had left the room.

"There's nothing to tell. Just for your information, it was more than one man beating on me, and it happened because I was in the wrong place at the wrong time. And that's all I intend to say about the matter."

Johnny narrowed his eyes as he gazed at Luke. "Luke, you've got to stop. I've told you before, leave the investigation to Lane."

"Yeah, because he's doing such a good job," Luke replied bitterly. "It's been a little over two months since somebody shot our father, and still nobody is under arrest. Hell, Lane doesn't even have any suspects."

"Luke, you've got to leave it alone. I don't know where you were last night or what you were doing, but you could have been killed. Do you hear me? You could have been killed."

"Okay, well, I wasn't," Luke replied.

"This time you weren't. Dammit, Luke, I need you on

the ranch. You're supposed to be coming up with a plan for us to move forward with a horse-breeding program."

"I'll get to it. I've been working the ranch every day. What I do in my spare time is nobody's business," Luke snapped.

"Dammit, Luke, do you hear the rage in your voice?" Johnny asked. "You're being eaten alive by it."

"I'm done talking." Luke lowered the head of his bed and closed his eyes. He didn't want his brother to tell him what to do or how to think. Of course, Luke had a lot of rage inside him. Somebody had killed his father, and even getting the hell beaten out of him wouldn't stop Luke on his mission to get the person responsible behind bars.

CARRIE CARLSON LEFT the house she rented with fellow nurse and her good friend Emily Timmons. She got into her car, pulled out of the driveway and then headed down the tree-lined street toward the main drag.

It was a beautiful early-summer afternoon. The trees were filled with big fat leaves, and the grass had all turned a lush green after the long winter. It all felt like new beginnings, and in keeping with that, Carrie was about to do the most brazen, most forward thing she'd ever done in her life. She was going to check on a former patient at his home. More specifically, she was going to check on the man she'd had a crush on forever, Luke King.

He'd been released from the hospital two days before, after being diagnosed with a concussion, three fractured ribs and bruised kidneys. He'd also had various other contusions, including a rather nasty bruise on his lower jaw.

Before his father's death, Luke had had a reputation as a ladies' man. With his rich dark hair, beautiful blue eyes and handsomely sculpted features, he'd never had to beg for a date.

He also had wonderfully broad shoulders, slim hips and long legs. Physically he was the whole package. But as far as she knew, he hadn't dated anyone since his father's murder. And in a small town like Coyote Creek, where gossip ran rampant, she would have known.

She'd always hoped he would ask her out. He was friendly when they ran into each other in town, but he never seemed to see her as a woman to potentially date. Still, since his father's death, Carrie hadn't been able to get him out of her head, especially since he'd left the hospital pretty banged up.

She turned onto the two-lane road that would take her out to the King place. She rolled down her window and breathed in the outside air. It smelled like rich earth and sweet grass and cattle.

This was ranching country, and Big John King had left behind an empire. The Kings were one of the most successful operations in the state. With Big John dead, the bulk of the responsibility for the ranching would now fall on Johnny and Luke.

She wasn't sure what role the younger brother, Caleb, or their sister, Ashley, would have in the day-to-day running of the ranch. From the gossip she'd heard around town, Caleb was a self-proclaimed artist who drank too much. She knew Ashley owned a store in town, Bling and Things, that sold items for the home and a few nice clothes.

As she turned onto the long driveway that would eventually lead to Luke's home, her stomach clenched with nervous energy. She told herself all she wanted to do was check in with him and see how he was doing physically.

But the truth of the matter was she just wanted to see him, and she was hoping he might suddenly see her as a potential woman to date. She knew it was probably a stupid idea, but she was doing it anyway.

She drove past the big King family house. It was a huge, rambling ranch. She had never been inside it before, but she'd heard it was absolutely beautiful. She couldn't help but think about poor Margaret King, who had not only recently gone through a bout with breast cancer but had then lost her husband in an instant to violence. The rumor in town was that she was absolutely broken.

All the King children lived on the ranch except Ashley, who had an apartment above her store. She'd had a house in town, but about a month ago she had sold it and made the move to her store.

The next house she passed was Johnny's. Although it was smaller than the big house, it was an attractive place. Her fingers tightened on the steering wheel as once again an attack of nerves fluttered through her.

Finally, she came to Luke's house. Tucked in among tall trees and with a pond nearby, the place looked like an enchanted cabin in the woods. Two wooden chairs with bright red pillows sat on one side of the covered porch, with a small table in between them.

She pulled up in front of it and parked. She'd worn jeans and a sleeveless pink blouse, knowing that it was a good color on her. She'd left her long hair loose and flowing around her shoulders. She'd also applied a little more makeup than she usually wore on a workday.

She turned off her engine and sat for just a few moments. She drew deep breaths in an effort to calm her nerves and then got out. It was two o'clock on a Tuesday afternoon. For all she knew, Luke was someplace on the ranch working—something the doctor had specifically told him not to do for at least a week to ten days.

Drawing another deep breath, she walked up to the front door and knocked. After a moment the door opened and Luke looked at her in surprise. "Carrie, what are you doing here?"

"I just thought I'd come by and see how you were getting along," she replied. Clad in a pair of worn jeans and with a white T-shirt stretching taut across his broad shoulders, he looked positively hunky. Even the purple bruise darkening his lower jaw couldn't detract from his handsomeness.

"Come on in," he said and opened the door wider to allow her entry.

As she swept past him, she caught the scent of minty soap mingling with a woodsy cologne emanating from him. It was definitely a pleasant scent. Once they were both inside, he gestured her toward a brown leather sofa, and he sat in a brown recliner facing her. Decorated in rich earth tones, the living room felt warm and inviting. There was a fireplace on one wall, and she could easily envision it filled with burning logs to warm a wintry night.

"Your home is really nice," she said.

"Thanks. I like it here."

"So, how are you feeling?" she asked.

"I'm feeling just fine."

She eyed him dubiously. "Luke, I know all the injuries you suffered. There's no way you're feeling just fine after two days."

He offered her a rueful grin. "Okay, I'm still hurting a bit, but I'll live."

Oh Lordy, when he smiled like that, he caused a warmth to pool in her lower belly. "Have you had any nausea or vomiting since you've been home?" she asked, momentarily putting on her nurse's hat.

"No, nothing like that. My only complaint is that I'm still pretty sore, especially in my ribs."

"Then you need to listen to your body and take it easy," she replied. "You went through a trauma, being beaten up like that, and the doctor told you not to do anything strenuous for at least a week."

"Trust me, I know, and I haven't done anything since I've been home. Uh…can I get you something to drink? Maybe a soda or some tea?" he asked.

"No, thanks, I'm fine."

For the next few minutes, they visited about the weather and things that were happening in town. The conversation flowed surprisingly easily, even though on some level she couldn't quite believe she was actually sitting in Luke King's living room and talking to him.

"I should get out of here and let you rest. I really just wanted to stop by and see if you were doing okay," she said after about half an hour of visiting. She certainly didn't want to overstay her welcome.

His features pulled into a frown. "I won't be okay until the man who murdered my father is behind bars."

"Luke, I'm so sorry for your loss," she replied with all the compassion she had for him and his family. "I can't imagine the pain you've all been in."

"Thanks. I think he was murdered over a stupid mayoral seat. I think he was murdered because Wayne Bridges wanted him out of the way before the election. If he hadn't been killed, Dad would have definitely become the next mayor, and that was something Wayne wanted desperately." He frowned. "Sorry, I shouldn't be talking about all this with you."

"Luke, you can talk to me about anything at all. I consider this conversation and any other ones we might have between us to be confidential, and I would never betray your confidence."

His blue eyes gazed into hers intently for several long minutes. "Do you know Peter Jeffries?"

"I know him as a nasty man who is usually drunk and obnoxious at the Red Barn," she replied. "Why?"

He held her gaze once again for several long moments before replying. "I believe he's the man who shot my father. I think Wayne hired him to do the job." He swiped a hand down his face. "God, I've never said that aloud to anyone."

Carrie slowly digested what he had just told her. "So, did you fight with him? Is that what happened to you?"

"Him and four other men. I knew the men sometimes partied in Wayne's barn after spending the evening at the Red Barn. So, for the last two weekends, I've been eavesdropping outside Wayne's barn door to see if Peter would get drunk enough to admit to the other men that he pulled the trigger. That night they caught me outside their barn."

"Oh, Luke, they could have killed you," Carrie replied fervently.

He sat up straighter in the chair. "I don't care," he said roughly. "I need to get the proof that will put my father's killer in prison. It's been a little over two months, and Lane hasn't done anything. He has absolutely no clues at all. This is something I need to do. I know sooner or later Peter will get drunk enough to boast about what he did. I just need to be there when he does."

He slumped back, as if exhausted by his short diatribe. Carrie's mind continued to whirl with everything he'd said. "You know, Peter drinks at the Red Barn almost every night of the week."

"Yeah, but I can't exactly sit next to him every time he's there. I would be really conspicuous."

"Maybe you wouldn't be as conspicuous if you were on a date," she replied. She was probably being stupid in offering what she was about to offer. He'd probably laugh in her face, but that didn't stop her from voicing what she was thinking.

"Luke, I'm starting a two-week vacation tomorrow.

I would be available to go with you to the Red Barn anytime Peter is there. We could pretend we're dating, and we could try to sit as close to Peter as possible."

He didn't laugh at her. Instead, he straightened up once again and eyed her with interest. "That just might work," he said slowly. "Nobody would look sideways at us if we were on a date. Are you sure you really want to do this for me?"

"If it helps put a murderer behind bars, then absolutely, I'm in," she replied.

"I should probably tell you something else. It might be possible another person is responsible for my father's death." His forehead creased in another deep frown. "It's slightly possible my brother Caleb shot my father."

Carrie couldn't help the gasp of shock that escaped her. "What makes you think that?" she finally asked.

"He and Dad had a big fight the night before, and I don't know how much you listen to gossip, but Caleb isn't always in a rational frame of mind." The words seemed to come out of him slowly...painfully.

Once again, he stared at her in open speculation. "Maybe while we're pretending to date, you could hang out around here and see if you can get close to Caleb, maybe get him to confide in you."

"I guess I could try to do that," she replied. "I'll do whatever I can to help you, Luke."

"Why? Why would you agree to any of this?"

The question caught her by surprise. She couldn't very well tell him she was agreeing because she had a wild crush on him and this would be a way to spend time with him.

"I'm a nurse, Luke. I like to help people out, and it sounds like you need help," she finally replied.

"I don't know why I told you all this."

"Maybe it was a burden you needed to share and I just happened to come along at the right time."

"You're very easy to talk to, Carrie." He smiled at her once again, and again that flutter of sweet heat swept through her.

"Thanks, Luke," she replied. "And now I'd better get out of here and let you rest." She stood from the sofa, and at the same time he rose from his chair to walk her to the door.

"So, how about you come by here tomorrow right after dinner, say, around six? You can hang out here for a while and then we can head to the Red Barn," he said. His eyes held a brightness they hadn't had when she'd first arrived.

"I can do that," she agreed.

When they reached his front door, he held out a hand to her. She reached out her hand, and he clasped it tightly. "Then we're partners, right?" he asked.

"Definitely," she replied.

"And we can't tell anyone about the true intent of us being together," he added.

"That will be our secret. I told you that you can trust me, Luke."

Once again, his gaze held hers for several long moments. "I... I've needed somebody I can talk to...somebody to be on my side."

"I'm on your side, Luke, and hopefully we can get the creep who killed your father behind bars," she replied.

It was only a few minutes later, when she was on the drive back to her own place, that she thought about what she'd just agreed to. She must have been out of her mind to agree to this scheme. It could be a dangerous mission they'd set forward for themselves.

But she wasn't sorry. She had just set in motion a plan to spend lots of time with Luke. She was just hoping that in the process, he would not only see her as a partner in crime solving, but maybe also as a desirable woman he needed in his life.

Chapter Two

It was one of the longest days of Luke's life. He wasn't used to just sitting around his house and doing nothing, but he was taking the doctor's orders seriously, because his body told him he needed to take it easy. Another couple of days and he should be ready to get back to work on the ranch...at least, that's what he hoped.

Today the hours couldn't move fast enough until the time Carrie would arrive. He still couldn't quite believe she was really into the plan they'd come up with. He was definitely eager to see if it worked the way he wanted.

He'd never really noticed Carrie before. Oh, he'd run into her at different places in town, but he'd never really *noticed* her like he had when she'd stopped by yesterday. He wasn't sure why.

She'd looked so pretty, with her dark hair loose around her shoulders and wearing a pink blouse and jeans that revealed a slender waist, slim hips and medium-size breasts. She had a heart-shaped face with beautiful violet-blue eyes and lush lips that looked very kissable.

He wondered if he would have found her as attractive if she hadn't offered to help him expose his father's murderer. Still, it didn't matter if he found her wildly attractive or not—there was absolutely no room in his heart for anything resembling romance.

The only thing that burned in his heart was the absolute need for revenge. He had to catch his father's killer to somehow prove to Big John that he'd been worthy of his love. But that wasn't a thought he explored too deeply. He just wanted his father's killer behind bars.

It was a few minutes after four when a knock fell on his door. He answered to see his brother Johnny and his fiancée, Chelsea Black, standing on his porch. It hadn't been that long ago that Chelsea's best friend had tried to kill her. Thankfully she hadn't succeeded, and Chelsea was safe and sound today, with her "friend" awaiting trial for attempted murder.

"Hey, we were just going to the big house for dinner and were wondering if you were coming, too," Johnny now said.

Since their father's death, whenever possible the siblings tried to eat dinner with their mother. But lately Luke hadn't been going. It ticked him off too badly to sit and eat at the long dining table, staring at the empty chair where his father used to sit.

"Luke, come with us," Chelsea urged. "It's been a while since you've eaten with all of us, and it would make your mom happy if you came."

Chelsea's mother, Stella Black, owned the ranch next to the Kings'. Chelsea had always seemed like a younger sister to Luke, and very soon she was going to officially be his sister-in-law. She already lived with Johnny, and they had loved each other forever. They were engaged but hadn't set a wedding date yet.

When John King had been murdered, Chelsea's mother had thrown her hat into the mayoral ring, running on the same platform Luke's father had run on. Last week Stella had won the election and was now the newly elected mayor of the small town of Coyote Creek.

"Tell her I'm sorry, but I can't tonight," Luke said. "I have a guest coming by soon, and she and I have plans to hang out together."

One of Johnny's dark brows rose. "She? She who?"

"Carrie Carlson," Luke replied. "She came out here yesterday to see how I was getting along, and one thing led to another and I asked her to come hang out and then later to go to the Red Barn with me."

"From what I hear, she's a nice person," Johnny said.

"Yes, she is," Chelsea added. "She's come into Ashley's store before. Just don't go breaking her heart."

"That's certainly not my intention," Luke replied with a dry laugh.

"That's never your intention, but you've left a trail of broken hearts behind you," Chelsea said chidingly.

Luke wanted to tell them it wasn't like that between him and Carrie. They were merely partners, not potential lovers, but he couldn't very well say that and keep his cover. Johnny would give him absolute hell if he knew what Luke was doing, and Luke wasn't in the head space to hear another lecture from his older brother.

"Anyway, tell Mom I said hi and I'll see her some-time tomorrow," Luke said.

He breathed a sigh of relief when they left. He didn't appreciate Chelsea making it sound like he broke hearts on purpose. He never intentionally meant to hurt any woman. He usually went out with a woman several times, and if no real spark happened with her, he then moved on. What else was he supposed to do? But all that was in his past now. He would be "dating" Carrie now, but it was only for pretend. This evening, with Carrie's help, he would truly begin his quest to get his father's murderer once and for all.

At five, Luke took a hot shower, wincing as the water sprayed against his bruised ribs. After shower-ing he changed into a clean pair of jeans and a royal blue polo shirt. He slapped on some cologne and then stared at himself in the mirror over the sink.

The bruise on his chin was beginning to turn an ugly light purple and yellow, but at least that meant it was healing. Still, it ticked him off every time he saw it. It had been such an unfair fight. He turned away from the mirror and returned to his recliner to wait for Carrie.

At precisely six o'clock a knock sounded on the door. Luke got up to answer, but before he did, a wave of nervousness tightened his gut. Was this a stupid idea? The last thing he wanted to do was put Carrie in any kind of danger. But what kind of danger could occur with them just having a drink at the Red Barn?

Before he could change his mind, he opened the door. "Hi, Carrie." She looked pretty in tight jeans and a purple blouse that hugged her body and turned her blue eyes to a deep, beautiful violet.

"Hi, Lucas." She offered him a warm smile.

He stepped out on the porch with her. "You look really nice."

"Thanks, so do you," she replied.

"Thanks right back. I thought maybe I'd show you around the place, maybe introduce you to my brothers if we run into them."

"That sounds great," she said agreeably.

They left the porch and began walking side by side up the lane that led to most all the other buildings on the property. "Did you have a good day?" she asked.

"It was all right," he replied. "I've definitely learned over the last few days that I'm not a man who likes to sit around and do nothing."

She flashed him another bright smile. "Luke, you weren't sitting around and doing nothing. You were healing, and that takes a lot of work."

He laughed. "It sure didn't feel like a lot of work." An awkward silence ensued as they continued up the lane. "Uh…nice evening," he finally said. The air still retained the warmth of the day and smelled of green grass and the various wildflowers that grew along the side of the lane.

"It's a beautiful evening," she agreed. "Early summer is absolutely my favorite time of year. I love seeing everything come alive after winter. I love the warm days and cool nights. What about you? What season do you like most?"

He frowned thoughtfully. "Definitely fall for me. I

love the leaves all turning different colors. I like cool nights when I can burn a fire in my fireplace." He laughed. "I don't think anyone has ever asked me what season I like before."

"Then you must be hanging out with the wrong crowd," she said with a teasing grin.

"Maybe so," he replied. "This is my brother Johnny's place," he said as they approached the next house. "I'd introduce you to him, but he and his fiancée, Chelsea Black, are at the big house eating dinner. I'll take you to the barn and we might find Caleb there. He's living in one of the rooms set up for our ranch hands, and he rarely goes to dinner with the family."

"I've seen him around town before, but I've never been introduced to him. I know you want me to try to make friends with him, so meeting him is an important first step in the process."

"He can be...uh...strange sometimes," Luke replied. Luke knew his brother was drinking too much and was smoking weed. However, he didn't know what else his brother might be doing or taking, and that worried him.

"That's okay. Everyone can be a bit strange at times," she replied.

So far, he was finding Carrie remarkably easy to get along with, which was good, since he was planning on spending a lot of time with her.

"Wasn't today your first day of vacation?" he asked, remembering something she'd said the evening before.

"It was," she replied as they headed toward the large barn in the distance.

"What did you do to celebrate?"

"The first thing I did was slept in sinfully late, and then I cooked myself a good breakfast. I then bee-lined for the sofa and watched television for most of the afternoon. I'll admit it was a lazy, completely un-productive day."

Luke laughed. "So, we both had relatively unpro-ductive days today."

They reached the barn and walked inside. To the left were hay bales stacked almost to the ceiling. To the right was a wooden staircase leading up to the sec-ond floor, where the other rooms for the ranch hands were located, and immediately in front of them was a wooden door.

"Caleb is living here right now," he said and then knocked on the door.

To his surprise, Caleb answered almost immedi-ately. "Hey, Luke. What's up?" He was clad in jeans and a white T-shirt that was spattered with paint in a variety of colors, and his long black hair, tied back at the nape of his neck, looked like it could use a good washing.

Luke was grateful that although Caleb smelled like beer, he didn't appear to be drunk or high...yet. "I thought I'd stop by to introduce you to my new friend Carrie Carlson."

"Hi, Caleb. It's very nice to meet you," she said.

"Yeah, nice to meet you, too," Caleb replied.

"I hear you're an artist. Do you paint in oils?" she asked.

Caleb's pale blue eyes lit up a bit, and he looked at her with more interest. "Yeah, definitely in oils."

"What about watercolors? Do you ever paint with them?" she asked.

"Nah, watercolors are for artists who want to paint in vague, nebulous colors and figures. I like the boldness of oil much better." He looked at her curiously. "Are you an artist, too?"

"Oh no, nothing like that," she said with a laugh. "But I do like art. I'd love to see some of your work sometime."

Caleb frowned. "I don't know about that. I'm not ready for him or Johnny to see my work yet." He pointed a finger at Luke.

Carrie laughed again. "Caleb, I don't have to share with them what you share with me. Anyway, I'm just putting it out there that I would love to see your work."

Caleb stared at her for a long moment. "I'll think about it," he finally said.

"Well, it was nice to meet you," Carrie said.

"You'll be seeing a lot of her around here," Luke said, and he reached out to hold Carrie's hand. Her fingers were warm, her skin surprisingly soft, and even as they walked away from the barn, he found himself oddly reluctant to let go.

"How did I do?" she asked softly once they had walked onward from the barn.

"You did excellent," he replied. "You didn't push him too hard, and that bit about not sharing with me whatever he shares with you was perfect."

They turned around and headed back toward his place. "So, I threw out some bait—let's just hope he takes it," Carrie said. "Hopefully not only will he show me his paintings, but with time he'll confide in me about his feelings and dealings with your father."

"And now we move on to the next phase of our operation," he said, finally releasing her hand as they reached his place. "In about an hour or so we'll head to the Red Barn, and hopefully Jeffries will be there, too."

Luke's heart clenched tight as he thought of the man he believed killed his father. Thanks to Carrie, for the first time since his father's murder, he believed he had a real shot at overhearing Jeffries saying something incriminating.

And it didn't hurt that Carrie was pleasing to the eyes and easy to talk to. So far this felt like a partnership made in heaven, but if there was anything Luke had learned over the past couple of months, it was that hopes and plans and dreams could be stolen away in the blink of an eye...in two shots from a gun. And heaven could quickly become a horrifying hell.

CARRIE HAD ALWAYS fantasized about spending time with Luke. Now her fantasies were coming true, but with one difference. In her fantasies he had desperately wanted to spend time with her; in her dreams he'd been totally smitten with her.

She was acutely aware right now that the only reason he was spending time with her was with the hopes of catching his father's killer. He saw her as a partner in his quest, but he certainly didn't see her as a desirable woman he wanted in his life...yet.

But to be honest, she wasn't sure if she really wanted to be desired by him. Certainly, she'd entertained thoughts of lust where he was concerned in the past, but her thoughts had been based solely on a kind of schoolgirl crush.

She would have to get to know him better, although right now it was so far, so good. Her body had even tingled when he'd taken hold of her hand, even though she knew he was only playing a role of pretend boyfriend.

After being introduced to Caleb, they had returned to Luke's place and talked about their plans for the night. Luke knew Peter Jeffries drove a dark blue pickup truck, and he also knew the plate number.

At eight o'clock they got into Luke's truck to head to the Red Barn. "If Jeffries is already there, then we go inside and get the closest table we can to his," Luke said. "And if he isn't there, then we wait in the truck until he gets there."

"Sounds like a good plan to me," she replied. "I know he seems to be at the Red Barn almost every night. At least, he's always been there when I've gone there with friends."

"I still can't believe you're doing this for me, Carrie." He cast her a quick sideways glance. "I'll never be able to thank you enough."

"You don't have to thank me. I'm just glad I can help you in this way." Darkness had fallen outside, making it more difficult for her to see his features.

"I… I've just felt pretty alone in all this. Nobody else feels the driving need that I feel to put my father's killer behind bars. It eats at me all the time. I can't think of anything else. Johnny keeps telling me to let

it go, to wait for Lane to do his job, but I've been waiting for that and nothing has happened."

She saw his hands tighten on the steering wheel.
"Sorry, I didn't mean to go off like that," he said.

"Don't apologize for speaking your feelings," she
replied. She reached out and touched his forearm. "I
hope this works, Luke. I really hope you get what you
need and can find some peace."

"I won't have any peace as long as the killer is out
there walking free," he replied. "He needs to pay for
what he did. It's important I do this for my dad, to
prove…" He let his voice drift off, making her wonder
what he needed to prove—and to whom.

The moon was bright overhead as he pulled into
the parking lot of the Red Barn. The lot was lit with
several lights, and even though it was a weeknight, it
was half-filled with vehicles, including Peter Jeffries's
pickup truck.

The bar/dance hall was housed in a large, bright
red barnlike structure. Neon signs advertising various brews flashed from all the windows. Luke threw
an arm around her shoulders as they headed for the
front door.

Oh, he smelled so good, and she fit so neatly against
his side. The thought flittered through her head but
was quickly replaced by the soberness of what they
wanted to accomplish.

Luke dropped his arm from around her as they
walked into the bar. Peanut shells crunched underfoot,
and the air was heavy with the scents of booze, greasy

bar food and a combination of different colognes and perfumes, with an underlying touch of perspiration.

The music from overhead wasn't as loud as it usually was on the weekends. Still, several couples were on the dance floor, dancing to the country-western tune that played.

Peter and several other men sat at a round table near the dance floor. Thankfully there was an empty two-top right next to where they sat. She and Luke made their way to that table.

"Whoa, look who it is…the loser Luke King," Peter said, and the other three men at his table laughed as if he'd said something particularly brilliant.

Peter was a thin man with short, dark hair and equally dark eyes. He had a wide forehead, a small nose and lips that were usually turned up in a sneer. Every time Carrie and her friends came here, Peter and his band of creeps sniffed around them like dogs in heat. As far as Carrie was concerned, they were all disgusting.

"Hey, I'm not looking for any trouble here. I just want to enjoy a few drinks with Carrie," Luke replied evenly.

"Knock yourself out, lover boy," Peter said. Luke took the chair facing their table, and Carrie took the seat with her back to the men. "Or maybe you'd prefer if we knocked you out," Peter added. Once again, the rest of the men at his table all guffawed.

"I'd like to punch him in his smug little face," Luke said, his voice a low burn of barely suppressed rage.

"That won't accomplish what you want," she replied.

"Luke." She reached out and touched his hand, hoping to reach him through his obvious anger.

He visibly drew in a deep breath. "What can I get you to drink?" he finally asked, his voice more even and measured.

"A beer is fine."

He raised one of his dark brows. "Are you sure? I would have pegged you as a froufrou kind of drinker."

She laughed. "You must have me confused with somebody else. I'm just a down-home kind of girl who enjoys a cold beer now and then."

"Then the woman shall have a beer. I'll be right back." He got up from the table and headed for the bar located against the back wall.

The minute he left, Carrie leaned back to see if she could catch any of the conversation at Peter's table. It was fairly easy to hear them. She knew from other nights that the drunker Peter got, the louder he became.

Right now, they were talking about women. They disgusted her with their sexist, filthy words about various women and their body parts. They were boasting about their conquests and whom they wanted to "nail" next. They were definitely all repulsive.

She watched Luke coming back to the table through the small crowd. Even if they weren't romantic partners, she hoped he got what he needed to get to a place of peace.

As a nurse, Carrie knew just how bad it was to stress and harbor the kind of anger, the kind of rage that radiated out from Luke. She'd seen firsthand how negatively those kinds of emotions could affect the entire body, and that's the last thing she would wish on anybody.

Still, she couldn't help but notice how utterly hunky he looked tonight. The royal blue polo did amazing things to his eyes. With his rich black hair and those beautiful eyes, he was definitely a piece of eye candy.

He sat back at the table, placed a beer in front of her and then leaned closer to her. "Anything interesting?" he asked.

"Not a thing," she replied.

"I didn't even ask you if you wanted something from the kitchen. Would you like something?"

"No, thanks." She took a sip of her beer and smiled at him. "I'm good for now."

He moved his chair so he was no longer sitting across from her but rather next to her. It would allow him to better hear the conversations going on at the other table.

"So, how did you get into nursing?" he asked.

"When I was thirteen, my mother was diagnosed with stage-four liver cancer. My father and I spent a lot of time in the hospital with her before she finally passed away. I saw how caring the nurses were toward my mother, how patient and kind they were to me and my dad. I knew immediately that I wanted to be one of those caring nurses for other people."

"I'm sorry. I didn't know about your mother," he said.

She shrugged. "There's no reason you should have known. Anyway, that's why I became a nurse. I have a genuine desire to help people who are ill."

"You were so young to lose your mother," he said.

She nodded. "For the first year after she was gone, I felt utterly lost without her." For just a moment she remembered the grief, the despair she had gone through when her mother passed away. "Thankfully I had a warm, loving father to help me through my grief."

"Is your father still alive?" Luke asked.

"He is." She smiled at thoughts of her father, who was her biggest cheerleader and advocate in life. "He works as a medical equipment salesman and travels the four-state area."

"Do you live at home with him?" he asked.

"No, I rent a house in town with Emily Timmons. Do you know her?" she asked.

"She's a nurse, too, right?"

"Right," Carrie replied.

"Yeah, I've seen her around town, but I don't really know her," he replied.

"She works in Dr. Morris's office and I work in Dr. Holloway's office, and we both work at the hospital whenever we get called in. We get along great, and she's an awesome roommate."

"That's nice," he replied.

They sipped their beers in silence for several moments, both of them listening to the conversation at the table behind them. The men were now talking about their work on the Bridges ranch.

"What do you like to do in your spare time?" Luke asked. She understood other women's attraction to Luke. Aside from his obvious physical attributes, when he gazed at her so intently, he made her feel as if she was the single most important person in the entire world. It was a heady quality for a man to possess.

There was no question he had a reputation as a heartbreaker. Carrie wasn't looking to get her heart broken by him. True, she'd entertained a crush on him for a while, but really, she just wanted to get to know him better.

"Carrie?"

Her face warmed as she realized she'd been staring at him and deep in her own thoughts. "I like riding horseback and having picnics. I enjoy reading and watching mysteries on television." She smiled. "And I also enjoy checking up with former patients to see how they're getting along."

He grinned at her. "Thank goodness for that last part. So, do you own a horse?"

"Sadly, no. When I want to ride, I go to Dickerson's ranch and rent one of his horses for an hour or two," she replied.

"Dickerson only owns a bunch of poor old nags. You'll have to come out one day and ride one of our horses. We've got a couple of good, sweet-natured ones."

"I'd love that," she replied.

"Then we'll definitely plan a day for that," he replied.

To her dismay, Peter and his friends got up from their table and headed for the exit. Luke watched them go with darkened eyes. "Well, this was a bust," he said.

"Luke, I have a feeling this is going to be more of a marathon than a sprint," she replied.

He sighed. "Yeah, I know. I was just hoping…" His voice trailed off.

"We'll catch him on another night," she said. "If he really fired the gun that killed your father, then eventually I believe he will get drunk enough, stupid enough to say something about it, and we'll be here to hear him."

"You're right. At least now we can relax and enjoy the last of our beers." She felt some of his tension ebb away.

"So, what do you enjoy doing in your spare time?" she asked.

"Lately I haven't enjoyed doing much of anything." He took a drink of his beer and then continued, "I used to enjoy a leisurely ride through the pastures in the evenings. I also like to do a little fishing in the pond next to my place. There are some fairly big catfish and crappie in there."

"That sounds like fun," she said, thinking about sitting next to him on the wooden dock she'd seen extending out over the pond. The sun would be warm on their shoulders, and his attractive scent would wrap around her.

"Most of the women in town don't think fishing is much fun," he said.

"And you would know that because you've dated most of the women in town," she said teasingly.

He looked at her in surprise and then laughed. "Okay, I'll admit I've dated quite a bit. What about you? What's your dating history?"

"I dated Rory Howard for a while, but we broke up a little over a year ago."

"I know him. He seems like a nice guy. Why did the two of you break up?" Luke asked.

"We wanted different things in life. Eventually I want a family, and Rory didn't know if he wanted children. He was still big on partying and hanging out with his friends. Anyway, the breakup was amicable. Since then, I've dated a few other guys, but nobody seriously."

"So, I'm not taking you away from any other man right now," he said.

She laughed. "Definitely not. If I had a boyfriend, I wouldn't have agreed to all of this." She took the last drink of her beer.

"And I'm still very grateful to you." He drained the last of his bottle of beer. "Are you ready to get out of here?"

"Ready when you are," she replied. It wasn't like this was a real date, where they might enjoy a second drink or hit the dance floor. The reason they were here had left, so there was really no reason for them to remain.

"Then let's call it a night." He stood from the table, and she did as well.

He took her arm and led her toward the exit. She liked him. Even though it was obvious he held a lot of anger inside him, he had said and done nothing to change the little crush she had on him.

They had just stepped out into the cool night air

when the boom of a gun split the air. A bullet whizzed by within inches of her head, and then she was thrown to the ground with Luke's body on top of her.

Chapter Three

Another boom sounded, and the bullet pinged precariously close to them. "Stay down," he shouted to Carrie, who wiggled frantically beneath him. Luke's gaze shot all around, trying to identify the location of the shooter.

What in the hell was going on? Dammit, he hadn't even worn his gun tonight. Whom was the shooter aiming at? Carrie? Him? Anybody? A frightened cry came from Carrie, and still he remained covering her, waiting for another shot to come.

Every muscle in his body screamed with tension. Adrenaline filled his veins, and he drew deep breaths in an effort to slow the frantic beat of his heart.

People from the bar began coming outside to see what was going on. "Get back inside," Luke yelled at them, not wanting anyone to get hurt. "Take cover and call Chief Caldwell. It's an active shooter."

Thankfully the others quickly went back into the safety of the bar. There was a squeal of tires in the far left of the parking lot. Luke tried to see the vehicle, but it was gone before he could get a visual on it.

Seconds ticked by…slow seconds that turned into

minutes. The silence became deafening as he waited to see if any more bullets would fly, but he had a feeling the vehicle he'd heard peeling away had been the shooter fleeing the scene.

It was only when he heard the sounds of sirens in the distance that he relaxed a bit. He got to his knees and waited. Nothing happened. No more shots fired. He finally got to his feet as Lane's patrol car and two others squealed into the parking lot. It was only then that he helped Carrie to her feet.

She slammed into his body, wrapped her arms tightly around his neck and buried her face in his shirt as she shivered and cried.

Luke held her close, knowing that she must have been terrified. Even with everything going on around them, he was vaguely aware of how nicely she fit against him and how wonderful she smelled.

She finally pulled away from him. "I'm sorry," she said as she swiped at her tears. "I'm… I'm so sorry."

"What are you sorry about?" he asked.

"I… I didn't mean to break down."

"It's okay, Carrie," he assured her.

By that time Lane had approached them as three other officers fanned out in the parking lot with their weapons drawn. "I got a call of an active shooter," Lane said and motioned for the two of them to get back inside the bar.

Once inside, he yelled to get everyone's attention. The music halted, and a silence fell over the room. "Nobody leaves this building until I tell you it's okay." He then turned to Luke and Carrie. "Tell me what happened?"

"Carrie and I walked out the door to leave, and somebody shot at us," Luke said. "There were two shots and they seemed to be coming from the left area of the parking lot."

"Did you see the shooter?"

Luke shook his head. "No. After the first shot, we hit the ground."

"And then…then the person shot at us again," Carrie added, her voice trembling. Luke threw an arm around her shoulder and pulled her closer for comfort. He hated that he'd put her in this kind of danger. But damned if he could have foreseen somebody shooting at them the minute they stepped outside.

"There were two shots and then it stopped," Luke said. "And then I heard a vehicle squealing out of the parking lot. I don't think the shooter is around here anymore."

Lane looked directly at him. "So, who have you ticked off now?"

"Nobody," Luke replied irritably. "I've spent the last couple of days in my cabin all alone. Tonight, I invited Carrie out for a drink, and unless she has an overly protective brother who likes to shoot at her boyfriends, I haven't done anything to anyone."

"We just had a beer and decided to leave and go back to Luke's place," Carrie said, her voice a little stronger now. She moved out from under Luke's arm. "And I don't have a big brother and Luke did nothing wrong. In fact, he protected me by throwing himself over me."

"Do you think you were the specific target, or was

the perp looking to shoot anyone who walked out the door?" Lane asked.

"There's no way to know," Luke replied. "But nobody should have a reason to shoot at me."

"Or me," Carrie added.

One of the officers came in the door. "We've swept the parking lot and didn't find anyone," he said.

"And you didn't get a glimpse of the vehicle you heard pull away?" Lane asked Luke.

"Sorry, I didn't. I was too busy trying not to get shot," Luke replied dryly.

Lane raked a hand over his thinning brown hair, his pale blue eyes troubled. "Let's hope this was just an isolated incident. Somebody got liquored up and decided to shoot randomly." He frowned. "There are too damn many people owning guns these days."

"Yeah, well, starting tomorrow there will be one more person with a gun," Luke replied. "From now on I'm not leaving my house without my weapon."

Lane turned back to the officer. "Do one more sweep of the area and then I'll start letting people go."

"There's a small group of people who have arrived since we've been here, and they are waiting to come inside. Right now, we've got them all sitting in their vehicles and waiting until you give us the go-ahead," the officer replied.

"One more sweep and then we'll be done here," Lane replied. "Is there anything else you can tell me about the shooting?" Lane asked Luke when the officer left.

Luke frowned thoughtfully. "Everything happened so fast. I can't think of anything else."

"What about you, Carrie?" Lane asked.

"I can't tell you anything except that I've never been so terrified in my entire life," she replied. She wrapped her arms around herself as if fighting against an inner chill.

A long forty-five minutes later, Luke and Carrie were in his truck heading back to his place. "At least you know I provide an exciting time on a first date," Luke said.

Carrie gave a small laugh. "Definitely almost too exciting for me."

"I'm so sorry, Carrie," he said.

"There's nothing for you to apologize for," she replied.

"If I hadn't brought you there, then you wouldn't have had to go through all this," he replied. Now that it was all over guilt weighed down on him. Thank God Carrie hadn't been hurt.

"Let yourself off the hook, Luke. I chose to be there. You didn't kidnap me and force me to go to the Red Barn with you. You aren't responsible for anything. I've gone to the Red Barn plenty of times without you. This could have happened on any one of those nights."

He shot her a quick glance. Her pretty features were illuminated by the soft light from the dashboard. "You're a nice woman, Carrie."

She released another small laugh. "I am pretty easy-going. I only get angry about things that really matter. Being shot at falls in the category of scaring me half to death."

"It scared me half to death, too," he admitted.

He turned into the long lane that would take them to his house at the end. "Why don't you come in for a little while?" he said as he parked in front of his place.

"Okay. I'm definitely not ready to go home and go right to bed. I still have too much adrenaline rushing around in my head and body."

"I hear that," Luke agreed. He parked his truck, and together they got out. He unlocked the door and ushered her inside.

"Have a seat," he said and gestured to the sofa. "Do you want something to drink?"

"No, I'm good," she replied and sank down on the thick cushions.

He sat down in his recliner facing her. "Do you think it's possible Peter waited for us to walk out and then shot at us?"

A tiny frown danced into her forehead. "No," she answered immediately. "First of all, there was no ill will between you and him when they left the bar. And from what I've heard about Peter's shooting skills, if it was him, he wouldn't have missed the shot."

"Peter's shooting skills are what put him on the very top of my suspect list," Luke replied, his stomach tightening at the mere mention of the man's name.

"Like Lane said, I'm leaning toward it being somebody drunk and reckless."

"Drunk and stupid," Luke added. "At least you survived your first date with me." He grinned at her, hoping to lighten the mood.

She laughed. She had a nice laugh. It was light and musical and easy on the ears. "I survived thanks to you protecting me." Her gaze was warm on him. "Thank you, Luke, for throwing me down and using yourself as a shield to protect me. That's real hero material as far as I'm concerned."

"Hell, Carrie. I'm no hero. I'm just a man on a mission to find my father's killer."

"Peter and his gang of misfits didn't stay long tonight. There will be another night where they'll stay longer and get drunker, and maybe then Peter will boast about what he's done," Carrie replied. "If he's a guilty man, then eventually we'll get him, Luke."

He liked the *we* in her sentence. For the past two months, since his father's death, Luke had felt so all alone. None of his family members seemed to feel the real burn for justice that Luke felt. Now he had somebody who seemed to understand him, who wanted to help him, and it felt good.

"I think it's time I get home," she now said and stood. Luke got out of his chair. Together they walked to his front door. "Same place, same time tomorrow?" she asked.

"Are you sure you're still in this after what happened tonight?"

"Definitely," she replied without hesitation. "As far as I'm concerned, what happened tonight was just a fluke—a drunk with a gun. I'm very much still in this."

She looked so determined, with her violet eyes shining brightly. Luke could smell the scent of her, that flowers-and-spice fragrance that he found wildly attractive.

For a brief moment, he wanted to kiss her. She looked so pretty and so damned kissable. They stood so close to each other that he could feel her body heat. He must have leaned forward, for her lips parted slightly as if in open invitation.

Kiss her, a little voice whispered inside him. He snapped back, ignored the inner voice and broke the crazy moment. The last thing he wanted to do was give her the wrong idea about their partnership.

"How about I pick you up at your place tomorrow evening?" he said and took a step back from her.

"That would be fine. Shall I text you my address?"

"Yeah, we should exchange phone numbers." They both took out their phones and took care of that issue.

"Okay, then I'll text you sometime tomorrow and we can finalize the plans for tomorrow night." She smiled. "Good night, Luke."

"Good night, Carrie. Drive safely." He watched as she got into her car and then headed up the lane. Once her taillights disappeared from his view, he went back into his house and returned to the recliner.

He thought about that moment when he'd wanted to kiss Carrie. It had definitely been a wild impulse. It had to be because he knew she was on his side and they had just gone through a frightening experience together. It had nothing to do with any real desire for her, he told himself. He had no time or energy for desire. He wanted nothing to do with romance.

Carrie was a partner, and she would never be anything more. He would forever be grateful to her if their plan worked and they caught Peter confessing that he'd killed Big John King.

Of course, Carrie hadn't said or done anything that would make him believe she was romantically interested in him. Thankfully they were both on the same page—she probably wouldn't have wanted a kiss from him anyway.

Now all he could hope was that the plan worked and they caught Peter saying something incriminating. Only that would ease the grief, the all-consuming rage that ate at him day and night.

EVEN THOUGH CARRIE was officially on vacation, she got a call early the next morning from Dr. Holloway begging her to come into the office. Two of the other nurses had called in sick, and he had a full schedule. He told her he desperately needed her help.

Although she had been exhausted from all the events of the night before, she'd come in to work. It had been a crazy, busy day in the office, but thankfully at five o'clock it was done.

She was in the small break room getting her things together to leave to go home when Dr. James Holloway walked in. He was a short man with thin brown hair, a slightly oversize nose and pale blue eyes.

Carrie knew he was thirty-nine years old, and he was a good doctor with a thriving practice. He also had a three-year-old little boy that he was raising from a previous relationship.

"Carrie, I can't thank you enough for coming in last-minute today," he now said to her.

"It wasn't a problem," she replied. She grabbed her purse from the locker that was assigned to her, hoping he would just go away.

Far too often her boss stood closer to her than was necessary, or he'd reach across her and brush against her breasts. She never knew if it was truly an accident or on purpose. What she did know was that he often made her feel very uncomfortable.

"I miss you when you aren't here in the office, Carrie," he said, immediately making her feel that discomfort again. He often teetered on the line of professionalism with her.

"Carrie, would you consider going out with me for a drink this evening?"

Every muscle in her body tensed. "I'm sorry, Dr. Holloway, I already have plans for this evening. I've been seeing Luke King, and in any case, I'm sure I've mentioned before that I don't believe in mixing business with pleasure."

His blue eyes narrowed. "I'm a much better fit for you than some dumb rancher. Carrie, you're way too smart for somebody like Luke King. You need a mature man like me."

"In any case, I'm seeing Luke this evening, and I'm ready to leave now." He stood between her and the exit, but thankfully after a moment of staring at her, he moved aside. "Good night, Dr. Holloway. I'll see you when I get back from vacation."

She didn't breathe until she reached her car in the

parking lot. She'd known for some time that he had a thing for her. The other nurses teased her about the crush their boss had on her. But this was the first time he'd taken it a step further and had asked her out. It had validated all those times when she'd believed he wasn't just "accidentally" touching her. Tonight, he'd gone way over the line.

He was a creep, and maybe it was time she looked for another job. Her boss had been making her uncomfortable for some time, but in a small town like Coyote Creek, jobs weren't exactly a dime a dozen. Still, the idea of going back into that office was repugnant to her.

She shoved these thoughts out of her mind and focused on the night ahead. She was going to have to hurry to get home and then get ready for Luke to pick her up at six thirty.

Luke. She couldn't help but feel a pull toward him. He was nice and could be quite charming. He seemed genuinely interested in getting to know her, and there had been a moment the night before when she'd thought he was going to kiss her.

She'd seen a flash of desire in his eyes. He'd moved in intimately close to her, and her heart had quickened with sweet anticipation. And then he'd stepped back and the moment had been lost.

Despite the shooting at the Red Barn last night, she wasn't afraid to go back there tonight. She'd thought about the shooting long after she'd gotten home the night before. She did not believe she and Luke had been the specific targets. She did believe, whomever the shooter was, he would have fired those shots toward whoever stepped out the door.

Besides, she wanted to be there for Luke. Aside from the fact that she liked him, she'd seen flashes of the pain he held inside, and she'd felt the grief that still clung to him. If anyone needed a friend, it was Luke.

It took her only minutes to get from the doctor's office to the attractive two-story house just off Main Street that she shared with Emily.

The house was painted a light gray with darker gray shutters. The street was lined with tall, mature trees, and a huge oak stood in their front yard. She pulled into the driveway next to Emily's car and got out.

"Hello," she called out as she stepped into the living room.

"In the kitchen," Emily yelled back.

The living room was decorated in a mishmash kind of style. Emily had brought with her a slightly broken-down, overstuffed beige sofa from her parents' basement, and Carrie had added a black and glass coffee table and matching end tables she'd bought at a garage sale.

The two women had pooled their money to buy a nice brown chair for the living room and a dining room table, dishes and pots and pans. Each of them had brought their own bedroom furniture, and for the last two years they had been good friends and great roommates.

Carrie walked into the kitchen, where Emily sat at the table with a sandwich and chips in front of her. She was clad in a pair of pink scrubs that complemented her light brown hair and pretty hazel eyes.

"Hey, girl," Emily greeted her. "How was your day?"

"It was fine until the end." Carrie went to the refrigerator and pulled out the sandwich meat and a piece of cheese.

"What happened at the end?" Emily asked curiously.

As Carrie made herself a sandwich, she told Emily about Dr. Holloway asking her out for a drink. "Oh, ick," Emily said when Carrie was finished.

"That's what I thought," Carrie said as she finished making her sandwich and sat in the chair opposite Emily.

"You said before that you thought he had a crush on you," Emily said.

"Yeah. I'd often feel him staring at me, and he often invaded my personal space, but he definitely confirmed my suspicions today when he told me I needed a 'mature man' like him." Carrie began to eat, watching the clock and knowing she still wanted to shower and clean up before Luke arrived.

"That's so disgusting. So, what are you going to do?" Emily asked. "Don't you think things are going to be really awkward now for you at work?"

"Definitely. In fact, things have been awkward there for quite some time now. Is Dr. Morris hiring?" she asked half-kiddingly.

"Actually, he is hiring. Sarah Benson just quit to be a stay-at-home mom." Emily grinned. "Just think of all the fun trouble we could get in working together."

Carrie laughed. "Maybe I'll put in an application with him while I'm on vacation."

"Seriously, I'd love working with you at Dr. Morris's office," Emily said. "He's a really nice man and treats all of us with respect."

"I'd like that, but right now, I need to choke down my sandwich and get upstairs to shower and change. Luke is picking me up at six thirty."

"How's that going?" Emily asked.

"Good. He really seems to be a nice guy, and I'm enjoying spending time with him."

"I wish Lane could find the person who killed Big John. I've heard that the whole King family is still grieving deeply," Emily said. "I feel so sorry for them all. And now I'll shut up and get out of here so you can finish eating."

Emily put her plate in the dishwasher. "I'll talk to you later," she said and then left the kitchen.

The two rarely cooked on the days they both worked. Sandwiches and frozen meals were their best friends on those days. When one of them had a day off, that person usually cooked a real meal for them both.

Carrie finished her sandwich and then headed upstairs to her bedroom. She had the master bedroom that had its own bathroom. She paid a little more rent than Emily did for the privilege. She took off the scrubs she'd worn all day, threw them into a laundry basket and then got into the shower.

As the warm water pelted her, she stifled a couple of yawns. Last night had been a fairly late night and she'd definitely been up and running very early that morning, leaving her a little tired now. However, thoughts of spending more time with Luke shot a welcomed rivulet of much-needed adrenaline through her.

She had no idea if he intended on taking her back to the King ranch to hang out before they went to the Red Barn or not. Six thirty was a bit early to head to the bar, but it was Luke's choice what they did. She was just along for the ride.

Once she was out of the shower, she pulled on a pair of jeans and a long-sleeved spring-green blouse that hugged her body in all the right places. She applied her makeup and then spritzed herself with her favorite perfume.

She was ready with fifteen minutes to spare. She went back downstairs and sat on the sofa to wait for Luke. A small knot of nerves tightened her chest. She couldn't help but feel a little nervous about seeing Luke again. The crush she had on him had only grown with each and every minute she spent with him.

When his knock fell on the door, she jumped up, grabbed her purse and then went to answer. As usual, he looked totally hot in jeans and a light blue T-shirt. "Hi, Carrie."

"Hey, Luke. I'm ready to go if you are," she replied. "I just need to yell up to Emily and let her know I'm leaving." As Luke stepped just inside the front door, Carrie went to the foot of the staircase and hollered up to her roommate. "Emily, I'm leaving now. I'll lock the door."

"Okay, thanks, Carrie. See you tomorrow," Emily yelled back.

Carrie turned back to Luke and smiled. "Now I'm ready." Together she and Luke left the house and headed for his truck parked at the curb.

"This is an attractive neighborhood," he said.

"Yeah, it's nice and peaceful, and we love living here." It was a quiet neighborhood—most of her neighbors were older couples with grown children.

"Your house looked nice from what little I saw of it." They reached his truck, and he opened the passenger door for her.

"It's actually a hodgepodge of styles that screams for an interior decorator, but it's comfortable. I should have invited you in to see it all," she replied as she got into the truck.

"Next time," he said and flashed her the smile that always shot a delicious warmth through her. He closed her door and then walked around the front of the truck to the driver's door.

"You know, I should have invited you to dinner at the café tonight before we headed to the Red Barn," he said as he pulled away from the curb.

"Next time," she replied with a grin.

He laughed. "You look like spring in that green blouse. It looks very nice."

"Thank you. I look like green grass and you look like blue skies," she replied.

"You're right." He headed down the highway. "I thought we'd hang out around the ranch until later."

"Sounds like a plan," she said, echoing his earlier words and making him laugh once again. He had a wonderful laugh, full and deep-bodied, and she loved hearing it.

He asked her about her day, and she told him about going into the office to help out and then her boss asking her out for a drink.

"Are you interested in him?" Luke asked.

"Heavens, no," she replied with disgust. "To be honest, I find him kind of creepy. He's always made me feel pretty uncomfortable. He's always brushing up too close to me or reaching across me and skimming my breasts. I kept telling myself those things were accidents, but today he definitely crossed the line, so I'll be looking for a new job in the next couple of weeks."

She hadn't realized she'd made up her mind to definitely look for another job until this very moment. She deserved better than working in a place that made her feel so uncomfortable and stressed. She deserved better than working for a man who obviously had little respect for her.

"Good for you," he replied. "You deserve much better than that."

"That's what I was just thinking," she replied.

By that time, they had arrived at Luke's place. "There's something I want to show you," he said as they got out of the truck.

She followed him to the front door. He unlocked it and held it open for her to enter the house. Once inside, he locked the door once again, something he hadn't done before. "I... I've been working on something that I want you to see," he said. "It's in my spare bedroom."

"Okay," she replied slowly. She'd never heard anything negative about the way Luke treated women, but inviting her into his spare bedroom seemed strange, and he was acting odd...like he was suddenly very nervous.

"Nobody else has seen what I'm about to show you, and I hope you won't mention it to anyone else," he said, further intriguing her and making her nervous all at the same time.

"Luke...what is it?"

He reached for her hand and pulled her down a short hallway. They passed what appeared to be Luke's master bedroom. She peeked in and saw a king-size bed covered in a navy bedspread. Navy curtains hung at the windows. From the quick glance she got, it looked neat and clean. Then they came to a closed door.

He dropped her hand and opened the door. "Welcome to my nightmare."

She stepped into the room and looked around in stunned surprise. Large whiteboards covered three of the four walls in the room, and on them were notes about his father's murder.

There was a list of suspects, some crossed out, while others were underlined. Every encounter he'd had with Lane was written down with notes to the side.

She'd known Luke was fixated on finding his father's killer, but this spoke to a depth of obsession that could make a person descend into utter madness.

"EAT, BILLIE. YOU know you have to eat, so open your mouth." He guided the spoon, but just before he could put the food in, the mouth snapped shut.

"Dammit." He threw the bowl of oatmeal across the room. The plastic bowl hit the far kitchen wall and slowly slid down to the floor, leaving a trail of lumpy oatmeal behind.

He got up from the table, too angry to sit for another moment and too angry to clean up the mess he'd just made. He went into the living room and threw himself on the sofa.

It wasn't supposed to be this way. Dammit, it wasn't supposed to be this…this hard. He was supposed to have a partner…a wife to help him. But he'd been cheated.

And soon he'd have to change a dirty diaper, and that would only bring his rage on all over again. It could have been different. It *should* have been different. His stomach clenched and his head ached as the anger continued to build inside him all over again.

That bitch. That snotty nurse—he'd make her pay. He'd tried the other night at the Red Barn. He'd sat in the parking lot and waited, hoping to get off one perfect shot. But he'd missed her, and then that pseudo-hero Luke King had covered her body with his own.

Now his anger toward her had only increased tenfold. He'd make her pay for what she hadn't done and all the lies she'd told him. He was going to enjoy making her pay—and the ultimate compensation to him for all her lies was her death.

Chapter Four

Luke had been afraid that by showing Carrie his murder boards, he might chase her away. He'd worried that she might think him completely insane and she'd run for the hills as fast as she could.

However, he'd been pleased that she'd not only not run from him, but she'd studied his work and talked to him about other suspects and why he had ultimately discounted or added them.

A week and a half had passed since that night—a week and a half of frustration, as far as the case was concerned. He and Carrie had sat for hours in the Red Barn, listening to Peter and his drunken buddies whoop and holler, laugh and crow. He'd heard them talk about everything but the murder of Big John King.

Luke's frustration, along with his rage, had grown with each day that had passed. That was why he had invited Carrie to come to the ranch for some horseback riding today. He needed something to ease the rage and the pain, if only for a couple of hours.

It was a beautiful Saturday afternoon, and Luke was hoping a little horseback riding would erase some of the pressure, some of the stress that rode his shoulders almost all the time.

The pressure definitely eased somewhat whenever he was with Carrie. It was strange, but spending time with her brought him a peaceful calm that was positively intoxicating.

He'd gotten to know her better with each evening they had spent together. She made him laugh, something he had forgotten to do since his father's death. And, to his surprise over the past week, she and Caleb had become quite friendly as well.

His brother rarely opened up to anyone, yet for some reason he seemed to be open to a friendship with Carrie. As far as Luke was concerned, it only spoke to Carrie's warmth and sweet personality that drew people to her.

He'd introduced her to his mother and his sister, and even Johnny had given Carrie his stamp of approval as a romantic partner for Luke. Of course, they weren't really romantic partners. They were just partners.

As he heard the sound of a car pulling up outside, he stepped out on the porch. He smiled as Carrie parked and then got out.

She looked pretty clad in jeans and a long-sleeved light pink blouse. Her dark brown hair was loose around her shoulders and sparked with red and gold highlights in the bright sunshine.

A swift and strong surge of desire suddenly punched him in the gut. It wasn't the first time he'd experienced it where Carrie was concerned, but it always surprised him when it rose up inside him. It was always unexpected and undesirable.

He just assumed it was because it had been a long time since he'd been with a woman and he and Carrie had been spending a lot of quality time together. Still, it was definitely completely inappropriate. He quickly squashed it down. There was no place for that kind of feeling where Carrie was concerned.

"Are you ready to do some riding today?" he asked as she approached him.

"I can't wait," she replied. Her eyes shone brightly. "As long as you don't intend to put me on the back of some wild bucking bronco, I'll be good."

He laughed. "I promise, no wild bucking bronco. Come on, let's head down to the stables." He grabbed her hand as they walked across the lane from his house and down a path that would eventually lead to more outbuildings. It felt natural to hold her hand even though it was just a ruse to make everyone they encountered think they were in a romantic relationship.

"Did you hear back from Dr. Morris's office yet?" he asked.

"Actually, I heard from him this morning. I start Wednesday morning for him, and I immediately called Dr. Holloway to let him know I wouldn't be working for him anymore."

"How did he take it?"

"I could tell he was pretty ticked off. He was very cool but civil," she replied.

"I'm glad you're getting away from him." Luke's hand tightened around hers. "I didn't like it that your creep boss made you uncomfortable and crossed all kinds of professional lines with you."

"I didn't realize just how uncomfortable I have been until this morning when I got the call from Dr. Morris. I've never felt such a sense of relief as I did when I realized I don't have to go back to work in that place anymore," she replied. "However, I do feel bad that I'm not giving Dr. Holloway two weeks notice."

"You don't owe that man any notice. You don't owe him anything. The minute he brushed up against you, the minute he asked you out, he broke the trust that might warrant him notice," Luke replied firmly.

"Thanks, Luke," she said with a bright smile that shot an explosion of warmth into his stomach. He wasn't sure why her smiles always warmed him, why they always made him feel very special and…happy.

Ahead, the large stables came into view. Luke's rib pain had finally quieted to a mere whisper, and he was looking forward to riding for the first time since his beatdown. He'd wound up taking far more time off than he'd ever intended because his ribs had continued to give him fits.

"I asked one of the ranch hands to get the horses ready for us," he said as they approached the entrance. "The horse I have picked out for you is named Sue. She's a gentle, sweet mare and shouldn't give you any trouble."

"And what's your horse's name?" she asked.

"Storm," he replied. "She's a feisty ride and takes a firm hand, but she trusts me and I trust her."

They stepped across the threshold of the stables.

Luke loved the scents of horse and hay and grain. Before his father's death, he'd always loved hanging out in the stables. But the place also held many memories of Big John that now brought a deep grief with them. He hadn't been spending much time out here since his father's murder.

It was here in the stables that he had spent quality time with his father. He and Big John had spent many hours in here talking about the horses and life in general. Luke had cherished those times with his dad.

Hopefully, the grief would eventually pass and he would once again enjoy being in this place with the horses he loved taking care of and being around.

"Hey, Rod," Luke said, greeting the man who stepped out of a nearby stall. "Carrie, this is Rod Jackson, one of the men who help us out around here. Rod, this is Carrie Carlson."

"Hi, Carrie. I've seen you around town before, but it's nice to officially meet you," Rod replied.

"You, too, Rod," she said.

"I've got the horses all saddled up and ready to go," he said to Luke.

"Thanks, Rod. Why don't you bring Sue around and I'll get Storm?" Luke dropped Carrie's hand. "Just wait here," he said to her.

Minutes later they left the stables on their horses and headed out into the pasture. "It feels good to be riding again," he said.

"It feels good to be on a horse that's tall and strong," she replied. She leaned forward and patted Sue's neck. "I'll behave if you behave," she said to her mount.

Luke laughed. "Trust me, she'll behave."

Carrie looked good on the horse. Her posture was perfect, and her hips rolled easily with the horse's gait. As they rode at a leisurely pace, he pointed out the large herd of cattle in the distance and various outbuildings and land features he found interesting.

"That area over there is Caleb's playground," he said, pointing toward a heavily wooded area. His stomach tightened as he thought of his younger brother. When his father had been shot, Caleb's alibi was that he was out in that area taking pictures of various flowers he wanted to paint. But it was an alibi that couldn't be confirmed.

"That field is too full of trees and brush and uneven terrain, so we can't use it as much of anything. Caleb spends a lot of time out in the woods there finding things to photograph and then paint," he added.

"I'll bet it's beautiful," she replied.

"I guess it is. I never go there. Are you ready to do a little galloping?"

"Ready when you are," she replied.

He took off galloping, pleased that she easily kept up with him. The breeze was pleasant on his face, and the sun was warm on his shoulders. Seeing Carrie with her long, dark hair fanning out and her beautiful smile in place as they rode filled him with a pleasure he hadn't felt for a very long time.

As he broke into a full run, her laughter rode the air as she urged Sue to go faster. They raced across the pasture for a short time, and then he reined in and she followed his lead.

"That was exhilarating," she said, and once again her smile caused a rivulet of warmth to rush through him. "I never get to run like that on Dickerson's horses."

"We'll walk them for a few minutes, and then I've got a place for us to dismount and relax for a little while."

They walked for a few minutes to cool the horses down, and then he led her to a small pond with trees all around and they dismounted. Before she'd arrived, he'd packed a blanket and two soft drinks in his saddlebag. He now spread the blanket out for them to sit on.

"This is nice," she said once they were settled.

"I used to come to this spot a lot to think and just chill."

"It's beautiful here and so peaceful." It was a very peaceful place, with the breeze rustling the leaves overhead and the birds singing their songs from all the trees.

"Yeah, although I have to admit there were times when I came out here to pout," he said.

"Pout? You? You definitely don't seem like the pouting type," she replied with a raise of her perfectly arched, dark eyebrow.

"There was only one thing I ever pouted about." He cast his eyes to the distance, finding it a bit difficult to look at her as he confessed to some of his weakest moments.

"What, Luke? Tell me." She placed her hand on his forearm in the silent encouragement he'd come to expect from her.

He returned his gaze to her. "I always knew that as the second son, I would come in second when it came to my dad's love, but that was always a hard pill to swallow."

He saw her about to speak, and he held up a hand to stop her. "I know what you're about to say, and I know my father loved me, but Johnny definitely was his go-to son. I'd see them out of horseback together and yearn to be out there with them. Dad depended more on Johnny than he did me. He...he..." Luke broke off, horrified that his emotions had climbed far too close to the surface.

He sucked in several deep breaths to steady himself, mortified by his momentary lack of control. "Anyway, that's what I'd come out here and think about. And now I feel the need to get Dad's killer, to prove to him that I'm the son who loved him more." He released a slightly embarrassed laugh. "Childish, huh?"

"Oh Luke, I'm not about to tell you that your feelings are childish or unwarranted or anything else." She moved closer to him, so close the evocative scent of her eddied in his head. "Your feelings are your feelings. But you must know on some level that your father loved you very much."

"Logically, I know that, but Johnny was a hard act to follow as an older brother. He's always been so sure of himself and his role here at the ranch. He's now pressuring me to get more involved and take charge of a horse-breeding operation here."

"And you don't want to do it?" she asked.

"Yeah, I do want to. It's something my dad wanted to see me do, but I'm just not ready to do it yet."

"Luke, don't put off your life while waiting to catch your father's murderer. I know how badly you want the man responsible behind bars, but life is far too short, and it's okay to find some happiness despite your grief."

He looked into her eyes…her beautiful violet eyes. Without giving it any thought, functioning only on sheer emotion, he leaned forward and captured her lips with his.

CARRIE HAD BEEN waiting for a kiss from Luke for what felt like forever. His lips were wonderfully warm, and she immediately parted hers to invite him to deepen the kiss.

Their tongues danced together in a hot tango as he slowly leaned her back on the blanket. What had begun as a simple kiss quickly turned into something hot and hungry and demanding.

The sound of the birdsongs faded away as she gave herself to the magic of Luke's kiss. Fiery heat flamed through her veins. She was surrounded by the scent of him, a heady scent of sunshine and the woodsy cologne he wore that she loved.

At the moment, if he wanted to strip her naked and make love to her right here, right now, she would welcome it. Over the past week and a half, her feelings for Luke had only deepened. As crazy as it seemed after such a short time, she was definitely on the verge of falling in love with him.

He suddenly released her and shot back up to a sitting position. He raked a hand through his hair and stared down at her, obviously appalled. "God, Carrie... I'm so sorry. That...that shouldn't have happened."

She sat up and held his gaze. "Why? Luke, why shouldn't it have happened? I have been wanting you to kiss me for a while now." She still wanted him to kiss her, to hold her and tell her that he cared for her.

He frowned. "That's not what this partnership is about."

"Don't worry. I haven't lost sight of what our partnership is about, but I like you, Luke. I like you a lot," she confessed.

"And I like you, too, Carrie. But I'm not in a position to have any kind of romantic relationship right now. I thought you understood that."

"I do understand that. I don't expect anything from you. It doesn't matter how many times we kiss. It doesn't even matter if we were to make love. I still wouldn't expect anything from you." She thought she saw a flash of desire in the depths of his eyes, but it was only there only a moment and then gone.

"I just want to make sure we're both on the same page," he said. "That's really important to me."

"We are, Luke," she replied fervently in an effort to reassure him. All she could hope for was that with more time, Luke would realize what they had between them was something special and romantic and wonderful.

"On that note, why don't we mount up and do a little more riding?" he said.

Minutes later they were riding once again. There

was no question she was a bit disappointed by the way their few minutes of passion had ended. But she knew Luke was single-minded in his quest. Still, he'd obviously wanted to kiss her in the first place and that thought shot a river of delicious warmth through her.

He might believe he had no time or energy for romance, but emotions couldn't be tamed. They could only be stuffed down for so long before they finally had to be acknowledged. If Luke was falling for her, then eventually he'd have to embrace those feelings. At least that's what she hoped would happen.

In the meantime, all she could do was continue to help him pursue Peter's admission of guilt, or help clear his brother once and for all from being a viable suspect.

They rode for another half an hour and then headed back to the stables. "How about I take you to dinner at the café?" he said once they were walking back toward his house.

"That sounds good. Since I didn't know for sure what the plans would be, I brought a change of clothes. Do you mind if I change and clean up a bit?"

"Not at all," he replied.

"Then I'll just grab my things from my car and meet you in the house."

As Luke headed inside, Carrie grabbed her fresh clothing and a travel cosmetic bag from the back seat of her car, then went into Luke's house.

"I'm going to do a little cleanup before we go, too," he said. "Why don't you use the bathroom in the hallway and I'll use mine in my bedroom."

"Okay," she agreed.

"If you want to take a quick shower, there are towels and washcloths underneath the sink."

Minutes later, Carrie stood beneath a warm shower with her hair pulled into a messy knot on top of her head so as not to get wet.

They had talked about going to the café over the last week but had never actually done it. So, tonight would be the first time they'd be out in public together in a place other than the Red Barn. Once again, they would be acting like they were a real couple.

It was a fast shower, and then she dressed in a fresh pair of jeans and a long-sleeved royal blue blouse. After applying fresh makeup, she left the bathroom and went into the living room to wait for Luke.

She didn't have to wait long. He must have showered, too for when he returned to the living room, he smelled of minty soap and that evocative woodsy cologne that stirred something deep inside her. He had changed into another pair of jeans and a navy polo shirt.

"All ready?" he asked.

"Ready," she replied.

"You look very nice," he said.

"Thank you," she returned. One of the things she liked about Luke was he was always quick to compliment her. She appreciated that, as most women would.

"Are you hungry?" he asked once they were in his truck and headed toward town.

"Actually, I am. All that fresh air and sunshine definitely stirred up my appetite," she replied.

He laughed. "It has a tendency to do that."

"It was fun today. Thank you for letting me ride one of your horses," she said.

He flashed that gorgeous smile at her. "You're a good rider. We'll plan to do it again soon."

"Thanks, I'd like that."

They rode in silence for a few minutes. It was a comfortable silence that didn't need filling with inane conversation.

It was Saturday, so hopefully tonight Peter would really cut loose and get drunk enough to confess that he'd fired the shots that had killed Big John King. She wanted that for Luke. She desperately wanted him to finally be at peace, with the killer behind bars.

However, it was a two-edge sword. While she wanted Peter to confess, she was also aware that it was possible that would be the end of any relationship with Luke.

They reached the Coyote Creek Café. Inside, the café was an homage to the area's ranchers. The walls were painted a calming green, and one wall was a painting of pastures with a herd of cattle in the distance.

They found a booth in the middle of the establishment. As they walked to the booth, several people greeted them. Carrie saw several former patients.

There was Jason Cartwell, whose wife had suffered a stroke a year before, and the Davidsons, whose little daughter had needed an emergency appendectomy, and several more who had suffered illness or injuries that had landed them either in the hospital or at the doctor's office at one time or another.

She cast a warm smile to Edward Munford, whose wife had died in the hospital three months ago from breast cancer, leaving him to raise his two-year-old son all alone. His wife, Lydia, had been pregnant when she'd been diagnosed and had refused treatment so she could deliver a healthy baby. By the time she got treatment, it had been too late. The cancer had spread throughout her entire body.

Once seated, almost immediately Stacy Wellington, one of the waitresses, appeared at their booth.

"Hi, Luke. Hi, Carrie," she greeted them with a friendly smile. Carrie had gone to school with Stacy, and she seemed to remember that Luke had dated her at one time. "What can I get for you?"

They both ordered burgers, hers with French fries and his with onion rings, and they each got a soda. Once Stacy moved away, they made small talk about the day and their plans for the next couple of days.

"If you're going back to work on Wednesday, will that interfere with our nights together at the Red Barn?" he asked.

"It shouldn't," she replied. "I might not hang out as late on the weekdays, but on the weekends, when our suspect usually gets smashed, I'll be right there next to you as long as you need me." She kept her voice low so nobody else nearby might hear her.

Luke's gaze was warm on her. "I appreciate you giving me all your free time."

She smiled at him. "Luke, you have to stop thanking me. I'm doing this because I want to do it."

"Okay, but I want you to think of something I can

do for you in return for everything you're doing for me," he replied.

Just love me. The words jumped unbidden into her head. Words she would never speak aloud to him. For sure they were inappropriate, and she still couldn't believe how quickly her feelings toward him had grown. "All right, I'll think about it," she replied.

Their meals arrived, and as they ate, they got into an animated discussion about a television crime drama they both watched. "I'm telling you, Powers is behind it all," she said, referencing one of the main characters on the popular show.

"No way. It's Milton. He's the man who ordered the hits on those two men. It's all about revenge."

Carrie laughed. "That's what they want you to think, but I'm telling you it's Powers. Sometimes the obvious isn't the guilty party. You just wait and see."

"I guess we'll know by the end of the season."

She laughed again. "Or they'll leave it as a cliff-hanger and drag it into the next season."

"That's probably what they'll do," he replied.

They ate for a few more minutes. "You mentioned that one of the reasons you broke up with Rory was because he wasn't sure he wanted children. So, just how many children do you want?" he asked.

"At least two. In a perfect world, I'd have a boy and then a girl," she replied. "What about you? How many children do you want?"

"I'd like five or six," he replied.

"Five or six? How many wives do you intend to have?" she asked with a laugh.

Her laughter died on her lips as Luke glanced over her shoulder and suddenly stiffened. "There he is…the snake behind my father's murder."

Carrie glanced behind her to see Wayne Bridges with his wife and two other couples. Wayne was a tall, brown-haired man with a big barrel chest. He was a bit of a blowhard and seemed to love the sound of his own voice. As far as Carrie was concerned, he talked too loud and laughed too often, and she was glad he hadn't won the mayoral election. The group took a large corner booth, laughing and talking as they sat.

Carrie knew Wayne Bridges had run against Big John King for the mayoral position, a position that Wayne had ultimately lost to Stella Black. It was hard to believe that a man would order a hit to obtain the position of mayor in such a small town. But she knew this was what Luke believed.

Luke tapped his fingers against the tabletop, a habit she noticed he did whenever he was particularly stressed or upset. She didn't know what to believe when it came to Big John's murder. She did know that Lane, as chief of police, had admitted that it was now a cold case, with no clues or leads to move forward.

They finished their meals, left the café and headed for the Red Barn. Once again, they sat at the table close to where Peter and his buddies were seated.

"Look, it's lover boy again," Peter said once they sat down.

"I've told you before, I don't want any trouble," Luke replied.

"You were definitely looking for trouble that night when you wandered on our property," Sly Baskum said.

Carrie knew most of the men because some of her girlfriends had dated them. For the most part, she knew that the men were dirtbags misogynists and lowlifes. She also knew now that they could be brutal. They had beaten Luke badly.

"I was waiting for Peter to get out his rifle and shoot me," Luke replied.

"From what I heard, somebody else tried to shoot you right here before," Peter replied. "Trust me, if it had been me doing the shooting, I wouldn't have missed you."

Tension filled Carrie. This was the kind of conversation Luke had been hoping for. Was it possible they were about to hear some form of a confession from the drunken ranch hand?

"Yeah, my boy here can shoot the eye out of a squirrel from a hundred yards away," Sly said and slapped Peter on the back.

"Or a man's heart?" Luke said. His words hung in the air for a long moment, until then Peter laughed uproariously.

"You think I shot your daddy?" Peter laughed again, and all the men at the table joined in. "You're barking up the wrong tree, King. But if I wanted to make that shot, it would have been a piece of cake for me."

Carrie felt Luke's tension wafting off him as the two men glared at each other. She held her breath as the stares continued. "You're some piece of work, Jeffries," Luke finally said.

"I'll drink to that," Peter said and downed his bottle of beer.

As the men at the other table returned to their own conversation, Carrie placed a hand on Luke's forearm. "Are you okay?" she asked softly.

"Yeah." He drew in a deep breath and released it slowly.

An hour later, they were back in his truck and headed back to his place. Peter and his band of creeps had left the bar fifteen minutes before.

"I thought it was going to happen tonight," he said. His voice betrayed his bitter disappointment.

"I did, too," she replied. "But I don't think Peter was really drunk enough to make a careless confession. I've seen him drunker."

"He said I was looking at the wrong person, but I still believe he did it."

"Then we continue to do what we've been doing and hope one night he gets completely smashed and accidentally confesses," she said.

"From your lips to God's ear." He turned onto the long lane that would take them to his house. "You want to come in?" he asked as he parked in front of his place.

She would have loved to spend more time with him alone, but it had been a long day, and it was late. "No, thanks. I think I'll just head on home."

He parked, and they got out and then he walked her to her car. "As always, despite what we're doing, I enjoy spending time with you," he said.

His words shot warmth straight through to her heart,

and suddenly she was thinking about the kiss they had shared earlier in the day.

"I always enjoy spending time with you, too," she said. She stopped by her driver door and hoped he would kiss her again.

"Why don't I pick you up about six thirty tomorrow and we can hang out here for a while before heading back to the Red Barn?"

"Oh, Luke, there's no reason for you to drive all the way into town to pick me up when I can just meet you out here," she replied.

His features were barely discernible in the glow from his porch light. He smiled at her. "Okay, then you meet me here and we'll go from there."

"Then I guess I'll just say good night." She hesitated another long moment, hoping for a second kiss.

"Good night, Carrie," he replied and took a step back from her so she could open her door. She got into the car and released a deep sigh.

The kiss had changed everything for her. It had given her hope that he might see her as something other than a partner—that he might be seeing her as a desirable woman.

On a scale of one to ten, his kiss had been off the charts. His lips had been so soft, yet they'd had a mastery that had been thrilling. It had made her want him more than ever.

She turned onto the long, dark road that would take her back to town. Like Luke, there had been a moment tonight when she'd thought Peter was going to confess that he'd shot Big John. As he'd talked about his shooting prowess, she was certain it was going to happen. It had been a big letdown that it hadn't happened.

Maybe even drunk, Peter knew if he said anything about shooting Big John, he'd wind up in jail. Maybe he would never get drunk enough to confess to the crime. She wasn't even sure if he was really the guilty one.

She understood why he was on Luke's radar. Wayne had had a motive to want Big John out of the way, and Peter had the skill set to make that happen. But that didn't mean that either of them was good for the murder.

She was reminded of the conversation about the crime drama they both watched. Luke was convinced the obvious person was guilty, while she wasn't so sure. Peter was the obvious person, but time would tell if that made him guilty.

"Darn," she said aloud as she suddenly remembered she'd left her clothes and cosmetic bag at Luke's place. Oh well, she'd just get them tomorrow night when she was out at his place again.

She shoved all these thoughts out of her head as she saw a vehicle approaching quickly behind her. It appeared to be a truck, and it was coming on very fast. She moved over as far as she could in the lane so the driver could easily go around her.

It continued to race up directly behind her, and she gasped as the vehicle bumped into the back of her car. The steering wheel momentarily twisted out of her hands. She quickly grabbed hold of it, corrected and sped ahead.

What on earth was wrong with the driver of the

truck? Was he drunk? Had he just mistakenly gotten too close to her? She stepped on the gas, wanting to get some distance from him. Before another thought could enter her mind, the truck hit her again, this time with enough force to snap her head back and then forward.

She cried out and reoriented herself just in time to see the ditch as it appeared directly in front of her. And then she slammed into it. Her body jerked around despite the seat belt, and her brain went blank.

Chapter Five

Slowly Carrie came to her senses. A hissing noise came from someplace in the front of her car. She assumed it was her radiator, but she wasn't sure. The darkness of the night fell around her, deep and profound and further disorienting her.

Her car had stopped running, and even the headlights had doused. Her seat belt had pulled agonizingly tight around her, squeezing her chest painfully. She quickly took it off, drawing several long, deep breaths in an effort to calm herself.

The airbags should have deployed, but they hadn't, and she was grateful that they hadn't. She'd always heard that airbags could hurt when they hit your face and chest.

Thankfully, she felt no real pain anywhere, so she didn't believe she was seriously hurt. She looked around for her purse, which had her phone inside, but she had no idea where her purse might be. It had been on the passenger seat before the wreck but was no longer there, and it was too dark to hunt around for it.

What she needed to do was get out of the car and

get to the road so she could flag down some help. At this time of the night, on this particular road, she realized, it might be some time before another vehicle came along.

Her eyes slowly began to adjust to the dark, letting her see a little better despite the darkness. Her door was crunched, but she pushed and shoved against it with all her might and somehow managed to get it open.

She half rolled out of the car, and as she straightened up to inspect the damage, she saw the black pickup truck that had hit her parked along the side of the road. The lights were off, and the truck was idling.

Why was it just sitting there like that? Something about it seemed strangely ominous, and the air suddenly smelled not only of hot steam and oil, but also of an unknown danger.

If the driver had stopped because he'd caused the accident, then why wasn't he getting out of his truck to check on her condition? Surely that's what a normal person would do. Why was he just sitting there?

Was the driver waiting to see if he saw her and knew she was okay? Was he then going to drive off? Was it a hit-and-run and he or she just wasn't running yet?

She crouched back down and moved to the back of her car to peer around the edge of the fender. Her heart had already been beating too quickly given the wreck, but now it beat even faster.

Things just didn't feel right. For several long minutes, she remained hidden behind her car, watching and waiting to see if the truck drove away or not. She sensed something about to happen, but she couldn't anticipate what it might be. All she knew was this whole situation didn't feel right.

The driver door of the pickup suddenly flew open, and a man got out of the vehicle. In the darkness she could only see a vague silhouette, but she saw enough to be afraid. Whoever the man was, he walked with slow, heavy steps across the asphalt road, and he was carrying a rifle. Why carry a rifle to check on the victim of a car accident?

"Carrie, Carrie. Gonna shoot you deady," a deep, singsong voice said.

She froze. Wha…what was happening? Her brain tried to make sense of things, but it couldn't. He knew her name, and from his words he intended to kill her. He knew her name! Dear God, what was happening? Why was this happening? Who was this man?

She shoved a hand in her mouth to stanch the scream that begged to be released. That voice…it was eerily familiar. But she couldn't think about that right now.

The footsteps came closer. Escape…she needed to escape. She desperately looked around for a place to hide. Would the darkness shield her if she ran away? If he did see her, a bullet from a rifle could travel a very long way far faster than she could run.

She had to do something, because he was nearly on top of her. She looked around frantically. Could she stay hidden in the deepest darkness of the ditch? Could she crawl away without him hearing her now?

She heard a faint click, and then a spear of light appeared. He had a flashlight. The words screamed through her head. *Oh God, he has a flashlight!* She now had no time to run. With the flashlight he'd find her if she hid in the ditch. He'd see her if she ran. He'd find her no matter what she did, and he apparently intended to kill her. Why? Why was this happening?

"Carrie, I'm coming for you," the deep voice said, and then he laughed. The deep burst of laughter was filled with glee.

Terror shot through her. Her chest tightened, and her throat squeezed so tight she could scarcely draw a breath. Closer…he was coming closer.

She moved as silently as possible and, not knowing what else to do, she slid beneath the car. She lay flat, a hand once again fisted against her mouth. Quiet. She had to stay completely quiet. She watched in horror as the booted feet walked slowly around her car.

Like a child, she wanted to squeeze her eyes tightly closed and become invisible. Yet at the same time, she wanted—needed—to see where he was going and what he was doing.

Could he hear her heartbeat? It pounded so frantically in her head. Surely he could hear it, too. He was now on the driver's side of the car. The flashlight shot all around, illuminating the ditch and nearby brush.

"Carrie." Her name was a soft hiss. "Carrie, I'm going to find you, and then I'm going to kill you."

Sobs of terror blurred her vision and rose up in the back of her throat. She held them in, knowing if he heard a single sound from her, he'd find her and it would all be over.

How long before he bent down and looked beneath the car? How many minutes did she have left of her life? Sooner or later, he'd look. When he couldn't find her around the car, he'd look under it and find her.

She was now a sitting duck. How easy she'd made it for him to just point his rifle beneath the car and shoot her. Maybe she should have taken her chances running. But it was too late now.

"Carrie, I know you didn't go far. You might as well show yourself and take your medicine," the deep voice said.

Another deep sob welled up inside her, and she shoved her fisted hand more tightly against her mouth. Why was this happening? Why? Who was this man and why did he want to kill her?

She was in a nightmare, a horrible nightmare, only she couldn't wake up. She was going to die, and she would never know why.

In the distance she heard the approach of another vehicle. The flashlight clicked off, and her attacker took off running. She heard his boots back on the asphalt road and then the slam of his truck door. He took off with a squeal of tires.

At the same time, she heard the second vehicle pull to a stop. She didn't move. Fear kept her in place even as a sob finally escaped her.

"Hello? Is somebody there? Does anyone need help? Carrie, is that you?"

She recognized that deep voice. It was Luke's brother Johnny. She scooted out from beneath the car and got to her feet, sobs now ripping from her throat. "Johnny," she managed to cry. "Johnny, I'm here."

"Carrie…are you okay?" Johnny hurriedly stepped down into the ditch to meet her.

"Ye-yes…no. He was go-going to ki-kill me. Johnny, he…he wanted to ki-kill me." The words jerked out of her amid her cries.

"Who? Carrie, what's going on? Who was going to kill you?"

"I don't kn-know. The man who w-was here before you," she replied. "Can you c-call Luke for me?" She leaned weakly against the back fender of her car.

She wanted Luke here to hold her. She needed him to wrap her in his arms and make her feel safe. Her terror still radiated through her, making it difficult for her to draw a full breath.

"The first person I need to call is Lane," Johnny replied. He pulled his phone out of his pocket and called the lawman. After telling Lane where they were on the road and that they needed a tow truck, he added that somebody had apparently tried to kill her. He hung up and then called his brother.

Carrie tried to pull herself together. Despite the heat of the night, shiver after shiver of cold chills shot through her. "Somebody should be here in just a few minutes," Johnny said. "Are you sure you aren't hurt?"

"Not physically, but I'm… I was…am…terrified."

"You're safe now." He awkwardly threw an arm around her shoulder and pulled her against his warm, strong body. "I'm not going to ask you any of the details of what happened. Lane will be here soon enough, and you can tell him everything."

She wanted to cuddle into his warmth in an effort

to stanch the icy chills that continued to grip her. She needed somebody to tell her what was going on, who that man was and why he wanted to kill her.

Headlights appeared in the distance, and she tensed with a new horror. Was the man coming back? Oh God, was he coming back to kill her?

"Johnny…he's coming back," she said frantically. "He's going to kill me, and now he'll kill you, too." She gripped his arm in renewed terror.

"Nobody is going to kill you while I'm here," Johnny replied firmly. "Besides, that's Luke."

Sure enough, it was Luke's truck that pulled to a halt on the shoulder of the road. His lights illuminated the area with a welcomed brightness, and he kept them on even after he cut the engine. As he got out of the vehicle, Carrie ran toward him. She slammed into him and began to sob all over again.

He instantly wrapped his arms around her and held her tight. She buried her face in the crook of his neck as tremors shook through her body. She finally released all the deep sobs that had been trapped inside her for so long.

"Carrie, don't cry. Baby, you're okay. I've got you," he said. He rubbed his hands up and down her back in an obvious effort to comfort her.

With his arms holding her and his familiar scent surrounding her, she felt safe for the first time since she'd careened into the ditch.

In the distance a siren wailed, letting them know Lane would be here within moments. Still, she clung to Luke as he attempted to calm her by murmuring assurances in her ear, assurances that she was safe now and he wasn't going to let anyone hurt her.

Lane pulled up, cut the screaming siren and flashing lights, and then got out of his car. "Carrie, are you okay?" he called out as he approached them.

She finally stepped out of Luke's arms. "I'm okay." She drew several deep breaths to steady herself. "A pickup truck rammed into me and I... I wound up in the ditch." Despite her best effort to stay calm and relay important information, new tears burned at her eyes as raw emotion once again surfaced.

"Then the driver...he...he got out of the truck and he had a rifle and he said he was going to kill me. And then I hid underneath the car and he had a flashlight and was looking for me. He wanted to kill me." The words tumbled out of her in a rush. "And then...then Johnny came along and the man ran back to his truck and sped away."

"Whoa, slow down," Lane replied. "Let's start at the very beginning. So, you believe this truck intentionally rammed into you to make you wreck?"

"Yes, it was absolutely intentional," she replied. "He hit me twice, and the last time I flew off the road and into the ditch." She wrapped her arms around herself as a new chill swept through her.

"Do you know the color of the pickup truck that hit you?"

"No, it was too dark to be sure, but I think it was black," she replied.

Lane looked at Johnny. "Did you see the color or recognize the vehicle?"

"No and no," he said. "The truck squealed away before I got close enough to see anything about it. I was just on my way home after playing some cards out at Sam Kaiser's place when I came upon the accident."

Lane returned his gaze to Carrie. "So, you hit the ditch, and then what happened?"

Slowly, she told him everything that had happened. As she got to the part where the man had told her he was going to kill her, Luke wrapped an arm around her shoulder and pulled her close against him once again.

"Are you sure he said your name?" Lane asked.

She nodded. "Positive. He said it several times. There was no mistaking it."

"Did you recognize the voice at all?"

She frowned thoughtfully. "I thought it sounded vaguely familiar, but I'm not so sure now. I'm not sure about anything except somebody wanted to kill me tonight." Tears once again stung her eyes and spilled onto her cheeks. She brushed them away. "I don't know who it was or why he's after me."

"Did you see anything about him?" Lane asked.

"I saw his feet. He was wearing either tan work boots or cowboy boots. That's all I saw. It was too dark to see anything else, and I was hiding under the car," she replied.

"What about height? If you saw him get out of the truck, how tall did he appear to you?"

She frowned. "I don't know…just medium height."

"What about his build? Was he heavy or thin?" Lane asked.

"I think maybe he was on the thin side," she said

and then shook her head. "But I can't be sure. It was just so dark."

"Carrie, have you had problems with anyone lately? Have you fought with anybody?"

"No, nobody," she said.

"What about Dr. Holloway?" Luke said, and then he filled Lane in on her work issues.

"I can't imagine James Holloway doing something crazy like this," Lane said. "But I'll definitely check him out."

The questioning seemed to go on forever. "I'll take you home with me for the night," Luke said to her when it was all over.

"You two go ahead. I'll wait here for the tow truck," Lane said.

"I'll hang around and wait with Lane," Johnny said.

"Thank you, Johnny, for trying to make me feel better, and thank you for coming along when you did," she said. "You probably saved my life."

"No problem, Carrie," Johnny assured her.

Minutes later she was in Luke's truck and heading back to his house. "Thank you for letting me stay at your place for the night. To be honest, I was afraid to go home. I know Emily planned on being gone for the night, and I… I don't want to be all alone right now."

"I know how shook up you are, and I didn't want you to be all alone," he replied. "At least in my house you'll be safe and can get a good night's sleep."

Her cosmetic bag and the clothes she'd worn horseback riding that day were still in Luke's house. She could wear her T-shirt to sleep in, but at the moment sleep seemed far away as the horrifying events of the night kept crashing through her brain.

It didn't seem possible that it had only been earlier in the day when they had been galloping across the pasture, carefree and happy. It felt like it had been years ago that they had sat in the peaceful spot in the pasture and Luke had kissed her.

How quickly things had changed. Now her car was wrecked and somebody wanted her dead.

WHO COULD POSSIBLY be after Carrie? She was the sweetest, most giving woman Luke had ever met. It was a question that rolled over and over again in his head as he drove them back to his place.

He couldn't believe this had happened to her, that somebody had forced her car off the road with the intention of shooting her. Who could be behind such a heinous thing?

He could feel the fear that still radiated from Carrie, a fear he wished he could take away from her. He couldn't imagine the terror she must have felt when she'd been under the car and afraid of being discovered. And he couldn't imagine sending her on her way to go home alone after such a terrible scare.

Once they were inside his place, he gestured her to the sofa. She sank down and stared at the coffee table before her. He'd never seen her so pale, so utterly lost-looking. His heart positively ached for her.

"How about a drink?" he asked.

She looked up, and the depths of her beautiful eyes still held her terror. "What do you have?"

"I've got beer, whiskey and scotch—just name your pleasure." She still looked small and afraid and so vulnerable. It squeezed his heart tight to see her that way.

"Normally I'd choose a beer, but I think the night warrants something a little stronger, so I'd love a whiskey on the rocks," she replied.

"I'll be right back." He left her and went into the kitchen, where he prepared her drink and one for himself. He took off his gun belt and set it on the counter, then returned to the living room and sank down next to her.

"Thank you," she said. Her hand trembled slightly as she took the drink from him. She took a big sip, then closed her eyes as she swallowed.

"Carrie, what can I do to help?" he asked softly.

She opened her eyes and smiled, but it was a smile that didn't quite reach her eyes. "You're doing it." Her smile fell away, and she released a deep sigh. "Luke, I've never, ever been so terrified in my entire life."

"I can't even imagine." He scooted a little closer to her. He figured the best thing he could do was listen to her, as it was obvious she needed to wind down before they headed to bed. Her jeans were grass-stained, and even though she was disheveled, she still looked pretty…but frightened.

"It was like a horrible nightmare, but there was no waking up from it," she continued. "I can't imagine who the man was. He must have followed me from here. Why would somebody try to kill me, Luke?" Her gaze searched his features as if she thought he might hold the answer.

"I don't know, Carrie. I can't imagine somebody wanting to hurt you in any way. I wish I did know so Lane could get him behind bars." Luke took a drink of the whiskey, its smooth notes a pleasant warmth as it slid down his throat and into his stomach.

"Lane won't be able to make an arrest. A man driving a pickup and wearing boots describes almost every man in this town. I wasn't able to give him any kind of a description to help him find the man." Her eyes darkened with each word she spoke.

"Lane is smart. Both you and Johnny said the person squealed his tires when he drove off. Lane might be able to get a tire imprint that will let him know what kind of tire was on the vehicle, and that would definitely shorten a list of suspects."

She released a deep sigh. "I'm supposed to be helping you find your father's murderer, not worrying about my own safety," she replied and then took another sip of her drink.

"If you're still in, then we continue to go to the Red Barn in hopes that Peter will somehow confess, and at the same time we try to figure out who is after you and why. I can promise you that nobody will hurt you as long as you're with me."

"I'm still in," she replied.

"I'm glad to hear that." There was a part of him that realized he was being a jerk in even asking her about continuing to help him with his desire to catch his father's killer.

"In the meantime, what you need to think about is who might hold some kind of a grudge against you.

It could be something small and insignificant to you. Also, you said you thought the voice sounded vaguely familiar. Can you try to figure out where you heard that voice before and who it belongs to?"

She released another deep sigh. "I need to think long and hard about those things, but not tonight. I just can't think any more tonight. My brain is utterly fried with everything that happened."

"Drink up, then, and we'll call it a night," he replied. He'd like to be able to tell her that everything would be better in the morning, but he couldn't say that because it wasn't true. Things would probably look just as dark for her in the light of day.

They finished their drinks. He carried the empty glasses into his kitchen and placed them in the sink. He then went back into the living room, where she had gotten up from the sofa.

Her clothes and cosmetic bag were on the table in the entryway. He grabbed them for her and then led her to the spare bedroom, hoping the whiteboards on the walls didn't bother her as she tried to fall asleep. "The sheets on the bed are clean," he said and placed the clothing and the bag on top of the light blue spread.

"Thanks, Luke…for everything." She held his gaze. In the depths of her eyes, her terror remained. Once again, she appeared achingly small and vulnerable, and his heart squeezed tight.

He reached out and drew her into his arms. She wrapped her arms around his neck and leaned her head against his chest. Desire suddenly reared up inside him, an emotion that had absolutely no place at this time—at any time. He'd pulled her close to him to comfort her, and he was a total jerk for feeling that kind of emotion right now. All he wanted to do was comfort her. He held her only for a few moments and then released her.

"If you need anything—anything at all—let me know," he said.

She nodded. "Good night, Luke," she said.

"'Night, Carrie," he said and then left the room. He went back into the kitchen and placed their glasses in the dishwasher.

He glanced up just in time to see somebody outside run past the window. He whirled around and grabbed his gun. What the hell? Nobody should be lurking around his home.

Was it possible the creep after Carrie had followed them back here? Was he now seeking a way in to kill her? With his gun tightly in his hand, Luke quickly moved through the living room and out the front door.

Moonlight drifted down, making the landscape fairly visible. Adrenaline fired through Luke as he held his gun before him. He ran silently to the corner of the house, whirled around it and saw a figure.

"Stop or I'll shoot," he shouted.

"Don't shoot. Luke, it's me. It's Caleb."

Luke released a string of curses as he lowered his gun. "Caleb, what in the hell are you doing lurking around my house?"

"I just wanted to see Carrie and make sure she is okay. Johnny told me what happened tonight, and I was worried about her," Caleb replied. "She's my friend."

"I know she's your friend, but I could have shot

you." Luke released a deep sigh. "You should have just called me if you wanted to know how she was doing."

"I'm sorry, Luke. I guess I wasn't thinking."

"It's okay, and I assure you she's okay. In fact, she just went to bed, and that's where I intend to go."

"Okay. Again, I'm sorry, and I'll just leave you alone now."

Luke watched as his brother took off toward the barn, and then he went back into the house and locked the door. The adrenaline that had rushed through him now slowly ebbed.

He headed into his own bedroom. Once there, he placed his gun on the nightstand, and then he took off his shoes and socks. He shucked his jeans and T-shirt and then got into bed wearing only his boxers.

He wasn't surprised that Caleb had been worried about Carrie. It spoke to the friendship the two of them had been building. There was no question Luke was worried about Carrie. Who had forced her off the road and then threatened to kill her?

He'd been seeing her for a couple of weeks now, and she'd never mentioned having any problems with anyone other than her boss. As far as he'd seen, she was kind to everyone. So, who was after her and why?

Was it possible it had something to do with them trying to find his father's killer? No matter how he twisted and turned it all around, he simply couldn't connect the two things.

All he could do now was make sure Carrie remained safe. From this moment on, he'd pick her up and take her home from his place. Now that he thought about it, he never should have been okay with her driving home all alone at all hours of the night in the first place.

It had been a hell of a day. First there had been the pleasure of being back on a horse again, then the mistake of kissing Carrie.

Her lips had been so soft and filled with such heat and invitation. It hadn't felt like a mistake until it was over and he'd realized just how much he wanted to kiss her again and again. Even now the idea of kissing her once again stoked a touch of desire inside him.

Then there had been that moment when he'd thought Peter was actually going to confess to pulling the trigger and killing his father. With Peter crowing about his shooting skills, Luke had been certain he was going to crow about making the two shots that had killed Big John. But it hadn't happened.

And now this.

He turned off the lamp next to his bed and his room was plunged into darkness except for a faint ray of bright moonlight that drifted in through the window. Thoughts continued to whirl around in his head, making sleep impossible.

Had it been James Holloway who had tried to kill Carrie tonight? It had just been that morning that she'd quit her job with him. He'd obviously wanted a relationship with her. Had her quitting somehow sent him over the edge? Had he snapped and decided if he couldn't have her then nobody would? It was damned coincidental that Carrie had quit working for him that morning and then this happened.

Or was there somebody else? Somebody who was

not on her radar at all? What worried him most of all was the fact that a man had tried to kill her tonight, and because he had been unsuccessful, he might try it again—the next time with success.

"Luke?" Carrie's soft voice came his doorway.

He immediately sat up. "Yeah?"

There was a moment of silence from her. "Uh…can I sleep in here with you?" The question was tentative.

He understood her need to be with somebody. Surely he could just sleep next to her with no real issues. "Come on, then," he replied.

As she went around his bed to get in on the other side, he caught a vision of her in the moonlight, her shapely legs bare beneath the T-shirt she had on. She got into bed and immediately cuddled against his side.

"Were you asleep?" she asked softly.

"No, I wasn't."

"I'm afraid to go to sleep. I'm afraid of what dreams I might have," she replied.

He threw an arm around her and allowed her to snuggle even closer to him. "I never told you that one of my secret talents is I can sniff out a nightmare from a mile away."

A small laugh escaped her. "Kind of like a drug dog?"

"Exactly like a drug dog, only I smell nightmares, and I'll wake you if I think you're having one."

"Thank you, Luke. You're the very best."

He wasn't the very best. In fact, he was the very worst. She was looking for his comfort, and he was acutely aware of each point of contact with her.

Her sleek, bare legs rubbed against his, and her full breasts were warm and soft against his side. Her breath was warm on the side of his neck, and despite all his valiant efforts to the contrary, he felt himself getting aroused.

"Luke?" She whispered his name softly.

"Yeah?"

She raised up and looked down at him, her eyes luminous in the moonlight. "Luke, I want you to kiss me. I want you to make love to me."

"Carrie, lay back down and go to sleep," he said firmly. "You're under a lot of stress right now." Her words only made the desire inside him burn hotter. But he was desperately trying to do the right thing, even though it was extremely difficult.

"I realize I'm under stress, but that has nothing to do with me wanting to make love with you. I want you, Luke. I've wanted you for some time now, and I think… I think you want me, too."

His heart suddenly beat too fast, flooding his veins with a fiery desire he couldn't fight any longer. Her words unleashed something deep inside him, something that had been burning inside him for some time. With a groan, he reached for her and surrendered to the want he'd been fighting against for days.

Chapter Six

Luke's mouth crashed down to hers, tasting of white-hot desire and just a hint of whiskey. As he kissed her, she lay back down on the bed. She opened her mouth to him, and he took her invitation by dancing his tongue with hers.

She'd wanted this…she'd wanted him for weeks. In fact, it felt as if she'd wanted him all her life. This had little to do with what had happened this evening, although she would admit it was a perfect time to lose herself in Luke's arms.

As the kiss went on, it was as magical as it had been that afternoon. His lips were soft but commanding, and she returned the kiss with all the fever, all the intense heat he stoked in her.

His hands began to move, stroking up her back and then around to her breasts. Her nipples instantly hardened beneath her T-shirt to meet his touch.

Within minutes she was tired of the cotton material that kept him from touching her more intimately. She pulled her mouth from his and sat up. In one swift move, she pulled her T-shirt over her head and tossed it to the bottom of the bed.

"Carrie, you're so beautiful," Luke said softly.

"So are you," she replied, loving the sight of his bare chest in the faint moonlight that lit the room.

Once again, their lips met, and as he stroked her breasts, she ran her hands across his firmly muscled chest. His skin was warm and smooth, and at the same time she was enjoying touching him, she also loved him touching her.

When their kiss ended, he dragged his lips sensually along her jawline and then slowly across her collarbones. She gasped when his mouth captured one of her nipples. He teased and nipped at it, creating electric currents that raced through her entire body.

When he was finished with one, he moved to the other, giving it as much attention as he had the first. She was on fire, and he was the only one who could put it out.

Her heart cried out his name as his familiar scent surrounded her. She was utterly lost in him. All thoughts of the accident and attempted murder faded away from her mind as she embraced all things Luke.

She moved her hands lower, running down his chest and across the waistband of his boxers. It was obvious he was fully aroused, and he moaned deep in his throat with his pleasure at her touch.

She loved the sound of his moans. She loved that he was fully aroused for her, that he obviously desired her as much as she did him.

He moved one of his hands down her stomach and

down to the waistband of her panties. His fingers danced there, teasing her until she was half-mindless. She held her breath, and then he was there, touching her where she most needed his touch.

More…she wanted more. As he slid her panties down, she raised her hips to allow him to draw them off her body. His hand returned to where it had been, and he began to move his fingers against her in a steady rhythm.

She raised her hips to meet his touch as a sweet tension began to build inside her. He quickened his finger movements, and she cried out his name as a sudden climax crashed over and through her.

"Luke… I want more," she whispered urgently despite the pleasure he'd just given to her. Feverishly she plucked at his boxers, wanting them off him so he could fully make love to her.

He obviously felt the same need, for he pulled his boxers down and off. He quickly moved between her legs, and she grabbed his buttocks, urging him forward.

As he eased into her, she cried out his name once again. For a moment he remained buried deep inside her, not moving but filling her up completely. "Ah, Carrie," he whispered on a groan.

Then he began to stroke into her…slow, steady strokes that made her breathless, and a new tension quickly built up inside her. His mouth took hers again in a kiss that left them both breathless and panting.

Faster and faster he moved, taking her on a ride of pleasure she hadn't ever imagined possible. The tension built and built, higher and higher, and then she reached the peak, and as she fell over the edge, he groaned her name once again and found his own release.

Afterward they lay side by side, waiting for their breathing to return to normal. Her entire body felt warm and relaxed. She'd spent lots of time imagining what it might be like to make love to him, but her wildest fantasies couldn't compete with the reality.

It had been wonderful and magical, and she didn't want him to talk and somehow ruin it. After several minutes, she finally stirred. "I'll be right back." She slid out of the bed and grabbed her T-shirt and panties and then left the room for the bathroom in the hallway.

Now she was ready to fall asleep in his arms. feeling safe and secure and loved—if only for a night. Once she was cleaned up and redressed, she went back to his bedroom.

She smelled the scent of minty soap and knew he had gotten up and cleaned up. He'd pulled his boxers back on. "Luke, please don't say anything," she said as she got back into the bed. "We can talk about all this in the morning if you really feel the need. I just want to go to sleep now." She moved close to his side. "Deal?"

He hesitated a long moment. "Deal," he finally said.

He wrapped an arm around her, and she snuggled into him. Within minutes she was sound asleep.

She awakened the next morning with bright sunshine streaming through the window. Luke was no longer in bed with her, but his pillow still held the imprint of his head.

She remained in the bed, thinking about the night before and what she and Luke had shared. He'd been a wonderful, generous lover, and she wanted him all over again. But now it was time to get out of bed and face the new day.

She was surprised that when she moved to get up, her body protested. She ached all over, and it wasn't from Luke's lovemaking. She assumed it was from the car accident. She must have been banged around more than she realized.

The accident…she needed to call her insurance company and arrange for a rental car. It would be nice if Lane contacted her this morning to tell her that he'd arrested the man who had caused the accident—the man who had wanted to kill her. Unfortunately, she knew that probably wasn't going to happen.

Despite the warmth of the bed, in spite of what she and Luke had shared the night before, a chill walked up her spine as she thought of the accident. Of course, it hadn't been an accident at all. It had been on purpose, with the sole desire to kill her.

Who? Who would want to kill her? And why? She thought again of the man's voice. She still had the feeling she'd heard it before, but where? She just couldn't make a connection right now.

With these disturbing thoughts rolling around in her head, she finally pulled herself up. When she went into the hallway on her way to the spare bedroom, the air smelled of freshly brewed coffee.

Once in the bedroom, she pulled on the jeans and blouse she'd worn to go horseback riding the day before and then went back to the guest bathroom to brush her hair and freshen up. Thank goodness she'd left her cosmetic bag here so she could now put on a touch of makeup.

When that was done, she headed into the kitchen, where she found Luke seated at the table with a cup of coffee before him. "Good morning," she said.

"Good morning to you," he replied and immediately got out of his chair. "Sit and I'll pour you a cup of coffee."

"Thank you," she replied and eased down into a chair.

"How did you sleep?" he asked.

"Good, except this morning I'm definitely feeling all kinds of aches and pains from the car crash."

He turned and looked at her in alarm. "Do you need to see a doctor?" His voice held a wealth of concern.

"No, nothing like that," she quickly replied. "I'm just sore in places I didn't know I had."

"I'm sorry to hear that." He placed a cup of coffee before her and then sank back down across from her. He eyed her with concern. "Are you sure you don't need to see a doctor?"

"I'm sure," she assured him. "I'll be just fine."

"God, Carrie, you could have been killed from the car wreck alone."

"I know, but I wasn't. I'm here and I'm alive, and I'm very grateful for that."

He smiled. "That makes two of us. Now, how about I make us some breakfast?" he said.

"I don't want you to wait on me, Luke. You've done more than enough for me already." Memories of the night before suddenly filled her head once again, reminding her of how much pleasure she'd found in his arms. "Really, all I need from you now is a ride home."

"Before I take you home, I'm making myself some breakfast, and it's no big deal to add an extra egg or two and some toast for you." He grinned at her. "It's one of my secret talents—I make really good scrambled eggs with cheese and some cut-up ham and a little red and green pepper. Surely you don't want to leave here without tasting them."

She returned his smile. "Okay, you talked me into it. Now I have to try your scrambled eggs, especially since making them is one of your secret talents."

"You got it." Once again, he got up from the table and went to the cabinet, where he took out a skillet, and then he began pulling ingredients out of the refrigerator.

"Do you cook often?" she asked.

"Before my dad's death, I almost always made and ate my own meals here. Since then, I often eat at the big house with Mom and my siblings."

"Are you a good cook?" she asked, hoping to head him off from any grief or anger that might fill him concerning his father's murder. She also didn't want to give him a chance to talk about what had happened between them the night before. He'd told her he regretted kissing her. She feared he'd tell her he definitely regretted making love to her.

"I like to think I am," he replied. "What about you? Can you cook?"

"I don't do it often, but yes, I can cook. After my mom died, I had to learn pretty quickly. My dad didn't know how to cook, so if we wanted to eat, I realized I'd need to do the cooking."

For the next few minutes, they talked about what kinds of food they enjoyed cooking and various recipes. "I have to say, I'm vaguely surprised by your culinary skills," she said as he poured the egg mixture into the skillet.

"Why?"

"I've always thought of you as this big, macho guy who didn't cook or clean," she replied. "I figured you probably had a small group of women who happily did those things for you."

He laughed. "That's really what you thought?"

"Definitely women lining up to help take care of you," she replied. "You have a reputation as a ladies' man."

He placed four slices of bread in the toaster and punched down the buttons and then returned to stir the eggs. "Before Dad's murder, I was dating to find my significant other. I would date somebody a couple of times, and when I realized she wasn't the one for me, I'd move on to date somebody else. I don't know how else to find the perfect mate other than doing that."

"I get where you're coming from," she said. "A man can do that, but if a woman dates a lot and too often, she's sometimes called rather nasty names."

"Yeah, and that's unfortunate. But I realize I got a reputation as a heartbreaker, even though I never, ever intended to hurt anyone that I dated." He removed the eggs from the burner at the same time the toast popped up.

At least she was happy that they were talking about things other than what they'd shared the night before. She didn't want to hear him talk about how wrong it had been or that it had been a complete mistake, like he had when they'd only shared that simple kiss.

They had just finished eating when a knock sounded on the door. Luke answered. It was Lane, and he had Carrie's purse in his hand. "I thought you might need this," he said as he gave it to her. "We recovered it from your car."

"Thank you," she said as she took it from him. She checked inside, glad to see her phone and her wallet. "Thank goodness. Now once I charge my phone, I need to make some phone calls to see about getting a rental car."

"Your insurance will probably declare your car totaled," Lane said. "It suffered pretty severe front and back damage. You were lucky to get out of it without any injuries. And speaking of injuries, needless to say I have nobody under arrest yet concerning the events of last night."

"I didn't think you would," she replied. Once again, a cold chill waltzed up her back. Who was the man been who wanted her dead?

"We towed your car to Myers's lot," Lane continued. Ty Myers owned the only car dealership and garage in town. "He's waiting to hear from you, and he'll be able to give you the rest of your belongings that were in the car."

"I'll call him as soon as I get home and charge my phone," she replied.

Lane raked a hand through his thinning brown hair, a frown creasing his wide forehead. "Carrie, until we find the person who attacked you last night, it's important that you keep yourself as safe as possible. I don't have the manpower to put a security detail on you. You have to pay attention to your surroundings when you're out and about and make sure you aren't putting yourself at risk. Try to make sure you aren't alone whenever possible when you do have to go out."

Each word he said only made the chill inside her grow colder. "Carrie, if that man's intent was to kill you, it's quite possible he'll try again."

Even though logically she knew these things, hearing them spoken out loud only made it all worse. The same questions whirled around in her head with an awful dread. Who wanted her dead? And why?

ONCE LANE LEFT, they cleaned up the kitchen and then got into Luke's truck so he could take her home. He made sure to have his gun and holster riding his hip. Nobody was going to take him by surprise, especially when Carrie was with him.

Throughout the morning he'd tried to find the perfect time to talk to her about their lovemaking the night before. But the moment hadn't presented itself. However, it was a conversation he intended to have with her before they said goodbye for the day.

Jeez, they hadn't even used birth control. Things had flared out of control between them so fast he hadn't even thought about a condom. Bad on him. But it was important she understand that it was a fluke and didn't change the way he viewed her. She was a friend, and that was all she'd ever be.

"I'm so glad to have my purse and phone back," she said as he pulled away from the King ranch. "I was dreading having to replace everything."

"Yeah, it's good you have it back. Replacing everything like your driver's license and credit cards would have been a real pain."

"So, what time are we planning to go to the Red Barn tonight?" she asked.

He shot her a look of surprise. "Are you sure you're really up for that tonight?"

"I'm not stopping my life because of what's happened," she replied firmly. "What am I supposed to do, cower in my house until Lane arrests somebody? Lord knows when that's going to happen."

"It's your call, Carrie. I'll tell you what—why don't I pick you up about four and I'll cook dinner for you? We can just hang out around the ranch and skip the Red Barn for tonight."

He suddenly thought about that night when they stepped out of the Red Barn and somebody had shot at them. Was it possible the shooter had made an attempt on Carrie's life that night? Had she been the shooter's target?

A new tension tightened his chest at the thought. He needed to mention it to Lane. Maybe Luke needed to keep Carrie as close to him as possible to make sure she stayed safe. Right now, he couldn't imagine what his life would be like without her in it. She'd not only been his partner, but she was also his very sanity amid the sea of rage and grief that still rocked through him.

"That sounds perfect," she replied and cast him one of her warm, beautiful smiles. "But tomorrow night we're back on Peter watch at the Red Barn."

He pulled up in front of her house. "Just sit tight. I'll walk you to your door," he said. He cut his engine, got out and hurried around to the passenger door.

As he did, he looked first to the left and then to the right, making sure there was nobody lurking in the area either on foot or in a car. Satisfied there was no danger to her, he opened the passenger door, and she got out.

"Remember what Lane told you," he said as he walked her to her front door. "Stay aware of everyone around you, and keep trying to remember where you heard that man's voice before. Keep your door locked—don't open it for just anyone, and I'll see you back here around four."

She unlocked her door and then turned back to him. "Thank you for everything, Luke. I don't know what I would have done without you last night."

Minutes later he was back in his truck and heading home. He'd find a time later to talk to Carrie about what had happened between them the night before. She was a chill woman and would understand that things had just gotten out of control and that it wouldn't—it *shouldn't*—ever happen again.

Dammit, he didn't want a girlfriend. He didn't have time to woo anyone. He didn't have time for romance. He just wanted to catch his father's killer. When he'd come up with the idea of catching Peter bragging about his gun skills and confessing that he'd made the two shots on Big John, he'd never dreamed it would take this long.

Maybe he was wrong about Peter being the shooter. He knew the ranch hand had no personal animosity toward Big John. Despite him being a drunk and disgusting, Luke assumed he didn't have much of a criminal record or Lane would be looking at him closely. But at the time of the murder, Peter's boss, Wayne Bridges, had had a major reason to want Big John dead. And Luke believed Peter's skills with a rifle could be bought.

No, he wasn't wrong…unless… He shoved thoughts of his brother away. He didn't want to believe that Caleb was capable of killing his own father.

And just who in the hell was after Carrie?

All these thoughts whirred around inside his head even after he got home. Once there he took two steaks out of the freezer for dinner that night and then headed outside.

He was on the way to the stables when he ran into his brother Johnny. For the past couple of weeks, Luke had been trying to avoid his older sibling whenever possible.

"Hey, Luke," Johnny said as the two got closer to each other. "Where are you headed?"

"I thought I'd ride a few fences and check for breaks," Luke replied.

"Ribs feeling okay now?"

"Finally, they're much better," Luke replied.

"It was a hell of a mess last night."

"Yeah, thanks for being there for Carrie. She told me you were very nice to her before anyone else arrived," Luke replied.

"It was no problem. You're spending a lot of time with her."

"Yeah, I like her."

"Have you given any thought to the horse-breeding information I'd like you to find?"

The question poked at the anger that was never far from the surface. "I've been a little busy, Johnny. I don't know if you care anymore, but somebody murdered our father."

Johnny's eyes flashed darkly, and he took an aggressive step toward Luke. "You need to stop saying that, Luke. Dammit, of course I care about Dad, but I can't do anything about it. Lane is continuing to investigate and I've gotten on with living my life, something we all should be doing now."

Johnny drew a deep breath. "Luke, I need you here at the ranch. I need you to be present both physically and mentally. I just had to hire another ranch hand because you've been so absent around here. And if you're still doing crazy things to find Dad's murderer, keep in mind that it hasn't been that long since you were half beaten to death."

"I'm not doing crazy things, and my biggest worry right now is about Carrie. Somebody tried to kill her last night, and I intend to keep her as close to me as much as possible."

It was Luke's turn to take a deep breath. "I'm sorry you had to hire another man to help out around here, but maybe that's for the best, because I have a lot on my plate right now."

Johnny held his gaze for a long moment. "You know I love you, Luke, and I don't like to see you still struggling with your anger over the murder. You need to let it go and move on with your life."

"I'm trying to do that," Luke replied with a touch of a new anger rising up inside him. "Just because I'm not doing it your way doesn't mean I'm not doing it the right way for me."

"Don't be angry with me for caring about you," Johnny retorted. "I want to heal my family. Dad would hate the way we've all pulled apart instead of all coming together."

"I'll be healed when Dad's killer is behind bars. I'll be good once the creep who tried to kill Carrie last night is in jail," Luke replied.

"You need to leave both of those things to Lane," Johnny said.

"Yeah, right." Luke released a small laugh. "He has no clue who's responsible for either crime. He doesn't even have any suspects in mind."

"Luke, I just want you to get back to enjoying life. You can't mourn forever. Dad wouldn't have wanted that for you. He wouldn't like to see you the way you've been."

"I know, and I am enjoying spending time with Carrie. Of course, now I'm worried sick about her safety."

It was true. If anything happened to Carrie, he feared he'd drown in his own grief. She was the only bright spot in his life right now, even though he wasn't romantically involved with her.

Johnny reached out and patted Luke on the shoulder. "Let me know if I can do anything to help you, Luke. I know we've been at odds lately, but I'm here for you if you need me."

"Thanks, Johnny, I appreciate that," Luke replied. "And now I better get going. I'm picking up Carrie about four today and bringing her back here to hang out."

Minutes later Luke was on Storm's back and riding along the edge of the huge pastureland. His thoughts were still on his brother. There were only sixteen months between him and Johnny, and the two had always been close—and competitive with each other.

Growing up, if Johnny did something, then Luke worked to do it, too. They both had vied for attention from their parents, with Johnny often winning that battle.

Luke loved his brother, but he was frustrated that Johnny didn't share Luke's rage, his driving need to find out who killed their father. Johnny seemed content now to work the ranch and share his life with Chelsea. Luke didn't understand how Johnny—how *anyone*—had just moved on from the murder.

He didn't know how his sister was dealing with things. Since Ashley had moved back to town and was working in her shop, he hadn't seen much of her.

He rode for almost two hours, checking the fence line and on the huge herd of cattle that called the pasture home. He then headed back to his place for a hot shower and to get ready to pick up Carrie.

At four o'clock he pulled up in her driveway. She must have been looking out for him, as she immediately came out of the front door and ran to the passenger side of his truck. She was clad in a pair of black jeans and a bright yellow blouse, and the smile she wore was like a ray of sunshine.

"Hi," she said once she was settled in the seat next to him.

"Hi. Don't ever do that again," he said with reproach.

Her bright smile instantly doused. "Do what?"

"You ran out your door without even looking around outside. A bad guy could have been waiting in the bushes next to your porch and grabbed you before I could even get out of my truck. You should have waited for me to come up to the door to get you," he said.

"Oh... I... I guess I wasn't thinking. I saw your truck and..." Her voice trailed off.

"I don't mean to scold you, but Carrie, you have to be on your toes all the time. I will walk you to and from my truck as long as this man in on the loose. Again, I'm sorry for coming down hard on you."

"No, you're right," she instantly agreed. "And I won't make the same mistake twice."

"Good." He flashed her a grin. "Now, how was your day?" he asked as he backed out of the driveway.

"Busy," she replied. "Emily called me several times when my phone was dead, so as soon as my phone was charged, I called her back."

"Did you tell her what happened to you?"

"I did, and she was horrified. We agreed that when our work hours are the same, we'll ride together."

"Good, that's smart," he agreed.

"After talking to Emily, I made the accident report with my insurance company, and I have a rental car set up for me to get tomorrow. I also had to call Dr. Morris to let him know I couldn't start for him Wednesday but instead could start Thursday. What about you? How was your day?"

"It was okay. I did a little riding and then had a minifight with Johnny," he said.

"A minifight about what?"

He told her about the conversation he'd had with his brother. "I guess I just find it frustrating that he doesn't feel the same way I do."

"You know he's only trying to look out for you," she said.

"Yeah, I know. He just doesn't understand the drive I have to solve Dad's murder. Speaking of murder, did you hear any more from Lane today?"

"No, nothing, but I honestly didn't expect to. I spent the day trying to think of anyone who might have an issue with me. I also tried to remember where I'd heard that voice before, but I had no luck on either count."

"Hopefully it will come to you very soon. You remembering where you heard that voice might be the only way to catch this guy."

"I know—don't remind me. So, I'm looking forward to a home-cooked dinner from you tonight," she said.

He grinned at her again. "I hope you're satisfied at the end of it."

"I'm not real critical when it comes to food. I just like to eat."

They talked about food until they arrived at his place. Once inside, he took off his gun and set it on the counter, then he offered her a seat at the table while he got busy on the evening meal.

Before he'd left to pick her up, he'd put two big potatoes in the oven to bake and had made a salad. All he had left to do was cook the steaks, dress the salad and warm up some garlic bread.

He'd also called Lane and told him he thought the gunfire at the Red Barn might have been the first attempt on Carrie's life—something he wasn't going to talk about with Carrie unless she brought it up. She had enough on her plate to worry about without that additional concern.

He worked while they talked, and before long the meal was ready and on the table. "Oh my gosh, Luke, this is the best steak I've ever tasted," she said after taking a couple of bites.

"Thanks. It's all in the secret seasoning I use."

"Are you going to tell me what it is?"

He grinned at her. "I'll have to think about it," he said teasingly.

He wanted to keep things light with her this evening. She'd been through a terrible trauma the night before, and he wanted to be her soft place to fall, like she had been for him in the past.

Even though he still needed to make her understand

that just because they had made love the night before, it didn't mean they were romantically involved or lovers in the true sense of the word. But tonight wasn't a good time to bring it up.

Tonight, she just needed to relax and chill out, so as they ate, he entertained her with funny stories from his childhood. He loved to hear her laughter, and he made sure to make her laugh over and over again.

He told her about funny fights with his siblings. There had been a time when they were all angry with their mom, and so they had decided to run away from home.

They'd only run as far as the backyard area. They had dragged lumber from the barn to the yard and built a sort of shelter with the old wood and bedsheets.

"We were determined we were going to live out there forever. We each had taken something from the kitchen before we left. We had one apple, a cupcake, a bag of pretzels and I can't remember what else, but I can tell you splitting an apple four ways doesn't give anyone much apple," he said.

She laughed. "Why were you all so mad at your mother?"

"I don't even remember now," he admitted.

"So, how long were you out there?" she asked.

"Until darkness started to fall and the night insects started to sing. Ashley was the first one to go in. She was sure something was going to eat us all. Caleb was quick on her heels. He was positive something was going to kill us. Johnny and I managed to wait it out until about ten or so. We were both sleepy and just wanted the comfort of our own beds. The next day we had to clean up the mess we'd made in the yard, and we didn't try to run away again."

"So, you all learned an important lesson," she replied.

"Yeah, we learned that our beds were softer than the ground and a home-cooked meal was better than an apple split four ways," he replied, making her laugh once again.

They finished eating, and together they cleaned up the dishes. "Now that I ate so much, I'm ready for a walk," she said.

"That sounds good to me." He pulled his gun belt back on, and as he did, her eyes darkened.

"I wish you didn't have to wear that," she said softly.

"Carrie, I'm going to wear it until Lane finds the man who's after you. I told you before, I will keep you safe as long as you're with me."

"Thanks, Luke. I can't tell you how much I appreciate you."

Her words warmed his heart. They stepped outside and he threw an arm over her shoulder as they began a leisurely walk toward the barn. As always, the scent of her eddied in his head, a slightly exotic scent that continually stirred him on a primal level.

"It's another nice evening," she said.

"It won't be too long before it's going to get miserably hot," he replied.

"Maybe it will be a mild summer."

"That would be nice," he said.

As they got closer to the barn, he saw Caleb standing outside with Leroy Hicks. Luke's chest tightened. Leroy had worked for the Kings, but right before Big John's death, he had fired Leroy for theft and being drunk on the job.

At the time Leroy had made all kinds of horrible threats against Big John and the King ranch, but he'd had an alibi for the time of the murder, which had been corroborated by several other people.

Even though Leroy hadn't killed Big John, Luke couldn't believe his younger brother was now friends with the weasel. Luke couldn't be sure, but he believed the two of them were into something they shouldn't be in, but hell if Luke knew what it was.

It was only a month ago that Caleb and Leroy had been hanging out by the barn when several men on horseback began shooting at them. Johnny and Luke had gone after the men but had been unable to see who they were or find out why they had been attacking Caleb and Leroy.

Caleb had insisted he had no idea why the men had been shooting at them, but Luke and Johnny weren't sure they believed Caleb. Something was going on with Caleb, but damned if Luke could figure it out.

One thing was for sure—Luke believed Leroy was a bad influence on his brother, but there was nothing he could do about it. He couldn't exactly demand his adult brother pick his friends better.

As they met the two, Luke introduced Carrie to Leroy.

"Nice to meet you," Carrie replied and then smiled

at Caleb. "How are you doing, Caleb? Are you still working on paintings for your show?"

"Definitely." He looked at her intently. "How are you? Johnny told me what happened last night."

"I'm doing fine, thanks to your brother." She smiled at Luke.

"You want to come in and see a couple of my paintings?" Caleb asked Carrie, totally surprising Luke.

"You know I'd love to," she replied. "I've been interested in your painting for a while now."

"Leroy, you wait out here with Luke. Carrie, come on in and I'll show you a few of them."

As Carrie followed Caleb into the barn, a new tension tightened Luke's chest. Was it possible Caleb would tell Carrie something about the day of their father's murder? It was possible that in the next few minutes Carrie might hear something that would either damn his brother or exonerate him.

Chapter Seven

Carrie followed Caleb through the barn and into the doorway of his apartment, a small room with a single bed and a chest of drawers. There was a doorway that she assumed went into a bathroom and a curtain, behind which she assumed he hung his clothes. The whole area smelled of booze, weed, oil paint and turpentine.

An easel in the corner held a large blank canvas. "Looks like you're getting ready to start on a new one," she said.

"Yeah, I finished my last one three days ago."

"How long does it generally take you from start to finish on a painting?" she asked. She was aware that this was a huge moment, and she had no idea what to expect. Luke had told her Caleb spent a lot of time in the woods taking pictures of flowers and that he'd never shown his paintings to anyone except Leroy.

She had to be careful what she said and how she acted in order for Caleb to be completely comfortable with her. She knew what information Luke wanted her to get out of him and she'd do her best, but she couldn't push it.

"Usually, it takes me three to four days per painting, but then it takes several days for me to fill my creative well again," he replied. He gestured her toward the bed. "Have a seat."

"Thanks." She sat gingerly on the edge of the bed. The sheet that covered the mattress appeared dingy and gray. There was no top sheet or bedspread.

"My painting has always been my therapy. My dad didn't understand me, and he didn't like me very much. He thought I was useless because I didn't want to work on the ranch like Johnny and Luke. He didn't understand the dreams I had for myself."

"Oh, Caleb, I'm sure your father loved you very much."

He cast her a crooked smile. "Yeah, well, I'm pretty sure he didn't. Anyway, this is one of the paintings I intend to be in my show." He went behind the curtain and returned with a small painting of a single flower. Dewdrops glistened on the reddish-pink petals, and each leaf was painted in exquisite detail.

"Oh, Caleb, it's stunning," she exclaimed. "I never dreamed you were so talented."

"Thanks, Carrie." He smiled at her, obviously pleased.

"This is part of a collection just titled Nature. It's a group of painting that are mostly flowers. Then I have another collection entitled Feelings."

"Could I see something from that collection?" she asked. She was genuinely impressed by his work.

"Uh…okay." He disappeared behind the curtain once again, and when he reappeared he had two larger paintings in his hands. Carrie caught her breath, hoping he didn't see her complete shock.

She'd been expecting more greenery and flowers, but these paintings were abstracts in bold black and reds. The strokes were strong and more like slashes. The paintings portrayed violence and anger, and she found them deeply disturbing.

"So, what do you think?" Caleb's pale blue eyes held her gaze intently.

"I think it's obvious they are filled with a lot of emotion," she replied slowly. "I see a lot of sadness and unresolved issues."

"Exactly," Caleb said, once again obviously pleased by her words. "I'm glad you get that, Carrie. It's exactly what I was going for." He smiled at her. "I knew in my gut that you'd understand them…that you'd understand me."

"Do you want me to see more of your work?"

Caleb frowned. "No, I think this is enough for today." He placed the paintings back behind the curtain as Carrie stood from the bed. "I'm so glad that you *get* me," he said as he opened the door for them to walk out.

"When are you planning your show?" she asked.

"I'm now thinking about having it during the big Fourth of July celebration in town."

On the Fourth of July, the town went all out, with a fair during the day where vendors sold their fares. There was a contest for the best apple pie and another one for eating hot dogs. It was a day of fun, and then at night there was a carnival and a huge firework display. The new mayor, Stella Black, had promised that this year would be even better than ever.

"That would be a perfect opportunity for you," she said.

"Just remember that what you saw and what I said is our business and doesn't need to be shared with anyone."

"I won't forget that, Caleb," she replied.

They stepped back out into the sunshine, where Luke and Leroy were waiting. "You should feel very honored, Carrie," Leroy said. "Caleb hasn't shown his paintings to anyone but me."

"I do feel very honored," she replied and offered a warm smile to Caleb.

"You're almost family," Caleb replied. "And I feel like I can trust you. You're a kindred soul, Carrie."

"Come on, kindred soul," Luke said. "We need to finish our walk before nightfall."

"We'll see you two later," she said, and then she and Luke continued walking in the direction of the big house.

"So, what did you see?" Luke asked as soon as they were out of earshot of Caleb and Leroy.

"First of all, he told me that your father never understood him and didn't love him," Carrie said.

"I think that's been his excuse for all his bad behavior over the years. Dad didn't love him, so now he's a drunk and a drug user. Dad didn't love him, so he never had to take responsibility for any of his actions. It's been a big song and dance from him since he was a teenager."

"I don't think it's a song and dance. I think that's what he truly believes. The first painting he showed me was of a flower. It was absolutely beautiful. He has real talent, Luke."

"You think?" he asked in surprise.

"Well, I'm not exactly an art critic, but that flower was completely, breathtakingly gorgeous." She paused a moment and then continued, "And now do you want to hear the bad news?"

He frowned. "There's bad news?"

She nodded. "He then showed me two paintings that were definitely disturbing."

"Disturbing how?" Luke asked, slowing his footsteps as they talked.

"They were all black and red strokes. They looked like they were filled with rage and darkness. Looking at them, I really think your brother maybe needs help from a real therapist. Have you ever tried to get him help?"

"Several times. I know my mother has encouraged him to get some help, but he refuses. He keeps telling us his art is his therapy. So, what do you think about the idea of him being the one who killed my father?"

She could feel the sudden tension that wafted from him, and she wished she could take it away but knew she couldn't. "I don't know, Luke. After seeing the rage in those paintings, I wouldn't exclude him from the possibility."

He sighed. "That's what I was afraid you would say. Dammit, why has this been so difficult? This is a small town, and not many people could have taken the shots that killed my father."

His anger quickly rose to the surface. "And why in the hell can't Lane find one sick twist who wants to attack you?"

"Luke…" She grabbed his hand and squeezed it. "Remember that anger creates stress, and stress isn't good for you."

"Carrie, tell me the truth. Aren't you angry that somebody is after you? Aren't you angry that some-body tried to kill you last night?" He stopped in his tracks and gazed at her searchingly.

"No, that doesn't make me angry. It makes me com-pletely stressed."

He stared at her for a long moment and then laughed. "Woman, you are something else," he exclaimed.

His anger seemed to completely disappear as they walked on. In fact, he was far less angry now than he had been when they'd first started their quest. His bursts of anger came less and less frequently and were shorter in length.

She was encouraged that he hadn't brought up their lovemaking. She was elated that he hadn't tried to di-minish it or take it back.

They walked to the big house and then turned around to walk back. "Why don't we sit on your dock and listen to the fish jump?" she suggested.

"We can do that," he agreed.

A few minutes later, they were side by side on the wooden structure that extended out into the water.

Trees surrounded them, and for the first time since her crash the night before, she truly relaxed.

"Sometimes you have to push all the bad stuff out of your mind for a while and just enjoy being," she said. "I have a feeling you don't allow yourself to do that very often."

"When I'm with you, it's easier to do, but when I'm all alone, the bad stuff always seems to win out," he admitted.

"You need to work on that."

He grinned at her. "Yes, ma'am."

They remained seated on the dock talking about all kinds of things until darkness fell. They talked about their politics—they were both independents. They discussed favorite music. He was country-western, and she enjoyed more pop. However, they both liked oldies. Each and every subject they talked about make her feel like she knew him better and he knew her more.

"I should probably get you home," he said once darkness began to fall. They rose from the dock.

"Yeah, the next couple of days are going to be busy for me before I start work again on Thursday morning."

"Do you need a ride to Myers's tomorrow to pick up the rental car?" he asked once they were in his truck and headed back toward town.

"No. Emily has the day off and is taking me to get it, but thanks for asking."

"Carrie, remember that you need to watch where you go and who you allow to get close to you," he said. "You need to be aware of your surroundings at all times."

She couldn't help the way her chest tightened. "I know." Just that quickly she was back under her car, holding her breath and waiting for a killer to bend down and find her. She couldn't breathe as chills raced up and down her spine.

Don't let him find me. Oh God, please, please don't let him bend down and find me. The words rolled around and around in her head. She was trapped in the memories in her mind.

She stared out the side window, drawing deep breaths in an effort to calm herself down. She reminded herself that she wasn't beneath the car anymore. She'd survived both the car accident and the man attempting to kill her. He hadn't found her and she was safe... safe here with Luke.

She couldn't do anything about what had already happened, but she could think about where she'd heard that man's voice before. Identifying the voice might be the only way he'd be caught.

"Are you okay?" Luke's voice sliced through her troubling thoughts.

"I'm fine. I was just reminding myself how important it is that I try to identify the voice of the man who wants me dead," she replied.

"It's probably one of those things that the harder you try to remember, the harder it will be to remember," he said.

"I have a feeling remembering is the only way to catch this man. He certainly didn't leave any clues behind."

As they pulled up in front of her house, she was

grateful that Emily had turned the porch light on for her. "Sit tight," he said as he parked in the driveway.

She watched as he walked around the front of the truck to her door. As he opened it, he had one hand on the door handle and his other hand on the butt of his gun. He looked big and strong and made her feel incredibly safe.

As they walked to her door, she found herself following his gaze from the left to the right, seeking any danger that might exist in the dark shadows of the night.

When they reached the door, she stood with her back against it, and he stood in front of her. "Thanks, Luke, for taking my mind off things for a little while. It was nice to just chill out for a bit and not think about anything too important."

"Back at you," he replied softly. "Carrie, if you ever feel unsafe or that you're in a dangerous situation, day or night, I'm just a phone call away. Even if for some reason you're just afraid, call me."

"I appreciate that." He stood close to her—intimately close.

Her breath caught in her chest at his nearness, and she raised her face to him, hoping that he would take her in his arms, hold her tight and kiss her. Oh, she wanted him to kiss her once again.

She parted her lips in anticipation as he leaned toward her, his eyes darkening with something delicious. At the last moment, he jerked back from her.

"Good night, Carrie." His voice was deeper than usual.

"Good night, Luke," she replied. "Are we still on for the Red Barn tomorrow night?"

"That's up to you. Why don't I call you tomorrow afternoon and we can talk about it?"

"Okay, then I'll talk to you tomorrow."

Once inside her house, she leaned with her back against the door and thought about that moment when she'd been sure he was going to kiss her. But he hadn't.

This had started out as a desire on her part to get to know the man she'd had a crush on better, but it had grown into something much more, something much deeper.

She felt as if she knew Luke better than she'd ever known a man in her life. He had been vulnerable to her with his innermost feelings, and she had been vulnerable to him in the same way.

She loved spending time with him. He made her laugh, and he made her think. He challenged her in good ways, and each touch from him warmed her in a way no other man's touch had ever done before.

She was in love with him.

The realization slammed into her with a huge joy and more than a little fear. More importantly, she believed Luke was falling in love with her, too.

However, she couldn't see how this all would end. When he tired of going to the Red Barn on the off chance he'd catch Peter confessing to shooting his father, would he then just kick her to the curb? Would he be in a head space to embrace any love he might feel for her, or would he allow his anger and his need for revenge to keep him isolated and all alone?

With a sigh, she pushed herself off the door and headed upstairs. Another thought jumped into her head, bringing with it a chill of fear. She would never know how her relationship with Luke wound up if she was murdered.

FOR THE FIRST time since his beatdown, Luke put in a full day of work doing chores around the ranch. It felt good being out in the sunshine and working again. He not only did chores, but he also rode with Johnny for about an hour to inspect the herd.

He'd forgotten how much he loved all things ranching, like his father had before him and his brother did now. He loved the smell of the pastures and working with the herd of cattle that provided their livelihood.

He and Johnny made good partners. They were almost always on the same page when it came to the business. His brother had mentioned the horse-breeding program again that day, and Luke had told him he'd get to it in time. Thankfully, Johnny had dropped the subject.

Luke finally stopped for a break at around two and called Carrie.

"Did you get your rental car all squared away?" he asked when she answered.

"I did. At least I have wheels now to start at Dr. Morris's office ," she replied.

"What do you think about going to the Red Barn tonight?"

"You know me, Luke. I'm in—just tell me what time to be ready."

He thought about picking her up early so they could just hang out and talk before going to the bar, but then he changed his mind. "Why don't I pick you up around eight? I promise I won't keep you out too late since you're getting ready to start your new job ."

She laughed, that musical sound that he never got tired of hearing. "I appreciate that, but I'm a big girl. I can stay out as late as you need me and still be on my toes for work."

"Okay, then I'll see you tonight at eight."

He frowned as he hung up. He was getting too close to Carrie. He was starting to miss her when they were apart. He hated when he had to tell her goodbye, which he'd never expected. He thought about her first thing in the morning, and she was on his mind when he fell asleep at night.

He'd almost kissed her the night before. It had taken all his willpower not to kiss her again. He told himself he didn't need or want her as a lover, and yet he couldn't forget how soft and warm and giving she'd been in bed.

She had been an incredible lover, and if he had his way, he'd take her to bed over and over again. He'd explore more depths of the passion he felt for her. But that would be an enormous mistake. He already feared he'd sent her some mixed signals.

Somehow, he had to keep his emotional distance from her from now on. He'd already shared too much of himself with her. He wanted to keep her as his partner in crime, but it was time he maintained a healthy distance from her emotionally so his signals weren't mixed and she definitely understood they were just partners and nothing more.

At four o'clock he knocked off work and went in to take a shower. When he was cleaned up, he decided to go to the big house to eat dinner. He hadn't seen his mother for several days and hadn't eaten with her for far too long.

As he walked toward his childhood home, Johnny and Chelsea joined him. "It's nice to see you coming to dinner," Chelsea said. "I know your mother has missed seeing you there lately."

"Yeah, I've missed seeing her, too." To be honest, it had been difficult for Luke to see his mother so broken after the murder. Before Big John had been killed, Luke's mother had survived two bouts of breast cancer.

The first time she'd gotten it, it had been treated with radiation and chemo. She'd lost all her hair and had been sick for months. When it came back the second time, she'd had a double mastectomy. His father's death on top of everything else had nearly destroyed her.

"How's your mom doing as the new mayor?" Luke asked Chelsea.

"You know Stella—she's loving her newfound power and being the center of attention everywhere she goes," Chelsea replied. "It's what she's always wanted."

Stella Black owned the ranch next to the Kings' place. She was a tough lady who had single-handedly run her ranch and raised two children. Her first husband, the father of her son, Jacob, had died in a farm accident. He didn't know who Chelsea's father was.

Luke also knew there had been many times in the past when Chelsea had run to the King home after her mother had been particularly unkind to her. Stella always put on a pleasant face in public, but according to Chelsea, her mother could be a real witch behind closed doors.

"How's your brother doing, Chelsea?" he asked.

Luke had been friends with Chelsea's brother, Jacob, in high school, but Jacob had decided to leave Coyote Creek soon after graduation. He'd gone to Kansas City and worked as a police officer.

"He's doing fine. I think he's making plans to move back here in the next couple of weeks," she replied.

"Really? It would be great to have him back in town. Is he planning on joining the police force here?" Luke asked.

"I'm really not sure. I'm just glad he's coming home," Chelsea said.

"How's Carrie doing? You two seem thick as thieves," Johnny asked.

"Naturally, she's nervous about whoever is after her, but I have to say she's one of the strongest women I've ever known," Luke replied. "I'm picking her up later to go to the Red Barn."

"You guys seem to be hanging out there a lot," Johnny observed. "Do I need to worry about you developing a drinking problem?"

Luke laughed. "Not hardly. Carrie and I just enjoy having a few beers, listening to the music and just chilling," Luke replied. It was true. There were times when he was so deep in conversation with her that he momentarily forgot what they were really there for.

When they reached the big house, the air inside smelled of savory roast and simmering vegetables. His mother was seated in the wing-back chair next to the sofa. She wore a blue dressing gown that hung on her thin frame, and a blue-and-white scarf was wrapped around her head. Luke knew her hair was just starting to grow back in after the chemo treatments she'd undergone.

Despite the fact that she was far too thin and looked achingly fragile, Margaret King was still a beautiful woman. Her heart-shaped face showcased her bright blue eyes and her warm smiles.

Her eyes lit up when she saw him. "Luke, it's so nice to have you here for dinner. It's been a minute."

He walked over to her and kissed her on the cheek. "Sorry it's been a while since I've been here, but I'm looking forward to eating with you tonight."

"Are you still seeing Carrie?" she asked.

"I am."

She smiled. "I like her, Luke. I think she's a keeper."

Guilt swept through him. He was deceiving everyone by pretending he and Carrie were romantically involved. At that moment the door opened again, and Caleb walked in.

He greeted all of them and thankfully appeared to be relatively sober. "It's wonderful to have all my boys at the table tonight," Margaret said as they all moved into the dining room and sat down.

As always, the empty chair at the head of the table

evoked a tightening in Luke's chest. His anger rose—anger that Big John wasn't in his chair where he belonged, anger that he was dead and they didn't know who had done it or why. More than anything Luke wanted to know why. What was the motive for killing such a good man?

"Where's Ashley tonight?" Luke asked. Since the murder his sister usually tried to come out and eat dinner with their mother.

"She had a lot of new items come in today, and she told me she wanted to log them into her inventory so she could get some of them out on the shelves by tomorrow," Margaret replied. "She said she'd try to get out here tomorrow night."

"And she didn't need your help?" Luke asked Chelsea. Chelsea had gotten a job in Ashley's shop a little over a month ago.

"Apparently not," Chelsea replied. "She didn't call me in to help her. But I do work tomorrow night, so she should be free to have dinner here."

Nellie Maddox appeared, carrying in steaming platters of food. Big John had hired Nellie to cook meals when Margaret had first been diagnosed with breast cancer. Since that time, Nellie had become part of the family. She was both the live-in cook and housekeeper.

Nellie was in her midsixties. She was a little bit chubby, with long gray hair that she wore in a tight bun at the nape of her neck. She also had kind brown eyes. She was not only an excellent cook, but she'd also become a confidante to Margaret.

Luke knew that often in the evenings Margaret and

Nellie relaxed in the living room and watched television together. It was nice for him to know his mother wasn't all alone in the big house.

Tonight, for dinner, there were thick slices of roast and a platter of potatoes and carrots. Thick, rich gravy and homemade dinner rolls rounded out the meal. As they ate, Caleb was more talkative than Luke could ever remember.

When Big John was alive, Caleb rarely came to dinner, and if he did, he was usually silent and sullen. But tonight he appeared energized and was in a good mood. He also didn't appear to be drunk or drugged up.

As Luke remembered Carrie's assessment of Caleb's work, a heavy dread settled in his chest. There was no question that Big John had often ridden Caleb's ass hard, but Caleb had needed a firm hand. He'd been irresponsible and rebellious and often straight up disrespectful.

Still, Luke couldn't help but wonder if his father's killer was seated at the dinner table and not in the Red Barn. It was a sickening thought and one he hoped and prayed wasn't true, but he just didn't know.

As he listened to Caleb talk about his plans for his art showing and Johnny and Chelsea laugh and joke about their wedding plans, it felt like an affront to the man who was absent from the table.

Dammit, Luke wanted to know why his father was gone. He wanted to know who had shot Big John twice in the driveway of his own home.

Was he the only one who had not been able to move on? Was he the only one in the whole damn family who felt the absolute need to put a killer behind bars before he could really move on with the rest of his life?

If he found out that Caleb had been responsible for Big John's death, then he would see to it that his brother was arrested and prosecuted for the crime.

It would destroy a big piece of his heart if Caleb was guilty. Despite their differences, Luke loved his younger brother, but the guilty party had to pay. And he was more determined than ever to find the person responsible for the empty chair at the table.

"I GOT TO go into town to get some groceries, and you know I got nobody to watch you," he said as he began to tape down the thin little arms. "You just be good, Billie. Be good while I'm gone and I'll buy you some of that banana food that you like. I'll be back here as soon as possible."

Billie mewled as if in protest. "Don't whine," he snapped. "You know how much I hate it when you whine. Use your words, Billie."

God, he was so damned aggravated. And it was all *her* fault. As he continued to tape down Billie's arms, he thought about his last attempt to kill Carrie.

He'd almost had her. He'd managed to wreck her car, and it had all been so perfect. Eventually, if he'd had some more time, he would have found the bitch wherever she'd hidden and put a bullet in her head. He'd been close…so achingly close to achieving his goal.

But she'd been saved by another vehicle showing up. Damn his bad luck. The last thing he'd wanted was for whoever was in the other truck to be able to identify him. And damn her good luck in that other truck showing up just in time to save her.

His rage toward her was now all-consuming. Killing her was the first thing he thought about in the morning and the last thing he thought about before going to sleep. The only way to rid himself of the rage that burned inside him was to take her off the face of the earth forever.

He needed to watch her die, slowly and painfully. She deserved to die for all the lies she'd told, lies that had destroyed his entire life. He finished taping Billie down. "Okay, I'll be home as soon as possible."

The mewling came again. "Dammit, Billie, stop whining. You know I have to tape you down to make sure you stay safe while I'm gone. I have to get some groceries. You want to eat, don't you? I told you I'll be back as soon as I can."

He grabbed his wallet and his keys from the edge of the kitchen table and then headed out the front door, locking it behind him. Thankfully there was very little damage to the front of his truck. Hell, the old truck was beaten up and damaged on nearly all four sides anyway. Nobody would even notice a few more dents and bangs.

There was no way anyone would know he was the one after her. It had been nearly a year since she'd told him all the lies. He'd been patient, but now his patience was gone, and it was time for her to pay.

There was only one thing he really regretted. He was sorry he'd spoken to her when he was hunting her down in the moments after the wreck. He hadn't worried about her hearing his voice then, because he believed he was going to kill her.

Apparently—thankfully—she hadn't recognized his voice, because nobody had shown up at his door to arrest him. If he was going to rid himself of the constant anger inside him, he had to kill her. He just had to get more creative in how he intended to complete his goal. He could do that.

He smiled to himself as he pulled into a parking space in front of the grocery store. He knew he could come up with the perfect plan to assure that bitch's demise. It was just a matter of time.

Chapter Eight

Carrie sat at the kitchen table with Emily. The two of them had gotten home from work a half an hour before and were now sharing a frozen pizza for dinner.

It had been a good day. Dr. Morris, who was much older than Dr. Holloway, had been married to his wife for thirty years. He was an infinitely kind man both as a doctor and as an employer.

"It was so nice to work today and not feel like I had to dodge and weave inappropriate closeness and touches from the doctor," Carrie said.

"I've been working for Dr. Morris for four years now, and there has never been an issue like that." Emily moved a second piece of pizza from the pizza stone in the center of the table to her plate.

"I didn't realize just how much I dreaded going into work each morning until now," Carrie admitted.

"I'm glad you're with Dr. Morris. He truly is a good guy to work for. All the staff absolutely love him."

"I'm glad I'm working for him now, too," Carrie replied.

"So, what are your plans for the rest of the night?" Emily asked.

"The usual—Luke is picking me up around seven thirty, and we're heading to the Red Barn to hang out."

Emily eyed her closely and with more than a bit of concern. "Are you sure you really should be doing that right now? Surely it would be safer to stay here or at Luke's place."

"If you're concerned about my safety, don't be. Luke is a well-armed bodyguard, and I feel perfectly safe when I'm with him."

"So, what's going on between the two of you?"

"What do you mean?" Carrie took a bite of the pizza.

"I mean, you two have been seeing each other every night for a while now. What's going on with the relationship? Where's your head where he's concerned?"

Carrie swallowed her bite and then took a drink of her soda before replying. "I'm in love with him." The words popped out of her mouth as her heart expanded with warmth. She knew with every fiber of her being that she was hopelessly, madly in love with Luke King.

"Oh Carrie, that makes me happy for you and worried about you at the same time."

"Worried why?" Carrie looked at her friend in confusion.

"Before he was dating you, he had quite a reputation as a heartbreaker. I don't want him to break your heart, too."

Carrie laughed. "Trust me, I'm not a bit worried about that. Has Luke dated a lot of women in the past? Absolutely. But all he was doing was looking for somebody he wanted to spend the rest of his life with. We talked about it, and I'm fine about it."

"Do you think you're that somebody for him?" Emily asked. "Are you the person he wants to spend his life with?"

"I hope I am." She desperately wanted to be that somebody in his life forever.

Emily picked a piece of pepperoni off her pizza and popped it into her mouth. "So, has he told you he's in love with you?"

Carrie frowned thoughtfully. "No, we haven't said the words to each other, but I believe he is. I feel it, Em. I feel his love for me in everything he does."

"Have you slept with him yet?"

Carrie felt the warmth that leaped into her cheeks.

Emily laughed. "You don't even have to answer that. It's written all over your face." She sobered. "I just hope you don't get hurt, Carrie."

Carrie released a dry laugh. "I've got some crazy monster trying to kill me. Right now, I'm not too worried about Luke hurting me."

"Point taken." Emily's eyes darkened. "And you still haven't figured out who the voice belongs to?"

Carrie shook her head. "I've absolutely racked my brain, and I still can't figure it out." It was so frustrating, because she knew if she could identify whom the voice belonged to, then Lane could make an arrest and she would no longer have to fear for her life. "It's like having something on the tip of your tongue but not being able to figure out what it is."

"Well, I hope you figure it out sooner rather than

later," Emily replied. "Just so you know… I would definitely beat somebody's butt if they came after you and I was anywhere around."

Carrie laughed and then smiled at her friend. "Thanks, Emily."

At seven thirty as she waited for Luke to arrive to pick her up, she thought about how much she appreciated Emily's friendship.

They had known each other in school, but Emily was two years older than Carrie, so they hadn't hung out together then. They'd reconnected and become close friends when they were working together at the hospital. That had been five years ago, and their friendship had only grown deeper and better over those years.

Emily knew her better than anyone else except for Luke. Emily had been by her side when she'd broken up with Rory. She knew all the things Carrie longed for in her life. More than anything, Carrie wanted a family. Losing her mother at such a young age had shortchanged her in the family department.

She wanted to build what she had lost when her mother had passed away—a family unit with a husband who loved her and children she could cherish.

When she saw Luke pull up in the driveway, her first instinct was to run out the door to greet him, but instead she remained inside, knowing he'd come up to get her and escort her to his truck.

Twilight had fallen, heavy and dark with purple shadows. She watched him get out of his truck, his hand on the butt of his gun as he looked to the left and then to the right.

Since the night of the wreck, the only place she truly felt safe was in Luke's presence. She knew when they were together, he was constantly looking out for her safety.

When he reached her front door, she opened it and stepped outside. "Hi," she said.

"Hi, yourself," he replied lightly. "Are you ready for another night at our favorite spot?"

"I'm ready." When they reached the truck, he opened the passenger door, and she slid inside and then watched as he walked around to the driver's door.

He looked as handsome as ever with his slightly shaggy dark hair complementing the bright blue of his eyes. As usual, he wore jeans that fit perfectly on his long legs and across his nice butt. He wore a light blue T-shirt that stretched taut across his broad shoulders and chest and made her remember stroking her hands across his naked body.

Her love for him buoyed up in her chest, making her feel half-giddy. Did he love her? Or was he just using her in the capacity she'd given him permission to do? Surely he had feelings for her after all the time they had spent together.

He got into the truck, and she shoved her thoughts out of her mind. Now wasn't the place or time to tell him she'd fallen in love with him—hard.

"So, tell me all about your first day of work," he said as they pulled away from her house.

"It was actually a great day," she replied and went on to tell him everything she had experienced with her new boss. By the time she finished, they had reached the Red Barn.

As always, they took the table closest to Peter and his cohorts, who already appeared more than a little bit buzzed. "Hey look, lover boy is back," Peter said, and the men at his table all guffawed as Carrie and Luke sat down.

Carrie immediately felt the tension that wafted off Luke. "I'd rather be a lover boy than a killer," Luke replied.

The laughter halted, and Peter glared at Luke, his dark eyes intense. "And just who the hell do you think I killed?" The air around them suddenly snapped with a whisper of danger.

"I believe you shot my father," Luke replied.

Carrie held her breath. She'd had no idea that Luke had intended to confront Peter openly this way. There was a moment of pregnant silence, and then Peter threw back his head and laughed.

"Now why in the hell would I kill Big John?" Peter asked.

"I think your boss hired you to do it. He knew my dad was going to win the mayoral election, so he wanted Dad out of the way," Luke replied.

Peter narrowed his eyes. "You're way out of line here, man. First of all, there's no amount of money that would make me murder somebody. Secondly, Wayne Bridges is the tightest man in the world. He wouldn't part with a dime of his money for a scheme like that. I might be a drunk, and some might think I'm a lowlife, but I'm not a damned murderer, and you better not be going around and saying I am."

"I'm not saying anything to anybody." Luke got up from the table and looked at him. "But let's be real here—you're one of only a very few here in town who could have made that shot."

"You got that right," Peter fired back. "There's only a few of us who could have made that shot, and if I remember right, you three King boys are all good shots, too. Maybe you fired that shot, Luke."

Luke lunged across the table, and Peter jumped up from his chair. "Take that back," Luke shouted as his hands curled into fists at his side.

Carrie's chest tightened with wild anxiety. Luke's anger was a palpable force in the air. But if a fight broke out, she knew he wouldn't just be fighting Peter—he'd be fighting all the men were with Peter.

"Luke," she said, hoping her voice would reach him through his haze of emotion.

However, he remained in fight mode and glaring at Peter. "You take that back," he repeated angrily.

"I was just making a point," Peter said. "There are plenty of people who could have made that shot. I'm not the only one, and I had nothing to do with your daddy's death." He sat back down at his table. "And that's the damned honest truth."

Slowly Luke's fists uncurled, and he drew several deep, audible breaths. He turned and looked at Carrie. "I'll be right back with our drinks."

She watched him weave toward the bar through the

small crowd of people. She released a shuddery sigh. She'd been sure there was going to be a fistfight.

There was no question Peter had been a jerk to say what he had said. And Luke had taken his bait, responding in anger. She didn't know how Luke felt about the conversation, but she believed Peter.

As much as she'd hoped their little scheme would work to get the closure Luke needed, she no longer believed Peter was behind Big John's murder.

Luke returned with two beers, and for the next half an hour or so they sat. Luke was quiet, obviously deep in his own thoughts, and she didn't know what to say or how to pull him out and up. For the first time since meeting him, she didn't know what to say to him, and she couldn't imagine what he was thinking.

"Are you ready to go?" he asked once their beers were gone.

"I'm ready if you are," she replied.

Together they got up and headed for the exit. The night was warmer than usual, and Luke immediately turned on the truck air conditioner.

"Talk to me, Luke," she finally said after several minutes of driving in silence.

He released a deep, audible sigh. "I'm totally ashamed of myself."

"What?" She looked at him in surprise. "Why?"

"I'm ashamed of how quickly I lost my temper in there. I'm ashamed of how far I allowed Peter to get under my skin."

"What Peter said was totally out of line," she replied firmly.

"Still, I shouldn't have responded to him in the way I did. I know he's a jerk, but that doesn't mean I have to be one, too." He flashed her a quick, contrite look. "Sorry about that."

"You don't have to apologize to me. I know how emotions run high around this particular topic." She was oddly pleased with his apology, even though she didn't think he owed her one.

"Now I don't know whether I believe Peter or not." He tapped his fingers on the steering wheel. "There's a part of me that wants to believe he was lying. I mean, why should I believe he'd tell me the truth about committing a murder?"

"I don't know what to believe," she replied. "But he certainly sounded like he was telling the truth. Maybe what you need to do is make a list of all the people in town who are excellent shots with a rifle."

"Yeah, that's definitely a good idea," he replied. "I don't know why I didn't think of that sooner. I just homed in on Peter from the very beginning and that was that."

He drove for a few minutes in silence, and she could feel the weight of his thoughts—thoughts she wished she could see. She wanted to support him in any way she could, but she couldn't do that if he didn't share with her. And at the moment he wasn't sharing.

It was only when he pulled up and parked in front of her house that he turned to look at her, his tension-filled features clear in the light from the dashboard. "You know what really stinks?"

"What's that?" She reached out and placed her hand

on his forearm. She could feel his muscles there were all bunched and knotted. His eyes looked positively feverish in the pale illumination.

"I *need* Peter to be guilty. I *need* to believe he's the one who killed my dad, otherwise I'm left with only one other suspect, and that's my brother."

He stared at her bleakly, and in that moment her heart absolutely broke for him. "Luke, have you considered the possibility that it isn't Peter or Caleb, but your father's killer might be somebody else who is not even on your radar?"

He frowned. "Dammit, Carrie, how am I supposed to solve this if it's somebody else? I don't know who else to look at for this."

"Luke, it's not your job to solve it," she replied gently.

"But it is," he said with a touch of anger. "It is my job, because nobody else cares about solving it. I have to do it to…to prove to my father that I am worthy of his love…that I am the son who loves him most."

"Luke, your dad is dead," she said softly. "He won't care who solves his murder. I'm sure your dad knew how very much you loved him, and you don't have to prove your worthiness to him or anyone else. And I'm sure your father loved you very much."

He stared outside the front window. "I know he's dead and he won't care who solves his murder, but I won't stop digging until the killer is found out and thrown in jail. I'll go home and write up that list you suggested." He turned and looked at her, his gaze intent. "Carrie, are you still with me?"

"Of course. I'm with you for as long as you want me," she replied. Her love for him begged to be released. She wanted to tell him the depth of love she had for him in her heart, but she knew this wasn't the time—not when they were talking about murder.

Once again, he released a deep sigh that seemed to alleviate some of the anger that had gripped him. "I still want you," he replied. "Now let's get you inside." He opened his truck door and got out.

I still want you. His words shot a delectable warmth from her head to her toes. She knew he meant he still wanted her to help him solve his father's murder. She just hoped he still wanted her because he was falling in love with her.

LUKE SAT IN one of the chairs on his front porch and stared off to where the sun was slowly sinking in the sky, painting it in shades of fiery reds and oranges.

He'd called Carrie earlier in the day to tell her he wasn't going to the Red Barn tonight and he'd see her in the next day or two.

There was no question that his confrontation with Peter the night before had messed with his head. He had been so sure the man was guilty. Of course, Peter would be a fool to admit that he pulled the trigger and had killed Big John. But Peter's voice had rung with more than a grain of truth.

Surely if Bridges had paid Peter to kill a man, Lane would have checked out the finances between the two men. Apparently, there had been no flow of money between Wayne Bridges and Peter. Unless of course it had been cash and Peter was now sleeping on a pillow full of money that he couldn't deposit in any bank.

But what if it wasn't Peter? After he'd taken Carrie home the night before, he'd returned to his house and spent the next hour or so writing down the names of all the people he knew were more than proficient with a rifle.

Every couple of years, there was a shooting competition out at Walt Zimmerman's ranch. Walt was in his midsixties and had been hosting the contest for the past twenty years. Targets were set up in his pasture, and people paid a fee to participate. There were usually some out-of-town people who showed up, hoping to win first-place bragging rights and the five-hundred-dollar prize money.

Luke had stayed up half the night thinking of all the names of the men and women who had been able to hit close to the bull's-eye. Peter had been right in that all the King brothers were good shots.

He didn't know the names of the out-of-towners who showed up, but he'd been able to list a dozen people right here in town. There were even two women who had made the list. Henrietta Bakersfield worked at the post office. She was a mild-mannered woman, but put a rifle in her hand and she became Annie Oakley. The other woman who made his list was their esteemed mayor, Stella Black.

However, he couldn't think of a single motive that anyone on the list would have to kill Big John. So, he was back to square one, still thinking that Peter was good for the crime.

He now looked up the lane, where Caleb and Leroy stood outside the barn drinking beers and laughing. He knew Leroy now worked on the Black ranch, which made it easy for him to walk here to hang out with Caleb when Leroy was off duty. He stared at his brother for several long moments.

Was it Caleb? Had he somehow snapped, or had he been high and decided to take out his own father? Luke had heard his brother and his father fight the night before the murder.

Caleb had wanted Big John to give him the money to open up a place in town for Caleb to sell his artwork. Big John had laughed in his face and told Caleb if he wanted money, then he needed to get off his butt and do some work around the ranch, that he could earn the money, but Big John wasn't going to just give it to him.

Caleb had stormed out of the house, as angry as Luke had ever seen him. Had that fight prompted Caleb to get drunk or high and then seek out revenge? The very thought made Luke sick to his stomach.

Luke had never felt as alone as he did at this moment. He knew he could call Carrie and she'd be up for spending time with him, but he didn't feel like he'd be good company for her or anyone else at this moment in time.

He watched as Caleb and Leroy finished their beers and then headed up the path that would take them into the woods. It was an odd time to go hiking in the wooded area, but then again, maybe Caleb wanted to photograph some of theflowers he foundat sunset.

What if Carrie was right? What if the killer was

somebody not even on his radar? What if he never found the murderer? Would he be able to live the rest of his life with this yawning emptiness in his heart? Would he forever feel as if he'd somehow let his father down? There was definitely a part of him that was just tired of thinking of it all.

He got up from the chair and walked toward the big house. He suddenly felt the need to talk to his mother. He hadn't talked to her privately since before the murder, but he felt the need to do so now.

He found his mother seated in her chair in the great room. She brightened as he walked in. "Luke," she said in surprise.

"Do you have a minute?" he asked.

"Honey, I always have more than a minute for you. Please, sit down."

He sank down in the wing-back chair across from her.

She frowned. "What's going on, Luke? You look like you have a lot on your mind."

"I do," he admitted. He hesitated a moment and looked down at the coffee table. He drew a deep breath and then looked back at his mother. "I miss him, and I know you must miss him terribly, too. How do you get through each day?"

"Oh, Luke. I'm going to miss him every minute of every day for the rest of my life. But I have so many wonderful memories of him and of us together."

"But aren't you angry?" Luke pressed. "Don't you want revenge?"

"What good would revenge or anger do at this point?

No matter how angry I am, that doesn't bring him back." She smiled at him gently. "And Luke, your anger won't bring him back, either."

"Logically I know that, but I feel like I need to keep searching for his killer so he'll know how much I loved him." Luke's voice broke as a wave of emotion gripped him.

Margaret got out of her chair and moved to the sofa, then gestured for him to join her there. Once he was seated next to her, she took his hands in hers.

"Luke, your father knew how much you loved him, and he loved you very much. He used to talk to me about how much he enjoyed it when it was just the two of you in the stables. He thought you were so bright, so knowledgeable about the horses."

"I... I never knew that," Luke replied.

"Johnny demanded your father's attention. He was so bold, and Caleb...well, your daddy didn't understand Caleb at all. Caleb demanded all negative attention. But you...you were quieter and didn't demand much of anything. Your dad actually admired that about you. He thought you were much stronger than both Johnny and Caleb. Oh Luke, he was so proud of you."

Tears burned at Luke's eyes as his emotions bubbled over. "That's all I ever wanted...to make him proud of me." To his horror a sob ripped out from deep within him.

"Oh, honey." Margaret wrapped her arms tightly around him, and suddenly he was bawling like a baby in his mother's arms. They were the first tears he had cried for his father.

He sobbed for the days he would never have again, for the laughter he'd never again share with his father. He cried because he didn't understand why such a good man had been killed.

"Tell me, how do we go on?" he finally managed to choke out.

Margaret patted him on the back. "We go on because Big John made us all strong, and he would want us to go on and live our best lives. We go on by remembering the laughter we all shared, the love he shared with us. We honor him when we remember him, Luke, not when we harbor anger and a desire for revenge in our hearts."

Luke finally sat up and wiped at his eyes, embarrassed by his breakdown in front of his mother. "God, I don't remember the last time that I cried like that."

"I remember the last time you did." She smiled at him. "It was when you were twelve years old and Melody Watkins didn't give you a valentine."

Luke laughed. "I had decided I was going to grow up and marry Melody, and then she broke my heart by not giving me a valentine."

"Speaking of your heart, how are you and Carrie getting along?"

"We're doing fine." He still hated that he was lying to his mother about the relationship.

"Is it a true love connection? You know I'd love to see you settle down with a wife. I'm more than ready for some grandbabies."

"Whoa, slow down," he said and laughed again. "It's not like that with us. We're just really good friends."

"That's the way it started with me and your father. I considered him my very best friend, and he felt the same way about me. Then one day we realized we never wanted to be apart from each other and what we really felt for each other was actually a deep, abiding love."

"I don't know where things are going between me and Carrie. We're just taking it one day at a time right now," he replied.

"As long as you're both on the same page," Margaret said. "You're such a good man, Luke. Don't let your father's death stop you from living your life to the fullest. That's what he would want for you."

Fifteen minutes later as Luke walked back toward his place, he felt lighter than he had since his father's death. He was embarrassed by his blubbering in his mother's arms, but it had definitely been cathartic.

Still, nothing had changed in his desire to find his father's killer, although the need to do so was a little less pressing. And now that some of the pressure was momentarily gone, his worries about Carrie filled him.

When would the creep who was after her be found out? He worried every day when he knew she was driving to and from work. It soothed him most days that she and Emily could ride together to work, but their work schedules would not always be the same.

He wished like hell she could identify the person behind the voice, but so far, she couldn't...just like he couldn't identify his father's murderer.

He had just passed the barn when Leroy and Caleb

came running out of the woods. They ran like they were being chased by demons out of hell.

They whirled into the barn and slammed the door behind them. A minute later another man came crashing out of the woods. He was a short, wiry man with dark hair tied back at the nape of his neck with a long leather tie. Tattoos covered his face and neck. He was missing one eye, and he held a gun in his hand. Luke immediately pulled his weapon, and for several long moments the two faced each other in a standoff.

"Who are you and what are you doing on our property?" Luke asked. Luke had never seen this man before. He wasn't a native of Coyote Creek. His heart quickened as he faced off with the stranger. What in the hell was going on here?

"You don't need to know my name." The man held his gun steady and pointed at Luke's chest. Luke returned the favor by keeping his gun aimed at the man.

The air snapped with danger as the two men faced off. Luke had no idea what was going on, but his entire body filled with adrenaline. "I need to know what you're doing on my property," Luke said. He narrowed his eyes as he watched the man closely.

Was he going to shoot? Who was this man and what was he doing here? Luke held his gun tightly, ready to pull the trigger if necessary.

After several long moments, the stranger lowered his gun and put it in the black holster that rode low on his hips. "I'm looking for Caleb King. I know he just came this way."

Luke slowly lowered his gun but kept it firmly in his hand. "Why are you looking for him?"

"I got some business with him."

Luke narrowed his eyes. "What kind of business?"

"None of your business," the man replied sharply. "Are you going to tell me where he went or not?"

"I'm not Caleb's keeper. I don't know where he went, but I know it's time for you to get off our property. Otherwise, I'll call the cops to get you off."

"Hey, I don't want any problems here." The man took several steps backward. "There's no need to get the cops involved. If you see Caleb, just tell him Joker is looking for him and will catch up with him later." The man turned and ran back the way he had come, disappearing into the falling night shadows.

Luke stared after him for several long moments. What in the hell was that all about? That guy didn't exactly look like an upstanding citizen, and he definitely hadn't wanted any cop involvement. The man had looked like a tough thug.

What business could Caleb have with a person like that? What on earth had his brother gotten himself into? And was it possible it hadn't been Caleb who had killed their father? Was it possible it was somebody Caleb was doing "business" with?

Chapter Nine

Carrie had been disappointed when Luke called to tell her he was taking a night off from the Red Barn, which meant he was taking a night off from her.

However, it had worked out well, for her father had been in town, and so she'd spent the evening catching up with him. As she'd talked with her father about all things big and small, she'd thought about Luke, who would never again have a chance to just sit and talk with his father. Her heart hurt for Luke and his loss.

When it was time to say goodbye, she hugged her father extra hard, recognizing that he could be taken from her in the blink of an eye. The death of Big John had reminded her that everyone was living on borrowed time and it was important to tell the people in her life that she loved them whenever she got the chance.

Today work had been as pleasant as the day before. She and Emily had picked up Chinese food for dinner on the way home, and then Luke had called to ask her if he could pick her up around six thirty.

There was something in his voice that made her

feel like he needed her. He hadn't mentioned going to the Red Barn, but she wanted to do whatever he needed to do.

At six fifteen dinner had been cleared up and she'd freshened up and changed from her scrubs into a pair of jeans and a sleeveless hot-pink blouse.

She sat on the sofa awaiting Luke's arrival, and as always when she had a moment to think, her thoughts went to the dark place of knowing somebody wanted her dead. Who did that voice belong to?

Had she heard it in town? Maybe somebody working at the grocery store or in one of the other stores she frequented? Had he been a patient of Dr. Holloway's practice? Or had one of his family members been in Dr. Holloway's office and she had been the attending nurse?

She got up from the sofa and moved to the front window to watch for Luke. She appreciated that he was a punctual man, and at precisely six thirty he pulled into the driveway.

As usual, he got out and she waited until he was at her front door before opening it. "I missed seeing you last night," he said once they were in the truck.

"I missed seeing you, too," she replied, warmed by his words. She decided not to tell him that she'd spent the evening before with her father. There was no reason for him to know that, and it would only rub salt in his wounds. "So, how was your night?" she asked.

"Both soothing and disturbing."

"Those words don't exactly go together," she replied.

He flashed her a quick smile. "Yeah, I know." The

grin was quickly swallowed up by a frown. "On the soothing side, I had a really good talk with my mother. She told me not only how much my dad loved me, but that he enjoyed the time he spent in the stables when it was just him and me."

"That's good, Luke. I hope you took her words to heart," she replied.

"I did. In fact, yesterday with her was the first time I really grieved, and now I feel like a big weight has been lifted off me."

She was happy for him. It was what he'd desperately needed, and now maybe he would be ready to move on with the rest of his life…be ready to move on with her.

"However, I still intend to hunt for his killer," he added, making her feel like he wasn't ready to move on at all. It definitely disappointed her a bit.

"So, does that mean we're headed back to the Red Barn tonight?"

"Not tonight," he said. "Tonight I just wanted to hang out with you."

"You know I always love spending time with you, Luke."

He was silent for a few minutes, and then he flashed her a quick glance. "We're friends, right?"

"Absolutely. I consider you one of my very best friends," she replied.

"Good, so we're both on the same page with that."

"Definitely." Was he intentionally friend zoning her, or did he just want to make sure she truly was his friend? She wasn't sure what his words meant, and she was afraid to ask him to make himself clearer.

He pulled up in front of his place and parked. "Why don't I grab us a couple of beers and we can sit on the front porch for a while?" he said as they walked to his door.

"That sounds good to me, and then you're going to tell me the disturbing part of your day yesterday." She sank down in the cushion of one of the porch chairs.

"Definitely. I'll be right back." He disappeared into the house.

It was a beautiful evening. The late-June sun was warm but not too warm as a light breeze blew. The breeze rustled in the leaves of the nearby trees, and birds chirped their happy songs, making a pleasant melody of nature.

Luke came back out the door with two beers. He handed her one, and then he sank down in the chair next to her. "By the way, you look really nice," he said.

"Thanks." He looked as good as ever in his jeans and a striped gray-and-white polo shirt.

He took a long draw from his beer and then released a deep sigh and looked off in the distance. A muscle ticked in his jaw, and she could feel a new intensity wafting off him.

"Talk to me, Luke. What's going on? What has you so disturbed?"

It was then he told her about the man who had been chasing down Caleb the night before. "Did you speak to Caleb about it?" she asked when he was finished.

"I spoke to him this afternoon. He insisted that he had no idea a man was chasing him and Leroy the night before and that he didn't know anyone named Joker."

"Did you believe him?"

"No. It was obvious he and Leroy were running back to the barn for a reason. They were running away from this Joker guy."

"So, what do you think is going on?" she asked.

He stared off toward the barn for a long moment and then looked back at her. "I might be jumping to conclusions due to the way this Joker looked, but I think it was maybe some sort of a drug deal gone wrong." Once again, he gazed off into the distance.

"Then you think your brother is into hard drugs?" she asked.

He turned and looked at her. "Hell, Carrie, I don't know what else to think. And now I'm thinking maybe Caleb had nothing to do with Dad's death, but maybe some low-life drug dealer that Caleb brought into his life killed him."

"So, are you going to take this all to Lane?"

He looked down at his feet and then took a drink of his beer, remaining silent for several moments. "I don't know what I'm going to do yet. I've been thinking about what to do all last night and today. I need to talk to Johnny about it, but he left early this morning for Oklahoma City. Some rancher there is auctioning off all his cattle and horses, and Johnny wanted to take a look at them. He won't be home until tomorrow afternoon, so I have to wait to talk to him until then."

"What does your gut instinct tell you to do?" she asked.

"I know how my father would want to handle it. He'd want to keep everything in the family. If Caleb is doing hard drugs, then he doesn't need to be hounded by Lane about a murder. What he does need is some sort of an intervention. As a family, we need to see if we can get him into treatment."

"Yes, but don't you also need to tell Lane that it's possible some druggie lowlifes might have killed your father?"

The muscle in his jaw pulsated once again. "I intend to find this Joker guy myself and have a little chat with him about my father's murder."

Carrie gasped. "Oh Luke, please don't do that. Listening to Peter in the Red Barn and hoping for a confession is one thing, but this is something much different—something much more dangerous."

"I still have to chase this down, Carrie. I *have* to. It might be the only way I get some answers and some closure in this whole mess."

She placed her beer on the small table, got out of her chair and knelt next to him. She reached out and grabbed hold of his arm and held on tightly. "Luke, if you pursue this, then I fear that the closure you'll get will be your own death. Please take this all to Lane. You don't have to mention Caleb's name. Just tell him about this creep lurking around your property. Leave this Joker guy alone."

"I'll take it to Lane when I know more, and only after Johnny and I decide to," he replied firmly.

Her heart raced with fear for him. If what he believed was true, then this Joker person was a drug dealer, and not the garden-variety kind who sold weed to his friends. Just from the way Luke had described the man, he sounded like he might be a hardened criminal.

True, she was doing something she'd always hated— she was judging a book by its cover. But given the circumstances, it was hard not to believe the one-eyed Joker with facial tattoos was a dope dealer and a criminal.

"But maybe this man is already wanted for something else," she continued, desperate to change Luke's mind about going after the man himself. She released her hold on his arm and returned to her chair. "If you'd take this to Lane, he might have the resources to hunt the man down."

"I told you this is something I have to do," he snapped, his tone immediately hurting her feelings. He raked a hand through his hair and shook his head. "God, I'm sorry, Carrie. I didn't mean to come at you like that. You're the last person in the world who deserves any of my anger."

"I accept your apology," she replied. She knew how high his emotions were at the moment. "But I can't help but be afraid for you, Luke. This driving need you have to find your father's killer is now taking you into what I consider very dangerous territory."

Once again, she wanted to tell him she was in love with him, but she didn't want to have that conversation in the midst of a talk about drug dealers and murder. And so she held her emotions in check. But sooner or later she was going to have to speak of her love for him.

If she wasn't killed by the man who had tried to kill her before, then she feared she'd die a different kind of death if Luke didn't love her back.

IT WAS THE next evening when Luke finally sat down with his older brother to tell him everything that had happened with Caleb. Just after dinner, Luke sat on the sofa in Johnny's house. Chelsea sat next to him, and Johnny was in his recliner.

Johnny's house had originally been the old foreman's cabin. He'd spent four years renovating the place and had turned it into a really beautiful home.

"How was the trip to Oklahoma?" Luke asked.

"It was a total bust," Johnny replied. "The horses were old nags, and the cattle looked even worse. All the equipment was old and rusty. There was absolutely nothing there for us."

"That's a shame," Luke replied.

"It was a pleasant drive and we stayed in a nice hotel for the night, so it wasn't a total bust." Chelsea shot a warm smile to Johnny.

Johnny laughed. "She thought the drive was nice because she had me trapped in the truck to discuss wedding plans."

"And what are the plans?" Luke asked and realized he was putting off discussing the real issue he'd come to talk about.

"We're planning on getting married in early September, and I just want a small gathering in the pasture where there's an old wagon on my mother's land," Chelsea said, her eyes shining brightly.

"What's so important about that wagon?" Luke knew which one she was talking about. It was a broken-down old wagon right along the property line between the Black land and the Kings' land.

"It's the place where I realized I was still in love with Johnny," she said.

"And the same is true for me," Johnny replied.

"September is only a few months away. Don't most people take a year or so to plan a wedding?" Luke asked.

"Johnny and I don't want a big to-do, so we should easily be able to pull together what I want in a short amount of time," Chelsea replied.

Johnny looked back at Luke. "So, what's up with you? You normally don't just pop in to visit."

Luke told his brother about the encounter with Joker. When he was finished, a grim frown cut across Johnny's forehead. "So, you're thinking maybe this Joker guy killed Dad over a drug deal with Caleb?" he asked.

"It's a thought," Luke replied.

"Luke, think about it. Why would a drug dealer kill the money man? Everybody knew that the only way Caleb got money was from Dad," Johnny said.

Luke frowned thoughtfully. He hadn't thought about that, but Johnny was right. It didn't make any sense for Joker to have killed Big John. Dammit, he'd been so sure he was onto something.

"What we really need to talk about is what we intend to do about Caleb," Johnny said.

"He obviously needs some help," Chelsea said. "He's needed help for some time."

"Definitely," Johnny agreed. "Do you want to take this all to Lane?"

"I don't know. I don't want to throw Caleb under the bus if the only thing he's guilty of is doing drugs.

Maybe we should get everyone together, Mom and Ashley included, and have some sort of a family intervention."

"It sounds like he definitely needs treatment. I'll do some research tonight and see what kind of in-house treatment facility we can get him into," Johnny said.

"So, maybe we can plan this for Sunday afternoon," Luke said. "That gives you all day tomorrow to be able to come up with someplace for him."

"Then why don't we all meet at around three o'clock? Mom can make sure Caleb shows up," Johnny replied.

"And I can work for Ashley so she can be here," Chelsea added.

"I just hope with all of us on the same page, Caleb will agree to get help," Luke said. He wanted his brother to reach his full potential, and Caleb couldn't do that with all the drinking he did or whatever drugs he was taking.

A half an hour later as he walked back to his place, he thought about what Johnny had said about Joker. Johnny might not believe that Joker would kill Big John, but he might have killed Big John as some sort of a warning to Caleb.

A headache tightened across Luke's forehead with nauseating intensity. Too many thoughts were crowding his brain. When he got to his house, he sank down in his recliner and closed his eyes.

Immediately a vision of Carrie filled his brain, and he felt himself relaxing. That's what she brought to him—a kind of peace no other woman had ever given him before.

He would have spent this evening with her, but she'd had a late night working at the hospital. She was supposed to get off at eight o'clock. Emily wouldn't be with her, so Luke intended to be in the parking lot to follow her home.

His family might be falling apart, but he was determined not to let Carrie down. Until the creep who was after her was behind bars, he would do whatever he could to keep her safe from harm.

IT WAS SUNDAY afternoon when all of the King family came together for the intervention. While they waited for Caleb to arrive, Margaret sat on the sofa. She appeared worried about confronting her youngest son. Ashley displayed a bad case of nerves by prattling about the latest inventory at her shop. Johnny looked grim and determined, and Luke just wanted to get it all over with.

He still found it heartbreaking to think that it was possible his brother was in any way responsible for Big John's death, but whether possible or not, he knew Caleb definitely needed help.

Luke still wanted to find out more about this Joker fellow and what role he might have in Caleb's life and Big John's murder. He still felt a burning need to solve his father's murder, but over the last couple of days, he'd just been tired.

He'd just been tired of thinking about murder and mayhem. He was exhausted by spending so long twisting and turning things around in his head. He told himself he just needed a night or two off—a night or two to rest his mind, and then he'd get back to things stronger than ever.

More importantly, while he believed Carrie supported him, over the past few days he'd sensed her growing impatience with his quest. The last thing he wanted to do was push her out of his life. She was far too important to him as a friend.

The room fell silent as Caleb walked in. "Mom told me there was some kind of a family meeting and I needed to be here," he said and sat down next to their mother on the sofa. "I hope you've all decided to back me in my art endeavors and we're here because you're all going to give me the seed money I need to open up a storefront."

"That's not why we're all here," Johnny said, obviously taking the lead.

"Then why are we here?" Caleb asked curiously.

"We're here for you, Caleb," Ashley said.

Caleb's eyes narrowed, and he visibly tensed as he looked at each and every one of them. "So, what exactly is going on here?"

"We all think you need help, Caleb," Johnny said. "You're drinking too much, and we know you're doing drugs."

"Are you wearing your daddy hat now, Johnny?" Caleb asked irritably. "He was always accusing me of doing all kinds of drugs."

"Are you, Caleb?" Margaret asked, her voice soft and filled with concern. "Are you doing all kinds of drugs?" She looked at him worriedly.

"No, Ma, I'm not. I like beer, and I'll admit I like

smoking a joint now and then, but that's the only drug I do," Caleb replied. "It's not a big deal that I like weed. Smoking helps me open my mind for my painting."

"Then how do you explain Joker?" Luke asked.

"I can't," Caleb said. "I have no idea who Joker is or why he was supposedly looking for me." Once again, he looked at everyone in the room. "Is this one of those interventions? Is that why you are all here?"

"I do have some information here about a great place in Kentucky," Johnny said. He reached for a handful of papers he'd carried in with him and had placed on the end table. "It's a nice place, Caleb, and they use art as a form of therapy. I think it would be good for you to get away from the ranch for a couple of months and just work on yourself."

"You've got to be kidding me. Wow. I thought my family couldn't betray me any more, but I guess I was wrong," Caleb replied in obvious irritation.

"Oh, Caleb, honey. We all just want the best for you," Margaret said.

"You, of all people are breaking my heart right now," Caleb said to Margaret. "I thought you understood me. All I want is seed money to open a store. Why can't you just do that and then leave me alone?"

Margaret dabbed at her eyes with a tissue.

"Caleb, this is what's best for you," Johnny said authoritatively. "We all want you to thrive in your own life, and you aren't doing that right now."

"I'm doing what I want. I'm working on my art to display and sell during the Fourth of July celebrations. I don't need to do anything else. I definitely don't need to go off somewhere for any drinking or drug therapy. I don't have a drinking or drug problem."

"Come on, Caleb, please consider it," Johnny said and held out the paperwork to him.

Caleb got up from the sofa. He slapped at Johnny's hand, and the paperwork flew all over the room. "To hell with you all. I know you all think I'm a damned embarrassment to the family and there's nothing more you'd like to do than hide me away in Kentucky. But I'm not going there. I'm not going anywhere. There's nothing wrong with me and no reason for me to go to Kentucky or anywhere else."

Before anyone could say another word, Caleb stormed out of the room and slammed the door on the way out of the house. "Well, that went well," Luke said dryly.

"I never should have agreed to this," Margaret said half-tearfully. "He's always been the most sensitive of all of you. Now he won't trust me anymore."

Johnny looked at everyone and shook his head. "He's a grown man. We can't force him to go anywhere or do anything." He heaved a deep sigh. "I guess all we can hope for is he'll eventually get to a place where he realizes he needs some help."

Luke was bitterly disappointed this had failed, but he wasn't really surprised. Caleb might be the most sensitive of them all, but he was also extremely hard-headed, like the rest of the King kids. Still, he definitely worried about what Caleb might have gotten himself into.

One thing he felt right now was the need to see and

talk to Carrie. It was funny, but whenever he was upset or angry, he needed his friend, and thankfully she was always there for him. However, if he kept pressing the issue of finding and questioning Joker, he knew he ran the possibility of no longer having her full support.

At five o'clock he left his place to pick her up, with the plans to go to the café for dinner. Because she had to go to work in the morning, he didn't intend to keep her out too late.

It would be easy to grow lax with her safety right now. Nothing more had happened since the car wreck. But Luke didn't intend to become complacent. The man who had tried to kill Carrie was still out there somewhere, just like Big John's murderer.

Luke had taken it easy for the last couple of days, but starting tomorrow, no matter how much danger he might face, he intended to continue his search for the man who had killed his father.

HE WATCHED AS Luke King picked the bitch up and the two of them drove away. He'd been watching her comings and goings from the house for the past week. He wasn't interested in trying to take her down on her way to or from work. Most of the time she wasn't alone, but rather had her roommate with her.

During the past week, while the house was empty, he'd checked every door and every window, seeking a way inside. Unfortunately, there were good, sturdy locks on both the front and the back doors. Even most of the windows held good locks. He didn't want to break a window to get in—he feared any broken glass would tip her off and she'd run out and escape before he could get her.

He'd been positively gleeful when he'd found a window in the back of the house with a faulty lock. Yesterday while they'd been gone, he'd rattled the window in the old frame until it had jiggled unlocked. It led into the kitchen over the sink. It would be relatively easy to climb into it and then jump from the sink to the floor.

He hadn't been prepared yesterday for her murder, but today he was definitely ready and eager.

He'd decided he didn't want to shoot her. Shooting her would kill her too fast, and besides, somebody might hear the gunshots. He'd much rather kill her up close and personal, so he had two deadly sharp knives in his pocket. He couldn't wait to sink them both deep into her flesh. His intention was to hide in a closet until she was completely vulnerable.

A giddy excitement roared through him. Finally, he would get what he needed—revenge for all the lies she had told him. He was aware that it wouldn't change things in his hard life. It wouldn't magically make things easier, but it would definitely give him the satisfaction he needed. She had to pay, and he was going to make her pay.

He'd wait until dark to make his move. Right now, he was hidden behind a bush in her backyard, waiting for nightfall. He was clad all in black, so once the night shadows fell, nobody would see him sneak across the yard and through that kitchen window.

He didn't know if the roommate was home or not. If she wasn't home, then it was her lucky day. If she was home, then she could become collateral damage. He had no reason to harm her, but he definitely would if she stood in his way of getting to Carrie.

He had already had to wait way too long for this. He wasn't willing to wait any longer. A sweet anticipation swept through him. Yes, tonight was his night to finally make her pay—and he couldn't wait.

Chapter Ten

Carrie didn't ask any questions of Luke until they were settled in a booth at the café and had placed their orders. She was eager to hear what had happened with Caleb.

On the drive to the café, they had kept things light. She talked about her late night at the hospital, and he told her about the new ranch hand Johnny had hired.

Now, Carrie's curiosity couldn't wait another minute. "So, how did things go with Caleb?" she asked.

A deep frown cut across his forehead. "It was a bust. Johnny found a good facility in Kentucky, but Caleb wanted nothing to do with any of it. All we managed to do was piss Caleb off."

"I'm sorry, Luke. I know how much you wanted to get him help," she replied.

"Ah, well. You know the old saying—you can lead a horse to water, but you can't make him drink." He drummed his fingers on the top of the table.

"Hopefully, Caleb will get to a place where he realizes he could use some help and reaches out for it," she replied.

"Hopefully."

They both fell silent as the waitress appeared with their orders. She had gotten a chicken salad platter with cottage cheese and chilled grapes, while he had ordered the heartier meal of meat loaf and mashed potatoes.

As they ate, she enjoyed him talking about the horse-breeding program that his brother had encouraged him to get together.

"I'm starting to wrap my head around the potential. Not only will it bring in a brand-new revenue stream, but I'm most excited for the kind of excellent horses I know we could produce."

"So, have you figured out how to get it all started?" she asked. She was thrilled that finally he was looking toward the future and not back into the past.

"I plan to start researching it all tomorrow," he replied.

"I'm so glad to hear that, Luke. I know it will make Johnny happy, and I'm sure it would have made your dad happy, too."

"Yeah, it would." His eyes looked clearer and more at peace than she'd seen them. "Mom told me Dad always enjoyed spending time with me in the stables. I've always loved being in the stables among the horses."

"Then maybe it's time you got back to the stables," Carrie replied with a smile.

He returned her smile with one of his own. "That's what I'm thinking."

"Tell me about horses... I don't know much about the different breeds and what kind you might be interested in. All I know is there are old nags like at the Dickerson ranch and there are good horses at your ranch."

For the remainder of the meal, Luke talked about horses. It was obvious he was very knowledgeable in the area, but what she loved more was the animation that illuminated his features as he talked about a subject he obviously loved.

He shared with her conversations he'd had with his dad about the various types of horses, their health and well-being. "At one time Dad called me his horse whisperer because I was spending so much time with the horses. The horses seemed to understand what I would say to them, and I understood them."

"All this time and I didn't know you had this hidden talent," Carrie teased. "What else have you been keeping from me?"

He grinned. "I guess you'll just have to stick around if you want to learn the rest of my secret talents."

She laughed in return, but the truth of the matter was she wasn't sure how long she could stick around with him with their relationship remaining static.

She was in love with him, and if he didn't feel the same way about her, then she wasn't sure how long she'd be willing to continue to see him. It broke her heart to think about no longer spending time with him, but in the end, she'd have to make a decision that was in her own best interest.

They lingered over coffee and dessert, and when they got up to leave, she realized this was the first time they'd spent time together and their conversation hadn't been about his father's murder or who might be after her.

Instead, they'd talked about things people on a date would talk about. It had been refreshing not to discuss murder or attempted murder with their meal for a change. For just a little while, she hadn't thought about the fact that there was a man out there who wanted her dead.

The conversation continued to remain light and pleasant as he drove her back to her house. It was only when he turned off the truck engine and he was about to open his door when she stopped him.

All evening her love for him had trembled on her lips, had burned in her heart, and she'd waited for the perfect moment to tell him how she felt—and that moment was now.

"Luke, before I go in, I need to talk to you," she said.

He settled back in the driver's seat and looked at her. His handsome features were visible in the bright glow of her porch light. "Talk about what?" he asked curiously.

"Luke, I… I'm in love with you." The words blurted out of her and hung in the air for several long moments.

His eyes widened. "No, you aren't," he finally said, obviously appalled by her words. "Carrie, we've been spending a lot of time together and you're just…just confused about things."

"It's because we've spent so much time together that I know for sure I'm in love with you," she replied. "Trust me, I'm not confused."

"But…but that wasn't part of our deal. We're friends,

Carrie. We're good friends, but it was never supposed to be anything more," he replied fervently. "Believe me, you're just confused."

"Stop saying that," she exclaimed in frustration. "You're right in that this wasn't part of our deal, but my heart doesn't care about our deal. My heart fell in love with you." Tears welled up inside her and burned at her eyes. "I love you, Luke King, and I think if you look deep in your heart, you love me, too."

"Carrie, I told you all along that I had no room for romance in my life. I made that clear to you time and time again. I need to solve my dad's murder before I even think about romance," he replied.

The tears spilled over and raced down her cheeks. She'd hoped…she'd thought…but each of his words broke her heart. It was obvious he didn't feel what she'd believed he felt about her.

"Ah, Carrie, don't cry. You know I can't stand to see you crying," he said.

His words only made the tears fall faster. "Don't tell me not to cry. Not only is my heart broken for me, but it's broken for you, too. Oh, Luke, if you cling to this idea that you need to solve Big John's murder, then eventually you'll push everyone who cares about you out of your life."

"It's something I have to do," he replied inflexibly.

"No, it's not," she countered with a touch of anger. "At dinner this evening, you talked about breeding horses, and it was the first time I've seen you really happy. For God's sake, Luke. You will always grieve for the loss of your father, but you need to move on with your life. You're stuck in revenge mode." She angrily swiped at her tears.

"I love you, Luke, and I was sure you felt the same way about me. If you don't love me, then I hope you'll open your heart to more than murder." She looked out the front window and then back at him. She had no more words to say. She'd told him what was in her heart, and now she just felt empty and broken inside. "And now I'm ready to go home," she finally said.

He nodded and got out of the truck. Moments later they walked silently up to her front door. When they reached it, she turned to face him once again. "Luke, I can't do this anymore," she said softly, wearily.

"Do what?" His voice held apprehension.

"I can't hang out with you anymore. I can't spend any more time with you, loving you, when you aren't ready to move on with your life, when you apparently don't love me. I just can't do it anymore."

Each word she said shot an enormous wealth of pain through her heart, but she knew in that same heart that she was making the right decision.

She couldn't keep seeing him day after day, spending time with him and laughing with him without falling more deeply in love with him. And he didn't love her back. She owed it to herself to get out now, no matter how painful it would be to no longer see him.

"Carrie, please don't say that." He reached for her hand, but she jerked hers away. Where once she had longed for his touch, she now found it too painful to bear.

"But…but I need you," he protested, his gaze appearing frantic.

"No, you don't, Luke. You really don't need anyone. You're perfectly satisfied with just you and your obsession. There's obviously no room for anything else in your life," she replied.

"But, Carrie…"

"Good night, Luke." She cut him off, turned back to her door and unlocked it. "I'm sure we'll see each other around town. Good luck with things."

Without giving him a chance to respond, she entered her house and quickly closed the door behind her. The tears she had so desperately tried to control now unleashed, pouring from her eyes as deep sobs racked her body.

Weakly, she leaned back against the door, crying at the death of her hopes and dreams where Luke was concerned. She'd been so sure that he loved her. She could have sworn she'd felt his love in his touches and seen it shining in the depths of his eyes when he gazed at her.

She couldn't believe she'd been so delusional. She'd been sure it was just a matter of time before he'd professed his love for her. But he didn't love her. He'd just needed her to keep alive his fantasy that Peter would eventually confess to his father's murder. He'd just needed a partner for his madness, and she'd been that for far too long.

With tears still streaming down her cheeks, she pulled herself off the door. She threw her purse on the sofa and then headed for the stairs. Sadness made her legs feel as if they weighed a hundred pounds as she climbed each step and headed for her bedroom.

She told herself she needed to stop crying. She'd always known that heartbreak might be in the cards with Luke. But as each day had gone by, she'd grown more confident that heartbreak wasn't going to happen. He was her person, and she'd really believed she was his person. But she'd been wrong...so wrong.

Dammit, she'd been so certain he loved her and just hadn't said the words to her yet. Her every instinct had told her he loved her. How could she have been so mistaken?

She reached her bedroom and continued to weep as she took off her clothes and changed into a nightshirt. Once she was changed, she sat on the edge of her bed and tried to pull herself together.

She drew in deep breaths and released them slowly. She finally stopped crying, but she wasn't ready to go to bed just yet.

Instead, she decided a talk with Emily might help. Emily would be sympathetic and a listening ear as Carrie talked about how she'd gotten things so wrong.

She knew Emily was at home and in her bedroom, because her car had been in the driveway and Carrie could hear Emily's television noise drifting out despite the closed bedroom door. She hesitated just outside and then knocked softly.

There was no answer. Carrie knocked again...harder this time. It wasn't so late that Emily would be sleeping. Still, there was no response from Emily. She twisted the knob and cracked open the door. "Em?"

Emily was usually a light sleeper. Carrie opened the door all the way and realized the bed was empty.

Apparently, Emily wasn't home. Maybe Craig, Emily's boyfriend, had picked her up and she'd just forgotten to turn off her television before she left the house.

Carrie was about to leave the room when she saw the pair of legs protruding out from the opposite side of the bed. "Emily," she cried, her tears about Luke instantly gone as worry about her friend welled up inside her.

She raced around the side of the bed and found Emily unconscious on the floor. "Oh God, Em." Carrie fell to the floor next to her, her gaze immediately going over the length of Emily's body as she sought any obvious injuries.

She saw nothing obvious. Had Emily fallen out of bed and hit her head? Had she suffered some sort of a heart issue? At least she seemed to be breathing, although her breaths sounded weak and shallow.

Carrie needed to call for an ambulance. Frantically she looked around for Emily's cell phone, but it was nowhere in sight.

Realizing her own cell was in her purse on the sofa in the living room, she left the room and raced down the stairs. She flipped on lights as she went. She'd just reached the sofa when a noise from the kitchen drew her attention.

Three footsteps, and then he appeared in the threshold between the kitchen and the living room. She froze at the sight of him. He was clad all in black and wore a ski mask over his head. He held a wicked-looking knife in each hand.

"Hello, Carrie."

LUKE DROVE SEVERAL blocks away from Carrie's place and then pulled over to the curb in front of somebody else's house. He shut off his engine and then unfastened his seat belt. He couldn't drive anymore. A tight pressure filled his chest, and a range of emotions flew through his head.

He felt sick to his stomach, and a band of tension wrapped around his head, squeezing tightly. He couldn't believe how the night had ended. He couldn't believe that Carrie really intended to not be in his life anymore. How could she just cut him out of her life?

She loved him. Her words thundered in his head. He tried to tell himself she was mistaken, that they were just really close friends. But she'd been clear she wasn't confused or mistaken about her feelings for him.

He hadn't seen it coming. But now that he thought back on things, maybe he should have. Maybe he should have recognized that her touches were filled with love, that her heart was all in on him when she gazed at him. He'd obviously been obtuse in not recognizing what was happening emotionally with her.

After they had made love, he'd never had the talk he'd intended to have with her telling her that it had been a mistake. Now he wished he would have had that conversation with her the very next moment.

Dear God, what was he going to do without her? Who would he have long, deep conversations with? Who would make him laugh? She was the best friend he'd ever had, and he couldn't imagine his life without her.

He couldn't believe she had made the choice not to

spend time with him anymore. His feeling of grief was profound. His heart was emptier than it had ever been.

What in God's name was happening to him? He'd stopped seeing women he'd dated before in the past, but nothing had prepared him for the kind of utter loss he felt at never being with Carrie again.

Whom would he think about first thing in the morning? Whom would he think about just before he fell asleep at night? Who was going to keep her safe from the madman who was after her?

His heart clenched with fear for her. If necessary, he'd be her bodyguard from afar. He knew her daily schedule, and he could follow her to and from her work. She'd never have to know that he was around, watching out for her.

Still, it didn't solve the problem with his heart. He was nowhere near ready to be without Carrie in his life. And it hurt so badly that she didn't want to be in his life anymore.

With a deep sigh, he started his truck once again and pulled the seat belt back around him. As he pulled away from the curb, his heartache rode with him.

Chapter Eleven

Carrie stared at the man as a million thoughts raced through her head all at the same time. Fear kept her momentarily frozen in place. Who was he? Oh God, what had he done to Emily? What was he doing here… in her house? This wasn't supposed to happen. She was all alone in a house with a man who wanted to kill her and a roommate who was unconscious.

Her gaze darted around, seeking something she could use as a weapon, but there was nothing. "Who are you and what do you want?" she asked.

Maybe she could get him talking and she could slowly get herself closer to the front door. It would only take her a second or two to unlock it and run. At least he wasn't advancing on her yet.

"I'll tell you who I am," he said. "I'm the man who is going to kill you."

"What did you do to my roommate?" She tried to keep the terror out of her voice, even though it screamed inside her.

"Ah, I was hoping the poor girl would be out of the house tonight, but she wasn't. Unfortunately, I had to give her a rather hard love tap on the back of her head to make sure she didn't interfere with my plans."

"So, who are you?" Carrie asked again, hoping and praying that Emily would be okay. His voice still sounded familiar, but she couldn't place it.

"I'm the man who you lied to over and over again." His voice raised a bit.

"Lied about what?" She took a small step to her left, moving closer to the front door.

"You told me she'd get better and she didn't. She didn't get better," he yelled.

"Who? Who are you talking about?" she cried frantically. "This has got to be some kind of a mistake."

"Trust me, it's no mistake. You told me after her stroke that she'd get better. You lied to me. Damn you for all your lies." He took a step toward her.

Terror roared through her, sending an arctic ice through her veins. She didn't know who he was or what he was talking about. All she knew was his knives looked deadly sharp and a sick rage emanated from him.

"I don't know who you are," she said and took another step, moving her closer to the door.

He shoved one of the knives in his pocket and then yanked off his ski mask and tossed it to the floor. She gasped in stunned surprise. Jason Cartwell. His wife, Elizabeth, had suffered a debilitating stroke about a year ago, but with therapy the prognosis for her to improve had been good.

"Now do you remember me? Or do you lie to so

many people you don't remember one of us from another?" he screamed, his face turning red with his rage.

"Jason, I told you Elizabeth should improve with
therapy, and that wasn't a lie. Did you get her into
therapy?"

"It's none of your business what I did or didn't do,
but it is your business that you lied to me. She's like a
damned baby. I got to feed her and change her diapers."
He took another step toward her. "And you know what
the price is for all your lies to me? It's your death." He
lunged toward her, and with a scream Carrie ran for
the front door.

Too late. She was too late. She didn't have enough
time to unlock the door. He slammed into her back,
grabbed one of her arms and violently flung her away
from the door. She half stumbled over the coffee table.
She fell to her knees and quickly got back to her feet
as tears of fear half blurred her vision.

"You're going to die the death of a thousand cuts,"
he said, suddenly gleeful as he charged at her once
again. He lunged forward, sliced her forearm and then
laughed uproariously.

Pain seared through her, and she grabbed her arm,
where blood had begun to flow. She released her arm
and instead grabbed a throw pillow from the sofa.

He stabbed at her, and she used the pillow as a
shield. As the knife buried itself in the pillow, he
laughed again. "Okay, let's play," he said.

He thrust the knife forward, and once again she
blocked it with the pillow. Stuffing began to fall around

her feet. It would only take another stab or two and the throw pillow would be utterly useless.

"Jason, please… I didn't lie to you," she said tearfully.

"Don't tell me. I got to feed Billie like a baby. I've got to change her diapers. She can't talk…she can't do anything for herself, and damn you, you told me she'd get better." He used the other knife and lunged out to stab her in the lower leg.

New, excruciating pain shuddered through her, momentarily stealing her breath away. "You don't want to do this, Jason. You'll wind up in prison, and then who is going to take care of Billie?" she gasped amid tears.

"I'm not going to no prison," he scoffed. "Nobody knows I'm here, Carrie. Nobody knows I'm the one who wants you dead." His dark eyes shone with malice. "Carrie, Carrie, you're going to be deady." He threw back his head and laughed. He dived toward her and sliced her arm once again. "Death by a thousand cuts, Carrie. I'm going to slice you up good before I bury my knife in your black, lying heart." He laughed once again. It was the sound of a devil at work.

She was now too far away to get out the front door. Her head felt fuzzy from the pain that burned in her arm and leg. All she knew was that somehow, someway, she desperately needed to get away from him.

The stairs. If she could just make it up to her bedroom, that door had a lock. She could lock the door and then scream out the window for help. She could barricade the door so he couldn't get in to hurt her.

Knowing it might be her only hope, she raced for

the stairs. She got up five of them before he stabbed her in the back of her leg. She screamed as the excruciating new pain shuddered through her. She quickly sat on one of the stairs, whirled around and raised her legs. With all the might she had within her, she kicked him in the chest.

He stumbled backward and fell to the floor beneath them. "I'll kill you for that, you bitch," he screamed.

She screamed as loud as she could as she scrabbled up three more stairs. She had to get to her bedroom. It was the only way she'd have a chance to survive. She was not going to let this monster of a man be the death of her.

Her chest tightened. Sobbing pants released from her, making it difficult for her to draw a deep breath. *Somebody help me*, a voice screamed in the back of her head. But she knew nobody was coming to her rescue. Luke was long gone, and nobody else would be showing up.

The knife once again sliced across the back of her leg. *Death by a thousand cuts.* The words thundered in her head. She refused to let that happen to her without fighting back. Once again she whirled around to face him, only this time her kicks were directed at the knives he'd used to hurt her.

She screamed in both pain and triumph as her foot dislodged one of the knives. It flew out of his hand and clattered to the floor below. She was ready to kick at his other hand when a knock sounded at her front door.

Jason froze, and so did Carrie. And then she screamed as loud as she possibly could.

"Carrie?" Luke's voice drifted through the door.

"Luke," she screamed.

Jason leaped into action. He went back down the stairs and disappeared into the kitchen. Carrie's heart pounded a million beats a minute. She waited several long moments, still frozen in place and unsure if he was really gone or not.

Luke banged on the door frantically. "Carrie? What's happening in there?" He banged again.

Finally, she ran down the stairs, unlocked and opened the door, and then collapsed in Luke's arms as she cried uncontrollably.

"Carrie, what's wrong?" He held her tight. "Carrie… baby, you're bleeding," he said in alarm.

"It's Jason Cartwell. He…he was h-here. D-death by a thousand c-cuts," she managed to say between sobs.

"Carrie, where is he now?" Luke asked urgently.

She pointed toward the kitchen. "He…he went in there."

"Go sit down," Luke said softly as he drew his gun and then disappeared from sight.

Carrie took two steps toward the sofa and then fell to the floor, still sobbing from the pain that burned through her. She was crawling to the sofa to get her phone from her purse when Luke came back.

"Baby," he said and then scooped her up in his arms and placed her on the sofa. He pulled his cell phone from his pocket and called for help.

Once that was done, he knelt in front of her and checked out the wounds on her legs and arms. "Honey, do you have any bandages here?"

She nodded. "In my bathroom upstairs. But don't leave me here all alone," she said with a new panic. "He co-could come b-back." She grabbed his hands and held tight. "Please, don't leave me alone, Luke."

"Okay, I'm not going anywhere," he replied. "But you're bleeding badly, Carrie." His features twisted in anger. "Damn him for hurting you."

"He…he was going to kill me. If you hadn't knocked when you did, he would have succeeded." The words came out of her amid sobs. "Oh God, Emily is unconscious upstairs. He…he hit her over the head. She needs help."

A siren sounded in the distance, letting them know help was on the way. As they waited, Carrie told him more about the encounter with Jason.

The ambulance arrived first, before any law enforcement. Carrie insisted that they go upstairs and tend to Emily before they helped her.

They brought Emily downstairs on a stretcher and loaded her into the ambulance and then came back inside for Carrie. They got her on a gurney and wheeled her to the waiting vehicle. Luke walked out with them.

"I'll be at the hospital as soon as I can," Luke said to her. "I need to stay here and talk to Lane."

"Okay," she replied as the paramedics worked to bandage her wounds. He leaned down and kissed her on the forehead and then stepped back as she was loaded into the ambulance.

It wasn't until the ambulance took off, the siren once again wailing, that she wondered, why had Luke shown up at her place at all?

LANE PULLED UP to the curb just as the ambulance sped away. Luke was angrier than he'd ever been in his life. Seeing the knife wounds on her beautiful skin, hearing Carrie's cries of pain and terror, had stirred up a rage he had never known before.

"It's Jason Cartwell," he said to Lane the minute the lawman got out of his car. "He tried to kill Carrie. He attacked her with a knife and escaped out her kitchen window. He allowed her to see his face because he intended to kill her. We've got to go after him, Lane. Maybe he's home now packing to get out of town."

"I'll head out to the Cartwell place," Lane said. "You sit tight here or go on to the hospital and I'll contact you when I have him in custody."

"I'm not sitting tight anywhere. I'm going to get Cartwell. You'd better hope you get to him before I do, because I'm going to beat the man half to death for what he did to Carrie," Luke replied.

He didn't wait for a reply but instead headed toward his truck. Lane hurried to his car and managed to take off before Luke.

Luke knew the Cartwell place. It was on the outskirts of town, a ramshackle house on enough land for Jason to keep a small herd of cattle. Luke knew he had a wife, but he couldn't remember the last time he'd seen either of them in town.

As he drove, he wrapped his hands tightly around the steering wheel. Carrie had told him why Jason had wanted to kill her. It had all been about revenge for her supposedly lying to him. It didn't matter what his reasons were—all that mattered was the man had hurt her. He'd taken a knife and had slashed into her flesh.

He had no idea how many cuts Carrie had suffered at the man's hand. One was too many. Dammit. Why hadn't Luke thought of getting her a home security system? He'd just assumed she'd be safe in her home with Emily there.

He hoped Emily was okay. Carrie would never, ever forgive herself if Emily wasn't. She would blame herself for whatever happened, even though it was nobody's fault except Jason Cartwell's.

Once again anger seethed inside him. He'd meant what he'd said to Lane. He wanted to punch Jason's face in. The thought of somebody finding her dead in the house shot icy chills through him. Thank God he'd returned to Carrie's house when he had.

He stepped on the gas, hoping and praying they would find Jason home, hoping and praying that the man was arrested and charged. As long as the man was on the loose, Carrie wouldn't be safe.

He followed behind Lane's car as close as he could. They turned off the main drag and onto a gravel road. The gravel pinged on the underside of the truck as he raced to catch the man who had tried to kill Carrie.

As they got closer to the Cartwells' property, Luke's heart beat a thousand beats a minute. They had to catch him. Carrie deserved to live her life without fear, and that could only happen if Jason was behind bars.

He breathed a sigh of relief as the Cartwells' house came into view with Jason's old, beat-up truck in the driveway. Hopefully that meant the man was here.

Lane pulled to a halt, and Luke parked right behind him. Both men jumped out of their vehicles. "I'll go around back," Luke said.

Lane nodded, pulled his gun and headed for the front door. Luke also drew his weapon as he rounded the house and found a back door. He stood next to it, ready if Jason should try to escape out the back.

"Jason, it's Lane. Come to the front door," Luke heard Lane as he yelled and pounded on the front door.

There were several moments of silence. "Jason, come to the front door," Lane called. He banged on the front door once again.

Luke heard a scuffling noise just inside the back door. He shoved his gun back in its holster, afraid he would actually shoot the man. He tensed, ready to spring. The back door flew open, and Jason came out.

Luke immediately tackled the tall, thin man to the ground. Jason fought to get free. He attempted to punch Luke in the face, but the blow went wild. Luke grabbed him by the arm and yanked him to his feet.

"You bastard," Luke said and threw a punch that connected with Jason's lower jaw. Jason reeled back, but Luke held on to him. He was ready to hit him again when Lane came running around the side of the house.

"Luke, that's enough," Lane said firmly. He grabbed Jason's arm away from Luke and snapped cuffs on Jason's wrists. "I'm locking him in the car. There's somebody else in there who needs help."

As Lane disappeared back around the house with Jason in tow, Luke entered through the back door. Somebody else who needed help?

The door led into a filthy kitchen. Dirty dishes were not only stacked up in the sink but also lined the counters and the table. Flies buzzed in the rancid-smelling air, and rotting garbage overflowed from a trash can in the corner.

He couldn't believe somebody was actually living here. He stepped into the living room and gasped. Jason's wife, Elizabeth, sat in a wheelchair. She was achingly thin, and her arms were taped down so she couldn't move them. Another piece of tape was across her mouth.

"Elizabeth," he said and rushed to her. As he tore the tape from her mouth and then her arms, she gazed at him with grateful eyes. "We're going to get you out of here," he said as he worked to get her free. "We're going to get you help."

All he could think about was getting her out of the hellhole of a house. Dear God, what had Jason done to the poor woman? How often had he taped her down?

The living room was as filthy as the kitchen. Fast food containers covered the coffee table, and trash was almost everywhere in the room. His heart ached for poor Elizabeth, who had been forced to live this way. He was sure Lane had called for an ambulance already.

Lane came back in through the front door, his features twisted into a frown of disgust. "Let's get her out of here and into some fresh air," he said.

"My thoughts exactly," Luke said, and he pushed the wheelchair toward the front door, which Lane held open. Once outside, Elizabeth raised her face to the skies above, as if thanking God for her rescue.

"Billie," Jason yelled from the back of the patrol car. "Billie, don't worry, I'll be home in no time."

Luke saw every muscle in Elizabeth's body tense. "He's not going to be home anytime soon," Luke leaned down and whispered in her ear. "And you don't have to go back in that house or be with him ever again."

Several sirens screamed in the distance. Jason continued to yell out the window to his wife as Luke kept a steadying hand on her thin, trembling shoulder.

Two patrol cars squealed into the driveway, followed by an ambulance. Luke waited to see Elizabeth safely loaded inside, and then he ran for his truck, eager to see the woman he most wanted to see.

CARRIE LAY ON the hospital bed in the emergency room. Dr. Morris had just been in to clean and stitch up all her wounds, and he'd finished up by giving her a tetanus shot and something for her pain. He also told her he was keeping her in the hospital overnight.

She'd asked him about Emily's condition. He'd told her that Emily had been hit over the head hard enough to knock her out, but she was now awake and, aside from a concussion, she was going to be just fine.

The pain medicine instantly helped and put her in a drowsy state. She closed her eyes and tried not to think about what she'd just endured and all the stitches she'd had to get on her arms and legs. If she dwelled on it, she would only start crying again.

Had the police caught Jason? Had Lane been able to arrest the man? Or was he still out there in hiding… waiting for another opportunity to kill her? She didn't want to think about that, either. Otherwise, she would be terrified all over again.

Luke. She'd think about Luke. If he hadn't shown up at her door when he had, she would have been killed. He'd saved her life. And he didn't love her.

Hot tears pressed at her eyes. Thinking about him only broke her heart all over again. She tried to empty her mind from any and all thoughts. She allowed the pain medicine to drift her away.

She must have fallen asleep, because she came awake suddenly, her heart racing until she realized she was still in the hospital and safe. Then she saw him. Luke stood just inside the curtain that kept her bed private.

He looked stressed as his beautiful blue eyes met her gaze. "Carrie," he said softly and walked to the side of her bed. "How are you doing?"

"Much better than I was doing an hour ago," she replied wryly.

"We got him, Carrie, and I managed to get in one good punch to his jaw before Lane stopped me. I swear, I wanted to beat him to death for what he did to you."

"I'm glad you didn't. I would have really been stressed out if you went to prison." She knew the grin she tried to cast his way probably looked goofy, but at this point she didn't care.

"Oh woman, what am I going to do with you? I guess the only thing I can do is marry you."

She stared at him. Was she having some sort of a delusional hearing issue? "Luke, I'm sorry. I'm on some pain medicine, and I must have misheard you."

"Then I'll say it in a different way. Carrie Carlson, will you make me the happiest man in the world and marry me?" he said. His eyes gleamed with warmth... with what definitely looked like love.

"Luke, I don't understand. One of the last things you told me was that you weren't in a place for any romance in your life, that you saw me as a good friend but nothing more." She searched his features.

"Oh, Carrie. I've been such a big fool." He reached out and took her hand in his. "After I left your house, I pulled over and really thought about my feelings for you. I love the sound of your laughter. I love the long talks we have about everything and nothing. I look forward to seeing you, and I dread the times when we have to say goodbye. I was only fooling myself with the friends-only thing. I love you, Carrie. More importantly, I'm in love with you, and I never, ever want to tell you goodbye again."

Each and every word he said seemed to magically take away the pain of the multitude of stitches she had just received. Each and every word he said eased the residual terror that had fluttered through her even though she was safe in the hospital.

"Luke, I need you to do me a favor," she said.

"Anything," he replied immediately.

"Will you tell me all that again tomorrow when I'm not on such strong pain meds?"

"Honey, I'll tell you again whenever you want to hear it. Now, will you do me a favor?" His gaze held the warmth—the love she'd always wanted from him.

"Of course," she replied.

"Will you answer my question?"

She frowned. "What question?" she asked. Darn the pain meds for making her more and more drowsy as each minute ticked by.

"Carrie Carlson, will you marry me?"

"Yes, yes, I will." Tears once again burned at her eyes, only this time they were happy tears. They lasted only a moment before a new worry filled her. "Oh, Luke. You might not want me anymore. I look like a rag doll that's been put together too many times. I've got stitches in both my legs and my arm."

"Carrie, I didn't fall in love with a pair of legs or an arm. I fell in love with you, and no amount of stitches is going to change that." He leaned down and took her mouth in a kiss of infinite tenderness and one that tasted of abiding love.

"Now, the doctor told me not to stay too long, so I'll be back here tomorrow when you get out of here, and then you're coming to my place after that."

She smiled at him, still half-unsure if this was a dream or not. If it was a dream, it was the best one she'd ever had in her entire life. If it was reality, then she was the luckiest woman in the whole, entire world. Her eyes drifted closed. She felt his warm lips graze her forehead once again, and then he was gone.

SHE AWOKE THE next morning to sunshine drifting through her window and her wounds all hurting at the same time. She'd been moved the night before from the emergency room to a regular room. She hadn't been awake long when Shannon Franklin, one of the other nurses, came into the room.

"Hey, Carrie. I'm so sorry to see you in that bed," she said.

"That makes two of us," Carrie replied ruefully.

"I'm used to seeing you taking care of patients, not being one."

"Trust me, I'd much rather be wearing my scrubs instead of this ugly hospital gown," Carrie replied.

"Well, you know the drill. I need to get your vitals, and then the doctor has ordered some more pain relief for you," Shannon said.

"I'm not going to say no to that." Carrie raised the head of her bed and then remembered the conversation she'd had with Luke the night before. Was she really an engaged woman this morning? Had Luke really been with her last night and professed his love to her? A wave of happiness swept through her at the very thought. Or had it been just a wonderful dream?

Luke showed up in her room just after she'd eaten breakfast. "How are you feeling this morning?" he asked and swept her forehead with his lips.

"I'm hurting and a little bit confused. Luke, this may sound crazy, but am I an engaged woman or did I just have a wonderful dream last night?"

He smiled at her, the smile that always warmed her in a way no man's smile had ever done before. "Well, I can't talk to you about the wonderful dream you had last night, although I sure hope I was in it."

She returned his smile. "You were a main player in it." Her smile faded, and she looked at him more seriously. "Did you visit me last night? And did you really mean the things you said?"

"I meant every word. In fact, I'm late this morning because I made a stop on my way here." He took a ring box from his pocket, and her heart instantly quickened. "I wanted you to know just how serious I was about what I said last night to you." He opened the box to display a beautiful princess-cut diamond.

"Oh, Luke," she said breathlessly.

"I'll ask you one more time… Carrie Carlson, will you marry me?"

"Absolutely, positively yes," she replied as her heart expanded with the depth of her love for him.

He slid the ring on her finger. "Now it's official."

"Looks like I'm just in time for the celebration," Dr. Morris said as he stepped into the room.

"As soon as she's better, we're going to have a big party," Luke replied and smiled down at her once again.

"Well, you can start celebrating a little bit now, because I'm letting her go today," Dr. Morris said. "All I need to do is check on her stitches and rebandage them, and then she can go."

"And then you're coming home with me and we'll never have to tell each other goodbye again," Luke said, making her heart leap with the happiness and the knowledge that the man who was her best friend—the man she loved—loved her back.

An hour later they were on their way to Luke's house. They'd left the hospital and filled a prescription for pain medication. When the doctor had changed her bandages, Luke had seen all the damage Jason had done.

How could a man do something like that to a woman? Her pain hurt Luke, and all he wanted to do was make her better. When he'd left her house the night before and pulled to the curb down the street, he had thought long and hard about his feelings for Carrie.

In the end, he'd realized that what he was feeling for her was love, the kind of true love that he'd been looking for. She was not just his best friend; she was absolutely everything he wanted for a life partner. All the time he was telling himself he didn't have time for romance, he'd been in a romance.

He'd driven back to her house, eager to tell her how much he loved her, and instead he had found her bloody and terrified. Even now, with her safe and in the passenger seat next to him, he wanted to wrap her in his arms and never let her go. He never wanted to see her hurting again.

The things she'd said to him still rang in his ears. She'd given him a picture of himself that he hadn't liked. He still wanted his father's murderer to be caught, but he wanted to have Carrie in his life more.

She'd been right…everyone had been right. It was time for him to leave the investigation to Lane. And it was time for him to let go of his need for revenge— justice—and get on with his life, a happy life.

"You're very quiet," she said, pulling him from his thoughts.

He flashed her a smile. "I was just thinking how

much I'm looking forward to having a wonderful life with you."

"Luke, I want you to be happy, and I want you to be at peace," she replied.

"I saw what revenge looked like last night when Jason came after you. I don't want to be that man. I've found my peace with you."

She reached out and placed her hand on his forearm, a familiar gesture that warmed him. "I love you, Luke King," she said.

"That's all I really need," he replied as he pulled up and parked in front of his home...their home.

The afternoon flew by. Lane showed up to get an official statement from Carrie, and as Luke heard every single thing that had happened between Carrie and Jason, he was awed by Carrie's strength and her courage in facing off with the madman.

Lane also told them that Elizabeth had been taken to the hospital. She'd been suffering from malnourishment and had been badly dehydrated. Jason had never taken her for any therapy after her stroke, but she was now set up to go into a rehab where she could get all the help she needed.

After he left, Emily called Carrie to tell her that she was doing fine but she planned to move back home with her parents for a while. She would pay her half of the remaining lease and make arrangements to move her things out of their house as soon as possible.

She had been apologetic to Carrie, but apparently her encounter with Jason had scared her badly. Carrie had assured her it was fine.

It worked out perfectly for Luke, who wanted Carrie to move her things into his house as quickly as possible. He wanted their life together to start immediately. With Carrie's permission, he would pay off her rent and arrange for her things to be brought here to the ranch.

Finally, things had quieted down. He made them a quick dinner of soup and sandwiches, and then Carrie took a pain pill and fell asleep on the sofa.

He watched her sleep, grateful that he'd come to his senses where she was concerned. It comforted him that she would fall asleep in his arms tonight and that she'd be the first person he'd see when he opened his eyes in the morning.

He'd realized the night before that he had loved her for some time—he just hadn't recognized it. He'd been too filled with his anger to see the love.

He wasn't sure how long he watched her before he finally got out of his chair. He wrote a short note for her in case she woke up, and then he left the house.

His feet took him on the familiar path down the lane and to the stables. He flipped on the overhead light to ward off the coming darkness of night and then sank down on a bale of hay near the center of the building.

The scents of the hay and the horses filled his head and instantly evoked memories of Big John. This time the memories came without the enormous stabbing pain and anger, but rather they fluttered through him on lighter notes of shared laughter and conversations.

For just a moment he smelled his father...the fragrance of sunshine and the fresh, crisp cologne he'd always worn. A deep grief swept over Luke, a grief he knew he would probably feel for the rest of his life. He would always mourn for his father. There would always be moments when he would feel the loss of Big John.

But how lucky he'd been to have had as much time as he'd had with a man who had been bigger than life, a man who had been a good father and husband. How lucky he'd been to have had a father he loved and who he knew loved him.

Still, it was time to let go and make time and energy for Carrie and the life they would be living together. Eventually they would have children and he would tell them stories about Big John.

"Luke?" Carrie appeared next to him.

He got up from the hay bale and turned to face her. "Honey, you shouldn't have walked all the way down here," he said to her.

"I thought you might need me," she replied somberly.

He smiled at her. "I need you every minute of the day and night, but I'm okay," he assured her. He pulled her into his arms. "We're going to have a great marriage, Carrie. We're going to laugh and love and build memories every day. Are you in?"

"I'm in," she replied with the bright smile he loved.

He took her mouth in a kiss that held all his love and desire for her. His father's murder still wasn't solved, and he didn't know what kind of trouble Caleb might be in. But when he held her in his arms, those things faded to background noise.

He could have chosen to stay stuck in his anger and obsession with finding his father's killer, but he'd cho-

sen love instead. The woman he held in his arms had
pulled him out of the darkness and into the light, and
he knew it was a light that would shine on them for
the rest of their lives.

* * * * *

OPERATION PAYBACK

JUSTINE DAVIS

I'm repossessing this space for a special canine dedication. People have different feelings about police K-9s. For me, the bottom line is this: these animals do what they do, what they're trained to do, for one reason. They don't do it to catch bad guys. They don't do it to find illegal drugs. They don't do it because somebody broke the law. They do it for us. For their handlers. The humans they have chosen to love and obey.

And sometimes doing what they do for us costs them everything.

Just a few of the loyal dogs who have lost their lives recently doing what we have given to them as their duty:

Buddy

Jango

Jedi

K.G.

Max

Mick

Sjaak

Miss them, honor them, in whatever way feels right to you, and never, ever forget they didn't do it for the law or the order…but for us.

Chapter One

This was without a doubt the craziest thing he'd done yet. Or the stupidest. Or both. And considering the mess he'd made of his life so far, that was saying something.

Trip Callen looked out the bus window. Even behind the sunglasses he wore, he winced a little at the bright sunlight, and the movement triggered the now familiar pain around his blackened left eye. It figured that on a day when he would welcome the usual April Northwest overcast, it was blatantly absent. He tried to gauge how far they'd gone. It was impossible, though, really, because the surroundings looked the same for so long, amid the towering evergreens. It was as if they were on some endless road that never went anywhere, just on and on. Or in a circle, maybe. Some endless round and round until he was old and gray and—

You're losing it, Callen.

Or maybe already lost it. No, that was an understatement. How many people his age ended up with exactly one thing on their to-do list?

But it was the only thing he wanted to do. He owed it to someone. One person, only one, had never abandoned him, never written him off. What he could offer, a heartfelt thank-you, wasn't much, but it was all he had.

He'd made a lot of vows in the last few months. All but

this one had been to himself. Vows that it would never, ever happen again. That he would never go through this again. That he would take what he'd learned and do something with it, build something, make a life, one worth living, not one he was ashamed of. Above all he'd vowed never to be so gullible as to believe a fast-talking, self-appointed boss like Oliver Ruff again, no matter how much he pretended to be a friend. Your very best friend. Until you outlived your usefulness.

Without much thought, he pulled off the sunglasses, wondering how much it would hurt.

"Are you all right?"

The quiet question from the older woman, who had been reading in the seat beside him since he'd changed buses in Port Angeles, startled him out of his fruitless memories.

He watched her, thinking she looked sort of like his mother had before she'd gotten sick. Not really old, just noticeably older than him. Her eyes were nearly the same shade of blue. And he realized he should have kept on the sunglasses he'd bought in Port Angeles with some of his small cash reserve. Because she was eyeing the shiner.

"Sorry. I know it's ugly," he muttered, and moved to put the glasses back on.

"Don't on my account," she said. "That wasn't what I was asking about."

Her expression was so gentle, so caring, he had to swallow before he could speak.

"I'm fine." Well, he was in the health sense except for the eye, so it wasn't one of those lies he'd also vowed to banish. He hesitated, then tried for a smile himself. Tried to remember what you were supposed to say at times like this. "Thank you."

She smiled back. It was full of warmth, and a touch

of sadness. "You just reminded me of my son, when he gets worried."

He wasn't sure why he kept talking. "I am. A bit. But it's in my hands now. It…wasn't." Even he could hear how odd, how choppy it sounded. But she didn't seem to notice or care.

"Then you have the chance to build something good," she said.

Build. Was it coincidence, that she'd used the very word he'd just been thinking?

"I'm…not sure I know how," he admitted, still a little stunned that he was carrying on this conversation with a total stranger.

She studied him for a moment before saying, with a nod of certainty, "You can learn."

He started to grimace, but it hurt, so he stopped. "You're awfully sure."

"I've been a teacher for years. I'm pretty good at assessing the learning capacity of people."

"Even strangers on a bus?"

"Especially," she said. "No preconceptions or expectations to discard."

He had to admit, he never would have thought of it that way. And that brought out more words than he'd said at once in a long time. "Wish you could teach me that. I apparently su— I mean, I'm lousy at assessing people, learning-wise or otherwise." Yeah, she reminded him of his mother all right. And she smiled at his abrupt change of wording.

"Oh, I don't know," she said rather breezily. "You're talking to me, aren't you?" He couldn't help it, he liked that one. "Where are you headed, after the bus?"

"To Redwood Cove," he said. "I have something I need to do there."

"Well, isn't that handy? That's where I'm going. I can give you a ride."

He blinked. Stared at her. "You don't even know me. I could be a serial killer, or a—"

"But you're not," she cut him off quietly.

It had been so long since he'd met someone like this, he'd almost convinced himself they didn't exist anymore. After a moment, determinedly, he said, "No. I'm not."

By the time they reached the bus drop-off near the ferry landing, he knew her name, Cynthia Larson, that she taught at the elementary school and her husband owned a small car repair shop in Redwood Cove where they also lived, that the son she mentioned lived in Port Angeles and she'd been there for a visit—and taken the bus even though it was about a half hour longer than driving herself because she liked to be able to look at the scenery or read—while her husband attended to some business on the other side. That had made him smile, the term locals used for the big-city side of Puget Sound. The side where he'd gotten into this mess.

In turn she'd learned only his name, that he'd grown up in Redwood Cove before moving to the city, and finally, the truth he'd felt compelled to tell her before he got into a car alone with her.

"Mrs. Larson, there's something you should know before you do this."

"What's that, Trip?"

"I just got out of prison."

He looked years older than he was.

Kayley McSwain knew the man in front of her was actually a few months younger than her own twenty-eight, but he looked like thirty-five was in his rearview mirror. It wasn't his actual physical appearance, because he was as tall and strong as ever. Stronger, in fact, in a lean, solid way, as if he'd been working hard or working out. Maybe both.

His hair even seemed the same. Although shorter, it was still thick, dark, and with that tendency to stand up on top. And it certainly wasn't his face, the right side at least; he was as handsome as ever. It wasn't the ugly bruise around his left eye, either. No, the extra years were in the shadows in those eyes. Eyes she had always remembered as a lovely deep green. Now they looked darker, shaded, like eyes that had seen too much, and too much of it bad.

And that black eye only emphasized it all.

He's been to prison. What do you expect?

"Trip," she whispered, for some reason unable to speak any louder.

"Kayley," he said, and his voice was a little rough.

The last time he'd been at this door, it had been to pick up Debra. Her beautiful, somewhat flighty then-housemate. She and Debra had grown up together, and had been friendly enough that when her parents had moved to take care of her grandmother, leaving Kayley to hold down the family home, Debra had moved in with her to share costs. Most of the time she'd managed to ignore Debra's parade of boyfriends—although to Kayley, being a boyfriend required more than a couple of dates—until the day she'd opened the door to Trip Callen.

One look at those amazing evergreen eyes and she was a goner. She knew it was crazy and tried to bury the reaction. She was shy by nature, and living with the almost frighteningly gregarious Debra had only exacerbated that. She was used to hiding things, so she was good at it.

He'd been a bit bruised up that day, too. It wasn't until later—this relationship of Debra's seemed to be lasting, since at least a month later he was still showing up—that she found out why. In the inevitable wait before the gorgeously prepped Debra made her entrance, he'd actually started talking to her a little.

She found out the bruises were the result of a fight with his father. Another fight. Or rather, another beating, since she also found out he rarely fought back. She hadn't understood why until Debra had mentioned one day before he'd arrived that his mother had died. When she later tried to express sympathy to Trip, he brushed it off.

"Is that why you stay, when he…hits you?" she couldn't stop herself from asking.

"I stay because if I left, he'd spiral out of control and end up dead, too."

The words had come out in a rush, as if against his will. And Kayley didn't quite know what to think about a guy who, instead of grieving his dead mother, spent his time trying to keep his father alive. And taking a beating to do it.

That had decided her about Trip Callen. And from then on she spent every moment of the time he waited for her housemate with him, talking, learning. All the while chanting in her mind that she had to remember he was taken.

Debra noticed, even teased her about it.

"After my man, McSwain?"

She'd blushed furiously. "Of course not!"

"Good thing," Debra had said, then sighed. "Because I think he's the one, Kayley."

Kayley had had to take the words seriously, given how long the relationship had lasted. A month was an eon for Debra. So she had buried even deeper the feelings that had been stirring within her. And in a way it made it easier; she was able to talk and laugh with Trip in a way she'd never been able to do with any other man. Because she knew he was not and would never be hers.

Chapter Two

Kayley swallowed tightly, realized he was standing out on the porch in the cold. April, in characteristic Northwest fashion, was turning out to be a battle between winter and the coming spring. The clear days like today were often the chilliest.

"Come in out of the cold."

For a moment his eyes closed, as if she'd said something far more momentous than she had.

Or maybe to him, an offer to get out of the cold was momentous. The thought made her shiver as if she were the one standing outside the door.

"Please," she said softly, moving aside to let him pass. He hesitated a moment longer, then stepped through. A wash of cold, external air came with him, and she shivered slightly again, although as before, she doubted it was in reaction to the temperature.

She noticed the pair of sunglasses hooked into his jacket pocket, and wondered if they were for the light or to mask the shiner. The jacket itself was a single layer of denim, not really enough for the chilly temperature today. She wondered if it was all he had. If it was even his. Did you get to take your own clothes into prison? For the day you finally got out? She'd never thought to ask things like that when she'd visited. She was too worried about how he was doing, how he was surviving, and would he make it through this without being forever damaged.

She hadn't seen him for a couple of months. She'd been buried with an influx of new clients, so last month she had missed her usual trek out to the facility in Forks. And she'd felt guilty, although he'd said not to.

But then, in the beginning he'd told her not to come at all.

She'd understood how he'd felt. How could she not, given what had happened to him? He'd ended up in prison, disowned not only by Debra, but by the father he'd tried to save, the father who had driven him over the edge and straight into trouble.

He stood just inside the door, not moving as she closed it. For a moment neither of them spoke. Then, awkwardly, he said, "I'm out. For good." He gave her a rather weak smile. "Early, even."

"I know. I mean, I knew. I called yesterday about a visit this week, and they told me. That you wouldn't be there, I mean."

"Oh."

He looked so ill at ease, she gave him the best smile she could muster. "Do you want some coffee? I promise it's not too old."

He let out a compressed breath. As if the idea of being picky about how old coffee was was silly. As it probably was now, for him. Even as many times as she'd visited, she knew she had no true idea what it must have been like for him. She doubted anyone who hadn't been there could really understand. Even in a minimum security facility, there was no comparison to the outside.

He hadn't said yes to the coffee, but she proceeded as if he had. And he followed her to the kitchen. He took the seat she indicated at the counter while she got two mugs out of the cupboard above the coffee maker.

"One sugar still?" she asked.

He looked surprised for an instant. That she remembered how he liked his coffee? *You'd be surprised—or embarrassed—at what I remember about you.*

He recovered quickly. "No, I—" He stopped. Almost imperceptibly gave a tiny shake of his head. "Never mind. That's fine."

Her brow furrowed. "It's okay if you want it different."

"No. I just…it took more sugar, and cream, to get it down…there."

"Oh."

She didn't know what else to say, so she left it at that. She finished fixing the coffee and slid his mug across to him. She wanted to go around and sit next to him, but he already seemed so edgy, so nervous, she didn't. Instead she stood with the counter between them, watching as he took a long, warming swallow. His eyes closed, as if he were savoring the taste. But then he winced, and she assumed the action had pulled at the swollen area around his bruised eye. She wanted to ask what had happened but was afraid she didn't want to hear the answer. Had he already gotten into a fight, fresh out of prison? Or had it happened before? But would they have still let him out if he'd been involved in a fight?

Instead she went for something she was sure must be true.

"I'm so happy for you, Trip. You must be incredibly relieved it's over."

He drew in a long breath. "I…don't think it's fully registered yet."

"When did you actually get out?"

"Noon."

Noon today? She mentally calculated the driving time from the facility in Forks. He had to have come straight here. That seemed very meaningful to her. Perhaps more than it should.

"How did you get here?"

"Bus, mostly. But…a lady gave me a ride here from the ferry landing. She sat next to me on the bus."

He both looked and sounded…bemused, she guessed. And it struck her that it was probably the simple fact of open human contact and friendliness. Something he'd been doing mostly without long before the unfortunate events that had landed him in the Olympic Corrections Center.

"One of my neighbors?"

"I…not close. I mean, she lives in Redwood Cove, but not here. She was in Port Angeles. Her son lives there. Her husband has a car repair place in town." He was speaking choppily, as if he weren't used to talking this much. She supposed that was true, too. "She's a teacher," he finished.

And suddenly all those pieces fell together in her head. Her eyes widened as she asked, "Mrs. Larson?"

He drew back, startled. "How'd you know that?"

She smiled. "You know how small towns are."

He grimaced. "Yeah. I just got out of a 'small town.' There were less than four hundred of us."

She didn't know what to say to that, either, so she just went on. "Mr. Larson works on my car, and she was my fifth-grade teacher. One of my favorite teachers ever. She was so nice, so kind, that everybody just wanted to please her."

For the first time, he smiled. It was tiny, a bare curve of his lips for only a second, but it was there. And even that tiny hint of the smile she used to love warmed her. She'd half expected him to not be able to smile at anything.

"I can see that," he said quietly. He lowered his gaze, then said, as if she'd asked, "And yes, I told her."

At first Kayley wasn't sure what he meant, but when she realized that he was saying he'd told Mrs. Larson he'd been in prison, she felt an odd sort of clutching in her chest.

"She wanted to give me a ride anyway." He said it even more quietly, but now there was an undertone of amazement in his voice.

"Why did you risk it? Risk her saying no?"

His head came up. "She's a nice lady. She…deserved to know what she was really offering to do."

"And that," she said, putting all she could of what she was feeling into her voice, "is why she did it. Because you're the kind of man who knows that."

He looked a little startled. "I'm an…ex-con," he said, and his expression as he spoke made her wonder if this was the first time he'd even thought it, let alone said it.

"Emphasis on the *ex*, and keeping it that way," she said briskly.

She thought she saw a shudder go through him. "I'm never going back."

"I know," she said. Then, impulsively, she said, "I was going to fix some chicken and veggies for dinner. Will you stay?" He blinked. Stared, as if speechless. "Please?" she added.

"I…yes." He lowered his gaze for an instant, but then it shot back to her face. "Thank you," he said, as if he'd only that moment remembered it was something he should say.

She smiled at him, trying to put everything she had of comfort, reassurance, and welcome into it. She didn't think it was enough, so she reached across the counter and put a hand over one of his.

He jumped. Barely visible, but she felt it. He didn't look at her, just stared down at their hands. She felt torn between wanting him to talk about what he'd been through, and not wanting to hear it because it would probably be horrible. It broke her heart to even think about it.

She normally wasn't one to sympathize with people who committed crimes, and she wouldn't declare he'd done no wrong, but she understood why he had, after what had happened to him. And while the time he'd served seemed an eon to her—it certainly must have seemed much longer to him—she knew it was the shortest sentence anybody involved had gotten, and she suspected the shortest allowable. Here he was, out six months early thanks to ERCs, earned release credits, mostly for good conduct, they'd said. That had to be a sign, didn't it?

She cut off her rambling thoughts as she gathered the items for dinner. They'd get to all that after he'd had a decent meal. Assuming he'd stay long enough.

He had to stay.

She couldn't lose him all over again.

Chapter Three

"I remember this," he said softly, glancing around the covered deck, open to a view of the trees beyond, but itself sheltered enough to be comfortable with the outdoor heater on. He would have thought the tall evergreens, which looked quite like the ones that surrounded the facility he'd just left, would have made him twitchy. But they didn't, because this was so different, felt so different.

Besides, Kayley was here.

She peeked over her shoulder from where she stood at the barbecue and smiled at him. It was the smile he'd always remembered, warm, kind, and genuine. He'd learned a bit about fakery over the last few years, and in his mind she had always stood as the opposition, the person who proved there were still good people around. Even before she'd proven it by doing what he'd never expected, visiting him one way or another, every week. At the least a video chat every weekend, phone calls—which he had to make so she had the option to turn them down when they were put through—but also in person. Once a month she'd made the nearly three-hour drive to Forks and back to visit him face-to-face.

Visits that were the only bright spot in his existence. Visits he'd come to not just look forward to, but...the only phrase that came to mind was *count on*. Sometimes he thought they were the only thing that kept him sane.

Your woman's pretty cute, Three.

She's not my woman. She's just a friend.

Robber had snorted with laughter and said something about wishing he had "just a friend" who looked at him like that.

When it came to friends, if he'd made one in that place, it was Robert Goodwin, known generally as Robber, a constant, painful reminder of the circumstances that had landed the man there: a robbery gone bad, a robbery he'd committed to pay for a last-ditch treatment for his little boy. Who had died anyway. It was Robber who had started the habit of everyone calling him Three for *triple*, instead of Trip. Considering some of the other nicknames he'd heard inside, he figured he'd gotten off easy.

He walked around a bit, just looking, still marveling at the fact that he was free to do so. Then he sat down, his back to the house, facing out to the open space beyond. It was habit now, always knowing what was behind him.

"I remember that first barbecue you came to here," Kayley said.

He drew in a steadying breath. "So do I. You cooked. And Debra did nothing."

She frowned. "As usual."

That startled him. Kayley wasn't usually one to bad-mouth anyone else. Or judge them. Wasn't the fact that she hadn't dumped him as fast as Debra had proof of that?

And then she turned to face him. "Is that why you're here?"

He blinked. "What?"

"If you want to know where she is, why didn't you just ask?"

He drew back. "No!" It came out a little sharply. "You think I'm here…looking for her?"

"You're not?"

He told Kayley the truth. Because that's who she was in his life. The one he told the truth.

"Looking for the woman who said she loved me and then couldn't drop me fast enough when I got in trouble? Hell, no. I'm here for the woman who stood by me. The only person who ever did."

He didn't think he'd said that much at once since… he couldn't remember exactly. Before he'd gone in, anyway. But it had flooded out of him as if a dam had burst.

"Oh."

It was all she said, but she said it in that shy but pleased tone he remembered so well. It had almost amused him back in the beginning, on those occasions, which were almost always, when Debra had kept him waiting. Back then it had started simply as a way to kill the time. But eventually he'd gotten to where, to his own shock, it had almost irritated him if Debra was ready too quickly.

He just watched her for a minute, carefully using tongs to turn over the chicken, a brush to spread on more sauce.

"I…can I…do something?" he asked belatedly.

"You already brought out the plates and utensils, and I've got this, I think," she answered, as if he'd spoken in a normal way. He'd definitely lost that knack. He hadn't talked much to anyone inside, except Robber. "Chicken should be done soon."

"Smells great." There, that had come out better.

"It's Mom's recipe. You liked it, I think."

He remembered that day again, how delicious everything had tasted. How he had felt compelled to clean up after. And had shamed Debra into helping, although she'd laughingly said Kayley was better at it.

He'd been so young and stupid then. He'd really thought Debra's looks and charm made up for the part of her that assumed Kayley was there to both cook and clean up.

Something moved on the edge of the open backyard. He managed not to jump, but he tensed. Any sudden movement made him nervous. Wary. Then he saw it was a dog coming through the trees and relaxed a little. And relaxed more when Kayley called out to the animal happily.

"Ah, there you are! Haven't seen you in a couple of days. Did you know I was grilling?"

The dog, tail wagging, trotted toward them. Odd, it looked sort of like the dogs the corrections officers used at the higher-security prisons, that they had sometimes brought to where he'd been for training on hunts through the thick woods. *Maligators*, they'd called them. *Don't mess with those guys*, they'd said. *They're tough and fearless.*

Except this one had thick, long fur, not the short, sleek stuff those other dogs had. The coloration was close, though, black head and shoulders gradually switching to a reddish brown from the shoulders back. As it came up the deck steps, he saw the ears were upright and alert-looking, the tail long and plumed.

Even as he noted that, the wagging stopped. And so did the dog. Stopped in its tracks, staring at him. There was something unnerving about those eyes, dark, deep, flecked with gold. Not in the way the K-9 guards were unnerving, but just as intense.

"He's not used to seeing anyone else here, especially a guy," Kayley explained quickly, putting down the tongs and walking over.

Trip registered what she'd said—and the implication that she didn't have guys hanging around, which was their loss—but he couldn't tear his gaze away from the dog. He felt almost pinned, as if he didn't dare look away.

"He's on his rounds," Kayley said, crouching to pet the dog.

The dog at last looked away from him to her, and Trip could breathe again. The dog swiped a pink tongue over her cheek in a dog kiss.

Lucky dog.

Where the hell had that come from?

And then it registered exactly what she'd said.

"Rounds?" It came out almost like a croak, because that sounded more like it would apply to those other dogs he'd been thinking about. The ones tasked with keeping people like him where they belonged, behind figurative bars.

"He checks on all the neighbors," she said, looking at him but still petting the dog. "He has a circuit he makes. We all look forward to seeing him." She smiled; she clearly liked the dog, and it was clearly mutual. "He's so well-mannered. And helpful."

"Helpful?" He was obviously back to one-word sentences.

"He finds things and brings them back to people. Things you've dropped, or lost pets, or even kids, sometimes. And he does…" Her voice trailed off, and when she finished with, "…lots of other things," he knew that hadn't been what she was going to say.

"Clever dog."

"You have no idea," she said. "So, Cutter, this is Trip. Trip, this is Cutter."

He almost wished she hadn't done it, because the dog was looking at him again. With that gaze that seemed to pin him there. He had the thought that this must be how sheep felt when that herding dog stared them down.

"You can pet him," she assured him. "You two get acquainted while I take the chicken off." She gave the dog a last pat. "Your piece is ready, too, boy."

"His?"

"I always set a little aside for him. He is the neighborhood guardian, after all."

"Who owns this…guardian?"

She started to answer, then stopped. "Let me get dinner served. Then we can talk."

She went back to the barbecue. The dog stayed where he was. Still staring at him. And he had the stranger thought that if a squirrel ran right over their feet, the dog wouldn't even glance at it. It would just sit there, eyes with the odd gold flecks boring into him.

He'd never had a dog—his mother had been allergic—so he didn't know that much about the ins and outs. Was this normal, for him to just sit there staring like this? Admittedly Trip was a stranger, but still… Maybe the dog was just keeping an eye on him, to make sure he wasn't a threat to Kayley, who was obviously a friend to the animal.

Maybe he can smell that place on you. Can smell it and knows it's bad. Maybe there's something in the air there, or even put on the surfaces, to make you easy to track if you tried to make a run for it.

He tried to shake off the absurd thought, although come to think of it, that would be a pretty smart thing for them to do. Although there weren't a lot of escapes from the place, despite the fact that there was no full perimeter fence, only one around the living quarters and dining facility. One guy who tried it a few years ago was caught less than two miles away, after they'd called in the teams put in place for just such an event. Minimum security didn't mean you could just walk away, even if you were basically there by consent. The threat of ending up in a much worse place kept most in line.

He'd never even considered it. Not only because it was crazy, and almost a given you'd be blasted all over the news and eventually caught, but he had nowhere to go. No one to go to. Besides, compared to most in the system, he was lucky. Minimum security was more like a work camp. Gang leader Oliver Ruff was doing fifteen years of hard time in a maximum security prison across the state. Trip knew he'd been lucky his record had been much cleaner, so he'd gotten a shorter sentence than Ruff had. Shorter than he'd expected—in fact, shorter than the public defender had told him to expect. It had been a pleasant surprise in a grim process, just as ending up in a minimum security facility had been.

When Kayley spoke, it snapped him out of the reverie. She was indicating it was time to move to the small, round, bar-height table. He did, again keeping his back to the house. Anybody coming that way, through the house, would make enough noise to be heard. Then she set a plate full of delicious-smelling chicken and grilled asparagus in front of him, and his stomach growled as ferociously as that dog watching him ever could.

Kayley laughed. "I thought so."

She set down her own plate across the table from him, while he toyed with the knife and fork before him. An ordinary place setting.

With two obvious weapons.

Life outside.

This was going to take a lot of getting used to.

Before sitting down, Kayley went back to the grill and picked up a finger-sized piece of chicken that looked as if she hadn't put any sauce on it.

"Here you go, Cutter," she said, and tossed it toward

the dog in a high arc. The animal caught it easily and chewed with gusto. With teeth that looked quite capable of sinking into other kinds of flesh.

Trip thought the dog would take off now that he'd gotten his treat, but instead he turned his gaze, that steady, penetrating gaze, back to the intruder—him—for a long moment.

"He probably won't leave until you actually pet him," Kayley said.

"Seriously?"

"He's a very, very clever dog."

Trip looked down at the animal again. *Clever* didn't seem quite strong enough to describe that look in those dark eyes. With a wry grimace he reached out, slowly, warily. The dog's head didn't move. No teeth were visible. Half expecting that to change at any instant, he kept going until his fingertips brushed the fur on the black head.

He froze. Surely it was too cold, too damp for static electricity? Besides, what he'd felt hadn't been a snap or a shock, but more of a…warmth. Almost a soothing warmth.

He moved his hand a little more, just an inch or so across the dog's head. The warmth grew, spreading somehow, making him almost relax a little. Was this normal? He didn't think so. He may not have had a dog but he'd known them—and envied his childhood friends who had them—and petted them.

But he'd never felt anything like this comforting sensation that seemed to be spreading through him. And he couldn't seem to stop himself from actually petting the dog in long strokes.

"Amazing, isn't it? How he makes you feel better."

"I…yes." It was a relief to hear her say that, to know somebody else had felt this…whatever it was.

"He's a certified therapy dog, too, and visits hospitals and nursing homes."

That put it all in a context he could understand. He actually did relax then, enough to actually enjoy running his fingers over and through the soft, dense fur.

"You're really something, mutt," he murmured as he gave the dog a final pat. As if the animal felt his job was done—now, there was a crazy thought—he got to his paws, went over to nudge Kayley for what was apparently a familiar goodbye nose-to-nose, then headed down the steps and back the way he'd come. Trip watched him go, beyond bemused. Before he disappeared into the trees, the dog looked back over his shoulder at him, and even from fifteen yards away the stare seemed as intense.

That was an unsettling sort of dog. Both in the intensity and that knack for…soothing.

They began to eat, and he savored using ordinary utensils almost as much as the delicious food. He thought he should say something about the great taste, compliment her on it, but he was so out of practice, it took him a while to put together the words, and he thought he'd sounded horribly awkward. But she gave him a smile that made all that fade away.

It wasn't until he was done, and he was staring down at the plate he'd scraped clean, that Kayley said, her tone casual, "By the way, I have no idea where Debra is. Nor do I care to."

His head snapped up as her words startled him.

"What?"

She smiled, as sweetly as if she were talking about some pleasurable memory. "I haven't seen her since the day I threw her out."

He blinked. "Threw her out?"

"Of this house, and my life."

"But…she was your friend."

"I thought she was."

"Then…why?"

"Partly because of the way she treated you."

He gave a slow shake of his head. "I understand, now, that she just couldn't deal. I don't blame her."

"Fine. I blame her enough for both of us."

"Kayley, no. She was your friend. Don't let me ruin that, too."

The look she gave him then churned up his insides. "And that's why, Trip Callen," she said softly. "You're worth more than her faux friendship was, because after all you've been through, you still think that way."

Chapter Four

Kayley thought about telling him the rest. About the accusation Debra had hurled at her when they'd gotten into that big fight, when Kayley had asked when she was going to visit Trip.

"To a prison? Are you insane?"

"But he needs to know you still love him."

"Don't try and snow me, Kayley. You want me to go so you can tag along."

"What?"

She'd been stunned. And she didn't think she'd ever seen a glare so angry or a tone of voice so vicious as what came next.

"Do you think I don't know you two were cheating on me?"

Multiple responses, from *no, we weren't* to *that's a lie*, had popped to her lips, but none of them made it out. Because underlying them all was the one truth that made any declaration shaky, the simple fact that she was in love with Trip. They'd never acted upon it, she never would and he never knew, but the truth was still there.

As was the truth betrayed by that glare, in that harsh, almost cruel voice; this woman wasn't and never had been truly a friend. At least, not the kind of friend she wanted in her life.

So Kayley had gone with the honest truth.

"If that's what you believe, then obviously you don't want to live here anymore."

Her supposed friend had looked startled. In typical Debra fashion, she had declared, "I'm not disrupting my life over that piece of garbage. Good riddance to him. He's right where he belongs. I'm over my bad-boy phase."

"What about your disloyal, boyfriend-stealing friend phase?" Kayley had said, her tone icy.

Debra waved a hand as if brushing off a gnat. "Oh, I didn't mean that. I was just upset. I know you wouldn't."

Funny how she'd been certain enough to declare it, until she thought it might inconvenience her.

"I never even kissed him." *But I wanted to.* "Nor did I sleep with him." *I wanted that, too.* "But more than anything, the fact that you accused me tells me the truth about *our* relationship. Find a new place to live, Debra. Go back to the city. You belong there."

She'd left the woman in shock, heading back to her room and shutting the door.

"Kayley? You okay?"

She snapped out of the memory. Looked across at Trip. He was looking at her with a concern she couldn't doubt was genuine. Unlike Debra's mockery of the feeling.

"I'm fine."

"You didn't look fine."

Again she thought about telling him. But she was a coward. She didn't want to see him laugh at the very idea of him cheating on Debra with…her.

"Just a bad memory," she said. "You know how that goes."

"Ya think?" he said dryly.

The way he said it, like the old Trip had, delighted her so much she couldn't help smiling, widely, the memory of Debra fading. His brow furrowed, and she said hastily, "I wasn't smiling at…your bad memories. I know you must have a ton. It's just…you looked and sounded like your old self just then."

He let out a long breath. "I'll never be that guy again, Kayley."

He'd said it almost like a warning. "I know. How could you be, after what you've been through?"

"I deserved what I got," he said flatly. "Probably more than I got."

"Don't," she protested. "Everybody could see what happened, why you went off course, and how you got sucked up into that group of lowlifes."

"I was one of those lowlifes, for nearly three years," he said, his tone still flat. "Don't kid yourself."

He was talking more normally now, in complete sentences. But she wasn't sure it was much better. "You were only on the fringes," she insisted. "More of an accessory than anything. You never initiated any of the crimes."

He shrugged. "I went along. If the man in that last house had died, I would have gone down for murder along with the rest of them."

"Except why didn't he?" she retorted. "Because you helped him. You stopped the bleeding, snuck him his phone to call for help once you were gone. And you risking Ruff killing you for doing it."

He appeared surprised when she said the gang leader's name. Had he really thought she hadn't paid any attention? She would have been in that courtroom every day if people she trusted hadn't warned her it wouldn't be wise to let Oliver Ruff see that Trip meant something to her, or think she meant something to him, to perhaps see her as leverage down the road. The idea would never have occurred to her until Hayley, the gentle-eyed but tough, spirited woman who was her neighbor and had become a friend, had carefully laid it out for her. After a bit of joking about them being destined to be friends, because how could two people named Hayley and Kayley not be?

"Your mind, thankfully, doesn't work in those ways," Hayley had said. "But you need to be aware."

That was probably the first time she'd realized just how much trouble Trip had gotten himself into. She'd thought at first he just ran with a wild crowd. She hadn't realized it was actually a criminal gang. She'd thought that maybe it was a reaction to the time his father had beaten him badly enough to land him in the ER. She could understand that. Who wouldn't rebel against that kind of treatment?

But at the time, all she'd done was wonder why he dealt with the man at all. She understood why he'd stayed when his mother had gotten sick. She knew he had helped her every step of the way down that long, painful path. But after she was gone, why had he stayed? He'd been old enough to strike out on his own, but he'd stayed in that house, with the man who seemed to be making a habit of beating him up.

She quashed the memory of how many times she'd expected—hoped?—that Debra would ask Kayley if he could move in with them. Or rather, knowing Debra, that she'd just move him in and tell Kayley after the fact.

She thought he had tried a lot longer than many would to save the man he'd once loved, admired, and respected. But in truth, that man had died the day they'd buried his wife, Trip's mother. Or rather, buried a skeletal imitation of the vibrant, lovely woman she'd been, judging by the pictures Trip had once shown her.

Dad went crazy after that. Didn't care about anyone or anything. Especially not me.

And finally, at twenty-one, Trip had stopped trying. And Kayley had often wondered, if he hadn't gotten sucked up into Oliver Ruff's pack of scum, if he would have just kept going, taking the beatings, because even as an adult he couldn't bring himself to strike back at his own father.

"How did you end up with Ruff's gang, anyway?" she asked now. "I mean, I think I know why in general, but why him? Them in particular?"

For a moment he just looked at her, and she thought he wasn't going to answer. Then he shrugged as if it didn't matter.

"They were the ones I knew."

Her brow furrowed. "Knew?"

His mouth twisted into a bitter smile. "They were my dad's dealers."

She blinked, drew back in shock. "He was…doing drugs, too? On top of the alcohol?"

The compressed breath he let out and the near eye roll he gave her then made her feel like a naive child. For the first time she saw the hardened side of him. The side she'd been warned likely existed—he'd survived in the brutal Ruff's world, after all—but she had never seen.

She hadn't been just naive.

She'd been a fool.

HE DIDN'T LIKE the way she'd looked. The way he'd made her look. Not hurt, but…wounded somehow. Damaged. He'd damaged her. Again.

She got up, gathered the plates and silverware. He had the thought that he could have actually stabbed her with the fork she'd just picked up and it might have hurt her less.

He knew she must have been shocked when he'd been

arrested because he'd never told her any of it, in any of those conversations they'd had in the living room of this very house, as he waited for Debra to do whatever it was she did when she was getting ready to go out.

No, she'd always thought he was just a guy—a nice guy, she'd said more than once—and he hadn't had the stomach or the courage to blow up that image by telling her the truth about who he was.

Yet he had told her so much. Things he'd never told Debra, about his mom, his father, and how he lived in constant fear he was going to lose his dad, too. He'd even, in a weak moment that evening when he'd showed up with a cast on his arm, admitted it was his father who'd broken his wrist.

That was the time she'd looked at him with those lovely blue eyes, so wide, so gentle, and said, "Maybe you need to stop trying to save him. Maybe only he can do that. Think about saving yourself, Trip."

She hadn't known that it was already too late. And she'd done what she rarely did. She reached out to touch him. And he'd felt…

Okay, now he was really losing it.

He gave a sharp shake of his head. He'd managed to break himself of the habit of lingering in the past, because it led down the path of what-if. There was no what-if, not a what if I hadn't done this, what if I hadn't gone there. It was far too late for that. And he knew that he indeed had been lucky, ending up at a facility like he had, where there was at least work to do, even things that helped the community. At a place where there weren't armed guards in towers at every corner, waiting to shoot you down if you tried anything. Nor had there been a lot of politics— what they called gang relations—or much fighting, and none he'd ever been involved in.

Well, except that little mess a few days ago. But given that it had resulted in his early release, he didn't put that in the bad category.

He hesitated before stepping back inside, as if her reaction to his harsh look had somehow revoked his welcome. But it was cold enough that he did, figuring if she told him to leave he'd need to get to the front door anyway.

He heard the ring of a phone, an actual landline. So that hadn't changed. People here still kept them, probably because of all the dead spots without a decent cell signal. The Center, as he called it in his head, had been like that. He'd heard the guards griping about it. The thought reminded him he'd promised to call Robber when he'd landed somewhere. The guy didn't have anybody either, and had no more idea than Trip had where he'd end up when he got out in a few months.

Kayley answered the call, although he couldn't hear what she was saying.

He saw she had set the dirty dishes—damn, that chicken had been good—on the counter to go over to the phone, so he picked them up and went to the sink. Washing dishes had been a regular assignment, so he was used to doing them by hand, but there was a fairly new and efficient-looking dishwasher next to the sink. So he waited. He'd gotten very good at that. Most of his days, if he wasn't out on a work crew, had been spent waiting for time to pass.

He suddenly remembered the day she'd shown up with a stack of crossword puzzle books. He hadn't thought they even printed them anymore, thought everything had been digitized. But he'd mentioned in passing they were prized possessions in his dorm, and one visit she'd shown up with them. One for everybody he roomed with. And not only that, she'd had the receipt showing she'd bought them mere hours ago, so the staff knew they were fresh and not with some kind of escape plot hidden in the pages.

"She's got quite an imagination, your girl," one of the officers had said with a grin.

Yes and she's not didn't seem like quite the answer to go with, so he'd merely nodded. By the time the books had been handed out, everybody in his dorm assumed he and Kayley were a couple.

And his first thought had been how much better off he'd be if they had been.

So now, here he was, in her house. She'd welcomed him, fed him, worried about him…and he'd put her down as hard as if he'd slapped her.

He sighed inwardly and waited for her to get off the phone, so he could apologize. Yes, he'd gotten very good at waiting. Sometimes he even managed it patiently.

She turned so that she could see him, probably wondering what he was doing in her kitchen. He resisted the urge to put his hands up so she could see he wasn't stealing anything. But the side effect of her turning was that suddenly he could hear what she was saying.

"—fine. Don't worry." She smiled, as if she were on a video call. "I'm sure he did. He's such a clever dog. Thanks for checking, though. Bye."

She put down the phone. Then she walked over to the counter, stopped, and just looked at him for a moment. Intently enough that he started to feel wary again.

"That," she finally said, "was Cutter's family."

"Oh. He got home okay? Crossing roads and all?"

She smiled at that. "Yes. He always does. After he's done checking on all his peeps he heads home, and never sets foot on the actual road. It's like he knows to avoid them."

He frowned then. "How did they know…he'd been here?"

She laughed. "I don't even ask anymore. He just has ways of communicating."

"You said he was smart."

"He's a few levels beyond smart, from what they've said. He finds cases for them."

His brow furrowed. "Cases?"

"Come in and sit down," she suggested.

He hesitated, but after a moment he followed her into the living room. There was a three-seat sofa against the wall opposite the front windows, and two single chairs facing it across a small coffee table. He chose the near end of the sofa with its back to the wall of the living room, and he saw that she noticed. He didn't explain, didn't want to go there. She sat down on the chair closest to him.

She took in a visibly deep breath before saying, "Cutter belongs to someone you know."

Now, that was impossible. Who on earth could she be—

"He belongs to the Foxworths."

And that simply she knocked every bit of air out of him.

Foxworth.

"That's really why they called. Quinn learned you were released early and wanted to make sure I knew."

An image slammed into his mind, of the tall, powerful, commanding man who had practically shamed him into handing over a piece of the loot they'd collected during one of the burglaries that he was about to go to jail for. A tiny piece, a child-sized locket Ruff had scoffed at as being worthless, but that Trip had looked at differently once he'd seen the inscription from mother to daughter engraved on it.

He still didn't know why he'd kept it. Why he'd carried it around, even taken it out to look at now and then, despite the fact that it made him faintly queasy. Ruff hadn't missed it, probably would have tossed it anyway. But it had been identifiable, enough to be in essence an admission of guilt. Yet he'd kept it.

Foxworth.

No wonder they'd asked if she was all right. No wonder they'd worried when they'd found out he was here at her place.

Quinn Foxworth.

The man who, in essence, had put him in prison.

Chapter Five

Kayley didn't even wince at the crude oath he let out under his breath. It had been barely audible anyway. Working on instinct alone, she kept talking, hoping that there was enough of the Trip she'd known left in him that he wouldn't simply walk out while she was speaking.

"She's doing wonderfully, by the way. Emily, I mean. The girl whose precious locket you gave back." Which had been the moment that had pulled her out of her own shock at what had happened, the moment that told her the Trip she knew was still in there somewhere. "She's seeing a really nice young man, Dylan. And you're part of that." He looked at her like someone who'd just heard a claim that the sky was green and grass blue. "You restored her faith in people. Quinn Foxworth says she never wears or talks about her mother's locket without thanking you."

She'd distracted him, at least. Because he was staring at her now. "You…say that like he's a friend of yours. Foxworth, I mean."

"They both are. He hadn't met Hayley yet when your situation happened, but they're married now, and the most solid couple I know. Quinn still intimidates me a bit, but only because he's so imposing. He probably has to be to run their organization—the Foxworth Foundation—the way he does. Hayley is the best kind of friend. And of course Cutter made everything easier, getting to know them. After all they did for you, I wanted to thank them."

His stare became one of astonishment. "Did for me? You mean landed me in jail?"

She assumed that was just a gut reaction. At least, she hoped so. But still, she said rather coolly, "While I understand why you'd say that, I believe you landed yourself there."

He let out an audible breath. "I know that. I didn't mean... I just didn't expect..."

"And I meant the good things they did for you."

"Good things?" He was shaking his head slowly, as if she were speaking a language he didn't understand.

"I mean talking to the judge and all."

He was gaping at her now, utterly confused. "What are you talking about?"

"I'm just saying, having Foxworth—the people or the foundation—in your corner around here is a pretty powerful thing. Anywhere they have a presence, in fact, which now is all over the country. Which is also in large part thanks to you. When you gave that locket back, Quinn found his calling. And Foxworth their mission."

"In my corner?"

He said it so blankly it belatedly hit her. It seemed impossible. But then, as she thought back, remembered how shut down he'd been, how closed off, and adding in how discreet she knew Foxworth was, had been even in the beginning, it seemed entirely possible.

"You don't know," she whispered.

"Don't know what?" There was a bit of a snap in his voice now. At first it made her think of that look he'd given her, but then she realized this was more a tone of pure urgency.

"Foxworth went to bat for you. Talked to the judge,

the prosecutor, your public defender. They even would have brought in another attorney to represent you if they hadn't reached the deal they had."

"Deal?"

"On your sentence, and where you'd serve it." She was feeling a bit tense herself now. "It could have been so much worse, a medium or even maximum security facility, since Ruff not only beat that man in the house nearly to death but was carrying a firearm. The one he claimed was yours."

His mouth twisted into a sour grimace. "Right. And that I brought to the scene against his orders."

"Yes. But Quinn told the judge he believed you, that it wasn't yours. He said he'd seen Ruff try to hand it to you, and that you backed away, wouldn't even touch it. His belief was justified when the only fingerprints on it were Ruff's. And of course, Ruff's record threw a lot of shade on all of his claims."

Trip grimaced. "Burglary was one thing. But when that old man was home and tried to resist…"

"Quinn pushed the fact that you had stopped Ruff from probably killing that man. Had taken steps to help him. And he insisted that you weren't the one armed. He wasn't positive you hadn't known Ruff was, but he was willing to give you the benefit of the doubt there. Because he knew."

"Knew?" he asked with a bewildered shake of his head.

She took a deep breath and plunged ahead. "Why you were there, tangled up with Ruff and his gang, at all. About your father. And your mom."

He went still. "And just how did he know all that?"

She drew herself up straight and faced him. She had

no idea how he was going to take this, but she had to give him the truth.

"I told him."

He stared at her, his expression unreadable. Funny, she'd always been able to read him, better than Debra, or so he'd told her back then. But not now. Maybe he'd learned the hard way to mask his reactions, his emotions. Maybe he'd had to. He hadn't been in a maximum security lockup, but it wasn't a Club Fed, either. It was still prison.

She hastened to assure him, "I knew you wouldn't want everything that went wrong in your life blasted to the whole world. I only told the one person I thought could actually help. And he did."

"I did the crimes, Kayley. I wasn't just an observer at that burg with the locket, or the last one where he beat up the man, or the others. I participated. Willingly."

She had to steady herself again. She'd imagined this conversation so many times, she'd thought she had it all worked out, what she would say. But now she was having trouble recalling all the calm, rational things she'd come up with. Emotion seemed to have taken over, and she couldn't hold it back.

"Willingly? Really? You're saying if your mom hadn't died, and your father hadn't spiraled out of control, if he hadn't become not just cold and withdrawn in his grief but abusive, you'd still have ended up running with Oliver Ruff?"

She could see the answer in his expression. But no one had ever been harder on Trip Callen than Trip himself.

Except the father he should have been able to trust.

"It was still my choice," he insisted.

"I know that. I'm not saying you're blameless. But

sometimes we make a choice because it seems like it's the only one we have."

He lowered his gaze, as if he couldn't bear to look at her anymore.

"You lost your *mother*, Trip. A different kind of grief, but no less powerful than what he was feeling."

"Not according to him," he muttered without looking up. "He said I had no idea, I couldn't possibly know."

"Is your father still alive?"

His head came up then. "What?"

"Just wondering. I'd like to go tell him off. Let him know at least one person knows that he's as much at fault for what happened as you were. That he took a wonderful guy, the son of the woman he's supposedly grieving so much, and threw him into hell."

"He didn't throw me," he insisted. "I jumped."

"But you wouldn't have if he had dug himself out of his pity party and seen to his son!"

He blinked, probably at the vehemence in her voice.

"I wasn't a kid, Kayley. I was nineteen when she died."

"And sixteen when she got sick. And you were there for her every step of the way, weren't you? To the very end." It wasn't really a question, because she knew the answer. And her voice went rough with all the pain she was feeling for him. "It must have been awful."

"It was. But at the end almost peaceful. When she went, I mean." He lowered his gaze again, as if it were too much to speak this and look at her at the same time. "She had a few minutes of near clarity, the evening before."

She hadn't known this. "Were you able to talk to her?"

He nodded. "They told me she was hanging on despite the pain. That I should tell her it was all right for her to go. Tell her that I'd be okay." She held her breath, afraid to speak and disrupt this painful flow of memory. "I didn't want to, I didn't want her to go, but she was in so much pain…so I did." His head came up then, sharply. "You know what she said? She said I had to take care of my dad. Made me promise, because he wasn't going to take this well." He let out a compressed, twisted sort of laugh as he leaned back on the couch, looking exhausted. "She was right about that, wasn't she."

It was no more a question than her earlier words had been. But Kayley felt a sudden rush of understanding. She should have guessed it was something like this, that a deathbed promise had kept Trip trying with his father. It all made sense now, why he'd stuck it out, trying and trying, even with the abuse.

A chill rippled through her as another realization struck. No wonder he'd gotten sucked into Ruff's dark, dangerous world. He'd already thought he was a failure, because he hadn't been able to keep that promise to his dying mother. She had been more right than she knew about who bore as much blame as Trip for what had happened to him.

Yes, she really wanted to find Mr. Jay Callen and tell him off.

It was a long time before she spoke again. He didn't seem to notice or mind, and she wondered if, in prison, they spent hours in silence. Feeling horribly naive, not for the first time, she tried the most obvious question she could think of.

"What are you going to do now? Is there a plan?"

"They gave me a list of groups to contact, that are supposed to help, but…" He shrugged. Gave her a glance that nearly stopped her heart, it was so like the old Trip in its sheepish charm. "I don't think I've really accepted it as reality yet."

"I don't blame you. Talk about culture shock."

He yawned, although she could see he'd tried to stop it. And it was nearly ten, which she knew was lights-out at the facility. Just as she thought it he said, "Feels weird, not being on a rigid schedule."

An idea occurred to her. She excused herself, saying his schedule comment had reminded her she needed to do something. She went back into the den that served as her office, idly tidied a couple of things on the desk, killing time.

When she finally went back out to the living room, as she'd hoped, he was dozing on the couch. He stirred when she came back in, but she softly told him, "Just relax. You've had a heck of a day."

"I shouldn't—"

"You're fine. Put your feet up and rest."

He hesitated, then shifted to where he could stretch out. She noticed he looked around almost warily as he did so. The action made her feel a sharp jab of sorrow; he now couldn't sleep in a different place without worrying?

"It's all right." She smiled at him as she grabbed up the knitted blanket that had been the sole result of her venture into the knitting world a couple of years ago. She draped it over him, and noticed he tensed as she did so. And had a sudden vision of him waking up in prison to find someone looming over him as she was now. That likely would not have been good.

"You're safe here, Trip," she promised.

His eyes widened. Those incredible dark green eyes. He stared at her. And after a moment, with a slight, slow shake of his head, he said, "Shouldn't you be asking yourself if you are?"

She straightened and looked down at him, putting as much insouciance as she could muster in her voice and her expression. "Going to attack me in my sleep, are you?"

"No!"

"I didn't think so. Get some sleep."

She felt his gaze on her as she left him there.

She wondered if he would still be there in the morning.

Chapter Six

Trip woke up with a jolt, every sense alert, awareness flooding him that he wasn't in his bunk, wasn't in the dormitory. A split second later the memories were there.

Kayley.

He was at Kayley's.

He'd fallen asleep on the couch. He had a vague recollection of her pulling this knit thing over him, the thing that was so soft and warm.

His heart slammed in his chest, because another memory hit him.

You're safe here, Trip...

The way she'd said it, the way she'd looked at him then, had been...he didn't know the word for it. He wasn't sure there was a word for it. Or for how it had made him feel.

Safe.

And his reaction had been gut-level. *Shouldn't you be asking yourself if you are?*

When he'd asked that question, he hadn't meant to imply she wasn't safe with him here. He'd just been, for the first time, really looking at this from her point of view. The point of view of a woman going about her normal life, opening her door to find an ex-con on her doorstep.

A good woman. A kind woman. A generous woman.

Your woman's pretty cute.

That, too. Robber had been right about the cute part.

But she wasn't his woman. Because he'd been too screwed up, or too plain stupid, to realize that the real value under this roof had been her, not Debra's phony flash.

A shiver went through him, and he pulled the soft knitted fabric up over his shoulder as he turned on his side, leaning against the back of the couch. It was comfortable, although surprisingly not as comfortable for sleeping as his bunk, which at least was long enough for him to stretch out to his full six feet, and wide enough to roll over. But the quiet, the peace...

Because this couch was in the free world, as he'd come to think of it, and that made all the difference. And as he lay there, his head on one of the decorative pillows, he realized his stupidity had continued. Getting here had been his only goal, and he'd spared little thought about what would happen after he'd said his piece. If she wasn't so kindhearted, if she wasn't who she was, he could well have ended up out on the street with nowhere to go. Getting even a cheap room somewhere would have eaten up too much of his limited funds.

But getting here to her had been almost an obsession. It was as if he couldn't take another step in any direction until he'd taken this one.

And you still haven't actually gotten it said.

Yes, he'd blurted out the bones of it when she'd thought he was here looking for Debra. But he hadn't said the words he'd rehearsed over and over in his mind. And he still didn't feel like he could go on until he did.

He sat up. It was still dark, but he felt as if it were close to the time he'd usually be getting up for cleanup duty in the chow hall. Since he had neither a watch nor a phone, he had no idea for sure. But there was a clock on the oven in the kitchen, he remembered, and he stood up.

Belatedly, he realized he had apparently gotten his cheap tennis shoes off during the night.

Or Kayley took them off.

The thought of her removing any item of his clothing, even something as innocuous as shoes, sent an electric sort of jolt through him. He laughed it off, or tried to, as the result of all those long, long months of isolation; he'd done without for a very long time.

It almost worked.

When he got out to the kitchen—just as well the shoes were off, since that let him walk silently—he saw that his internal clock was right on; it was 4:32 a.m. But there was no trek to the chow hall to make, no cleanup to do, no five in the morning breakfast.

He just stood there, feeling lost. He'd meant what he'd told Kayley last night. He had no one else to blame for the wrong turns he'd taken, the lousy choices he'd made. His father hadn't made those choices for him, hadn't made that wrong turn. People had gone through things as bad as he had, and worse, and hadn't ended up as he had, tangled up with the wrong kind of people and doing things he never would have imagined before that day when Mom had slipped away from him, from everything.

And now here he was, an ex-con, about to learn just how hard it was to walk the straight and narrow with a felony rap and a prison term on your record.

He went over to the sink, found a glass in the adjacent cupboard, and got a drink of water. He stood there looking out the window that gave him a view of the deck where they'd eaten last night.

Where that dog had appeared.

The Foxworth dog.

Everything she'd told him about them, about what the man he should probably hate had done to help him, things he had never known until now, rolled around in his head, making him feel even more tangled up and confused. It just seemed impossible that the simple act of handing over that locket—how had they kept it out of the police's hands, anyway? Did they have that much pull?—could have landed someone with the apparent sway Quinn Foxworth had on his side.

Not that he'd had any choice. Foxworth had known Ruff's gang had been behind the theft, had in fact set himself up in the neighborhood hoping they'd strike again. It had worked. Ruff hadn't been able to resist turning what had been planned as a single burglary into two when he'd seen a window open in a house on the next block. Trip hadn't wanted any part of another crime, but after what Ruff had done to that old man who hadn't been any kind of a threat, he didn't feel like he had much choice; clearly Ruff would turn on anyone who got in his way.

Unfortunately—or fortunately—that house had been temporarily occupied by a former Army Ranger by the name of Quinn Foxworth. A tough, steely Army Ranger who had a soft spot for the little girl down the street, whose locket Trip had had tucked into his wallet. And that night, Foxworth had told him the story of the locket, how it was the only keepsake a child had of her dead mother. Which had gotten to him as nothing else could have. And he'd handed it over, right before the cops had arrived.

Everything after that was a bit blurry. The long, awful process, the arrest, booking, all of that, was clear enough, but then the long haul had begun. He'd had some idea that you got arrested, got booked, went to court like the next day and to trial shortly after that. But it seemed when someone the level of Ruff was involved, someone they'd been after for so long, it was much more complicated. He'd spent months waiting, and since his father wasn't about to bail him out, he'd spent them in custody. True, they'd counted it toward his eventual sentence—he wondered suddenly if Foxworth had had something to do with that, too—but that hadn't made it any less nerve-racking.

He'd figured out long ago that it had been a trap, Quinn being there, in that house, in that neighborhood, with that tempting open window. And Ruff had fallen for it. It had been an odd sort of comfort during those long months inside.

A slight sound behind him spun him around. A split second later, the figure that had made a tiny noise whirled around where she stood, at the end of the hallway where it entered the living room. She'd apparently been looking at the vacated couch. When she spotted him in the kitchen, she seemed to relax.

"Oh! I was just—I was afraid you'd—"

"Thought I'd decamped in the middle of the night?"

She gave him a slight smile. "Something like that."

I have a thank-you to say first.

But once that was done, there would be no reason to stay any longer. And while he knew that was for the best, he wasn't quite ready to face the world out there, a world he had no place in, nor any idea how to find one.

So instead he said something else. "I was just thinking about that night. The night Foxworth caught us." He grimaced. "Or rather, the night ol' Ruff walked right into what turned out to be an ambush."

"Quinn didn't ambush you!" she exclaimed. She was quick to the man's defense. But then, she was quick to Trip's, too.

"It might as well have been, because he's so damned tough and fast."

"He had years of training."

"He never forgot a bit of it." He gave a wry chuckle. "Ruff thought he was the baddest guy around, but Foxworth took him down so easily he didn't even have time to react."

"And you didn't react," she said quietly. "Quinn told me you never tried to stop him from taking Ruff out."

"I was…stunned. At how fast he did it. And, I think… relieved."

"Relieved?"

"That it was over. The life I hadn't really enjoyed much. I knew the life that was coming, behind bars, would probably be worse, but at least…"

His voice trailed off. He didn't really want to admit to her how much of that life he'd spent second-guessing his every step and spending endless nights either sleepless or enveloped in nightmares.

"Quinn told me that once he asked you about the locket, you never hesitated to give it back. That you even had it on you, right there. I told him I wasn't surprised, that if there was anything in the world you'd have complete empathy with, it would be a kid who'd lost their mother."

Words broke from him almost against his will. "When he told me how old she'd been when her mother died, and I thought about how much worse that would have been, I…"

"I understand," Kayley said gently. "Again you proved

who you really are, Trip. And now you have the chance to be again."

She sounded so very certain. She had too much faith in him.

Certainly more than he had in himself.

Chapter Seven

Kayley was a little shaken, although she thought she'd hidden it well enough. For a moment she'd really thought that he had, as he'd put it, decamped. And if he had, leaving her with no idea of where he was going or what he would do, she wasn't sure how she'd have dealt with that.

"I guess I can clear my calendar next weekend. I was planning a visit," she said, keeping her tone purposefully light. He'd been studying his shoes, what looked like a cheap pair of tennis shoes, thinking who knows what, but at her words, his head came up.

"I remember looking at the procedure you had to go through to do that," he said. "The forms you had to fill out, the questions you had to answer, all the rules you had to follow... I don't know why you did it."

She had quite a list of reasons, but she decided he probably wouldn't want to hear most of them, at least not now. So she said only, "I figured your father wasn't likely to come."

He snorted at that. "Hardly."

That made her heart ache, but she tried to lighten things up, talking cheerfully. "It just took a few times to get used to everything. At first I kept having to check it to make sure I hadn't put on something that wasn't allowed, like if I had a belt on and the buckle was too big.

And that I had all the requirements like sleeves, and the right money, nothing bigger than a five and no more than twenty total. But socks were the most important."

He blinked. "Socks?"

"You have to take your shoes off to go through the metal detector. Like at the airport. Some floors you just don't want to walk on barefoot."

He grimaced. "I should have said no in the beginning. I had to make the calls, so I could have. Should have, since I didn't want your name tied to mine. Like I said, I don't know why you did it. Why you bothered."

She decided to explain after all, in the hope that it might make him see himself in a slightly different light. "I bothered because while your bad choices landed you there, your bad choices were understandable to me. And because Quinn told me about the locket. I knew then that the Trip I'd come to know was the real one, the guy who got sucked into a tornado because he'd been standing on the periphery, and had nothing to anchor him."

He lowered his gaze again, but she thought she saw the hint of a smile. "That was quite a metaphor." He hesitated, and she stayed quiet, curious to see if he would go on. After a brief moment, still looking down, he said, "I'm glad—no, more than glad—that you did it, Kayley. Sometimes those calls and your visits were the only thing that kept me going."

"Then it was time well spent."

His head came up again. He met her gaze, held it. And the words came out sounding as if he'd rehearsed them repeatedly. "You stuck by me, when no one else did. You didn't write me off, you didn't turn your back on me. You're the only one. I can never repay you for that."

"Yes, you can. Go on from here and live the life you should have had all along."

The upward curve of his mouth was definite this time, although a bit crooked. "And that pays you back how?"

"It tells me I was right about who you are inside."

He started to respond, stopped, gave a sharp shake of his head, and then said only, "Thank you. That's all I really wanted to come here and say. Thank you."

"And you have." She smiled back at him, letting a little—but only a little—of what she was feeling show. "And that you came here first means a lot to me, Trip."

He looked as if he didn't know what to say to that, so she was glad she'd held back. Likely the last thing he'd want right now is her gushing out how she felt about him, how she'd always felt about him. She was even more certain of that when he quickly changed the subject.

"I'm sorry if I messed up your sleep. I'm just conditioned to getting up the same time every day. Or do you normally get up this early?"

She didn't, but she didn't want him feeling bad about it, so she waved it off. "It doesn't matter. Since I work from home, my time is pretty flexible."

He smiled again, and this time it was better, steadier. "Be funny if someone who helps people find jobs they can do remotely didn't do hers remotely."

She smiled back, and her own was steadier this time, too, because that was something the old Trip would have said. "Exactly."

"You ever come up with a job title for yourself?"

They'd had this discussion on one of her visits, when she'd made the momentous decision to strike out on her own, after what she'd begun doing part-time had grown to the point she thought it could support her. Essentially serving as a human resources department for small businesses who couldn't afford one, she matched skills with opportunities, and it was working well for all concerned.

"I didn't have to," she said. Then added, with a grin this time, "You did."

His brows rose. "You used that?"

"I did. Because 'employment facilitator' was the perfect name for what I'm doing."

He looked pleased enough that it warmed her inside. "It's working out, then?"

"Nicely," she said. "Thank you for the encouragement." Her parents had been wary, being from the steady salary school of working, although they'd come around after the first few months. But Trip had seen the potential, and supported her decision from the beginning.

"Not sure it's wise to take career advice from somebody sitting in a state prison," he said dryly.

"I didn't take advice. I took support. Different altogether," she said. Then, briskly, since he seemed level enough, she asked, "What's the first thing you want to do?"

He looked a little taken aback, and she wasn't sure if it was because of her tone or her words. And his tone was a bit sour when he said, "Forget my DOC number."

She knew that was the ID number the Department of Corrections assigned every inmate. And she couldn't blame him for wanting to forget it, or that it had ever existed.

"That will probably take a while," she said, understanding. "I meant, what do you want to do today?"

"I don't know. I didn't think much beyond getting here."

She kept her tone casual. "Well, it's your first real day of freedom, so your choice. Maybe you'd like to drive around a bit, see some familiar places?"

He stared at her. "What, are you offering to chauffeur me around?"

"Easier than the bus," she said lightly, as if it were nothing, when in fact it was tremendously important that he not just vanish on her. She was glad she had a very light work week ahead of her. "Or you must need some things, clothes, maybe a phone?"

"Don't think the budget will run to a phone," he said with a wry twist of his mouth. "I didn't have much of my own left, and they only give you so much gate money. But maybe some clothes, if there's someplace cheap around."

"New or used?"

The wry twist became rueful. "Can't afford to be picky. Used is fine, if it's clean."

"Got it," she said. "But breakfast first. Fix here, or go out?"

A rather endearingly sheepish look came across his face. "You know what I'm dying for?"

"What?"

"One of those darn fast food egg and biscuit things."

She laughed, and for the first time since she'd opened the door to see him standing there, she felt a blast of hope that he'd be all right.

"That," she said happily, "can be arranged."

He smiled, another good one. "Your canine friend doesn't come by for breakfast?"

"Cutter? No, he won't be around today. Quinn and Hayley are heading to Foxworth Southwest, to visit Hayley's brother, who runs their operation there. He's married to her best friend, so it's a twofer."

He looked startled. "Foxworth Southwest? And here is what, Northwest? How many are there?"

"Five now, I think. Headquarters in St. Louis, and an outpost, as Quinn calls them, in all four corners."

He was staring now. "I...they're that big?"

She nodded. "Apparently Quinn's sister is a financial

genius, so they have amazing resources." Her expression shifted as she remembered the sadness of their beginning. "She started with the insurance from their parents, who were killed in a terrorist attack. The perpetrator was let go for political reasons. Which is another reason they do what they do, get justice for those who deserve it."

He gave a slow shake of his head. "And here I thought he was just a badass."

"Well, that, too," Kayley said with a grin, glad of the shift in mood.

It was a couple of minutes later, as she was getting out her favorite rain jacket, that Trip let out an "Oh, yeah," as if he'd just remembered something.

"What?"

"I promised I'd let Robber know I…got here."

"Your friend?" She'd met the man briefly, which was all that was allowed when she was there to see Trip, but he'd seemed nice enough. On his best behavior, anyway, in the visiting room. Then the complications hit her. "But you can't call him. He has to initiate a call, like you did."

"Right. I could email him. He wouldn't get it for a while, but at least he would eventually."

She knew all "eMessages," as they called them, went through a process before they were delivered. That could take up to seven days. "Might be better off sending him a postcard," she said. "They have to deliver that within a couple of days. Which makes no sense, which in turn figures."

He looked at her as if he'd just realized something. "Is that why you sent all those cards? So I'd get them sooner?"

"I wanted you to get something every day."

He stared at her yet again. And then, in a wondering tone, he said, "There are wives and girlfriends who didn't do that much."

"Maybe they didn't have the time," she suggested. "Especially if they had kids."

"You always see the other side, don't you?" The look he gave her then was almost sad.

"I just assume everybody has their own battles we don't know about," she said.

"How did you get so...like that?"

She met his gaze head-on then. "I was lucky. I had a father who loved me and taught me."

He looked thoughtful, as if he were considering his next words carefully. She didn't care if he said something that made her angry, because he was talking almost normally now, not with that awkwardness of someone who hadn't had ordinary conversations in a long time.

When he did speak, she knew he'd been trying to find a non-antagonistic way to ask. "So...the battles we don't know about doesn't apply to my father?"

"Not when the main casualty is his own son, no."

For a long moment he just looked at her, with a combination of surprise and warmth that she couldn't quite interpret. Unless it was as simple as him not being used to anybody caring.

And then he gave her a full, genuine smile. And for the first time it really reached his eyes.

She would do a lot more than just fill out a bunch of forms and drive a few hours a month to see that smile.

Chapter Eight

He had just gotten his shoes back on—still wondering if he'd kicked them off while half-asleep or she'd taken them off—when Kayley came back down the hallway from the closet, where she'd apparently gotten the jacket she held.

"I just had a thought," she said. "Do you suppose they'd let your friend call me, since there's still some credit on my prepaid account?"

"You're not on his PAN list," he said, wishing he'd thought before he'd left to see if she could be on Robber's personal allowed number list. But then, he hadn't expected the kind of welcome reception he'd gotten, either. He'd thought he'd just say his piece and be on his way. To where, he still had no idea.

"But they have the number, and they know me. Maybe they could just add me to his list and give him what credit is left so he could make the call. Or he could call the landline here at the house collect. We'd just have to get him the number."

"I'm not sure," he said. "Maybe."

"Worth finding out, isn't it? I could call Officer Moreland. He was always nice."

"Sure." *Because he thought you were hot.*

He stifled a grimace. It was nothing less than the truth,

because David Moreland had told him so, and he'd seen the way the corrections officer had looked at her, surreptitiously flirting with her. But he'd also told Trip after her third visit that he was damned lucky to have a good woman who cared about him. And the flirting and looks had stopped. Which told him, he supposed, as much about Moreland as it had about Kayley.

Except he'd already known Kayley was the real deal. She was there to see him, not get picked up by some other guy. Even if Moreland would likely be a much better bet, if she were in the market.

"I'll call after his shift starts. If he can't okay it, maybe he can aim us toward who can, or at least start the process."

That could take some time, as most everything to do with government seemed to. He wondered just how long she figured he was going to be here. And it hit him suddenly that there might just be somebody who'd already taken her off the market. And that somebody, if he was smart enough to pick Kayley, might not be real happy about his presence here in her house.

"What?" she asked, and he realized he'd been looking at her rather intently as that idea had occurred to him.

"Just wondering," he said, "if I need to worry about your boyfriend showing up mad about me being here."

He thought he noticed a tinge of pink in her cheeks. But she answered easily enough. "Not at all, since he doesn't exist."

He didn't want to try and analyze the relief he felt at that. "So they're all stupid around here?"

Definitely pink this time. "I haven't exactly been looking."

Why?

Damn, he'd almost said it. Scrambled for something, anything else to say. "Oh. Okay."

Well, that was inane enough.

Her tone was brisk when she spoke again, as if she wanted to put his question well behind them. And he couldn't blame her for that; it was none of his business, except for the fear of causing her a problem.

"Let's get breakfast, and by the time we finish, the thrift store in town should be open. Here," she said, holding out the jacket he'd thought she'd gotten out for herself. "It's my dad's, so it might fit you, although you're taller."

"Your father's jacket?"

"He keeps it here for when they visit." She smiled. "Not much need for a heavy jacket like that in Florida. And it might rain later, so you'll need something waterproof."

"I...thanks."

The thought of having something more than one layer of quickly-gets-wet denim was more than appealing. And he was only borrowing it. Although he couldn't help wondering how her father would feel about her loaning his stuff out to an ex-con.

He wanted to ask if her parents knew what she'd been doing, calling and coming out to visit him. But he decided he didn't need to hear an answer he could guess. Any father as loving as hers would probably have a fit if he knew.

His own father could give less than a damn about anything connected to his son, and that had started long before he'd wound up behind bars.

He veered off that useless path and focused on the simple fact that he was getting in a car of his own free will, and was about to go somewhere he'd chosen. The novelty of that was nothing short of exhilarating.

She had a different car than the rather weary old sedan

she'd had before, although the same key chain. A silver thistle he supposed was a salute to her ancestry. The dark green compact SUV wasn't new, but much newer, and in very good shape. In the small town of Redwood Cove, it only took a few minutes to get to the single fast food outlet in town. As they approached, he felt a slight qualm as he looked at the almost full parking lot. He wasn't used to this, being around a lot of people in the free world. He'd felt the same getting on the bus yesterday, although it had been quashed a bit by the knowledge he was leaving that place for the last—and by God it would be the last—time.

And then she turned into the drive-through lane, and he felt himself relax. Had she known somehow? He wouldn't put it past her.

"I thought we'd grab this and head down to the marina. You like watching the ferries, too, right?"

She'd remembered that? Debra had joked about it, calling it silly, when Kayley had said she enjoyed watching the big green-and-white boats carry their passengers, both on foot and in vehicles, across. That was what had driven him to say he enjoyed it, too, drawing a look from Debra that he now, far too late, realized was derisive.

"Yes," he said, "I did."

She lifted a brow at him. "Past tense? You don't anymore?"

"I don't know." He let out a long breath. "I don't know what I like anymore."

Except you.

And it would be true in one form or another for the rest of his life. Because even that wouldn't be enough to pay her back for what she'd done.

A bare three minutes later, they were sitting at one of

the tables at the small marina, and he had a mouthful of the longed-for breakfast sandwich. Not something he'd be indulging in often, given how the price had gone up. And he felt awkward that she had insisted on paying.

"I wouldn't be where I am without your encouragement, so consider this thanks."

And what do I consider all the trips from here to Forks?

A vivid memory formed in his mind, of the first time she'd come in person. He'd been edgy, not sure why she'd visited. He hadn't known what to say, so he hadn't said anything. It seemed at first she wasn't certain either, but after a silent moment, she had given him a smile and said, "If I promise not to make any sparkly vampire jokes, will you talk to me?"

He'd let out a short chuckle, surprising himself. He hadn't even realized until he'd gotten here that the place he'd been sent was near the setting of that famous string of books and movies.

"It is a bloodsucking kind of place," he'd finally said.

And as if the exchange had broken some kind of barrier, they were back to talking as they always had, easily. He'd been relieved that she didn't push him about what his life was like now, what it was like to be an inmate, but instead talked about the things they used to talk about, from books to philosophy.

And when he'd once, eventually, asked her, not why she was here but why she made it so…normal, she'd said simply, "I don't want you to lose touch with the world you'll be coming back to."

And now here he was, in that world, sitting across from the same woman who had cared enough to keep him connected to it. And he could barely think of a thing to say to her.

He looked off to the left, because if he kept staring at her, he was going to say something really stupid. The ferry dock was empty at the moment, but he could see one heading out, and slightly farther north the other heading in from the other side.

"Too bad it's cloudy," she said, "or you could see the mountain from here."

He glanced to the south, where on a clear day the massive shape that was Mt. Rainier would be unmistakably visible, looking too impossible to be real, rising above the flat at over fourteen thousand feet. That was what most meant when they said "the mountain," although he personally had always liked Mt. Baker to the north just as much.

The ferry horn blew its coming-into-port signal, a long blast followed by two short ones. This one was a long one and two quick, almost chipper-sounding ones. And he remembered the time he and Kayley had talked about how something that seemed like it would sound the same every time didn't, and wondered if it was the personality of the captain or whoever sounded the horn coming through.

"He sounds cheerful," she said, and when his gaze went back to her face, he knew she was thinking of the same thing by the way her eyes practically twinkled.

By the time he was finished with the two sandwiches and halfway through the big dose of coffee, the ferry was sliding into the dock. They were close enough he could hear the informational recording playing over the loud-speakers. One short ride across Puget Sound and he could be back in the city. The city where his life as he knew it had ended for a very long time.

No big loss.

"Missing the city?" she asked quietly.

"No!" It came out suddenly, sharply, almost fiercely, surprising even him.

And for some reason it made her smile.

Chapter Nine

He ended up with a decent pair of jeans, bringing him to two, a pair of khakis and three shirts. Two long-sleeve T-shirts and a dress shirt that looked as if it had never been worn. He'd been iffy on the dressier stuff, but Kayley suggested he might need them for a job interview. He'd looked so stunned she knew he truly hadn't thought that far ahead.

Or was convinced no one would hire him.

Which was what made her ask after they got back in the car, "I thought the plan was that you'd go out to the work release place down in Port Orchard?"

"It was, but…they're full up. And…" He hesitated, then gestured at his black eye. "This happened."

"I've been afraid to ask," she said honestly, turning to face him. "Afraid you'd already been in a fight."

His mouth quirked. "Fight was last week. That is, if you think standing there and letting some clown punch you is being in a fight." She tilted her head questioningly, and he shrugged. "Guy we call Touchy, with a short-man complex and a hair trigger. I bumped him accidentally, and he launched. Which was stupid on his part, because there were two guards in the room at the time."

She remembered Touchy. Remembered the way he

leered at her when she visited, even calling her by name when he saw her. "The short guy with the New York accent?"

"That's him."

She grimaced. She could see how he'd be easy to get into a fight with, but she would have thought fighting would have messed up Trip's release because—

Realization cut off her thought. "You didn't fight back," she said softly.

"That close to getting out? I wasn't about to blow that."

"And the guards saw it."

He nodded. Then, sounding reluctant, he added, "One of them was your friend Moreland. He took me to the infirmary. On the way he told me that was the best thing I could have done. I thought he was just talking, but...he made a report, and here I am."

"I knew he was a good guy," she said.

And she had the feeling he was going to help Trip connect with his friend, too; he'd seemed willing enough when she'd called a while ago. He'd said to give him a day or so to see what he could do.

They spent another hour in a discount store, where he picked up some necessities, socks, underwear—she wished she hadn't been there for that selection—and a pair of nail clippers. He'd seemed a bit overwhelmed by everything, although she didn't know if it was the amount of offerings or the simple fact that he was free to choose.

"Toothbrush?" she asked when he said he was done.

"They gave me one. And a little tube of toothpaste."

"Nice to know they focus on dental hygiene," she said, so primly he gave her a startled look. She grinned at him and was delighted when he smiled back. She wondered if she'd ever stop marveling that he could smile at all.

They looked at the prepaid phones near the checkout,

but he was reluctant, and she didn't push. She couldn't blame him for wanting to limit his expenditures, since he'd indicated he didn't have much in the way of cash reserves.

The next stop was a grocery store. She'd just been a couple of days ago but didn't mention that. She had the feeling he wouldn't like her buying extra food for him, but she wanted to. She wanted him to have home-cooked meals, something she doubted he'd had much of since his mother had died. He'd told her in one of those waiting-for-Debra sessions that in the time he just called "after," his father had relied mostly on takeout, and Trip had gotten the leftovers. If there were any.

Of course once he'd gotten sucked into Ruff's gang, eating was no longer an issue; they just took what they wanted. And she was sure the stolen articles they pawned or fenced had put a nice bit of cash in his pocket, once the take was shared out.

She was pondering just how much chicken to buy— that meal they'd shared along with Cutter used up her last—when it became clear they needed to have that talk she didn't want to have. As in, what he was going to do now, if he was going to stay. With her.

It was odd. Before when she'd thought about him getting out, she'd thought about what would happen. But somehow now that it had happened so unexpectedly and he was really here, she didn't know how to broach the subject. She hadn't gotten that far since it had been, she'd expected, months away yet.

And now, sillily, looking at a display case of chicken, she was face-to-face with it.

She glanced to her right, where Trip stood looking at a rack of spices as if it were the most bewildering thing he'd ever seen. Then, as if he'd sensed her gaze, he turned his head toward her. It was probably crazy, but she got the feeling he'd reached the same point she had, the realization that they were going to have to Talk with a capital *T*.

And to her surprise, once they were back at the house, he brought it up himself, while he was unloading the grocery bags so she could put it all away.

"I didn't come here intending to move in on you," he said abruptly.

"I never thought you had." She put the last of the cheese she'd bought in the deli drawer of the fridge and turned to him. "But I've always thought that if you needed to, you could stay here until you got your feet back under you."

He stared at her. "Do you know how crazy that would sound to...almost anybody?"

"Anybody who doesn't know you, maybe." She took a breath, then plunged ahead. "I wish I'd been...braver back then."

"Kayley," he said, then stopped as if he didn't know what else to say.

"I knew you were headed for trouble, but I didn't have the courage to stand up, to try and help."

"You couldn't have. I knew better, knew I was out of control, heading down a really bad path, but I couldn't seem to stop." This time the words sounded as if they'd been ripped from him. "I was beyond help then."

"So let me help now. That way you don't have to make any hasty decisions that might not be the best for you."

"You did more for me than anyone," he said, his voice sounding rough, as if it was an effort to get the words out. "You're the best person I know, Kayley McSwain. And deep down, I think I knew it back then. All I had to do was compare you to Debra. You're a stronger, better person than she ever was."

Her throat tightened. This was obviously not easy for him, but he was doing it. As if it were part of the vows she knew he'd made to himself that he would never let his life careen so out of control again. And everything she'd ever felt for him but suppressed, all that time ago, came rushing back at the sight of his weary face and shadowed eyes.

"And you," she said, the words sounding nearly as rough as his had, "are a stronger, better person than you were when you got sucked into that nasty crowd. So stay, Trip. As long as you need to. Get used to things. And we'll get some warm compresses on that eye, get that cleared up. Then you can start…thinking about the future." For a long, silent moment they simply looked at each other. She saw the touch of doubt still in his gaze. So, with a smile she'd practiced in her mind countless times, she added, "There's even a guest room, so you don't have to sleep on the couch."

There, that had come out nice and light. Nothing more than a friend offering to help. Not even a hint of the silly woman who'd been in love with a man who wasn't hers.

HE SHOULD FEEL RELIEVED. He'd gotten it done, gotten the words he'd rehearsed so many times said. He'd told her what he'd wanted to, had thanked her as best he could. Yet he felt wound up tighter than he had been before.

He looked around the small but welcoming room. A dresser. A chair and a table that could serve as a desk. He looked at the bed that was twice the size of his bunk. The nightstand beside it with a lamp. The bright blue curtains at the window.

And the door. The door he could close, giving him the thing he'd missed almost as much as freedom. Privacy.

He let out a long breath, trying to release some of the

tension along with it. He set his backpack on the foot of the bed and walked over to the window. He was guessing it looked out on the backyard. He tugged back the curtain and saw he was right. It felt odd, to see the corner of the deck, the yard and the trees beyond, not the prison yard, that barren spot under watchful eyes.

Eyes. Like that darned dog.

The Foxworth dog.

Which brought him to Quinn Foxworth, who had taken pseudo-tough-guy Ruff down like a toasted marshmallow.

Yeah, Ruffle—he used the nickname the man so hated intentionally in his mind—had had that one coming. He got greedy. Or his violent blood was up after beating that old man. He couldn't be satisfied with what they already had, a nice haul of easily fencible stuff, and a bag full of medicine bottles that the boss had grabbed once he saw the prescription painkillers. That had turned Trip's stomach, when he'd realized the old man Ruffle had just beaten to the floor was already in that kind of pain.

In fact, that was the moment he'd known he was done. That he couldn't be part of this anymore.

Unfortunately that decision had come one job too late.

He wondered idly how the man Ruffle had left in charge, his cousin Boyd, was doing at trying to hold the crew together. The stocky, rather squat guy who had always run muscle for his powerful cousin wasn't much on smarts.

He dropped the curtain and turned around. There was a bathroom with almost everything he'd need right across the hall, Kayley had said. Towels, soap, shampoo. No shaving cream, though.

"Don't need it. I got used to the electric razor, and they let me keep it." He'd rubbed at his chin, which was already rough, since he hadn't used that shaver yet. "They're not big on issuing us razor blades."

"Oh." She had looked as if she felt silly for not realizing that. But then she'd given him an odd sort of half smile as she'd added, "Doesn't matter. I kind of like a little stubble."

With that she'd left him there at the doorway, almost gaping after her as she went down the hall. And wondering if she'd meant that generally or specifically. As in did she like it, period, or...she liked it on him?

He didn't know, and wasn't about to ask. The last thing he needed or wanted right now was to offend her. He didn't think she'd kick him out, not once she'd offered him shelter, but that warm welcome might chill a bit. And he did not want that. Not from her.

What he did want from her was something he didn't dare think about.

Chapter Ten

"If you hadn't made that deposit to be sure I got that tablet from the JPay system, I think I would have gone completely insane."

Kayley looked at him across the table, over the plates that had held scrambled eggs. Some of the best she'd ever had, thanks to Trip's unexpected suggestion of tossing in a bit of honey mustard.

"My mom used to do that," he'd said.

He had so rarely even mentioned her, and never actually talked about her, so this had caught her a little off guard. But she didn't think pushing through that opening would be the best thing so soon after he'd gotten out of prison, so she'd just said, "Sounds like a great idea," and gone to the fridge for her bottle of the condiment.

"I just knew I'd go crazy if I couldn't read," she said now, "and then you could have music and other things, too."

"I ended up reading more than anything," he said with a wry smile. "The books were free, at least."

"What was the selection like?" She felt safer now asking, because he'd opened up a bit in the last three days, was talking almost normally. Or at least, more like they used to talk, when he was waiting for Debra. And his eye was looking better. The swelling had gone down, and

she could see yellowing where the bruising was starting to fade.

"Lots of classics. I decided to start with anything
where I'd seen the movie."

She smiled at that. "You know what they say, never
judge a book by its movie." That got a small laugh out
of him, and she added that to her mental treasure box.
"So, what did you start with?"

"Lord of the Rings."

"Wow," she said. "Now, that one would be a hard call
between books and movies. Then what?"

"Moby Dick. I read it in school, and they showed us
the old movie, but it was…in a year where I don't remember much."

And there it was again. A reference to the year his life
had started on this downhill slide. She opened that treasure box again and slid this one in.

"It's worth reading twice. Then what?"

He gave her a sort of sideways look. "You'll laugh."

"Nope," she said. "Cross my heart. I might smile, but
I won't laugh. What?"

"Sense and Sensibility."

She did smile. Widely. But she didn't laugh. "I love
that. Although I admit I'm surprised you saw the movie."

"It was my mother's favorite." There it was a third
time. She wondered if he'd ever spoken about her even
this much before. Or at least since her death. "I finally
saved up and bought it for her birthday one year, so she
could see it any time she wanted. She watched it a lot.
Especially after…"

His voice trailed away, and she finished softly, "After
she got sick?"

He nodded, looking down at his empty plate.

She took in a deep breath before saying, "I'd tell you

how sorry I am, but the words just seem empty. Useless. It doesn't change anything. Won't make you feel better. And I can't even tell you I know how you feel, because I don't. I've never had to live with that kind of pain. The only thing I can say is that knowing what you went through makes me appreciate how lucky I am."

About halfway through the little speech she'd never intended to make, he looked up at her. And when she finished, he gave her a tiny smile. "Oddly, that does make me feel a little better. About that, anyway. Or maybe it's just talking about her. Acknowledging she existed."

"Unlike your father?" she guessed.

He grimaced then. "My father pretended she never had. He burned or threw out everything that was hers and took her name off of everything. If mail came addressed to her, he burned that, too. It used to make him mad when he came across something he missed." He stopped, and she thought she saw a little shudder go through him. He lowered his gaze again. "He seemed to calm down after he'd erased her. But eventually he found my stash of her stuff that I'd grabbed up and hid when I realized what he was doing."

She didn't want to know what the bitter, cruel man had done. But if Trip needed to talk about it—perhaps, judging by his awkwardness, for the first time—she wasn't about to stop him.

"What did he do?" she asked, her voice as soft as she could make it.

"He burned it, too, then asked why the hell I'd want to keep anything from the woman who abandoned us."

Her breath caught. "He blamed her? For getting sick?"

"Just as if she'd done it on purpose." She saw his jaw clench. "As if she'd had any say in it."

"How old were you at that point?" she prompted gently, although she knew the answer.

He looked up at that. "Thinking I should have bailed on him?"

"Wondering," she admitted.

"I could have. I would have. Except for the last thing he said then."

"Which was?"

"That he wondered if I'd be as loyal to him after he died. And that we'd soon find out."

Her eyes widened. "Soon? Was he sick?"

"No."

"So he was threatening—"

"Yes."

"And that's why you stayed. You'd promised your mom."

His voice changed, took on a slightly urgent tone, as if he were desperate for her to understand. "He wasn't that way before. He wasn't a touchy-feely kind of dad—he was pretty strict—but he took care of us. He loved Mom, and he was even proud of me a few times. I couldn't lose him, too."

"So you put up with his abuse. Because you were afraid he'd kill himself?"

"I thought if he had that to focus on he wouldn't do it."

She stared at him for a long moment, searching for words to say. Finally she spoke the only ones that came to her. "So when you could have been sharing the burden, instead you were carrying it all, for his sake. That's one of the noblest things I've ever heard, Trip."

His gaze narrowed. "Noble? You're saying that to the guy who just got out of prison?"

"I'm saying it because it's true. If you weren't, you

would have been long gone by then, and not have stuck it out another four years."

"He just…never seemed to get past it. Every time I thought he might have, I found…something. An article on a carload of people that went off a cliff into the ocean. A stash of pills he'd stockpiled. A hose in the garage big enough to fit over his car's exhaust. Always something."

"I can't imagine living like that." And she had the answer to her last question about how he'd ended up on the path he'd taken. No wonder he'd chosen a gang who at least claimed to have his back. Because the person who should have never did.

He jammed a hand through his hair, then tightened his fingers against his head, as if it ached and that could ease it. She thought of offering aspirin, but then the tension seemed to ease, and he reached for his mug of coffee to finish it. Then, without another word, he got up, collected her plate and utensils, and took them along with his own to the kitchen.

"I can just wash them if you want," he said when she followed him over to the sink. "I got a lot of practice at that."

"Actually, I do often do that. With just me, it takes a long time to fill up the dishwasher. But it's almost ready now, so they can go in."

He loaded them up, then stepped back so she could add the soap and set the cycle she wanted. When the sound of the water flowing started, he just stood there for a silent moment. Then he looked at her.

"Why is it only you? I expected some smart guy to realize how lucky he'd be and grab you up long ago."

She didn't know how to feel about him asking that. So she shrugged, as he tended to do when he didn't know what to say. But then words she hadn't expected to utter came out. "I was close, a year or so ago. But it turned out when it came to how we wanted to live our lives, we were too opposite."

"City boy?"

"Among other things."

"His loss. I—"

The landline phone's ring cut off words she thought she might have liked to hear. She walked over to the handset on the counter and picked it up. Hitting the talk key, she answered.

A female voice identified the call as coming from the prison and then said briskly, "Will you accept a call from inmate Robert Goodwin?"

Robert Goodwin. Robber. "Yes, I will," she said quickly.

"Kayley? Trip's girl?" the voice on the other end said.

She pushed aside the little thrill that phrase gave her and said only, "Yes."

"Thanks for this. I need to talk to him."

"He's right here," she said, gesturing Trip over.

"Good," his still-imprisoned friend said. "Because he's got trouble. Big trouble. Ruff put out a hit on him."

Chapter Eleven

Trip didn't know why her eyes had gone so wide, because she didn't say anything, just held the receiver out to him. And it hit him who must be on the other end.

"Robber?" he asked.

"Yeah, it's me."

"You okay?"

"Status quo," Robber said. He was looking at another eight months inside, and was as dedicated as Trip had been to let nothing interfere with that. Which meant keeping your head down, your words and tone polite and respectful, and doing what you were told.

"I'm glad they let you call."

"Moreland. He got your girl on my list."

Your girl. "Figures," Trip muttered, giving Kayley a sideways glance. She'd moved far enough away to give him at least the illusion of privacy. Since he hadn't even had the illusion for a very long time, he appreciated it.

"Yeah, he always did have the hots for her," Robber was saying. "But I liked the way he backed it down to just appreciation when he saw she was focused on you."

"Yeah. He's...all right."

"Yeah. And you're a lucky shit to have her. But listen, I heard something you need to know about."

He didn't like the sound of his friend's voice when he said that. "What?"

"New officer came in, from over on the dry side." Trip knew that meant the east side of the state. Where Ruff was in prison. His stomach clenched. "Moreland says he told him Ruff put out a hit on the guy who turned on him in exchange for a cushy sentence."

Trip frowned. His stomach eased up a little, since that clearly wasn't him. "Turned on him?"

"Yeah. He thinks thanks to the rat, he's now looking at charges for other things, including rape and murder. You know his type. He can't accept that it was his own stupidity that landed him where he is."

Yes, he knew the type. He'd been that type for a while himself. "So he's blaming somebody else, as usual?"

"Three, he's blaming you."

"Me? But I never—"

"I know."

Trip's brow furrowed. This made no sense. They'd been caught together. Quinn Foxworth had taken them both down at once. There'd been nothing to bargain with even if he would have.

"But why wait until now?" he asked.

"I asked Moreland that—he really is an okay guy, for a guard—and he said he didn't really wait. He just couldn't get anybody in here to do it."

"But now I'm out…?"

"I don't think Ruff knows that yet. It's just a blanket kind of deal out there among his contacts that anybody who puts you down gets a nice payday and Ruff owing him."

"Great," Trip muttered.

"But it'll get back to him eventually that you got out early. Because he'll pay for that info, too."

Of all the things he might have expected, this wasn't even on the list. He thanked the one friend he'd made in that place. They talked for a few more minutes until the allotted twenty was almost up. Robber told him things hadn't changed much, and to make his life work, whatever he had to do. Trip told him to keep his nose clean and not mess up his own upcoming release. They promised to connect when he did.

And all the while, Trip fought down the nausea in his gut.

"Think I could call again?" Robber asked. "Would she mind, your lady?"

Trip felt a kick of wishfulness, that she truly was his lady, in the sense Robber assumed. "I think it would be okay. Until I get a number myself, anyway." *Or until I do what I have to, and leave her in peace.*

"Burner phone?"

"Maybe. Gotta watch the bucks."

"You need?"

He knew Robber wasn't in much better financial shape than he was. Still, he'd offered to help before Trip had been released, but he didn't want to become any more of a charity case than he already was.

"Not yet," he answered. *Hopefully never.*

He couldn't state any absolutes right now, save one. He was never going back into the system again.

But once the time had run out and the call ended, he knew there was another absolute.

If Oliver Ruff was after him, he needed to vanish. If he stayed anywhere Ruff had pull—which pretty much meant most of the state—his days would be numbered.

And anybody close to him, anybody who dared help him, could easily end up hurt or worse. Ruffle never worried much about collateral damage.

And he could not, would not let anything happen to Kayley.

"DON'T EVEN THINK IT," Kayley said warningly the moment Trip put the phone back on its charger.

He didn't look at her, just stood there, one hand still on the receiver. As she walked across the room, she could almost feel the tension radiating out from him, and somehow knew he was thinking about running. No, probably closer to actually bolting right now.

Finally he let go of the phone and turned around to face her. "I... Robber said—"

"I know why he called. He told me."

"Damn." Clearly he'd been hoping his friend hadn't mentioned that little detail. "Kayley, I have to go."

There was no missing the urgency in his voice. The worry. Not quite panic, but she couldn't picture him panicking anyway. "How could he possibly find out where you are?" she asked.

"I—"

"Did he even know about Debra?"

"I have no idea. But I can't take that chance."

"She's been back in the city for a long time. There's no way he'd know to look here."

"But Ruffle's still got connections all over."

She couldn't help the startled smile that crossed her face at the unexpected name. "Ruffle? How fitting. Bet he hates the nickname."

"He does. But Kayley, listen to me. He might not have

connections right here in Redwood Cove, but he does in the county. Unless I never set foot outside—"

"Which would be as bad as being back in prison."

He gave her a sideways look. Almost a smile, which seemed very odd, given the subject of the conversation. Maybe it was because she'd been interrupting him, as sometimes had happened back in those days when their conversations had ranged far and wide and she couldn't wait to express the thoughts his words triggered.

"Not hardly," he said softly. Then, with a little less urgency in his voice, he said, "It might be safe enough here, but anyplace else somebody could see me, recognize me—"

"Eventually, maybe. But not today. Or even this week."

"Kayley, I can't—I won't—risk you. Your safety. You've done too much for me."

"It's not a risk if he doesn't know where you are right now. You have time to breathe, Trip, to think."

A long, silent moment spun out between them. Trip just looked at her, and she saw turmoil in those deep green eyes. As if he were fighting some inner battle. The question was, was he fighting leaving, or staying?

She couldn't help herself; she reached out to him, as if her touch could anchor him somehow, could ease that tumult inside him. Although very brief hugs had been allowed when she visited him, after the first time when she'd impulsively taken advantage of the rule, he'd seemed so startled she'd never repeated the embrace again. For her own sake if nothing else, because any contact with him at all got her thinking things she shouldn't be thinking. Just as it had back when he was Debra's and she'd thought of Debra as her friend.

But that five-second hug had haunted her. Because she'd felt more in that brief contact than she had with any other man, ever. Nowhere else had she found that jolt of sensation, that electric sort of charge that had rippled through her.

"Don't," he whispered, lowering his eyes as if he couldn't even look at her. She yanked her hand back, beyond embarrassed.

"I'm sorry. That was…" *Presumptuous? Invasive?* "I know you don't want…" She couldn't finish it. She just couldn't. Because she was afraid the last word would be a pitiful *me*.

"You have no idea what I want." It stung, his voice was so harsh. But it enabled her to rein in her own silly emotions.

"No, I don't."

She was grateful when her phone chimed a text. It was her mother's notification tone, so she grabbed it quickly. Mom's mother had been doing better after a fall, but she was eighty-four now, and it was scary. However, this was just a morning check-in. Well, morning for her. It was now afternoon in Florida.

She swiped out an answer quickly, put the phone back down, then looked up to see Trip watching her.

"My mother," she explained.

"Ashamed of you, letting an ex-con stay with you?"

This time it was her voice that was harsh. "My mother would never be ashamed of her own child."

He let out a long, compressed breath. Closed his eyes for a moment. And when he opened them again, she would swear there was the sheen of moisture there, even though he wasn't looking at her. And when he spoke she was certain of it, because his voice sounded utterly broken. "Mine would be."

All her hurt feelings vanished. No matter how she felt, there was no way he didn't feel worse. And that knowledge put certainty in her voice when she said firmly, "Your mother would be ashamed, but of your father, not you."

He went still. Slowly shifted his gaze to her face. She couldn't read his expression. With an effort she made herself stay quiet, not trying to fill the silence. And it spun out long and taut between them before he finally gave a slow, weary shake of his head.

"Thanking you for…everything was the only thing I wanted to do when I got out. I never expected or planned on staying. And if I do, I could bring trouble down on you. I couldn't live with that, Kayley. It's better if I go."

"Where?"

He shrugged. "Somewhere. Anywhere. Anywhere that won't lead him to you."

"And how will that help you?"

He gave a bleak laugh. "Nothing and no one can do that."

She felt as if her heart were breaking all over again, as it had when she'd learned he was actually going to prison. *No one?*

The answer came to her in a rush. It seemed so obvious she wondered why she hadn't thought of it before. She grabbed her phone and swiped out a text, and sent it before she could change her mind. She didn't say anything, figuring he'd assume she was texting her mother again.

He was up and pacing now, his jaw tight. Trying to figure out where to go and how to get there? Probably. And she wasn't sure how to stop him. Or even if she should. Maybe a clean start somewhere else would be better for him. Except, did an ex-con ever get a truly clean start? Maybe some didn't deserve it, the ones who were bad by nature. But the ones who were forced into it by circumstance, the ones life had hit so hard, so unfairly—

The answer to her text came back, more quickly than she'd expected. But the answer was exactly what she'd come to expect. She read it and smiled.

"There is help, Trip. We're going there right now."

He spun around mid-pace. "What?"

"We're going to see people who can and will help."

He frowned. "What are you talking about?"

"We're going to Foxworth."

Chapter Twelve

"What?" He gaped at her, certain he couldn't have heard her right.

"You heard me."

"Are you crazy? Go to the guy who essentially put me away?"

"Well, not him specifically, I told you Quinn and Hayley are down in California." She was already bustling around, putting away things in the fridge and turning out the lights in the kitchen. "But there's somebody at their headquarters here, so that's where we're going."

"But—"

"Oh, and Cutter's there, so you can say hello," she went on, sounding almost cheerful as she grabbed up her phone. "I'll just go brush my teeth and get my jacket—"

"Stop!" he yelped as she headed down the hallway. "Kayley, what the hell?"

She did stop. She turned to look at him. "They'll help if they can." She held up the phone. "Hayley said so."

His mouth twisted. "Does her husband know she volunteered them?"

"Of course he knows. Hayley would never keep that from him, just like I would never try to trick them by not saying who needed their help."

He blinked. "You told them it was me?"

"Of course. I knew they'd help, because they helped you before."

They helped you before.

He'd forgotten. Or maybe still hadn't processed what he'd just learned, that they were what had really gotten him the "cushy" sentence. Not that Ruffle would believe that.

"And," she added, "when they find out why Ruffle is after you, I'll bet they'll be even more inclined to help. Come on, let's go. It's not raining now, but it's cold, so grab the jacket."

He found himself swept along as if in her wake, like a skier pulled by a powerful boat. And she was powerful, at least when it came to him. Because she had never denied him, he found it impossible to deny her. He didn't have much hope this would accomplish anything. There was no reason this Foxworth crew would want to help him again, after all this time, but he couldn't say no to her. Not after all she'd done.

He was still surprised at how little Redwood Cove had changed. Businesses had changed, and there were some new buildings, but not all that much. It was still a two–traffic signal town, and he knew the residents had always preferred it that way. They made a turn at that second signal and headed into a more rural area. Kayley obviously knew where she was going.

"You've been there before? This Foxworth headquarters?" Had that been where she had poured out his pitiful, miserable story to Quinn Foxworth? Not that he wasn't grateful, if that was what had kept him out of a higher-security facility, but still, it was…unsettling to think about.

"Yes," she said, her tone cheerful, as if buoyed by her certainty this would somehow fix everything. "Cutter invited me."

He blinked. Then said, a bit carefully, "The dog invited you?"

She laughed. "I know, I know, it sounds crazy, but that dog is something else. I was out for a walk, and Hayley and Quinn were driving past. I waved, since I recognized them, and thought that would be it. But apparently Cutter threw a barking fit until they stopped. They were on their way to their headquarters, and Cutter simply insisted I come along. He actually herded me over to their car."

"And they just...went along?"

She laughed again. "Hayley said they'd learned it was best. Quinn just rolled his eyes and said he didn't even question anymore. Apparently Cutter is really good at finding cases for them."

Okay, that was over the top. "Finding cases. A dog."

She nodded as she slowed to switch into a left-turn lane. "Like I said, crazy. But they swear he knows who needs their help."

They made the turn down an even more isolated road. A couple of miles later, she turned off the road onto a gravel drive that wound through a thick stand of evergreens. It wasn't until about the third curve that he spotted a three-story building through the trees. It was nearly the same green as the trees, and for a building that size, blended in well.

The gravel drive curved once more, and he could see that up ahead it opened out into a wider parking area a few yards from the building. There was a rather beat-up-looking silver sedan parked further down, in front of a second building to one side of the main one. This was a single-story place, but rather tall, and metal. It looked like a warehouse or very large garage.

And in between it and the green main building was... a helipad?

"They have a helicopter?"

"Yep. And an airplane, although that's what Quinn flew them down to California in. Or maybe Hayley. She got her pilot's license for the plane a while ago."

"So, who's the helicopter pilot?"

"Quinn flies that, too. And one of the other guys as well."

"One of? Just how many people are there?"

"Here? Five, I think. I haven't met all of them."

They'd turned into the parking area now, and the door on the larger building that faced this way swung open.

It was the dog. By himself. Which made no sense. How had he—

"They installed a handicapped door system," Kayley explained as if she'd read his look. "And Cutter learned to use it in about eighteen seconds."

The distinctively colored dog was bounding down the walkway that traversed the grassy area in front of the building. He greeted Kayley happily, tail wagging. After receiving her greeting and a scratch behind the ears, he turned to Trip. The dog's gaze was as steady as before, but oddly felt different. Not less intense really, just…different.

And then the door opened again, and a man came out. Tall, as tall as his boss, Quinn Foxworth, but rangier. His stride was long, and steady, although Trip thought he detected a slight hitch on the left side. As the man got closer, Trip saw that the expression on his lean, rather rugged-looking face was impassive. He wasn't concerned about their arrival. Or surprised. Although he guessed this guy would be very good at hiding either. So had Hayley Foxworth warned him they were coming?

Or maybe it was just the dog.

He nearly laughed at his own thought, and looked

down at the animal, who was now sitting at his feet. Thinking he was waiting for a Kayley-like greeting, since they had met before, Trip reached out and stroked the dog's head. And felt it again, that odd sort of soothing he didn't understand.

"Kayley McSwain?" the man said as he came to a halt before them; clearly the Foxworth woman had told him she was coming.

"Yes," she said, smiling, and held out her hand.

"Rafe Crawford," he said as he shook it; his smile was much more fleeting than hers had been. He was like the most wary of prisoners he'd ever encountered, shielded, on guard.

"Mr. Crawford," she began, but he shook his head.

"For you, Rafe'll do."

Then the man shifted his gaze to Trip. And Trip felt a shiver go down his spine; those steely gray eyes were as intimidating as any prison guard's he'd ever seen. In a crazy way, they reminded him of the dog's, in intensity, not color. This was a hard guy. And he knew somehow, just as he'd known which guards were the toughest, that this was not a man he'd want to fight. He'd be fierce, and relentless.

And suddenly he was regretting having let Kayley talk him into this.

"Rafe, then," Kayley began again, clearly about to introduce him, but before she could say any more the dog let out a low whuff, cutting her off. Instinctively Trip looked down at him, as did the newcomer. As if he'd waited to be sure he had Crawford's attention, the dog then got up, turned, and sat right back down where he'd been, only now with his back to Trip. He was looking up at Crawford, as intently as he'd once stared at Trip. The man's brows rose. When he looked back at Trip, his expression had changed. Not softened—Trip doubted that was possible—but as if he'd understood something.

One corner of Rafe Crawford's mouth twisted, and he let out a breath. "All right, dog. Got it."

Another woof, and the dog got up and trotted back toward the door he'd come through.

"We…met before," Trip said, feeling like some sort of explanation was needed. "The dog, I mean." Not that that explained the dog's odd action. Or this man's response.

"You might as well come on in," Crawford said. "No sense talking about it out here in the cold."

Not quite sure what had just happened—impossibly, it seemed like the dog had convinced this man to talk to them—Trip followed when the man and Kayley headed for the building. The dog had reached the door, rose up on his hind legs and batted the metal square beside the door at handle height, and the door swung open.

They stepped into a tiled entry, with a rack for coats and jackets to one side, and a couple of pairs of rain boots beside a drain in the floor. There was a basket of towels there as well, handy here in the Northwest. Once they were past that, Trip stopped dead, startled.

He'd been expecting a business-style office or something. But instead he was looking at what could have been the interior of a spacious home. There was a seating area with a large, comfortable-looking couch, four chairs, and a sizeable coffee table set on a colorful rug in front of a large fireplace, which was topped by a flat-screen TV. Further on was a compact modern kitchen. Off to the right was a pair of doors, one closed, one open and leading to what looked like a full bathroom, and a set of stairs went up the back wall.

"Coffee?" Crawford asked as they entered the big room. Then he added, with a wry smile that was as fleeting as the welcome had been, "Although fair warning, I'm the only one here at the moment, so it's my brew. Meaning it could strip paint."

"Sounds right up my alley," Trip answered. He'd gotten used to drinking whatever was there. Which made him wonder if the man would be so welcoming if he knew who he was or where he'd been just days ago.

"I'm fine," Kayley said, and she was smiling widely, in that generous, warm way of hers. "Hayley warned me about your coffee. She told you we were coming?"

"She said you'd be bringing someone who might need our help." Oddly, he glanced at the dog again, and the wry smile reappeared.

"Have a seat, and I'll get the coffee," Crawford said.

Trip followed Kayley over toward the fireplace, which was gas-fed and on, throwing out a nice level of heat. He guessed she felt the warmth, because she headed to the end of the couch closest to it and sat down. He stopped at the other end and started to sit, but suddenly the dog was there, and had jumped up and plopped in the very spot he'd been aiming for. A bit awkwardly he had to shift at the last moment to avoid sitting on the animal, and ended up sitting closer—much closer—to Kayley than he'd intended.

"Sorry," he muttered. "The dog."

She just smiled at him. That sweet, warm, generous smile. Then he looked up to see Crawford standing there, two mugs in hand, looking at the three of them on the couch with an expression that seemed almost resigned.

I don't get this. Any of it.

Trip took the offered mug, deciding the best course now was to shut up and wait. The coffee was indeed some of the strongest he'd ever drunk, but he'd had worse. Or maybe it was just freedom that made it taste better.

Or sitting next to Kayley?

He shook that one off rapidly. Once the other man was seated, Kayley went back to the introduction the dog had interrupted. "Rafe, this is Trip Callen."

Crawford drew back slightly, the first betraying reaction Trip had seen from him. Clearly he knew his name, but the real surprise was the way, with a slight nod, he said "Ah." He didn't add "That makes sense of it," but he might as well have. But why it made sense Trip had no idea.

Crawford shifted his gaze from Kayley to him. It was even more unsettling than having the dog staring at him. Because as dangerous as he imagined the dog could be if inclined, Trip sensed this man could be much, much more. If inclined.

So don't incline him.

It seemed simple enough, but Trip had no idea what might tip this guy into the wrong mood. And then, quietly, Crawford said two words.

"The locket."

Trip blinked. "I…"

"What do you need?"

He gave a short, bitter laugh. "Doesn't matter." He glanced around at the expansive room. "I can't afford this kind of help."

"We don't take money for what we do. We might call on you down the line to help someone else, but there's no fee for our help. So," he repeated, "what do you need?"

"That's it?" Trip was gaping now. He could feel it. Just like that, they were going to help him?

"You gave Emily's locket back."

Emily. He remembered the engraving on the inside of the golden heart. *To my beloved daughter Emily, with all my love, Mom.* The only memento the orphaned little girl had had of her dead mother.

"Yeah," he muttered, not liking the sudden tightness in his chest, an echo of what he'd felt in that moment. The sensation that had driven him to give the little piece of loot back. He'd been told he was just a sucker for a sob story, but...

That action had made the clearly influential Foxworths go to bat for him.

Which had ended up making his prison time a lot less ugly.

And it apparently was still having aftereffects.

How could things so small, the locket and the act of giving it back, be so powerful?

"Best decision you ever made," Crawford said quietly, as if he'd read his thoughts.

Trip gave a slow, wondering shake of his head, then met the man's steady gaze. And knew it was nothing less than the truth.

Chapter Thirteen

"Hayley's text said full bore, so you've got all of Fox-worth at your back," Rafe said.

"Just like that? You know…who I am, what I did, but…"

Kayley heard the note of incredulity in Trip's voice, and smiled to herself. Rafe took out his phone, tapped the screen a couple of times, and held it out to Trip. Since he was so close—and she couldn't say she was sorry Cutter had accidentally gotten in the way and he'd ended up right next to her—she could read the text as well.

Kayley McSwain is on the way. Full bore on helping however we can.

"She didn't even tell you it was me," Trip said, sounding puzzled. "Or why you should help."

"She knew I'd recognize the name when I heard it. And that's all that's necessary."

Trip gave her a sideways glance. "Told you," she said with the warmest smile she could manage. "They'll help."

She hadn't met this particular Foxworth operative be-fore, but she'd heard about him. Knew he was the one the others worried about most, although she hadn't known exactly why. Hayley had said unless forced to do otherwise, he tended to withdraw, and she was working hard on getting him to interface with people more.

But now that she was here, now that she'd looked into his eyes, she understood the concern. Those stormy gray eyes were shadowed, haunted, in a way she'd never seen before. And she wondered what he'd done, what he'd seen, in the days he'd worn the uniform of his country. Decided she didn't really want to know.

And was quite aware that she owed the chance to make that decision not to know to men like him.

"So, what do you need?" Rafe asked again.

Trip was still looking at her. "I don't think I even know where to start. Would you?"

She could understand that. He had to still be feeling a bit at sea, unanchored. So she quickly gave Rafe the basics, from his early release, and why, to the news they'd just gotten, that Oliver Ruff—hereafter to be known as Ruffle, she added derisively—had decided Trip had made some kind of deal, had turned on him, and that was why he was in the state penitentiary in Walla Walla and Trip was in a minimum security camp on the other side of the state. And as a result, Ruffle had put out a blanket contract, an offer of considerable remuneration for anyone who took him out. Permanently.

Rafe leaned back in his chair and sipped at his coffee as he listened. When she finished, he gave Trip a look. "Not sure any state prison facility and the word *cushy* aren't mutually exclusive."

Trip grimaced. "Relatively. A lot more than where he is."

"Which I'm sure is all that counts, in his view," Kayley said.

"How did you two meet?"

One dark brow was raised at her, and she knew he was

wondering how somebody as benign as she obviously was had ended up with someone as wild as Trip. Well, not *with* in the couples sense, but friends. And the memory of how much she'd wanted it to be in the couples sense made her, for the moment, unable to answer.

And she was very afraid it showed in her face, because her cheeks felt suddenly hot. She lowered her gaze, wishing in that moment that she was the one who had Cutter's comforting touch.

Finally, when she didn't answer, Trip said dryly, "I had the further bad judgment to date her roommate. Who dropped me like a hot rock when I got in trouble." Kayley sensed his gaze, and lifted her head to see him looking at her, his jaw tight again. She understood his tension, after the way Debra had treated him. But why was he looking at her? She glanced at Rafe, who was watching Trip as if studying him.

Then, turning back to Kayley, Rafe said quietly, "Sometimes people have trouble seeing what's right in front of them."

Her breath stopped for a moment. He didn't mean… her, did he? That Trip should have seen her? No, of course he meant Trip hadn't seen Debra's perfidy.

"Tell me about it," Trip muttered, now staring down at Cutter. He was silent for a moment, then took a deep breath, looked up, and met Rafe's steady gaze. "I didn't know until Kayley told me, when I got to her place Monday, what Foxworth did for me. I was pretty out of it, in shock, through the whole process, for a long time."

"It took a long time, from what Quinn told me," Rafe said. "A lot of delaying and fancy lawyering."

"Ruff—" Trip paused, glanced at Kayley, then adjusted and went on "—Ruffle was sure he'd slip through the jaws again. He bragged about it, how he'd get a short sentence, the equivalent of a slap on the wrist. You guys also have something to do with the fact that he didn't?"

"You'll have to ask Quinn that. I wasn't here yet."

"Kayley told me that—the locket thing—was what started all this." He gestured around the spacious room.

Rafe gave a small smile and nodded. A lock of his dark hair fell over his forehead as he did, and Kayley was a little amazed at how two such simple things changed his look; he went from tough, rugged, even harsh, to... something else altogether.

"Quinn says nothing in his military career ever made him feel good in the same way as giving that locket back to that little girl did," Rafe said.

"And he built a wonderful thing on it," Kayley said. "Helping people in the right, who can't fight anymore on their own."

"As Liam would say, it's the foundation of the Foundation."

Kayley smiled. "He's the Texan, right?"

"And the one who persists in naming inanimate objects," Rafe said, sounding like he was talking about an annoying but loved kid brother. Then he smiled, and it was a better one this time. "And who just got engaged."

Kayley's own smile widened. She'd liked them both, the ever-joking Texan with the slight drawl, and the young woman she'd met that day she'd come here. "The teacher? Ria, right?"

Rafe nodded. And then shifted his gaze back to Trip. "Ria, who brought Emily back to us."

Trip blinked. "Locket Emily?"

"Yes. She had a friend with a problem."

"The friend who's now her boyfriend?" Kayley asked.

"That's the one."

Trip looked confused. "So your guy's fiancée brought locket Emily back to you?"

"She wasn't his fiancée at the time. That's how they met," Kayley explained. "Just as Hayley and Quinn met on a case."

"They did?" Trip said, not looking much less confused.

"He kidnapped her," Kayley said serenely. Trip's expression became suspicious, and she knew he thought she was putting him on. "Rafe?"

"True story."

Trip went utterly silent, and Kayley took pity on him. "He had no choice, really. They were protecting a big witness, and she got caught up in it." She gestured with a grin at Cutter. "Thanks to that guy. And obviously it worked out for the best, since they're wild about each other."

Trip gave a slow shake of his head. He looked as if he thought none of this made any sense at all. She could understand that. But he also looked as if he were wary enough to bolt. And she tried to think of a way to fix that. She had to, because she knew, she just knew, that Foxworth could—and would—help him. She searched for words, any words, that would calm him, convince him.

But then Cutter, who had been quietly sprawled on the couch beside him, lifted his head and moved so he could rest his chin on Trip's leg. In the instinctive reaction of most people who liked dogs, Trip moved his hand to pet Cutter's head.

As she watched, she saw it happen again. Saw Trip's expression change as he stroked the soft fur. She could almost feel him relaxing. He was staring down at the dog with no small amount of wonder.

Kayley glanced at Rafe. He was watching man and

dog, but as if he felt her gaze, he shifted his eyes to her. And he nodded, as if to confirm what they both knew was happening.

She could tell simply by looking at those eyes that he'd been through a few kinds of hell himself. Had he, too, found comfort in the simple offering of a bit of peace in the form of a loving dog? Or—she turned back to Trip and Cutter, saw how Trip's expression had changed—could it be more than that? Hayley had told her Cutter was also a trained therapy dog, and that he regularly visited hospitals and nursing homes, and was welcomed happily.

"He's got something," Hayley had told her. "Call it *magic*, for lack of a better word."

Looking at that pair now, she almost believed it.

Chapter Fourteen

"How sure are you Ruffle doesn't know or can't find out where you are?" Crawford asked.

"Pretty sure," Kayley said.

Simultaneously Trip said, urgently, "Not enough."

The cool, gray eyes of a warrior looked at him. How could a guy seem so scary just sitting there with a mug of coffee in his hand? Trip held that unsettling gaze, somehow convinced that he had to. He'd survived all that time in lockup, but here he was, shaky at the thought of something happening to Kayley because of him.

"Not enough," he repeated, more calmly. "He might not know now, but he could find out. He's got connections all over."

"But does he have power?" Rafe asked.

Trip studied the man for a moment, but trying to read his expression was futile. He had the feeling with Rafe Crawford you saw what he wanted you to see, and nothing more. "He may not by the time he gets out, but right now I'm guessing he's still remembered and feared. His cousin Boyd, the guy he left in charge, will see to that."

"Loyal?"

"To the death," Trip said grimly. "And Ruffle's got money, stashed. Cash money. He'll be able to pay." He suppressed a shudder. "If he thinks I turned on him, he'll pay a lot. He's big on settling scores."

Crawford nodded. "All right. First thing then, safe shelter."

"He can stay—"

"No!" Trip cut Kayley off. He knew it had sounded sharp, almost angry, although he wasn't. No, he was worried to the edge of panic that he might bring the misery of his life down on her. So he reached for her hands, squeezed them gently in his. "No, Kayley. I can't risk it. Risk you. I won't."

"But…where will you go?"

He felt an odd sort of tightening deep in his chest. She sounded worried. About him. But then, Kayley had always worried about him. And a memory shot into his mind, as vivid as if the conversation had just happened. The day she'd found out he'd hooked up with Ruffle's crew.

It's true? You're running with that…criminal?

He hadn't liked the way she'd said that, so he'd turned to sarcasm. *Worried I'll steal something from you?*

I'm worried you'll end up in jail, the hospital, or the morgue!

It had been so long since anyone had worried about him, he hadn't known how to deal. Looking back, he realized that was the moment he'd started to realize the shallowness of Debra's attachment to him. When they'd first started seeing each other, he'd thought the beautiful blonde might be the answer to the yawning emptiness inside him. But that was before he'd found out it was the walk on the edge of the wild side she'd wanted. But only the edge; when he'd tumbled headlong into that wild side, she couldn't run fast enough.

Don't you see, Trip? She's empty inside. All she wanted

from you was a taste of a world that made her hollow self feel alive.

He remembered that day vividly, too. The first and only time, on a visit at the prison, that Kayley had brought up Debra. After that she refused to even talk about her.

"—here."

At Crawford's last word, Trip blinked and snapped out of his reverie. *Watch it, Callen. It would not be smart to zone out around this guy.*

"What?" he said, trying to sound like he'd heard what he'd said, just didn't understand it.

Crawford looked at him as if he knew perfectly well he'd been off in the clouds. "You can stay here," he said.

Trip blinked again. Had he lost every bit of his ability to understand a simple conversation? "Here?"

The man nodded toward that back corner where the two doors were. "There's a bedroom. Most of what you'd need's already there. Hayley sees to that."

"So what, I just move in?"

"For now. Until we figure out what has to be done."

What has to be done. How about going back in time? Can you manage that?

"I didn't realize the bedroom was there," Kayley said.

"This kind of situation is what it's there for," Rafe said.

"But what if Ruffle finds him here?" she asked, sounding anxious again. Which caused that same tightness deep inside him again.

Crawford smiled at her. It was that slight, quick curve of his mouth that Trip was beginning to think was the best he could manage. So maybe they had something in common.

"Liam and Quinn put a security system on this place that would stop Houdini. Don't worry about it."

At that moment, Cutter's head came up off Trip's leg.

The dog looked at Crawford and gave a short, sharp bark. Trip's first thought was that he needed to go outside. But Crawford—who must know, since he was apparently taking care of the dog while the Foxworths were gone—only shifted his gaze to the animal.

"Oh?" he said mildly, as if he expected the dog to—

Cutter barked again, differently, softer, a bark that crazily sounded…satisfied, as if he were happy that the man had understood.

"Looks like you'll have a four-footed bodyguard, too," Crawford said, as casually as if he often handed over the dog that wasn't even his. *Hell, maybe he does.*

"Oh, good," Kayley said, sounding genuinely relieved. "I'll feel better if Cutter's here with you."

"I don't know how to take care of a dog," he protested. "I've never had one."

The closest thing to a grin he'd seen flashed briefly across Crawford's face. "Don't worry about that, either. He's a very good teacher. And I'm bunking out in the other building, so I'll be close."

Trip's brow furrowed. "Wait, am I taking your room?"

"No. I stay out there when I'm here." He glanced at Cutter. "Hey, dog, is that the real reason? That little room out there not cushy enough for you?"

Trip almost laughed when the dog let out a combination bark and growl that actually sounded disgusted. Kayley actually did laugh.

"He's so expressive," she said.

"He gets his point across," Crawford agreed. He looked back at Trip. "He'll bring you his bowl if he's hungry. He'll sit by the back door if he wants out. Yip if you take too long to notice. If he's got a ball in his mouth, he wants you to throw it. If he sits in front of the fridge, he wants carrots."

"Carrots?" The dog ate carrots?

"Hayley says he likes the crunch," Kayley put in.

"I'm seriously going to be...dog-sitting?"

"Cheap rent, don't you think?" Kayley said.

He hadn't thought about it like that. "I didn't mean—I just don't know...what if I screw up?"

"I think you're laboring under a misapprehension," Crawford said, and despite his unreadable expression, Trip would have sworn he was laughing inside. "He's going to be taking care of you."

Trip looked down at the dog, who was back to resting his head on his leg. The amber-flecked dark eyes were fastened on him in that steady stare. Except this time it wasn't unnerving. It was almost comforting. As if the dog were reassuring him that Crawford was speaking truth, that he would be taking care of him.

"Guard dog, huh?" he murmured to the animal.

"Best I've ever seen," Crawford confirmed. "And that includes some that were trained to it." He got to his feet. "We'll organize getting you settled in here in a bit, but first I need to make a couple of calls and do a little research. While I do that, you need to make a list." He leaned down and slid a notepad on the coffee table toward them.

"A list?" Trip asked.

"Of everybody from Ruffle's gang who knew you. Then anybody outside who knew you were with them." The man's gaze flicked to Kayley for a moment. "Then anyone inside or out who might know Kayley was your ex's roommate."

"That...could be a long list."

"Then you'd better get started," Crawford said. He turned and walked toward the back of the room and started up the stairs. Trip noticed the slight hitch in his gait again, although it didn't seem to slow the man any. Cutter sat up and watched him go. Trip felt the loss of contact with the dog, and had a little trouble convincing himself it was just the physical warmth of the furry beast he was missing.

"That," he muttered once Crawford was out of sight, "is one coolheaded dude."

"Snipers usually are, I'm guessing."

His head snapped around. "What?"

"He was a sniper. In the Marines. Quinn says one of the best ever. Trophies and everything."

Trip stared at her. Witness protection, kidnapping, an airplane, a helicopter, and now a sniper? What kind of operation was this Foxworth, anyway?

"Are they all ex-military?"

"No. Liam's not, or Cutter. That they know of."

He couldn't stop the short laugh. "You say that like the dog is one of their…operatives."

She didn't smile, or laugh. "After what you've seen Cutter do, can you really say you don't think he is?"

Trip looked at the dog. Who was looking back at him, head tilted, mouth open, tongue lolling sideways.

Trip would swear the damn dog was grinning.

Chapter Fifteen

"Well, if it ain't Miss Kayley McSwain!"

Kayley laughed as the man with sandy brown hair—hair he took great glee in saying he had cut by a dog groomer—and golden-brown eyes caught her up in a bear hug. She knew the exaggerated drawl was for her benefit; there was usually only a hint of his Texas origins when he spoke.

"Hi, Liam," she said. "How's Ria?"

"My fiancée, you mean?"

She grinned at him. "*I do.* So to speak."

He laughed. "Rafe let the cat out, I see."

"Congratulations. She's an amazing lady."

"That she is."

She saw his glance shift over her shoulder as Trip put down the list he'd been working on and stood up. She introduced them. And saw that Liam recognized the name as quickly as Rafe had.

The Foxworth man studied Trip for a moment before saying quietly, and now with the barest hint of the drawl, "You're the locket guy."

She could see Trip's bemused reaction in his face, but after a moment he just said, "Yeah, I guess I am. Around here, anyway."

"That meant the world to Emily. She wears it to this day," Liam said. "That was a good thing you did."

"First time for everything," Trip muttered.

Liam tilted his head slightly as he studied Trip. "You always that hard on yourself?"

Trip shrugged. "Prison'll do that." He glanced at Kayley, who tried for her most encouraging smile.

"I'll bet it does," Liam said, rather fervently. "About time to thank Quinn again for saving me from that."

Trip's gaze snapped back to Liam. "What?"

Liam shrugged in a perfect imitation of Trip's earlier action. "I would have been locked up myself if it wasn't for him."

At Trip's startled look, Kayley said, "Liam was—and still is—a very efficient computer hacker." She gave the Texas guy a grin. "He told me so."

"You were going to go to jail for hacking, but Foxworth got you off? How—and why—did he do that?"

"Well, being the victim, he got some say."

Trip blinked. "The victim?"

"He hacked Foxworth," Kayley said with an even wider grin.

"Long story," Liam said as Trip stared. Then Liam looked at Kayley. "Where's Rafe? He sounded pretty adamant I get my butt over here fast."

"He's upstairs. Calls—one of which was you, I gather—and some research, he said."

"Research? Uh-oh. That means he's messing with my computer. I'd better go rescue it. Him. Both." He walked quickly toward the stairs. But before he started up, he looked back over his shoulder at Trip. "We'll make things right, Mr. Callen. It's what we do."

Trip stared after him. Then he slowly gazed around the big room. "I don't…" He stopped, took a deep breath she could both see and hear, then looked at her. "I can't believe something like this really exists."

"Hayley told me Quinn was a little lost before he found this cause. But once he realized he could help people who felt like he had felt when the man who had murdered his parents was let go, he found his true north, as she put it."

"So…it's like a mission, for him."

She nodded. "Helping people who have tried on their own but run out of options. People who are in the right, but up against more powerful forces, forces that won't listen to them." She smiled at him then. "Or maybe just a heartbroken little girl who wanted her only keepsake from her mother back."

He stared at her for a moment, and something showed in those green eyes that she couldn't quite put a name to. Some combination of amazement and…shock? He shook his head, looking around the big yet homey room again, more in wonder than disbelief this time.

"That sister must be a serious financial genius, if they're funding five places like this, all over the country. And they do this…for nothing."

Kayley leaned against the counter that delineated the small kitchen. "She is, I think. She helped their uncle raise him, after their parents were killed, even though she was practically a kid herself. And now she's a taskmaster who thinks of everything, according to Quinn. Anticipates everything. In the end they all answer to Charlie, he says." She smiled. "Just think of a woman who could intimidate the likes of Quinn Foxworth."

"Hard to imagine." His gaze flicked over and upward, toward the stairway. "And it's hard to imagine that Rafe guy would be intimidated by anyone or anything."

"He does seem like he'd be on the other side of that equation, doesn't he? Maybe he's the exception to Quinn's rule." She nodded toward the coffee table, where he'd put down the list he'd been working on. She could see there were two columns of names on the top sheet, one full, the second one about half. "How's that coming?"

He gave a one-shouldered shrug this time. "That's everybody I can think of right now, but I'm sure there are more." He grimaced. "I've tried pretty hard to put all that out of my mind."

"And I'm sure you don't like trying to remember it now. But it will be worth it." She felt a ripple of sadness that came out in words. "I'm sorry that what should be a joyous time for you, being, is being messed up."

His gaze flicked away. And the slightest of smiles lifted one corner of his mouth. "Some of it's been pretty amazing." He looked back at her. "You're amazing."

"I wish I'd done more. That I'd been there, during the trial, or—"

"No! No, if you'd been there, Ruffle would have seen you. He'd wonder, and find out who you were."

She nodded. "I know. I didn't think of it, but Hayley explained it wouldn't be wise. And so I'm safe now, thanks to Foxworth."

"Then I already owe them, even if they can't pull this off."

"They will. Quinn doesn't brook failure."

"Seems like you've gotten to know them pretty well."

"Well enough to know that." She smiled at him. "They're the kind of people you want in your life."

He studied her for a moment before he quietly, but with an ache in his voice that made her throat tighten, said, "They're the kind of people you should want in your life. Not people like me."

She couldn't stop herself. She reached out and grabbed his hands. "They're the kind of people you would have been, Trip, if your life hadn't taken that awful turn. The kind of person you can be now."

He stared down at their hands, but he didn't pull away. And despite the instinctive urge to avoid certain embarrassment, neither did she. Instead she took the chance to truly look at him again, this time focusing on the thick, dark, twin sweeps of his eyelashes. But then all she could think of was that beautiful deep green of his eyes, as rich as the evergreens just outside the window.

Slowly, as if he were fighting it, he lifted his gaze to her face.

"You have too much faith in me."

"It's to make up for the faith you don't have in yourself. Yet."

"You sound…so sure."

"I am." She hesitated, not certain she should do this, but hoping it would help him start down that path. "Why did you give it back? The locket?"

His brow furrowed, and yet again he shrugged. She was going to adopt that habit. It was so handy to avoid answering.

"Why?" she repeated.

"It wasn't worth much to pawn," he said, avoiding her eyes now.

"Right. You want me to tell you the real reason?"

His gaze snapped back to her face. His eyes had narrowed. Insulted, was he, that she dared tell him why he'd done something? Tough.

"You gave it back because you knew how much it would have meant to you to have something of your mother's to hold on to."

As if he'd shouted it, she could see the memory of what he'd told her, about his father burning everything of his mother's, hit him. He physically winced.

"I meant what I said before, Trip. The word is *noble*, and it applies. Whether you want to admit it or not."

He looked away, as if holding her gaze was too much. "You're crazy, McSwain. You know that?"

"Possibly. Maybe even probably. But I am what I am."

That made him look back at her. "You are, aren't you? You know who and what you are. You're steady, solid, unshakable."

"You forgot one."

He blinked. "What?"

"Stubborn. You left out stubborn."

She got what she'd wanted, a laugh. It was light, and short, but it was a laugh, and she counted that a win.

Chapter Sixteen

Trip heard someone on the stairway, and seized on the distraction to look away from Kayley. He'd already guessed it was Crawford by the barely perceptible unevenness in the footsteps. Apparently whatever injury he'd suffered made coming down a little more difficult than going up, which he'd done in long, steady strides.

"Liam's doing a deep dive," he said as he came back into the great room area. Then, with a wry twist of his mouth he added, "Which is why I'm back here. My style of input is more hunt, hunt, hunt, and peck than anything. And sometimes his searches involve doing things I'm better off not knowing about."

"Sounds like a good skill to have on tap," Kayley said.

Crawford nodded. "And the few things Liam can't handle, our guy in St. Louis can."

"Quinn told me about him. Ty, isn't it? He said if Ty told him he could change the weather, he'd believe him."

"Probably be more a case of changing worldwide weather reports, but yes," Crawford said.

He gestured them back to the sitting area. This time Trip thought he'd make it to the other end of the couch, but once again the dog got in the way. He felt a little bit herded, and wondered if that's what the breed, whatever it was, had begun as. He was already on the couch, in the same too-close-to-Kayley place he'd been in, before it occurred to him he could have taken the other individual chair opposite.

But then Crawford would have to turn away from Kayley to talk to him, and that would be awkward. So he started to apologize again, as he had before, but something about the way Kayley was smiling at Cutter stopped him.

When they were settled in again, Crawford looked at Trip. And something in that steely gaze warned him there was going to be something coming at him.

"We have someone else we often collaborate with. Besides his own encyclopedic knowledge and great gut instincts, he's got contacts throughout the county and state, and could probably get us a list of active members of Ruffle's gang in a day or so. Along with a ranking of who'd be most likely to make a move if the man ordered it, even from inside."

"I knew you'd be able to help!" Kayley exclaimed.

"Hold on," Trip said, eyeing Crawford. "There's a reason you're not telling me who this is before you told me what he could do."

"His name's Brett Dunbar."

"And?" Trip prodded, knowing that wasn't all. Crawford nodded as if in approval, and Trip thought he saw a brief flash of acknowledgment in his eyes.

"He's a detective."

His gut knotted. He should have known. Maybe on some level he had. That's why he found the temerity to push this guy who half scared the crap out of him.

"A badge-carrying detective," he said flatly. "A cop. You're calling in a cop."

"A cop Quinn would hire in an instant if he ever

wanted a change. Because he believes what we believe. And he's helped us on multiple cases."

"Wait," Kayley said suddenly, "Brett Dunbar...isn't he the guy who essentially took down our crooked, murderous governor?"

"That would be him," Crawford said. "With some help from a certain dog."

Trip drew back slightly. He'd heard about that. The entire corrections staff had been talking about it, and many of them had been none too happy to find out they'd been essentially working for a man who murdered his way into the top office in the state.

"And if that's not endorsement enough," Crawford added, with a look at Cutter, "he's got his own bark."

Kayley laughed as Trip's brow furrowed. "What?"

"They all have their own bark," Kayley said. "All the Foxworth people."

"Their own bark?" He was feeling slow on the uptake. This outside world seemed to be moving a bit too fast compared to the dull grind of life inside.

"I'd go through them all for you," Crawford said dryly, "but then I'd have to try and explain how mine's a yip, a yowling bark, and a yip, like a short, a long, and a short. Which coincidentally happens to be Morse code for *R*."

Trip laughed then. He felt almost relieved that it was obviously a joke. He was starting to feel a little weird about all the things they attributed to this animal who was no doubt clever, but still just a dog. But at the same time, he remembered the oddly rhythmic series of woofs and barks that had preceded Liam Burnett walking in the door.

Crawford didn't laugh. Or even smile.

"You're...serious?"

"I learned long ago not to joke about what that dog

can do. Or about his judgment, which has been infallible. And he trusts Dunbar."

"Not sure that means I should," Trip muttered. "All things considered." Including the simple, unavoidable fact of what he was, an ex-con.

"I think he's a good guy. I read something after," Kayley said, her tone clearly admiring, "about how he walked away from all the acclaim, and even people wanting him to run for office, because he just wanted to get back to work."

"As a cop," Trip couldn't stop himself from pointing out. "Why on earth would a cop want to help me?"

"But this cop took down a totally corrupt governor," Kayley said.

Trip shifted his gaze to the dog because he simply had to look away from Kayley. She was so honest, so earnest, that he felt as if he weren't good enough to even be in her company.

"And what makes you think he'd look at me any differently?" Trip said, his voice getting tighter.

"Because," Crawford said levelly, "he's capable of seeing more than one side. Plus he knows about the locket story. And," he added with that same twitch at one corner of his mouth, "Cutter's vouching for you."

The moment Crawford said his name, the dog nudged at him, bumping the hand he hadn't even realized he'd clenched into a fist. Instinctively he relaxed his fingers and ran them over the dark fur, only realizing when he felt it again that he'd been seeking that odd sense of comfort, of reassurance, that the dog seemed capable of delivering.

"Would it really be so different," Kayley asked quietly, "to accept help from a detective than to accept it from Foxworth? Since Quinn is essentially who caught you in the first place?"

He had to swallow before he could speak. "It's accepting they have the same goals that's the problem."

"Have you done anything since you got out that he'd have to arrest you for?" Crawford asked, his tone neutral.

"In four days? Not even I managed that."

"Anything from when you were with Ruff—Ruffle—that they didn't find then, that he might have to look into?"

He took a deep breath. "They found everything. Except maybe that I broke a neighbor's window with a baseball when I was twelve."

"Pay him for it?" Crawford asked, as if he were only mildly curious.

"Mowed his lawn and washed his car for a month."

"That'd do it," Crawford said.

"Whose idea was that?" Kayley asked, also sounding merely curious.

When he looked up and met her gaze, he knew what his answer would tell her. That it would show her he'd once had a normal, everyday life, with parents doing their best to teach him. Which only made it seem, to him at least, that going so far off the rails was his own fault, and his alone.

"My father," he said.

She held his gaze for a silent moment before she said softly, "I'm sorry he couldn't hang on to who he was. But I'm glad you're stronger."

He gaped at her, aware on some level that he'd spent a lot of time doing that since he'd arrived on her doorstep. "Stronger? I freaking went to prison, Kayley."

"And survived. And came out with your sense of principle intact."

"Principle?"

"The thing that made you give the locket back. You hung on to that, despite everything."

"You don't know that," he said, still unable to process the amount of faith she clearly had in him. He sounded as incredulous as he felt at this moment. He was vaguely aware that Crawford was watching them, but the man said nothing, didn't intervene or try to get them back on track. Which seemed odd, but he couldn't focus on that now.

"Yes, I do." She said it so serenely that he knew she believed it to the core.

"How?"

She smiled at him, and he felt an odd sort of flutter in his chest. "Because the very first thing you did when you got out was come to pay what you thought was a debt. It wasn't, it isn't, but you thought so, and you did."

Trip tried to speak, but the words weren't there. He could only look at her. And wonder how on earth he'd wound up lucky enough to have her so firmly on his side.

And *lucky* was not a word he often used about himself.

Chapter Seventeen

Rafe had stayed quiet through their conversation, although he had also stayed present. Kayley could sense him watching, taking in, but he said nothing. She remembered again Hayley telling her he was the most reticent and laconic of all of the Foxworth people here—probably in all the offices, Quinn had added wryly—but that he was getting better. That they were in essence forcing him to, by leaving him in charge when they had to go somewhere.

She was curious about the man, but right now her focus was, and had to be, on Trip. He'd had so much dropped on him, and she could sense he was having trouble processing it all. For the first time, she really thought about what it must be like, going from a totally controlled, endlessly the same life to out here in the world where, by comparison, chaos reigned. No wonder some people who were released actually wanted to go back.

But not Trip. She wouldn't let that happen, or even occur to him.

As if you can control what the man thinks. What any man thinks.

She shoved away that inner voice. Maybe she couldn't, but she could try. She had to try. And the best way to do that was to help him start a new life, and to make it as easy as it could be made. And Foxworth could help. Of that she was certain.

"Will you let Detective Dunbar help?" she asked.

"Do I have a choice?" His tone wasn't just sour. It held the ring of someone who hadn't had choices about much of anything for a long time.

Kayley glanced at Rafe. She'd learned a lot about what they did from Hayley, but not about how they did it. This was going to have to come from Foxworth.

"We don't force anyone to do anything," Rafe said, stepping in at last. "We do, however, point out what we think is the quickest and best plan of attack to resolve your situation."

"To bring in a cop who'll probably start looking for ways to put me back in prison, because he'll think I'm still part of Ruffle's gang."

Rafe studied him for a moment. Kayley held her breath. Then the intimidating man said, in an almost amused tone she never would have expected to hear from him, "I'm thinking the fact that ol' Ruffle put out a hit on you is pretty solid proof you're not."

Trip started to speak, then stopped, giving Rafe a side-ways look, as if he hadn't thought about it quite like that.

"Foxworth is vouching for you," Rafe added. "That carries a great deal of weight with Dunbar." Kayley saw Trip's jaw tighten, and wondered if he'd ever had anyone vouch for him in his adult life. "And he—" Rafe nodded toward Cutter "—will seal the deal."

"A cop will believe your dog?" Trip sounded incredulous. Even Kayley wondered at that; she knew the dog was different, special, but...

"He has firsthand experience with Cutter's...expertise," Rafe said. Kayley got the feeling there was much more to that statement under the surface. "But in the end, it's your call."

Trip looked as if he didn't quite believe that. "You're saying that if I don't want you to, you won't call him in?"

"It'll make things harder, and probably slower, but we're doing this to help you, not us."

Kayley watched Trip anxiously as he stared at Rafe. He was obviously having a difficult time believing any of this. Knowing what she knew of his history, she wasn't surprised. And then he looked at her, and she saw something in his gaze that made her speak.

"I know it's hard to trust anyone or anything, after what you've been through." She tried to put understanding into her voice. "It's a very big leap."

Silence spun out for a moment, but then, his voice low and a little rough, he said, "I trust you."

"And I trust Foxworth," she said simply.

For a moment longer he held her gaze, until she felt as if she were swimming in the dark green depths of his eyes. She saw the doubts there, the worry, even a touch of fear. But he didn't look away, as if he thought she held the answer to all of those. And in that moment, she couldn't look away, even though the feelings were almost overpowering.

Then he let out a short breath and looked back at Rafe. "All right. Call your cop."

He sounded like a man surrendering. And Kayley felt a rush of tangled emotions, an ache at that note of giving up, dismay at the resignation, and above all amazement at the simple fact that he clearly thought this was likely to end with him back in trouble, maybe even back in jail again somehow. But he was going to do it anyway.

Because he trusted her.

That realization stirred her up inside in ways she

couldn't even name. As did the next couple of hours, when they went back to her place to pick up his things and move them to Foxworth.

She knew it was the wisest course, for both his protection and hers, but she had the feeling her house was going to feel terribly empty when he was gone. And she was afraid she would feel the same way. Empty. How had that happened in just a few days? How had he so filled the place that it already felt hollow just knowing he would be gone? Had it really only been Monday that she'd opened the door to see him standing there, hesitant and wary? At least that seemed to have abated a bit. He was still wary, but the hesitancy had lessened.

Because he trusted her.

When he came out of the guest room with his backpack—something that should be far too small to hold everything a person owned—she almost wished she'd taken Rafe up on his offer to follow them here and take Trip back to Foxworth. But she hadn't, because she'd foolishly wanted a few more minutes alone with him. She wasn't sure why. He hadn't said more than ten words the entire drive back here, but it was better than driving back alone.

She stood there looking at him as he shifted the pack, looking as if he felt as awkward as she did. And suddenly words tumbled out.

"You'll still be there in the morning, when the detective comes?"

"I said I would." His voice was gruff, edgy again.

"I… I could come back over. Be there." His gaze lifted to her face. And she couldn't read his expression. "Unless that would make it worse," she ended rather lamely.

"Don't you have work to do?"

"Nothing that requires me to be here. I keep Fridays

light." She tried to smile. "What's the point of being your own boss if you can't set your own schedule?"

He let out a breath, and his eyes went distant, as if he were seeing something else, someplace else.

"Your own boss," he murmured. She understood his tone of wonder; he hadn't been his own boss for a long time. Maybe ever.

But he still hadn't answered. "I won't come if you'd rather I didn't, but… I'd like to."

Looking as if it had just occurred to him, he said, "Shouldn't you be asking Crawford about that?"

"You should call him Rafe," she said. "And I already asked."

He drew back slightly. "You did? And he said it was okay?"

"I did. He did."

She tried a smile, feeling a little distressed at how obviously disconcerting this all was for him. But he'd get used to it. The longer he was back in a normal life, the easier it would get, surely.

A normal life? A lifetime criminal wants to kill him!

She supposed, in a way, she was in part responsible for that. If she hadn't gone to Foxworth, if she hadn't convinced Quinn to help him, then Ruffle would have no reason to come after Trip for payback.

And Trip would have done longer, rougher time, probably someplace she wouldn't have been able to see him as often, if at all. And he might have come out a completely changed man, hardened beyond recognition. Permanently in Ruffle's mold.

But he wasn't. She was sure of it. Because a man truly like Oliver Ruff would never have come here to thank her. Would never have felt the need. And he certainly would never have returned a little girl's precious memento of her dead mother, just because he knew how that loss felt.

No, Trip was who she'd always thought he was, a guy who'd in essence suffered a doubly tragic loss, the death of his mother and his father's subsequent descent into cold cruelty and abuse. Abuse he'd tolerated for fear he'd lose that parent, too.

Kayley thought he probably would have been better off himself if he'd walked away from the disaster his father had become. But that, too, proved Trip was who she'd thought he was; he hadn't abandoned his father, not as he had been abandoned. Because he wasn't that kind of man, no matter what Ruffle's world had sucked him into.

She stood there silently, waiting. She wouldn't push. He'd spent too long not having any choice about where he went, what he did, or who he was with. She wasn't about to take those choices away from him again.

He let out a long, audible breath that sounded as if he'd been holding it. He was staring at his shoes again. That was one habit he'd picked up that she wouldn't mind seeing gone.

"Come," he said. Then, after a tight-looking twitch at one corner of his mouth, he added, "Please."

"Thank you," she said.

The twitch came again, only this time it almost seemed like the beginning of a smile. And he looked up at her. "Isn't that what I should be saying?"

"The thank-you is for trusting me."

This time he held her gaze. "How does it feel to be the only one?" he asked softly.

She was so distracted by that steady look, the softness of his voice, and the almost-smile, it took her a second to get there.

The only one he trusted.

She couldn't really describe how that made her feel. Pleased. Flattered. Honored.

And compelled to make sure it didn't stay that way.

Chapter Eighteen

Trip woke up with a start, but didn't move. He simply stayed still, his brain running through the process he'd gotten used to, trying to ascertain what had awakened him. First, he didn't sense anyone too close. That made things easier. The work camp might have been minimum security, but that didn't mean some scary guys hadn't managed to get there. Waking up to find someone hovering near your bunk wasn't a good thing.

And then, of course, there had been the days at Kayley's place. That safe, quiet little house where he should have been able to relax, knowing that if he woke up to someone in the room, it would most likely have been her. Somehow that wasn't relaxing at all.

But he was at Foxworth now. He opened his eyes. The room seemed still dark, but when he rolled over to look toward the single window in the surprisingly spacious and comfortable room, he saw the light beginning. Sunrise wasn't officially until about 6:30 a.m., but it started to get light well before that. Which he knew because inside, they were already up and working.

But here at Foxworth, he didn't really know what was normal. Was it a sound that had interrupted the odd dream about chasing something unseen and unknown through an endless forest of evergreens? Which in itself was strange. When he had dreams like that, they were more likely to be about being the chasee.

But then, that he'd slept at all was strange. Sitting up now in the still-dark room, he rubbed at his eyes. He was feeling tumbled, out of control, like a pebble being battered and rolled by high surf. He'd been warned, by the pre-release counselor, that feeling like this was common at first, but he'd foolishly believed that the pure relief of being out would overpower anything else.

Wrong again, Callen.

And at the feel of a cold nose nudging his hand, the other memory jolted back.

Cutter.

"Hey," he said, not knowing what else to do. The dog nudged him again. That at least he understood. He stroked the dark fur on the animal's head. It was as oddly soothing as it had been before. And he felt calmer. Crazy.

It had seemed strange when the dog had followed him in here last night. He'd spent a ridiculous amount of time trying to decide whether to leave the door open for the dog to get out, or close it. He'd decided on closing it because he knew he had no chance at all of sleeping if he didn't. And the dog didn't seem at all disturbed about being closed in here with him. He assumed if the dog needed out, he'd let him know, as Crawford had assured him.

Maybe that was why he'd slept. Because he'd known the dog was here. Maybe he'd felt...safer.

He heard the slightest of sounds, and now that he was sitting up and oriented, he guessed he'd been right about that being what had awakened him.

Kitchen and coffeepot.

Maybe it was Crawford. He looked like a guy who didn't sleep in much. He said he bunked out in the other building, but maybe there was no kitchen there, and he needed coffee.

Which was not a bad idea. He could use some serious caffeine himself. But he just sat there on the bed, still adjusting to the idea that he could simply get up and do what he wanted—or not do anything if he wanted. Choice was something he'd done without for a very long time.

Finally he rolled out, pulled on his jeans and the denim shirt he'd washed just yesterday at Kayley's. He looked around at the quiet room that was in fact nicer than any place he'd ever stayed in, other than Kayley's guest room. Except maybe his childhood bedroom, which his mother had furnished and decorated with such care and humor—that wall of superheroes had been the envy of his friends.

The inner ache at the thought of her was still there, and he knew it always would be. But the slamming grief that took his breath away happened less often, and he recovered faster than he had in the days when it had practically put him on his knees.

And wouldn't she be proud of you now, Callen?

He shoved the thought aside and yanked at the door handle at the same time. Cutter was at his heels, but once the door was fully open, he trotted past him and out into the big room. Trip followed.

It was Crawford in the kitchen, doing exactly what he'd suspected. Coffeepot was already filling.

The man didn't even look up before asking, "Wake you?"

"I'm not sure," he said tactfully, certain he didn't want to irritate the guy with an accusation.

That got him a look. "I figured you'd be used to hitting the floor before now."

"I...don't know what time it is."

Crawford glanced at his bare wrist. "No phone, either?"

He shook his head. "Not in the budget," he muttered.

"Five to six," Crawford said, with a gesture toward the time readout on the oven against the far wall.

He tried for a smile, wasn't sure if he made it. "I'm late, then."

"Five-thirty reveille? Or earlier?"

"Weekdays four thirty."

"Coffee's ready, and it's a bit lighter than paint remover again today, in your honor."

Trip managed at least a half smile this time. "Not sure I don't need the paint remover."

"Tomorrow, then." Crawford reached to an upper cupboard, got down a second mug, and filled it. He slid it across the counter toward Trip. Then he gestured toward the fridge and the cupboards next to it. "We're pretty well stocked. Anything in particular you want, write it down and somebody'll pick it up."

Choices. Again, choices.

"Feels strange?" Crawford asked.

"Yes. Very. Sir," he added, not sure what else to say. He picked up the mug and took a long swallow. It was hot and hit hard. Just like he wanted.

Crawford took a smaller sip himself before saying, "In a different sort of way, it was like that when I left the Marines."

Trip thought about that, and decided it was probably true. As he'd just thought, choices. Something you had less of in either case.

"Why did you?" Trip asked, since the guy seemed open to talking. "Leave, I mean? Sir," he added again, since something seemed necessary.

"We started to go in different directions. And Quinn offered me this." He had that twitch that was almost a smile again. "He was an Army Ranger, but I like him anyway."

Trip tried to smile back, but it was a little wobbly. "I thought about that. Joining up. Back when...things fell apart." He grimaced. "I should have done it."

"Back then, I'd have agreed. Now, not so much," Crawford said. "But it's time to look ahead, not back. You have a plan?"

Trip hesitated. He'd learned a lot about self-preservation, and instinctively knew it would not be wise to lie to this man, or try to feed him a line. He covered his hesitation by taking a seat on one of the stools pulled up to the counter. Crawford waited, leaning back against the counter by the coffeepot, working on his own brew.

"My plan was to get to Kayley and thank her for everything she did," he finally said frankly. "After that... no, not much of a plan."

"First things first," Crawford said, surprising him. He would have expected an opinion on how stupid he was not to have thought beyond that. "You stick by the people who stick by you," the man added, as if he'd read his thoughts.

"She did," Trip said, letting some of the wonderment he still felt into his voice. "What she went through, the paperwork, the long drives, sending stuff, always making sure I had mail, worrying about me—"

He broke off when the cell phone on the counter sounded a notification. Crawford set down his mug to pick it up. He tapped the screen, and when an app opened, he read what it displayed.

"She still is," he said, indicating the screen. He tapped in a response—efficiently enough, despite the Texan's jab—and a moment later another text came in.

"Well, that makes the morning nicer," Crawford murmured as he responded. Then he looked up at Trip. And this time the smile was fully formed. "She'll be here in an hour. She's bringing breakfast."

Trip looked at the clock on the oven. A little after six now.

"Definitely still worried about you," Crawford said as he took up the coffeepot again and refilled his mug. Then he looked at Trip. "Top that off?"

"Yes. Thanks, sir."

He filled it nearly to the rim, set the pot back on the maker, then looked back at Trip. "You just ran through your quota of 'sirs,'" he said. "Rafe'll do for you, too."

"I...all right. Rafe."

"You're a lucky guy, Trip. To have a woman like Kayley care that much about you."

"Yeah. I know," he said softly.

"You've got somebody else caring now, too," Rafe said, with a gesture of his coffee mug toward Cutter, who was now plopped on the floor, practically jammed up against the legs of the stool. "Let's just say I don't envy anyone who tries to get to you through him."

Trip gave the dog on the floor a considering look. As if sensing his gaze, Cutter looked up at him. But he did it by tilting his head way back, in essence looking at him upside down. For some reason that made Trip smile, which in turn, who knows why, made the dog plop his head back down again. As if all he'd needed was that smile.

He was, no doubt, totally wrong about it. Most of what he'd known about dogs as an adult was to avoid houses that had them when it had been time to pick targets, but he couldn't deny the feeling.

He'd finished his second cup of coffee before Cutter got up and trotted over to a door at the back of the big room. Trip assumed it led outside, since there were more towels and a basket of tennis balls that looked a bit worse for wear sitting beside it. The dog sat in front of the door, then looked back. Not at the guy he knew, but at him.

"Might as well get used to it," Rafe said, with a hint of a humor in his voice that didn't quite make it to his face. "He's yours for the duration."

"I...okay." He got up, still doubtful.

"You can either let him out on his own, or go with him."

"He won't run off?"

"Not unless he needs to for your sake."

Trip blinked. "What?"

"If he takes off, it'll be because some aspect of your situation is here." Trip just looked at the man, searching for some sign he was putting him on. There was nothing. The rugged face was impassive, the seen-too-much eyes unreadable. But then he seemed to relent, and with a half shrug, added, "Just trust him. I'll be out in the other building if you need anything."

In the end, Trip stepped outside with the dog, for a very simple reason.

Because he could.

Chapter Nineteen

Kayley was barely out of the car when Cutter came racing around the big green building toward her. Head down, tail out, and his tongue lolling happily, as if nothing else in his world mattered except getting to her as fast as he could. It made her smile widely, and she thought, as she often had since she'd realized she'd created a working concern that would allow her to continue to work at home, that she should get a dog of her own. She hadn't had one since childhood, but had never lost the longing.

She bent to greet the delighted animal, but straightened when she caught sight of someone jogging around the corner of the building pretty much on the same path the dog had taken.

Trip.

It was Trip, and he was grinning.

She couldn't describe how that made her feel. To see that expression on his face, to mentally compare it to the hollow, haunted look she'd confronted when she'd first opened her door to him. He looked like the drop-dead gorgeous guy she'd first met, with the incredible eyes and the hair so perfect everyone teased him about it.

She bent to Cutter once more. "You, my furry friend, are a miracle worker," she murmured, stroking the dark

fur, feeling the warmth and soothing that was unbelievable but unmistakable.

The grin had faded by the time Trip reached her, but
he was still smiling.

"That dog," he said as he came to a halt, "is something else."

"Besides a dog? I wouldn't argue that. Liam says his
family raises dogs, has for years, and he's never known
another one like Cutter."

"He did the whole Lassie thing when you got here.
Barked, tail wagging, then ran a few steps, looked back
at me, and didn't move until I started to follow, then ran
again." He gave her a look that seemed...softer somehow.
"He knew a friend was here."

It seemed so hard for him to admit he had a friend.
And once again she reminded herself that's all she was
to him. If he ever found out how she'd yearned for him,
back in those days when he'd been with Debra, he'd probably be totally embarrassed.

So he can't ever know. Remember that.

Briskly, she turned and leaned back into the car. She
picked up the bag and the small foil pan she'd brought,
and turned in time to catch a strange look on his face. But
he said nothing, so she just handed him the pan.

"I'll carry the muffins, you can do the rolls." He stared
down at the foil baking tin, then looked up at her again.
She grimaced. "What can I say? I bake when I'm worried. It helps."

"You...made these?"

"They're not as good as the ones at the bakery over
in—"

"They look incredible. I haven't had a cinnamon roll
in...forever, it feels like."

"Then they're all yours. Maybe save one for Rafe, though. If he even indulges in such things."

As they started walking toward the door, Cutter trotting ahead, Trip said, "I get the feeling he doesn't indulge in much."

She sighed. "I don't like even thinking about some of the things he's had to do. So that the rest of us can live our safe, secure lives."

"Or ruin them," he said sourly.

She put on her best imitation of her mother's most instructive tone. "You're far too young to consider your life ruined."

She saw a slight smile flicker. And his tone was a bit lighter when he said, "I don't know. I feel pretty darn old these days."

"You're younger than me," she pointed out just as Cutter reached the door ahead of them, rose up, and batted at the door pad.

Trip gave her a startled look as the door swung open. "I am?"

She felt her cheeks heat slightly. Was it odd, or too personal, that she knew that? She tried to make it a joke. "Debra said she was cradle robbing, but I thought it was a joke. Then when I met you I was surprised, and I asked. She usually went for older men."

"Men who could spend money on her in the way to which she was accustomed, I think the saying goes."

"Yes," Kayley admitted. As they stepped inside, she added sadly, "She wasn't always that way."

He gave a sharp snap of his head, as if shaking off even the memory of the woman who couldn't shed him fast enough. Then, as the Foxworth door swung shut behind them, he asked, "Just how much younger am I than you?"

She managed a credible grin at him then. "Oh, a lot. Almost six."

His brows lowered. "Bull," he said. "You can't be."

"Months," she said.

For a frozen second he just looked at her. But then he rolled his eyes and let out a smothered chuckle. "Walked into that one, didn't I?"

"You did," she said, and the joy she felt seemed all out of proportion to the silly joke that had brought it on. "Where's Rafe?" she asked as she set the bag of freshly baked muffins on the counter.

"He said he'd be in the other building." Trip looked slightly bemused. He nodded toward Cutter, who was gazing toward the baked goods on the counter, his nose twitching. "I seem to have inherited him while I'm here."

"Nice to have a guard dog, under the circumstances."

"Among other things, according to Rafe. He—"

He broke off as Cutter jumped to his feet, letting out an odd series of barks. A short, sharp yip, a sort of half yowl, half bark, and another yip. Trip stared at the dog, and she heard him murmur, "A short, a long, and a short."

She remembered what Rafe had told them about his own particular bark. Morse code for *R*. She was amazed, and grinning as she said, "He must be coming."

A moment later the tall, rangy man walked in the back door.

"Heard your car," he said after greeting Kayley.

"And you were properly announced," she said, bending to plant a kiss on the dog's head.

"You're not really saying he knows Morse code?" Trip asked.

Rafe gave the eyebrow equivalent of a shrug. "Coincidence," he said. "Nobody else has a bark that matches their initial."

"Or maybe you're just that special to him," Kayley said.

Something flickered in his gaze, as if he found the idea of being special to anyone, even a dog, hard to believe. No wonder he was the one they worried about the most. And maybe that was why she felt a particular pleasure when the man took the cinnamon roll Trip offered him, and complimented her on them after his first bite.

As did Trip, who seemed to hold his own first bite in his mouth for a long time, as if savoring every flavor, from the dough to the cinnamon to the frosting.

"Wow," he said when he finally swallowed.

And once more she found herself pondering what it must have been like to do without something so simple for so long. She thought the expression on his face pretty well demonstrated it. Again she ached for him, but quashed it with the knowledge that it was over now, and her belief in his determination that he would never go down that path again.

Cutter seemed once again determined that she and Trip sit next to each other on the big couch that could easily have given them four feet between them. And she couldn't help remembering the tales Hayley had told her, how the dog had been the reason she'd ended up with Quinn, and their operative Teague with Laney, and Liam with Ria. She'd thought them just cute stories, but there was no denying what the dog did every time they went into the Foxworth great room to sit down.

Or maybe you're imagining it because you want it. Maybe that's just Cutter's spot on the couch. Maybe his goal is to keep you off it, not drive you and Trip to sit together.

Certain she'd arrived at the proper conclusion—and the safest one—she tried to ignore the simple fact that neither she nor Trip had done the obvious and chosen to sit in one of the individual chairs around the big coffee table. She even dared to hope that Trip hadn't done that because he wanted to be close to her. Not, of course, for any reason based in attraction, but because he needed her support. After all, before long he'd be facing a sheriff's detective, someone with the power to send him right back into the nightmare he'd just escaped.

She felt a moment's qualm that she'd gotten him into this, but the bottom line was she trusted Foxworth. And she believed Trip when he said he'd done nothing that wasn't already on his record, nothing that would make the detective take action. So this was all for the best, to help him put this messed up chapter of his life behind him and start fresh. What she'd been waiting and wishing for ever since the day they'd led him away in handcuffs.

Cutter's head came up off the couch, and he let out another distinctive combination of barks and other sounds that made Rafe get to his feet.

"Brett's here," he said.

She felt Trip tense beside her. She reached over and took his hand, squeezing it in support.

"It'll be all right," she said softly.

He didn't look at her. Didn't say anything. But he didn't pull away.

And after a moment, his fingers curled around hers.

Chapter Twenty

Detective Brett Dunbar was both like and unlike any cop Trip had ever encountered. Tall, lean, strong, putting the lie to the touch of gray at his temples. He had a casual, unhurried sort of air about him, belied by the shadows in his eyes. Echoes of grim things witnessed and not easily forgotten. Trip had seen eyes like that before, on both sides of the badge. He had the feeling others might see those same shadows in his own eyes.

That he'd responded first thing the morning after Foxworth had called told him that what Crawford had said about them carrying weight with the man was true. But his actual arrival hadn't been a surprise, thanks to Cutter, who not only announced it—with one of those customized barks?—but ran to the door and batted the metal pad to open it well before Dunbar walked in. The dog greeted the man enthusiastically, and it was apparently returned as the tall man bent to scratch behind both canine ears in greeting.

He wore a knee-length dark coat that was sparkling with the raindrops that had begun to fall again. He pulled it off and hung it on the rack inside the door with ease and familiarity. Trip noticed that he wore not dress shoes but lug-soled boots with the dressier slacks and button-down shirt. An adaptation to the surroundings, he sup-

posed, and had a sudden vision of the guy trekking deep
into the woods after some bad guy.

Like you, you mean?

He watched as the man greeted Crawford with a nod,
then turned to look at Kayley. "Nice to see you again,
Kayley," he said.

"I wasn't sure you'd remember me," she answered with
a laugh. "We barely met at Liam's engagement party."

As if anyone could forget her. Trip had to fight off
memories of that moment when she'd turned to get the
things she'd baked out of her car, when she'd bent over
and presented him with the sweetest of sights, her trim,
taut backside in snug jeans. He was having more and
more trouble convincing himself that the long enforced
dry spell was the reason for his instant, fierce response
to her.

"It's a knack," Dunbar said.

Of course it was. He was a cop. And Trip was fully
aware of that as the man's attention shifted to him. It took
more than a little effort to hold that penetrating gray gaze.

Dunbar smiled. And now, up close, Trip saw something else in those eyes, a kind of happiness, holding the
shadows at bay. He wondered if it had something to do
with the new-looking wedding ring on his finger.

"And you must be the locket guy," Dunbar said.

He blinked. He hadn't expected that, either the quiet
tone or the smile. Because it wasn't the kind he'd seen
on cops' faces before, wasn't one of triumph and catching that bad guy they'd been chasing, or sneaky, as they
tried to trick that guy into admitting something, or even
the kind he'd seen when they'd put some pieces together
to realize who had committed some crime. No, this was
a genuine smile, a friendly one.

"I...yeah." It was all he could manage at that moment.

"Brett Dunbar," the man said, holding out a hand.

A cop wanted to shake hands with him? Like he would with anyone else he'd meet, as if he hadn't just gotten out of prison a few days ago?

It took him a moment to respond. "Trip Callen," he said belatedly.

The handshake wasn't overpowering, nor was it weak. It was just…normal. As if they were two ordinary guys who would be dealing with each other meeting for the first time.

"I lightened up on the coffee for you," Crawford said.

"You mean it won't take paint off today?" the cop said, grinning at the other man, who only shrugged, but one corner of his mouth was twitching.

As Dunbar got himself a cup of coffee—clearly this place was familiar ground—Trip tried to think if he'd seen a happy, cheerful cop in the last ten years. He didn't think so.

The man joined them in the seating area, taking one of the single chairs. And for the fourth time, Cutter did his little maneuver, pushing Trip to sit next to Kayley. He gave the dog a wry look.

Notice you're not trying to push the cop around, dog.

As if he'd heard and understood the thought, the damn dog grinned at him. Again.

And when Trip looked up, he saw Dunbar watching at the two of them, him and Kayley, with an odd expression on his face. He glanced at Crawford, who gave him a raised brow and a nod. Then, unexpectedly, Dunbar grinned, as if an unspoken message had been clearly received.

Trip had to remind himself that this was what it was like among friends who knew each other well, this kind of communication, often without words. And even as he thought it he realized how, despite the amount of time he'd spent with Ruffle and his crew, he'd never felt that kind of camaraderie with them. He didn't think any of them did either; everyone was too busy covering their own backside to open up in that way.

"So, what do we have?" Dunbar asked.

Rafe told Dunbar the story. Trip was a little amazed at how the man boiled down everything that had happened to a few concise sentences. And more amazed at how he said it with utter conviction. The man believed him. He really believed him when he said he was done with that life. Even knowing his record, and how he'd spent all that time running with that crew, he believed him.

Or he believed him because Kayley did. That was more likely. And even more amazing, that she would risk this relationship she had with people she obviously liked and admired, for his sake. What if he blew it? What if he slipped back into the old ways? What if—

No!

He stopped the thoughts, the runaway train of his own fears, before it could build up steam. He would not slip back. He might not know where he would go or what he would do, but he knew what he wouldn't. Not for anything would he squander this chance. Not for anything would he return to the life that had landed him in such chaos.

Not for anything would he let Kayley down.

Trip was surprised when Brett's first question was about the night Quinn had caught them in the act, trying to break into the house he was staying in.

"I'm curious. That crew didn't usually do strings of burgs in one neighborhood in one night," the cop said. "Why the double that night?"

He should have known the guy would have done his

homework before coming. He wondered what else he knew. Maybe he'd encountered members of the crew personally. Maybe even arrested some.

Trip really didn't want to talk about that side of things, but he'd agreed to meeting with the cop, so he couldn't back out now.

"Ruffle had rules," he said, and when he saw Dunbar's eyebrows rise at the nickname Kayley had gotten them all using, he glanced at her. She was smiling, although looking down into her mug of coffee. He looked back at Dunbar. "He did a lot of research. He was very computer-savvy, especially when it came to picking targets. He put out strict orders, never the same place twice, and at least three months between hitting neighborhoods. But that night, he saw that open window in that second house, and... I guess he couldn't resist the temptation."

"And therein lies the downfall of many a man," Dunbar said, rather philosophically for a cop.

It sure as hell was mine. "He expected some oblivious citizen stupid enough to leave a window wide open all night."

"And unluckily for him, instead he got Quinn Foxworth. Just as Quinn planned all along," Dunbar said, and there was no denying that his expression was one of satisfaction. And given everything, Trip couldn't hold that against him.

He drew in a long breath, then met that steady gaze head-on. "And, I realize now, luckily for me."

"Now?" Dunbar asked.

"He didn't know," Kayley said. "Until I told him after he...got here—" she'd been about to say *got out*, Trip knew, but had changed it at the last second "—he had no idea what Quinn had done, how he'd stepped in."

"Because he gave back Emily's locket." Dunbar said it

familiarly. As if he knew the girl. Maybe he did; seemed he was pretty tight with these people.

"And he did it because he knew how she felt. That's why—" Kayley broke off suddenly, and when she stole a glance at Trip, her cheeks were pink. "I'm sorry. It's not my place to talk about that."

You can have any place you want.

Trip gave himself an inward shake. It didn't work very well. Just as telling himself it was simply that he'd done without for a very long time wasn't explaining why he was reacting to her this way.

Dunbar looked back to him. "What did you think when he tried that second burglary?"

He stared at the man. No one, especially no cop, had ever asked or cared what he'd thought about that night. When in fact it had been, to him, momentous. He hesitated in answering, but he'd said he'd do this. And he had to start as he meant to go on. Keeping his word.

"I thought he was crazy. But I already thought that, before he headed for that open window. That night was when I knew." He took yet another deep breath, then plunged ahead. He doubted the man would believe him, or care, but it was the truth, and that's what he'd vowed to tell. "I was done. I knew, after he beat that old man almost to death. That poor old man who was already really sick, judging by all the medication on the counter, which of course Ruff—Ruffle—grabbed. I knew that I couldn't be a part of that anymore."

He heard Kayley's breath catch, and a moment later felt the warmth of her as her fingers wrapped around the hand that was closest to her. Involuntarily his own fingers curled around hers, and it was amazing the strength he took from the small contact.

"I didn't see that in any of the reports or supplementals I read," Dunbar said. Trip knew enough to know that supplemental reports were where cops recorded things that were other than concrete evidence and strict facts.

"I never told anyone." From Kayley's touch he drew the strength to keep facing the man as he added, "I assumed no one would believe me. They'd write it off as... as..."

"A foxhole conversion?" Crawford suggested, his tone wry.

"Yeah," Trip said.

Dunbar seemed to consider this before saying, "I heard another inmate tried to provoke you into a fight right before you got out."

Trip blinked, surprised they knew even this. "He was trying to mess this up. Me getting out, I mean."

Dunbar's glance shifted. "So you didn't bite. Even after he gave you that eye."

With all his nerves on edge, and now that it wasn't hurting much, he'd forgotten about what he looked like, with that bruise fading to ugly shades of yellow and almost green.

"I'd have taken worse," he said, his jaw tight.

Dunbar glanced at Crawford, and nodded. Then he looked back to Trip. "Let's get down to it," he said. "I'll need that list of people, so I can see if any of them have had contact with... Ruffle directly. Then we'll go to one step removed, and further if necessary. And I'll run the names past some people. We need to know if he's got the juice to arrange a hit even from prison across the state. Rafe says he left a relative in charge?"

"His cousin, Boyd," Trip said.

"Strong enough?" Dunbar asked.

"Strong, yes. Smart? Not so much," Trip said with a shrug.

"But you have a feeling." Dunbar said it without doubt. It wasn't even really a question.

Trip took another deep breath to steady himself. It felt so odd, to be talking to a cop like this. Not right, but not wrong, either. "He's intimidating enough to maintain control, for a while anyway."

"Top of the list, then. I'll talk to our gang unit, see what they know." He glanced at Crawford. "You got him covered?"

The taciturn man nodded. "He's going to stay here, for the moment."

"Better than a safe house," Dunbar said as he got to his feet.

A little boggled that the cop would even consider he rated a safe house, Trip stood up as well. Dunbar studied him for a moment, then said quietly, "I trust Foxworth, so I'll back you. As long as you stay straight. Weave even a little, and I'll take you down."

"Assumed," Trip said, holding the man's gaze with no small effort.

Dunbar nodded. Another glance at Crawford as he said, "I'll be in touch."

Trip noticed the man walked by Cutter as he left, giving the dog another scratch behind the ears as he passed. And then he was gone, leaving Trip feeling exhausted, and more than a bit stunned.

He'd just sat here talking to a cop for who knows how long, and he was still free. His mind hearkened back to the days when that likely wouldn't have been the result. And yet again he swore to himself, and silently to Kayley, that those days would never come again.

Chapter Twenty-One

Saturday morning.

Saturday morning in freedom.

Trip woke up early again, and lay listening to the quiet. It had never been truly quiet in the dorm. Somebody was always moving, rustling around, or worst of all, snoring. There'd been a couple of guys who, as Robber put it, could wake his dead grandfather.

Cutter, on the other hand, slept quietly. Trip knew that because the dog had never left his side. Even now he could feel the warmth of the dog curled up beside him. After Kayley had—reluctantly it seemed, although he feared that might be wishful thinking, something he'd thought burned out of him forever—gone home last night, and Crawford had left, he'd wandered the building. Cutter had been beside him at every step. If he stopped, just to look at something, the dog seemed to have a time limit before he nudged his hand for a scratch behind the ears. Which in turn had that odd calming effect.

He hadn't gone upstairs because that seemed off-limits, although no one had actually said so. But he'd inspected the living area, figuring if he was going to be here a while, he might as well know where everything was. The big flat-screen was tempting, and had him thinking about movies that might take his mind off all this. He inspected the far wall, which was mostly book-cases, holding everything from classics to popular fiction and kids' books, making him wonder who all had taken refuge here.

The kitchen had everything necessary, and a couple of gadgets whose function he wasn't sure of. The cupboards and fridge were stocked with basics from soup to eggs to bacon, and the freezer held meat and other delights he hadn't seen much of for a long time, including ice cream.

Most importantly, the coffee maker was straightfor-ward enough. As he thought it he yawned, as if the idea of caffeine had triggered it. And as if that were a signal, Cutter's head came up. The dog had never hesitated to jump up on the bed with him last night, and what Trip had thought would make his night restless had in fact been the opposite.

Now the dog seemed to wiggle forward a little, until he could lower his head onto Trip's chest. The faint light reflected off the dog's dark eyes, which were fastened on him as if he were the most interesting thing the animal had ever seen. And since it seemed the only thing to do, he lifted a hand to pet him.

And there it was again, that…comfort, he decided, for lack of any better description. He was really something, this dog. On the thought Cutter made a tiny sound, not a whine or whimper, but something that sounded cra-zily like he was trying to talk. Trip's brow furrowed, then it hit him.

"You need to go outside?" he asked.

Cutter's dark head came up sharply. And he was instantly on his feet and jumping down from the bed. Which was as definite an answer as he could get, and Trip was smiling as he sat up.

He dressed quickly, not sure how much he should

hurry. He paused for a split second to start that coffee maker Crawford had set up last night, but hustled after that since he didn't know how urgent the dog's need was.

And once again, despite Crawford saying letting him out and in was all that was necessary, he went out with the animal into the predawn light, simply because he could. It was a heady feeling, being able to walk outside of his own volition, with no one around, no one watching, no fence marking his limits. He could, if he wanted, just keep walking, and no one would chase him down, hunt him with dogs very much like this clever one at his side now.

Of course, one of Ruffle's old crew could put a permanent end to that if they found him. If, as Dunbar had asked, Ruffle still had the pull to give the command and have it immediately obeyed.

Once his business was done, Cutter came trotting back, and stayed by his side as if on a leash. Trip walked through the meadow, even in the faint light noticing the daffodils already poking up out of the earth. His mother's favorite flower, for that very reason, she'd told him. They were the assurance that spring was coming. The plants were everywhere, and he couldn't even imagine what this all would look like when they were in full bloom. A yellow sea, maybe.

Cutter nudged at him, as if trying to turn him around, toward the gravel drive. Wondering if maybe someone—Kayley?—was coming, although that seemed unlikely at this early hour, he turned and looked. But there was nothing but the empty parking area, and the trees between them and the road. Smothering the feeling of letdown, as if he'd really expected Kayley to be showing up even before the crack of dawn, he looked down at his furry companion.

"What's up, dog?"

Cutter sat, practically on his feet. And suddenly Trip was thinking of yesterday, when the dog had taken off at a run to greet Kayley.

If he takes off, it'll be because some aspect of your situation is here.

Crawford's words echoed in his head. He supposed in one sense it was true. She was an aspect of it.

The very best aspect of it.

Even as the admission formed in his mind, a brilliant blast of light shot through the trees ahead. It flared, seemingly in all directions, lighting up the sky and the few clouds in an eruption of color. Orange, gold, even pink. He could see the actual rays as they speared through the evergreens, and above the trees the bottom side of the clouds seemed to glow. It was an amazing sight, and one he hadn't had the time, location, or inclination to be still and watch for a very long time.

Cutter had moved him to here. He'd thought of Kayley. And this incredible show had begun. He knew he was being ridiculous, but couldn't help thinking the dog had known he'd want—he needed?—to see this. At this moment. The beginning of a new day. Burgeoning hope. A new life.

Emotions he hadn't allowed himself to feel, hadn't dared unleash for fear he'd wake up back inside, all this a dream, suddenly boiled up, unstoppable. His throat, then his chest, tightened, almost unbearably. Stupidly, his eyes welled up, and he had to blink rapidly.

He was free. A free man. Out. Cut loose. No longer a prisoner.

He was also, apparently, a sap. He tried to shrug off the emotions, but they were too strong. Or he'd already lost that iron control he'd developed inside, where it was never wise to let weakness show.

Cutter leaned against his leg, hard enough that he reached down to touch the dog. And again it was there, that comfort, that ease, and suddenly he could breathe again.

Grateful, he sank down to sit on the ground beside the dog, who tilted his head to swipe his tongue over his cheek. It almost made him laugh, and the switch from those roiling feelings to amusement was so fast it almost made his head spin. He did the only thing he could manage to do. He hugged the clever creature beside him as they both sat watching the changing sky.

The sun had cleared the horizon and the show transitioned to full daylight when Cutter turned his head to look behind them. Trip looked as well, and saw Rafe walking toward the main building. He gave a casual wave, telling Trip he knew they were there. He doubted much got by the guy.

When he walked back inside, Rafe was already working on his first mugful, and had a second mug set on the counter for him. He filled it and took a long, deep swallow. Definitely a higher class of coffee than he was used to. Not that that would take much.

Cutter sat in front of the refrigerator, tilting his head way back to gaze at them. Trip found himself smiling at how comical it looked.

"Your job," Rafe said.

"Oh. Carrots." He'd forgotten. He walked over and opened one of the upper doors, and saw a bag of the small orange veggies in one of the drawers. "How many?"

"Three or so. He's not greedy. He'll let you know when he's done."

He'd never heard of a vegetable-loving dog, although

the crunchy part made sense. The dog indeed did get to his feet after three of the little orange bits, and nudged his hand in apparent thanks.

"He's...quite a dog."

"He is."

"I swear, it seemed like he...herded me around to see the sunrise out there."

"Wouldn't be the first time."

Trip blinked. "He...does that?"

"He always seems to know when you need to see the world has survived another day."

Trip hesitated, but the man seemed willing enough to talk, so he asked, "Do you live here all the time?"

"Not usually." He stopped there, but after a moment, almost as if he'd realized that was a bit short, added, "My old landlord died. His kids sold the building. Some guy from the other side who wants to remake the world his way."

Trip grimaced. "Great. Another one of those. Sorry about the landlord, though."

"Me, too. He was a good old guy."

Something belatedly struck him. "Would you normally be staying in here instead of me?"

"Nope. Relax."

"Not sure I remember how," he admitted. "And I don't feel right, staying here on your dime."

"Foxworth's dime," Rafe said, "but point taken."

Trip thought he heard a note of approval in the man's voice, but the guy was so gruff it was hard to tell. "So... is there something I can do? Around here, I mean?"

"You want chores?"

Trip was sure of the approval this time. "Something," he answered.

Rafe studied him for a moment. "Anything you were made to do before that you actually liked?"

That surprised him a little. "I…didn't mind the cleanup stuff." He grimaced. "Better than filling potholes with a road crew. All that did was make me think how long it would be before I ever got to drive a road again."

"Understandable."

"Actually, I kind of liked when we went out and planted trees on a DOC crew. At least it was outside, and felt like I was doing a good thing."

"Well, now," Rafe said, considering, "it just so happens Hayley is always looking to spruce things up, garden-wise. She wouldn't mind at all if you did a little tidying up around here."

"I'd like to do that."

"Maybe you could even plant a couple of those maple trees she's been wanting. Something about fall color or some such. Oh, and some flowery thing she wants out by the patio."

"I'd like that, too."

"Then we'll have to see about getting those arranged."

"Thanks."

"You're thanking me for making you work?"

"Giving me work," he corrected Rafe, wondering where he'd found the nerve. "Big difference."

"Work you asked for," Rafe corrected him in turn. Then, with a nod that was definitely approval, he added, "Proving you're who we think you are. Now, let's figure out breakfast."

It was crazy how praise from this essentially unknown man, working for totally unknown people, and this unusual organization, made him feel so good. So encouraged. As had sitting out there watching a sunrise, arms around a dog with a mystifying effect.

He'd landed in a very strange place. But some tiny, long-buried part of him dared to expand again.

The part that was swelling with hope.

Chapter Twenty-Two

Kayley spotted Cutter racing around the corner of the building the moment she cleared the trees. By the time she pulled the car to a halt and shut it off, he was there, dancing outside the driver's door as if he'd been waiting his whole life for her to arrive. It made her smile, and she was still smiling as she got out to greet the happy dog. And amused when he circled behind her and nudged her. Gently, but definitely. She took a step, and Cutter darted out in front of her. He looked back, went a few more steps, looked back again.

He did the whole Lassie thing when you got here...

The memory of Trip's words made her smile all over again, and she willingly followed the dog around the corner of the building.

It had taken a great deal of restraint not to show up here at Foxworth the first thing this morning. She'd had trouble concentrating on her usual Saturday morning chores, which consisted of both contacts with clients who were looking for a better position and couldn't reach out from their current workplaces, and plain and simple housework. She kept thinking about Trip, and wondering how he was doing at Foxworth, if he and Rafe were getting along okay, and if he'd even want to see her there again today.

She wished he had a phone she could call him on. She could call Foxworth, but that would make it…official, sort of. Also, she wanted to ask personal questions, like how he was feeling, did he need anything, want anything…

Like you?

She had bitten her lip until the pain distracted her. And decided then and there that she was going. If he didn't want to see her, then she'd just leave. She'd decided to combine it with a trip to the market in town, so it wouldn't be a fruitless effort no matter what.

I was in the neighborhood sounded a lot better than *I couldn't wait to see you again.*

But somehow, now that she was here, now that she'd seen Cutter so clearly happy, almost jaunty, and now that she'd petted him and gotten that feeling she always got from the animal, she knew it would be all right.

"You're a miracle on paws, dog," she murmured as he disappeared around the next corner, to the back side of the big green building. She followed, and the moment she cleared the corner stopped dead.

Trip was here, all right. Clearly working, and just as clearly working hard. She noticed—barely—the jacket he'd shed tossed on the flagstones of the patio. He was in those cheap running shoes and jeans, which had both gathered some mud. And a T-shirt that was damp enough with sweat to cling to his broad shoulders and flat belly and set off ideas she was trying to avoid. It wasn't at all warm today, barely breaking sixty, but the sky was clear for a change, and she could see why he'd taken off the jacket, as hard as he was obviously working in direct sunlight at high noon.

You're lucky he didn't peel off the shirt, too. Or is that unlucky?

Cutter had reached him, and nudged at his knee just as he was about to dig in with the shovel he was holding. He stopped the motion and reached out to pet the dog. Then suddenly, as if he'd sensed her presence, he looked up.

He straightened. And smiled. Slowly, like the sun breaking through the clouds. Kayley felt her heart give a little skip. She felt a burst of joy all out of proportion to a simple smile of greeting. And she moved toward him, eagerly now.

"Hi."

"Hi."

It was, perhaps, a silly exchange, but Kayley heard more than the simple word. She heard in his voice the same kind of feeling that had echoed in her own.

"You're working hard," she said.

"It feels good." *It looks good.* She bit back the words—barely—and was glad she had when he added, "It's good to do it because you want to, not because you have to."

"I get that," she said. "I'm surprised Rafe put you to work, though."

"I had to ask him to," he admitted.

That sparked her curiosity. *Right. Like everything about him doesn't?* "Why did you?"

"It didn't feel right, just staying here, eating their food, without doing something in return." She smiled at that, and his mouth twisted. "I know, weird, after I spent all that time with the state feeding and housing me."

"I was smiling in appreciation of your principles," she explained. "But as for the other, you worked for that, too. And it's hardly the same. For the exact reason you said. It's good to do it because you want to, not because you have to."

He stared at her for a long moment. "Only you," he murmured with a wondering shake of his head.

"Only me what?"

"Only you could make an ex-con sound like a straight arrow."

She pondered that for a moment, then said, "I think you are a straight arrow. Your course just got bent for a while by circumstances beyond your control."

"I'm the one who decided hanging with Ruffle was a good idea," he pointed out sourly.

She sighed. "I hope someday you're able to forgive yourself."

"Kayley, you shouldn't…" He stopped.

"Going to tell me I need to toughen up?" It wouldn't be the first time she'd been told that. In fact, Debra had told her that several times. She'd considered the source and ignored the advice.

"No!" It came out sharply. Then, softer, "Don't. Ever."

Her smile felt much better this time. "You look like you could use a cold drink." *And a cool shower.* She again had to bite off the thought. She wasn't quite so successful in stopping the runaway train of images of him naked under streaming water that barreled through her mind.

"I grabbed a drink out of the hose. Didn't want to go in with mud all over my shoes. When I'm done I'll take them off to go in."

That is awfully polite, for this ex-con you keep talking about, she thought. But she said only, "I'll get some better water for you. Where's Rafe?"

"Out picking up the tree I'm digging this hole for." He glanced at Cutter. "He trusted me with him." He sounded a bit amazed still. Cutter nudged him again, and his fingers trailed over the dark fur. "Anyway, it's something your friend Hayley wants here by the patio."

"The magnolia? That's great. They have one at their house, but she's wanted one here for a while."

"I guess. All I know is it has to be close enough to the building and on this side for protection."

"The flowers have a kind of lemony scent. It will smell so good later."

"Hopefully I will, too." He gave her a crooked grin that made her heartbeat kick. And those shower images come back.

When she came out from inside with a glass of ice water, he'd put down the shovel and was sitting on the patio next to his jacket. Cutter was over investigating the hole he'd dug. Trip took the glass carefully. "Thanks," he said, and drank half of it down in a couple of gulps as Kayley sat on one of the chairs close by.

He nodded toward the hole and said, "Best I can do until I see the tree, and the size of the root ball."

She wondered if he thought it necessary to explain to her why he'd stopped working. But she only asked, "Then what?"

"Hole should be three times wider, but only deep enough to put the tree at its prior level. Or higher, and pile the soil up to cover the roots before you mulch."

She was staring at him now. "Then what?" she repeated.

He gave her a curious glance, but answered readily enough. "Check the roots, make sure they're not container-bound, break them loose if they are, before you actually plant it."

"Where did you learn all this?" she finally asked.

He looked away, as if embarrassed, and shrugged. "Guy who led the crew when we'd go out to plant trees on state land. He didn't mind answering questions, as long as he thought you really wanted to know."

"I didn't know you'd done that."

"It was the only thing I really enjoyed." His mouth

quirked. "Which is what landed me here. Rafe asked if there'd been anything I liked doing."

She smiled at the thought of the gruff former Marine sniper asking that question. Remembered Hayley's description of how he used to be, barely communicative, beyond laconic, so much that they had to practically force him to speak in full sentences. "I'm almost as proud of how he's changed as anything else we've done," Hayley had told her.

It wasn't hard to imagine him that way, now that she'd met him. If only because the effort he made not to be that way was almost visible.

"He was a warrior, Hayley said, down to the bone. So in a way, it must have been as big an adjustment to a normal life for him as it is for you."

He tilted his head as he looked at her. "He actually said something like that. I'd never thought of it that way."

She tilted her head in turn. "You're good at realizing things like that." She meant it. More than once he'd not rejected out of hand a new way of thinking about something he already had an opinion on. He'd been that way back in the beginning, and hadn't lost the capacity despite everything.

Something shifted in his gaze as he glanced up at her from his seat on the ground. He seemed to hesitate, then said, "I used to think, back when I first met you, that you were…like Debra. Don't be insulted," he added hastily. "I just meant she called it her 'bad boy' thing. I thought that was why you talked with me."

Several responses leaped to her lips, but she held them all back and asked only, "Used to think?"

"I know better now. You're not like her in any way. Lucky for me."

"No, I'm not," she confirmed. "I was never a sucker

for a bad boy." *But I think I could be one for a reformed bad boy.*

"Then…why are you helping me now?"

"Because you're not one. I don't think you ever were, really. Not deep down where it counts."

He lowered his gaze. Stared silently down at his muddy jeans and shoes. Without looking at her, he took a small step toward that view of his life.

"I hope you're right."

Chapter Twenty-Three

Trip leaned back in the patio chair, a mug of hot chocolate in his hand, looking at the tree he and Rafe had planted. It gave him an even greater sense of satisfaction than the other planting jobs had, because this was for someone who mattered, someone who was helping him. Even if it was specifically for someone he hadn't even met yet.

Rafe had gone back to what he called his quarters in the outbuilding, leaving them alone, albeit with Cutter in attendance. Trip had been afraid Kayley would leave, too, but she hadn't. And when he'd finished with his hasty shower and come back out, she had the hot chocolate steaming and ready.

Not the only thing steaming and ready.

He watched her take and savor a sip of the sweet brew, and the words were out before he thought. "I wanted to hug you when you got here. But I was all sweaty and muddy."

She met his gaze. A slow, sweet smile curved her mouth, that luscious mouth. "I wouldn't have cared."

He couldn't quite believe that. She looked too neat and sharp in a pair of greenish-blue jeans and a matching sweater.

She also looked damned sexy, with both garments hugging curves in just the right places.

He tried to fight down the urge to hug her now, because he had the feeling he wouldn't be satisfied for long with merely hugging her. And he was so hot for her, he'd probably scare to death. That was the absolute last thing he ever wanted to do. No matter how long he'd been without, no matter how much he wanted to ease this growing need, scaring or hurting Kayley was as off-limits as hitting Touchy in prison had been. And for the same reason: it could ruin the rest of his life.

His breath caught, and he had to look away.

The rest of my life.

He stared at the tree he had carefully planted and was watering with the slow soaker hose he'd also asked Rafe to pick up.

Had he really thought that? The rest of his life, whatever it might entail, in conjunction with Kayley Mc-Swain?

No, be honest, as you've sworn you'll be, and admit you were thinking of a future with *Kayley.*

A future at all was a treasured enough idea. At least, he'd always thought it was. But a future with Kayley? There were no words big enough to hold that idea.

It was the cold that finally drove them inside. He turned off the water to the tree since it was supposed to freeze tonight. The slow soak was much better than the occasional burst from a regular hose, especially in the beginning, so he'd turn it back on regularly until the tree got established.

Regularly. Well, at least for as long as he was here. And he had no idea how long that would be. Foxworth might be an amazing operation, but he couldn't hide out here forever. And that he had no idea what he would do when he left here was his problem, not theirs. Hell, the problem they were working on for him wasn't theirs, either. But they were doing it. All because of a decision his heart and gut had made long ago.

As he sat down on the couch, he remembered the locket. Remembered opening it to see a tiny photo of a lovely woman holding a little girl with flyaway blond hair, and opposite it that loving inscription from a loving mother. What would he give to have something like that of his mother's? Anything. He thought of the things he'd stashed away. The carved jade ring she'd always worn, that had been her mother's before her. Her favorite glasses with bright blue frames, "to remind me what color the sky will be again when winter's done," she'd always said. Or most of all, the photo of them together, her holding the little boy he'd been as if he were the greatest thing in her world.

Anything. He would have given anything to still have something of hers, but his father had seen to it that it was all destroyed. He had—

"Do you mind if I turn on the fire?"

He snapped out of the fruitless parade of thoughts to look at her. "No, but it's not mine to say."

"It is at the moment. For the duration, anyway."

The duration. "However long that will be," he muttered.

"If I know Foxworth, however long is necessary," she said nonchalantly as she adjusted the control that turned on the gas fire, which quickly began to put out warmth. He'd never dealt with one before, so he watched how she did it, filing it away to remember because that heat was nice. So were the flames, even if they were behind a glass screen.

She started toward the chair opposite him, but Cutter got in the way. Her legs came up against the couch seat and she wobbled slightly. Trip was about to jump up and help her when she simply sat down. He suddenly realized that Kayley had been herded just as he had been, so that they ended up sitting right next to each other on a couch that had room for four. Cutter looked…smug. How could a dog look like that?

"If I'm not mistaken," Kayley said, looking at the dog, "he's pulled that stunt on you a few times."

"Yeah," Trip agreed as the dog plopped himself down on their feet, as if to keep them from moving from where he'd put them.

"Apparently he likes people together."

"So it seems."

"I'll move—or try to," she amended, looking at the too-pleased dog. "If you'd rather."

"I'd rather you stay right here."

He wished he hadn't let that slip out and looked away quickly. He didn't want to see her reaction.

"I'm glad," she said quietly, and his head snapped back around.

"Kayley…"

He wanted to kiss her. More than he wanted anything in this moment, he wanted to kiss her. But if he did, he wasn't sure he could stop there. No, he knew he would, if that was what she wanted. He was not and had never been that far gone. So he guessed the truth was that if she didn't want it, too, he didn't want to know. And if he tried, he'd find out. In a hurry.

Coward.

In desperation he turned to the big-screen above the fireplace. Using the excuse of having been fairly limited in viewing options for a long time, he grabbed the remote and turned the system on. But he was quickly lost amid the sea of options, and amazed at how swiftly things had changed. He handed her the controller and told her to pick something. Anything.

But preferably nothing with a lot of kissing.

To his surprise, she picked a movie he'd actually seen once, a classic science fiction adventure he'd liked well enough to not mind seeing it again.

"Okay?" she asked.

"Absolutely," he said.

"Good. Dog, off my feet. This will require some of that popcorn I saw Hayley had stocked in the cupboard."

Trip grabbed her hand at the last second. "Don't make him herd you again."

She gave him that smile that kicked up his pulse. "I won't. You have to help me eat the popcorn."

And so they spent a luxuriously leisurely two and a half hours on the epic, eating the excellent popcorn, and spending several minutes of that time making comments on the plot holes that he'd never noticed the first time through.

"I think that means they made a good movie, if you don't care at the time," she said, and he couldn't argue with that. Not that he would. He didn't think he'd argue with her about anything at this point.

The extensive credits started to roll by. Kayley had leaned forward to put the now nearly empty popcorn bowl on the coffee table, just as Trip reached for the remote. Suddenly they were face-to-face, mere inches apart.

And, all his caution blown to the winds, he kissed her.

It was more than he could have ever imagined. It made the fireworks and special effects of the movie pale by comparison. Nothing he'd ever experienced could have prepared him for the explosion of fire and heat that swamped him at the feeling of her lips against his.

For a brief moment she didn't move, and a tiny, still-functioning part of his brain was sending out a warning to stop. But then, incredibly, she was kissing him back, willingly, warmly. And the feelings rippled out in all directions, swamping every part of him with fierce, almost cramping need.

He felt one of her hands at his face, cupping his cheek, and thought he might just lose it altogether at the simple touch. She wasn't pulling away, wasn't recoiling at being kissed by him, and that alone was enough to send awe spiking through him. On top of the heat and need, it was almost unbearable.

It took everything he had in him to remember this was just a kiss, and a first kiss at that. That a kiss wasn't permission for anything else, no matter how much his aching, deprived body might want it. Which in turn told him he simply had to stop this. And now.

He broke the kiss. Heard an odd, rasping sound, realized it was his own harsh breathing. He stared at her as her eyes slowly opened and she looked at him, seeming a little stunned.

He knew the feeling.

Silence spun out between them for a long, taut moment before she said, her voice tight, "Was that because I've given you a little help?"

"A lot of help. And no." It was all he could manage to say.

A fanfare of music billowed out of the TV's sound system as the next movie, the sequel to the one they'd just watched, started to play. He seized on the distraction because he didn't know what else to do. He was beyond out of practice with this. He was…afraid. Afraid because this was Kayley, and he'd slit his own throat before he'd hurt her.

She moved beside him. He thought it was because she

was going to get up, was going to leave after he'd dared to kiss her.

Still staring unseeingly at the screen, he said rigidly, "Please, stay. I promise I won't do that again."

"Not much of an incentive, Callen." His gaze shot back to her face. Did that mean…kissing her again would be an incentive to stay? She couldn't mean that. Could she? "But I wasn't leaving anyway. Just heading for the bathroom before chapter two starts."

"Oh."

He wasn't sure how that made him feel. What any of this meant. Hell, even the idea that the bathroom she was headed for was the one he'd taken that shower in rattled him. But a couple of minutes later, when he looked over as she came back, as he watched her walk across the room toward him, he could put a name to what it all felt like.

Fate.

Chapter Twenty-Four

When Kayley woke up, she felt odd. Not bad—in fact, utterly right—just odd. The room seemed different, oriented differently, as if she were a compass needle pointing the wrong way. But the right…the right was the solid heat behind her, the feel of strong arms around her. And in that sleepy moment, she thought it was the rightest thing she'd ever felt.

Trip. It was Trip holding her so close as they lay on the couch where they'd obviously fallen asleep. The sequel hadn't lived up to the promise of the original, and the last thing she remembered was groaning at a deus ex machina appearing just in time to save the hero. And now here she was, cuddled up against Trip, his gentle hold keeping her tucked up against him on the couch.

Was it morning? She didn't think she cared. She wanted to go right back to sleep in his arms, wanted that overwhelming feeling of rightness again, but a little sound from the kitchen made her eyes snap open. She felt Trip stir behind her, murmur something she couldn't quite hear, then go rigidly still.

"Sorry if I woke you. Didn't realize you were there until it was too late." Rafe's quiet voice from the kitchen sounded a touch amused and…something else she couldn't put a name to.

Trip jolted upright, almost forcing her to do the same. He appeared...not embarrassed but rattled, and she had to remind herself he was still in his first week of freedom. Rafe, on the other hand, now that her bleary eyes had cleared enough to see him, looked as amused as that tone she'd heard in his voice. She wondered if the other thing she'd heard was the wry acceptance that seemed to show in his rugged face.

What she didn't see was surprise. Of course, if he'd had time to get into the kitchen and start the coffee, he'd had time to get over any surprise at finding them sleeping together on the couch.

At least we're still dressed.

Even as she thought it, she had to ruefully admit that if it had been up to her, they might not be. Only constantly reminding herself of how new this all was to Trip had restrained her. She cared for him, a great deal, but she wasn't about to become his first woman after getting out of prison simply because she was the first woman handy.

Assuming, of course, that he wanted her to be. But the kiss had gone a long way toward proving that.

"We were watching a movie and fell asleep," Trip said, sounding a bit like a kid caught breaking the house rules. Which only reminded her of the rules he'd had to live by for so long.

"You don't need to explain," Rafe said, with more gentleness in his tone than she would have expected from him. "Besides, I knew it was coming."

Kayley blinked. "What?"

Rafe grimaced slightly, took a sip of the coffee he'd just poured, then said only, "Long story. His fault." The last came with a nod toward Cutter, who was curled up peacefully on his bed beside the fireplace, eyes open and ears alert, but not bestirred enough to lift his head.

"His fault?" Trip repeated blankly.

"That story's for another time. I'm heading over to Quinn and Hayley's to open up the house. They'll be back late tonight, for a day or two anyway."

"Your job…is that the kind of thing you do?" Trip asked.

Rafe lowered the mug. And Kayley was rather glad she wasn't on the receiving end of that look. Or the steel that had come into his voice. "No. It's the kind of thing I do for the best friends I've got, and the two best people I know."

Trip went still. But she noticed he didn't look away. Which was rather amazing, all things considered. And when he spoke, his voice was more than a little respectful.

"Sorry. I stand corrected."

After a moment Rafe nodded, and his voice this time held a kind of knowing undertone. "Just think of what you'd do for Kayley if she needed it."

"Anything," Trip said, his voice low and the tiniest bit unsteady. And a rush of something she couldn't deny was pleasure rippled through her. A different kind than his kiss had caused, but no less fierce.

After Rafe had gone, leaving Cutter to Trip's care—as if he'd had a choice, since the clever animal had made it clear where he was staying—they were in the kitchen contemplating breakfast. As Trip fed the dog, Kayley realized that in a way, Rafe's presence had helped them get through any awkwardness they'd felt after sleeping together in the literal sense. They settled on bacon and eggs, although Kayley made a mental note to augment the supplies the next time she came over, not wanting the Foxworths to feed her, too.

"Can't believe how much better this tastes," he said as he devoured the last of his two eggs.

"Seasoned with freedom," she said, smiling.

He gave her a startled glance, then smiled back in that way she loved, one corner of his mouth rising higher. "Yeah."

They had just finished clearing away when her phone rang. She knew who it was.

"My parents," she said at his glance. "They always call on Sunday. And if they haven't by noon here, I call them."

When he only nodded and looked quickly away, she felt almost guilty for that expression of the wonderful normalcy of her life. And when he went outside, Cutter in tow, to turn the water back on for the newly planted tree, she wondered if it was truly to give her privacy or to avoid hearing more of the same.

After catching up on her grandmother and the situation there, she told them that Trip was out. Their first reaction was a bit wary. She'd expected that. But they knew of Foxworth, and their reputation and mission, and when she told them they were directly helping him, that eased their fears. She didn't want to share the details he'd confessed to her, so she said only that she knew more now, and understood completely how he had gotten on that bad path, and that she, or anyone, might have done the same under the same circumstances.

"We trust your judgment, baby girl," her father said, using the nickname he always did with her and probably would when she was fifty. "If you say he's a good guy, then he is. So tell him we'll be rooting for him."

"I will. Love you. Bye."

Kayley slipped her phone back in her pocket, then walked over to the back door, and felt a burst of warmth at the sight of Trip throwing a rather grungy yellow tennis ball for the delighted Cutter. She stood there for a moment, just looking, loving to watch the way he moved as he threw it, again and again.

Finally she gave in and went outside. He had just released the ball, which went its longest distance yet, with Cutter in hot pursuit, when he looked back over his shoulder at her.

"Your folks okay?" he asked, his tone rather studiedly neutral.

"Fine."

"They know you're hanging out with an ex-con?"

She gave him a steady look and said, "Someday I hope you'll believe that the *ex* part is more important than the *con* part."

Trip seemed completely disarmed. He looked as if he was grateful when Cutter arrived back in that moment. And surprised when the dog didn't surrender the ball for another throw, but trotted to the door and then looked back at them.

"He must be thirsty after all that running," Trip said.

She wasn't sure the dog didn't have some other motive, then laughed at herself for assigning human thoughts to the animal. Then again, Hayley said they'd come to believe just about anything about the creature who'd turned up on her doorstep one day.

Cutter did head for his water bowl, after dropping the tennis ball neatly in the basket by the door.

"He's such a tidy thing," Kayley said with a laugh.

"He," Trip said wryly, "is scary."

"Hayley says he can be. That he can snap from goofy playmate to trained K-9 in an instant."

"Quinn train him?"

"She says no. That he came that way. She spent a lot of time looking for his owners, all the while hoping she wouldn't find them."

"I can understand that," Trip said. Cutter came back to them and sat, looking up at them. "I swear, he actually smiles sometimes."

"He does, doesn't he? And Hayley swears when they don't catch on to what he wants soon enough, he rolls his eyes. She calls it his 'dealing with dopes' look."

"I think I've seen that look," Trip said, his mouth quirking. "Aimed at me."

Since it seemed he was kidding, she took it as such, glad it wasn't more of him being down on himself. "I've been thinking about getting a dog, now that I've got a sort of routine going at home."

"That," he said, "would be a very lucky dog."

She smiled, but before she could respond, Cutter was back on his feet, letting out a short bark. Not an alarm sort of bark, just...an alert? No, more an announcement, she decided as she watched the dog, tail and ears up, trot toward the front door.

"I'd say that's a friend," Trip said. "But Rafe can't be back already, can he?"

"No. It would take longer to get to their place and come straight back."

"What if it's somebody looking for someone from Foxworth?" He sounded worried.

"It is Sunday," she said, "although when they're on a case, that doesn't matter. But the only case they're on at the moment here is yours."

He looked as if he still hadn't quite absorbed that. And she was almost certain he hadn't absorbed the entirety of what having Foxworth behind you meant. Then he drew back, startled, as Cutter rose up and batted at the metal pad beside the door and it started to swing open.

"Damn, that's putting a lot of trust in a dog," he muttered.

"He's never let them down," Kayley said, although even she had to admit it was a little disconcerting.

But Cutter was clearly greeting someone known and liked, so she started that way. The moment she moved, so did Trip, until he was walking beside her. Almost as if he didn't want her to go alone. Before she could slide into that kind of wondering, a young couple, teenagers she guessed, stepped inside. The girl was a sweet-faced blonde, the boy taller, a little thin, with darker hair.

The girl walked toward them quickly, her eyes bright and fastened on Trip. The boy followed closely, protectively.

Just like Trip had followed her.

"You're Trip?" the girl asked, almost eagerly. And suddenly Kayley knew. And couldn't help smiling at what she guessed was coming.

"I...yes," he said, clearly puzzled.

"I'm Emily Parker." She smiled a little self-consciously, putting a hand to her throat and the little golden heart that hung there.

She heard his breath catch, felt him go still. "The locket," he said.

The teenager smiled at him. And then she grabbed his hand and squeezed it. "I've waited for this chance for so long. Thank you. Thank you so, so much."

"I...you're welcome. I'm glad...something good came out of that mess."

Kayley knew he meant the mess his life had become. He would probably say the mess he'd made of his life, even though she felt it was much more complex than that.

"How did you even know I was here?" he asked, still sounding a bit bewildered.

"From Ms. Connelly. She's one of my teachers."

"Ria, Liam's fiancée," Kayley supplied at his blank look.

"Oh."

"She knew I'd want to know, from all the times I've said I wish I could thank you."

Kayley kept her eyes on Trip's face, saw the emotions he was trying to hide. She guessed Emily had put a face to that long-ago night, when he'd made the decision that had changed everything. And to see her, this sweet-faced, open and clearly caring girl, had to make him realize just how big that decision had been. At least, she hoped it did.

"Consider me thanked," he said, and by the slight gruffness in his tone, she knew she was right. "I'm sorry I ever touched it."

"But if you hadn't, I never would have gotten it back."

"I'm still sorry. That I was there at all."

"Good," Emily said brightly, and Kayley saw surprise flicker in his expression. "If you're truly sorry, it won't happen again, right? So, apology accepted."

A trace of a smile lifted the corners of his mouth. And Kayley had the thought that he couldn't have landed in a better place just now than Foxworth, with the kind of people they surrounded themselves with.

And the dog, of course. Who was watching all this quietly, patiently, with an expression that for the world looked like satisfaction.

"Liam said you've got some trouble," Emily said. Kayley felt Trip stiffen beside her, as if he were wondering if the friendly Texan had blabbed it all. "But he said Foxworth is helping you with it."

"I…yes."

"You're good, then." It was the first time the boy with her had spoken.

Trip shifted his gaze to the boy, and Emily hastily introduced him. "This is Dylan Oakley. And he knows firsthand about Foxworth's help."

"I do," the boy confirmed, meeting and holding Trip's gaze. "They saved me. And especially my little brother, Kevin. My father was a murderer," the boy said bluntly, and Trip drew back slightly, clearly startled. Dylan glanced at Emily, with a smile that spoke volumes. "But Kevin's okay, and so am I. Thanks to Emily, who knew we were in trouble and came to them."

Trip gave her a sideways glance. Kayley knew he was thinking about how she had come to Foxworth for him. "That's a good friend," he said, again with that touch of gruffness, as if it was hard for him to speak.

"Yeah," Dylan said. "Anyway, if it can be done, Foxworth'll do it."

The boy said it with utter confidence. His brusque admission about his father had registered hard with Trip. She could feel it.

And when Trip turned to look at her, she saw it in his face, his eyes, again. Stronger this time.

Unmistakable hope.

Chapter Twenty-Five

Trip wished there was a way out of this.

Because you're still a coward? Afraid of facing the guy?

His mouth twisted into a grimace as he buttoned the one shirt he had that wasn't a T-shirt variation. That it was of blue chambray and reminded him of the prison attire he'd seen all too much of, he tried not to think about.

Telling himself anybody who wasn't wary of a man like Quinn Foxworth was a fool, he managed to finish. He'd showered, shaved, spent a moment glad for once for his hair. It had garnered him some flak inside, because it looked as if he'd used some fancy product on it to make it sort of stand up, but it was just the way it grew and always had. All he'd done was wash it and toweled it as dry as he could.

He didn't usually spend this much time worrying about how he looked, but he was about to be face-to-face with the head of Foxworth, at the man's house, and he had to admit he was nervous. This wasn't just the guy who had taken down Ruffle—and him—the night Ruffle had beaten up that old man. He was the guy who could call a halt to everything, if he decided Trip wasn't worth helping. So it was almost like a job interview, wasn't it? Or just a business meeting, slipped in between business trips, since Rafe said they were heading out again in a couple of days to their national headquarters in St. Louis.

He told himself his nerves had nothing to do with the fact that he was going there with Kayley, who was due to pick him up any moment now. After all, it wasn't like it was a date or something.

A date was something he hadn't thought about in a very long time.

A date with Kayley was something he didn't dare think about at all.

And maybe Quinn Foxworth really will decide you're not worth helping after all. If you're going to stress out, do it about that.

Rather grimly calmer now, he walked out into the main room. Cutter, who had been sprawled in front of the fire, rolled to his feet and looked at him, head tilted in that quizzical way he had. Then he moved his head in what almost looked like a nod and plopped back down again.

"Pass inspection, do I?" he said.

The dog let out a little woof that Trip thought could have been interpreted as anything from a simple yes to *if that's the best you can do...*

He almost laughed at himself, carrying on a conversation with a dog, even if half of it was in his head. He spent a moment wondering just how big the dog's vocabulary was, since he seemed to understand almost everything, in fact seemed sometimes to practically read minds.

"You want out before we leave?"

The dog never moved. Trip knew he knew the word *out*, so took that as a no.

Rafe had thanked him for saving him a second trip to Quinn's place, since Kayley had agreed to take Cutter with them. Trip had said he'd pass that on to the one who should really be thanked, Kayley. Rafe had added emotionlessly he would not be joining them as he'd already given Quinn a full report when they'd arrived home late last night.

There, see? It is a business meeting. Not a date. Just because it's dinner at someone's house doesn't make it a date.

Being with Kayley doesn't make it a date. No matter how much you might want—

Cutter's head came up sharply, and he let out a bark that sounded nothing less than happy. He was on his feet a split-second later and headed for the door.

A butler. Damn dog was a freaking butler, opening the door for visitors, and no doubt effectively turning away unwanted ones. If he ever opened the door for those in the first place. He had the feeling that rarely happened, if ever.

Trip gave himself a moment to get himself settled, to try and slow the crazy ricocheting his mind had been doing all afternoon. He heard Kayley cheerfully greeting the delighted dog, then her footsteps as she started toward him. He braced himself and turned around.

And forgot to breathe.

She looked…incredible. She was wearing a dark green dress that flowed over her like a caress, hugging breasts he'd never quite realized—or at least hadn't dared to—were so full and perfect. The soft fabric stopped a couple of inches short of her knees, baring a lovely length of slender legs. Her hair was down, flowing in slight waves past her shoulders. He'd never seen it like that before. It was usually straight and often pulled back with some hair thing women used.

And her face. She'd put on more makeup or something. Her cheekbones stood out, and her already thick eyelashes looked even thicker and longer. Her blue eyes had somehow taken on a touch of green, as if picking it up from the dress. And her mouth, that luscious mouth was a dark pink and utterly tempting. It all made her... breath-stealing, he thought as he finally remembered how to take in some air, a good thing since he was feeling almost light-headed. But then when he did, he caught a scent, something luscious that reminded him of fresh peaches. It made his head spin all over again.

How had he never realized how gorgeous she was? He'd always thought of her as, not plain, but certainly not glamorous. More of the girl-next-door type, that all-American, fresh, innocent type. But right now she could have walked off the cover of some women's magazine. Right now, she'd turn heads anywhere. Right now, she left him speechless.

And strangely unsettled. Not in the way any straight guy seeing her would be, but almost unnerving. Hot, yes, body waking up in uncomfortable ways, but something else as well, something he couldn't put a name to just now.

Because all you can do is gape at her, dumbstruck?

"Something wrong?"

He tried to answer. It didn't work. He swallowed, tried again. "I...no. I just..." He grabbed some air. "You look great."

The smile she gave him then was worth all the breathlessness and the stumbling words. "Thank you. Hayley said I had to wear this. She was with me when I bought it, and she wanted to see it on. Of course it'll make Quinn cranky because she'll wear a dress, too, which will make him feel like he needs to wear a tie."

He grimaced. "I don't even own a tie."

"Would you wear one if you did?"

He looked at her again, in that dress. "Probably. Because now I look like some stray you brought along."

"You don't, but if it will make you feel better," she said as she dug into the small handbag over her shoulder, "here." She held something out to him. Something blue with a sheen to it.

A tie.

She'd brought him a tie to wear? And one that—coincidentally?—went with the one slightly formal shirt he had?

Not to mention, where had she gotten a man's tie?

Left behind by a former boyfriend? She'd only said there wasn't one now.

"I don't know if I even remember how to tie one."

"That's okay. I do. Used to do it for my dad, because he hated messing with them."

"I can relate."

And then she was standing right in front of him, so close, reaching up to put the strip of fabric around his neck, then moving to tie it with those long, graceful fingers. In the process she brushed his neck, and he nearly shivered. When she was done she patted the tie, and thus his chest, and even through the layers of tie and shirt, he felt a ripple of heat.

His denim jacket spoiled the effort at dressing up a little, but it was all he had. It wasn't cold enough for the jacket she'd loaned him before. Which made him wonder if the tie was also her father's.

"You'll start a new trend," Kayley said with a smile that sent that ripple of heat through him again.

They headed for the door, and she called to the dog. "Ready to go home, Cutter?" The dog let out a combination of bark and happy whine that made Trip smile and Kayley laugh.

The drive was scenic, but then everything around here was, to him anyway. He supposed anything that didn't involve guards and fences would be, but he did love this part of the country. And if he never set foot in a big city again, that would be fine with him. On the other hand, this was rural enough that it was easy to miss a turn unless you knew where it was in advance, but Kayley was obviously familiar with the route.

As they went, Trip felt the pressure building. All he could seem to think about was that night when what Ruffle had thought would be an easy score had turned to chaos as Quinn Foxworth had erupted into action, taking them both down as easily as if he'd had a battalion at his back. It had been a pitch-black night, and all he'd really been aware of was the power and speed and size of the man.

As if she'd sensed it, Kayley spoke.

"I know Quinn's pretty intimidating, but he's a good man. A really good man. And Hayley's the kindest person I know."

"Mmm."

"What are you worried about?" He gave her a sideways look. She had to ask? "Afraid when they see you they'll think you're a horrible person and decide not to help after all?"

He blinked. Maybe that dog wasn't the only mind reader around. "Maybe," he admitted.

"You've met Emily now," she said. "Can you really think they'd turn on someone who did something so wonderful for that sweet girl?"

"I was in the gang stealing that locket, remember?"

"And you alone gave it back."

She sounded so confident it actually eased his qualms. And he even laughed when Cutter barked from the back

seat, where he was sitting looking out the window, and
Kayley said it was because the next driveway was the
Foxworths'.

But the moment she made the turn and started down
the long drive that wound through thick trees much like
at the headquarters building, the tension started to build
in him again.

When he got his first glimpse of the house, he was
surprised. He'd somehow expected, given Foxworth's
obvious resources, something bigger, fancier, more man-
sion-like. This was a well-kept but not huge home, built in
the Northwest style of fairly steep roofs and cedar siding.

But as they went down the long driveway the tension
Kayley had distracted him from came rushing back when
he saw a man outside he knew had to be Quinn Foxworth.
Even from a distance he knew it, in the same instant he
realized Cutter was on his feet, tail wagging madly. The
man was tall, built, and carried himself like the commanding officer Kayley had told him he once was. And
he moved with that kind of controlled power that again
reminded him of the night that had changed everything.

"There's Quinn," Kayley said, confirming his deduc-
tion. "Let Cutter out, will you? I want to grab the flowers out of the wayback."

Flowers? Belatedly it hit him that was the kind of thing
people did, outside. Brought flowers to your hosts. One
more thing in the world he'd left behind. He'd left it behind long before he'd ended up in prison. It was the kind
of thing his mother would have done, though. In fact,
he vaguely remembered her doing it at least once, when
they'd gone to visit friends.

It only figured that Kayley would do the same.

He got out and opened the back door. Cutter leaped out
and raced toward the man joyously. Foxworth crouched

down to greet the dog, his smile changing his face amazingly. Trip heard him murmuring to the animal as he scratched behind his ears, Cutter wriggling from nose to tail with obvious delight.

Then he stood up and turned to look at Trip. Who felt suddenly frozen in place. Foxworth's eyes were an icy blue that sent a bit of a chill through him. It was just as well he hadn't been able to see that stare in the dark that night. For an instant they were both motionless, Foxworth clearly assessing, Trip fearing that assessment.

"Been a while," Foxworth said.

Trip couldn't read anything into his tone, but there was nothing of the snap of authority he had heard in his voice that night. He answered only, "Yes." Then, driven by the same urge he'd felt with Rafe, he added, "Sir."

Something glinted in that icy gaze. But then Foxworth nodded and held out a hand. "Good to see you under better circumstances. Come inside and meet my wife."

He said it as if Trip were anyone he was welcoming to his home and offering to introduce to his wife. As if he weren't the guy he'd caught that night, trying to break into that borrowed place, to steal anything of value he could find.

And then Kayley was beside him, slipping an arm through his as if she'd again sensed—as she always seemed to—he needed a bit of prodding support. He heard Foxworth greet her with warm welcome in his voice and his smile. And suddenly the normalcy of this hit him, and he had a flash of how his life might have been if his mother hadn't died and his father hadn't gone off the deep end of grief and stayed there.

He was torn between a fierce sensation of loss, and the recurring flash of hope that hinted that maybe, just maybe, he wasn't adrift forever.

Chapter Twenty-Six

Hayley worked her usual magic. Quinn had told Kayley his wife was a wonder with people, especially nervous or scared ones. Hayley said it was because she'd been terrified herself when Quinn had grabbed her and spirited her off in his helicopter because she got in the way of them protecting a crucial witness. Before, of course, she realized he wasn't just one of the good guys. For her he was *the* good guy.

Kayley wasn't sure if Trip was genuinely scared or just nervous. He'd admitted to the latter, but she had the feeling he never would to the former. And that made a sad sort of sense to her; she imagined admitting you were scared in prison was not a wise move. In her mind she again voiced the hope that he would one day be able to put that completely behind him.

But in the meantime, Hayley had put him as much at ease as she thought he could be. When Kayley asked them about coming home only for a day, she'd laughed and said San Diego was personal, to see her brother and her best friend—who happened to be married, and about to make her an aunt—and St. Louis was business.

"Which I'm dreading," Quinn said with a grimace. "My sister's annual assessment of the books. Where I have to sit and look at all her numbers and pretend I get it. I understand ancient Sanskrit better than her when she gets going on that stuff."

Kayley was watching Trip as Quinn spoke, saw his surprise at the admission. She supposed Ruffle would have counted any such confession as a sign of weakness. But Quinn Foxworth had no such qualms. Because no one in their right mind would ever think that of this man.

After a while Trip seemed to relax, at least enough to speak on his own. He complimented them nicely on the delicious dinner—grilled steaks handled adeptly by Quinn and a luscious potato-and-peppers concoction from Hayley—and once he'd done that, Hayley actually got him to join in the conversation. Although Kayley noticed Quinn was doing more watching—judging?—than participating.

But Hayley had even gotten Trip talking about his childhood hopes and dreams, in the time he usually just labeled "before." Hayley even shared her own loss of her mother a little over three years ago, saying she'd been so much luckier than he, to have had her longer. Just when Trip had started to look uncomfortable, she'd shifted to the tale of how Cutter had simply turned up on her doorstep two weeks after her mother's passing, and how he kept her distracted enough that she didn't drown in the sewer of grief.

"We all find ways to survive," she said. Her eyes, a meadow green, lighter than Trip's, were warm with empathy. "Some good, some not."

"Yeah. Expert at that last one," Trip muttered, staring down at his hand as he ran a thumb over the handle of his fork.

"And now that you're an expert at that," Kayley said briskly, "you can start working on forgiving yourself and moving on."

Trip turned, his gaze meeting hers. She saw the doubt in those deep green eyes.

Then Quinn spoke, and Trip's head snapped around to look at the powerful man. "I'm not much on self-analysis," he said. "But I'm all for taking good advice when you get it."

Sitting beside Trip at the table, Kayley knew she was the only one who could see his left hand, down at his side, clenched. Scared or just nervous, she still didn't know.

"I got pretty good at ignoring it," he said.

"You can learn," Quinn said. Then, with a look at his wife and an incredibly loving smile that almost made Kayley tear up, he added, "I did."

"I'll bet you get a lot of good advice," Trip said quietly.

Kayley didn't know if he'd guessed that the best thing he could do to impress Quinn Foxworth was to compliment his wife, or if he'd just meant it, but either way, the result was the same. Quinn nodded, and this time it was decisive.

"You've got the full force of the Foxworth Foundation behind you now, Trip. We're leaving again tomorrow and will be in St. Louis for the next couple of weeks, but Rafe and Liam can handle whatever turns up, and Teague will be back in a week or two."

"A week," Hayley said with a grin. "Or Laney will have his head. They have wedding plans to wind up." She looked at Trip. "One of our guys is marrying Cutter's groomer next month. I'd tell you how that came about, but you wouldn't believe it."

Kayley found herself smiling even though this was a member of the Foxworth team she hadn't met yet. "After how you guys met, I'd think anything would be believable."

"There is that," Quinn said, and again he gave his

wife that loving look. And Kayley felt a little burst of longing inside, wondering if a man would ever look at her like that.

Don't kid yourself. You want it from Trip, not just any man.

She smothered an inward sigh. She couldn't help remembering that he was the guy who'd gone for Debra, and if there was anyone she was further from, she couldn't think who.

But he'd kissed her. He'd kissed her, and everything she'd ever thought she knew about kissing had been wiped away in the fierce heat of it.

And ever since he's pretended it never happened.

She quashed her hurt feelings with a stern reminder that Trip had had a lot on his mind, like this first encounter with the Foxworths.

She found herself smiling when, after dinner, as they'd adjourned to the living room that had the same comfortable, homey feel as the unexpected room at the Foxworth headquarters, Cutter pulled his herding routine again, making sure she and Trip wound up together on the couch. She saw Hayley and Quinn exchange a glance that seemed rather pointed.

"Seems Rafe was right," Quinn said to his wife.

"Indeed," Hayley agreed.

And neither of them explained any further.

She could almost feel Trip's relief when Quinn didn't probe into how he'd landed in his situation, but stuck to the details of Oliver Ruff and his operation. Trip had told most of this to Rafe, and Detective Dunbar, but he answered the questions again, without protest. Then, when he'd finished, he gave Quinn a wry look.

"All this about how much power he has probably sounds silly to you, after you took him down in an instant."

Quinn only shrugged. "He's like most criminals of his ilk. He never expects anyone to fight back."

"You sure surprised the he—heck out of him." His mouth twisted. "And me."

"You showed better judgment," Hayley said.

"I'd never seen anyone put someone on the ground so fast."

"And you made the right decision," Quinn said, without an ounce of braggadocio.

Quinn left it there, and Kayley could see Trip's relief. When Hayley mentioned something about their early start tomorrow, she knew it was time for them to leave them to prepare. What she hadn't expected was, when they got up to leave, Cutter at their heels. As if he'd expected all along to go back with Trip.

"I thought he'd think he was back home with you now," she said. "It's like he knows you're leaving again."

"Not exactly," Quinn said.

Hayley smiled. "He knows Trip is his job right now."

Trip looked from Hayley to Cutter and back again, brows furrowed as if he were trying to figure out if she was kidding or not. Kayley knew she was absolutely serious.

Once they were in her car and on the way to Foxworth headquarters, he said with a glance into the back seat where Cutter once more sat looking out the window, although it was dark now, "They're really serious about this dog, aren't they?"

"They are. And rightfully so, from some of the stories I've heard. He's the one who keeps finding people who need Foxworth help. And then helps them help them," she finished with a grin. He chuckled at the phrasing as he looked back at her, which enabled her to add softly, "Just like he found you."

He went still for a moment. "What?"

"He found you. And knew right away you needed Fox-worth's help."

He looked at the dog again. Then back to her. "That day he came to your place. The way he…stared at me."

"Exactly."

"You're saying…what are you saying?"

"That he has a way of sensing not just trouble, but the kind Foxworth can help with."

"You realize how crazy that sounds?"

"Oh, absolutely," she said blithely. "So do they. But they've learned to accept it. They've had to, because he keeps doing it. At least a dozen times since he showed up on Hayley's doorstep. Not to mention leading Hayley to Quinn in the first place."

He laughed again. She decided it was her favorite sound. "You say it like that was intentional, too."

She'd heard some things, here and there, bits and pieces that made her wonder if perhaps it was. Then there was that comment about Teague and Laney, and what Rafe had said when he'd found them asleep together on the couch…

I knew it was coming…

She shook her head, deciding she was getting too fanciful, that what had happened in the last week had turned her logical mind to mush.

Or else it was just the presence of the one man who'd ever managed to do that simply by being there.

Chapter Twenty-Seven

Trip had the feeling Kayley had been going to drop him off and leave, but it seemed Cutter would have none of that; the dog stationed himself at the driver's door of her car and refused to move until she got out. Trip wasn't about to complain, not when her leaving was the last thing he wanted.

But still, he was amazed anew when, once she was out of the car, the dog trotted happily toward the door of the building. He batted at the pad by the door, and it started to swing open.

"Rafe must still be up and around," Trip said. "He said if no one's here, he locks up when he goes to bed."

"What if we'd been later, how would you get in?"

"I… Liam gave me a pass card. To swipe through the slot beside the pad."

He was still a little astounded at that, being given full access to a place like this. With all the equipment they apparently had upstairs—he still hadn't strayed up there, feeling that would be a violation of this tremendous trust they'd had in him—and who knows what else, being given the right to come and go was a wonder second only to being free to do so.

Kayley, on the other hand, seemed to accept that he'd been given that access as a matter of course. More importantly, she came inside with him, and as she passed, he got another whiff of that luscious scent that made him hungry all over again, and not for the peaches it smelled like.

It was slightly chilly inside, and he seized on the task of turning on the heat as a way to get himself in hand. But then he turned around and saw her standing there, lit by the newly launched fire, and knew it was hopeless.

At the same time, as he saw her standing there looking every inch as gorgeous as Debra ever had, he felt a qualm.

"What's wrong?" she asked.

"Nothing," he said, startled. He hadn't thought he'd let anything show. But hadn't she already shown she read him like a book?

"You looked bothered."

He nearly laughed at that. "Oh, I'm bothered all right. But…" His voice trailed off. He knew there was no way he could explain without messing it up.

"You don't trust me enough to tell me?"

The absurdity of that tipped him over the edge. "I trust you more than I trust anyone, including—" he corrected himself "—especially myself. It's just that all dressed up and made up and fancy like that, you remind me of how stupid I was. To fall for the flash, with nothing behind it."

She stared at him, and he was certain he'd done just what he'd feared, and insulted her. He scrambled, trying to fix what he never should have started.

"I just meant that…as beautiful as you look now, I prefer the regular you. The you I know. And trust."

"So you're saying I do have something behind the flash, as you call it?"

"You've got more substance than anyone I've ever known. If I'd had the brains to go for you instead of that hollow shell, my whole life would have been different."

She blinked, drew back a little. And her voice was a little unsteady when she said, "That's a pretty extreme assessment."

"Truth," he countered. "You're the kind of woman who could keep any man, even the dope Cutter knows I am, centered."

Something came into her gaze then, something that sent a delicious shiver down his spine and made the blood rush south. "You're not a dope," she said softly. "I would never fall for a dope."

Fall for? Her, for him? Did she mean back then, or... now? She couldn't mean now. Could she? She—

She closed the distance between them with one leggy stride. And then she was kissing him, standing there in front of the fire. That warmth suddenly seemed insignificant compared to the heat she was kindling in him.

Her mouth was soft, warm, and as sweet as the scent of that perfume. His mind felt paralyzed, but his body knew what to do, and did it in an almost cramping rush. His hands reached up to cup her face, to hold her so it wouldn't stop, that glorious tasting, probing. When her arms wrapped around his neck as if she wanted that same assurance, it kicked his pulse into high gear. Less afraid she'd pull away now, he slid his hands down, along her slender rib cage to her waist. Almost convulsively he pulled her closer, making sure he never lost touch with that incredible mouth.

The feel of her pressed against that near-instant erection warned him. It had been so long, and he was so hungry for her, he could embarrass himself in another minute or two. Then she made a low, husky sound that had him thinking that estimate was a little high. And he finally broke the kiss.

"Kayley," he gasped out.

"You stopped," she pointed out unnecessarily, a hungry sort of undertone in her voice that made him wish he hadn't.

"Because I was about to go off like a rocket," he said baldly. "It's been a long time for me, remember."

"You know," she said casually, "it's been almost as long for me."

He blinked. Was every man in this stupid state blind? *As blind as you were?*

"Kayley," he said again, unable to think of anything else. But then, did anything else matter?

"It's your call, Trip. Do I stay or go?"

"Isn't that backwards?"

"No. Because I've made my decision. Now you have to make yours."

"Kayley," he said, his body still aching until he thought he was going to keel over here and now. But he had to think about her. No matter how much he wanted this, he had to think about her first. "I'm not…prepared for this."

"You mean condoms?" She said it so easily he blinked. "I knew you wouldn't dare, so I did."

She'd bought condoms? Didn't that have to mean she really, truly wanted this? Wanted him? But then the doubts slammed back into his head. She couldn't, really. Not him, with all his baggage.

She watched him, and as if she'd read his thoughts she said softly, "I know who you really are, Trip Callen. And who you can be again, once you put this behind you. That's the man I want."

He gave up. He simply couldn't hold out any longer. His resistance crumbled so fast it was as if she'd blasted it away. He wasn't sure how they'd made it to the bedroom, and only the knowledge that Rafe was around somewhere had pushed him to it. He wasn't even sure how they'd ended up naked, except he had a vague memory of hearing something tear. And the fact that he didn't know if it was his shirt or her dress somehow fired him even more, because it meant she was eager, wanting. And when he kissed her again, she responded so fiercely that he could no longer doubt what had seemed impossible.

She'd meant it. She wanted him.

She tasted so sweet, so good, he felt as if he could happily drown in the feel of her. The first touch of her hands on the bare skin of his abdomen made him shiver, which was crazy since it was pure heat.

When her hand slid down below his waist, it just about ended things right there. He pulled back just enough to take them both down to the bed. Biting the inside of his lip, needing the pain to give him a tiny bit more control, he pulled back again and fumbled with the condom she'd gotten out, barely managing to get it on. He rolled back to her, then dared to slide his hands up to cup her breasts. They were so warm, so soft, so real, he again almost lost control right there. Then he slid his fingers to her nipples, and finding them already taut made his breath catch. Hearing her moan in pleasure at the touch had him biting down harder, until he thought he tasted blood.

She reached down between them until there was no doubt where she was headed. He grabbed her wrist to stop her.

"Trip?"

"There are no words for how close I am," he muttered. "You touch me and it's all over."

She seemed to consider that for a moment, then smiled. It was a smile unlike any he'd ever seen in his life. And then she twisted her hand around until it was she holding his wrist. She guided his hand down between their bodies instead. It took him a moment to realize, and he was very much afraid this was going to end it just as her fondling his erection would. Because when he touched her, stroked her, he found her hot, wet, and ready. And she gave another little moan when he did it.

"And that's how close I am," she whispered. "Please."

"This is going to be fast," he warned her.

"It's already been too slow."

He moved then, because he had no choice. He wanted to go easy, because she was tight, but she was also hot and slick, and he couldn't. He pushed a little more, and when she didn't protest but gave him a cry of welcome, he drove home. And that's what it felt like, home. As it never had before, with anyone else.

He would have been embarrassed at how fast he hit the peak, except she seemed to be right there with him. In the instant he knew he couldn't stop it, she cried out his name, and her body clenched fiercely around him. He exploded inside her, thought maybe he'd sworn, but knew he'd shouted her name as the waves of impossible sensation swept over him.

Chapter Twenty-Eight

Kayley wished she hadn't had to leave. She would have loved nothing more than to spend the entire day with Trip. Talking, encouraging, planning...and making love. *Oh, yes, don't forget that.* Her hands tightened on the steering wheel as remembered heat and sensation flooded her mind, causing a reaction in her body that, powerful as it was, was only a faint echo of last night.

He'd warned her the first time would be fast. What she hadn't expected was that she'd been right there with him, as though her body had been as close to the edge as his. The second time had been a little slower, but just as explosive. The third time had been...incredible. Amazing. Unbelievable. Or any other superlative she could think of. And she knew she would forever carry the image of his body driving into her, the sound of his voice groaning out her name as he pulsed inside her, proving beyond a doubt it was her he wanted so desperately, not just the release after long deprivation.

But she had three appointments on her schedule for this morning, and they were all return clients who had been happy enough with her results to come back again looking for more people. She couldn't risk losing them. She'd been distracted enough already in the last week.

A week.

It really hit her then, that she'd gone to bed with him after a week. That was so not her style.

But you've wanted him for years.

That had to be the answer. She'd finally gotten what she'd wanted since the day she'd opened the door to Debra's date and forgotten to breathe. He'd proved last night that it was truly her he wanted. In fact, he'd proved it the moment he'd asked her to go back to her real self. He didn't want, didn't trust the flash anymore. He'd learned. Just as he'd finally learned he couldn't save his father from himself.

And she wondered why some people had such harsh lessons in their lives.

She had to force herself to focus on the upcoming online appointments, running through in her mind the candidates she was going to propose to her clients. Two would be good fits. One would be perfect on both sides. It was always exciting to her to find someone the exact person they needed, made better by helping someone who was willing to work find the kind of job they'd not just do well but enjoy.

Which reminded her that she also needed to go over her notes and start writing her talk for the seminar she was scheduled to speak at next Monday, about working from home. Another benefit of one of those return clients, a local company who had recommended her as an expert on the subject of that, as well as finding good job candidates.

It belatedly occurred to her that, with the more immediate threat of Ruffle hanging over him, what Trip would do when that threat was over hadn't really been a topic of conversation. Perhaps she could find him something, once she knew what he wanted to do with the rest of his life. It would take some careful searching, and an employer willing to take a chance. And she had to admit how difficult it would be, what he was really facing. No wonder he kept hammering that ex-con appellation.

Her neighbor's terrier let out his usual string of yaps she chose to consider a welcome home as she pulled in. And that made her remember Cutter, planting himself in the drive and refusing to move. In a way, that had turned last night into what it had been, the most wonderful night of her life. And she smiled at the thought that she had the dog to thank for breaking that barrier Debra had put between them.

THE STRANGENESS TO Trip wasn't that he was curious; he'd always been curious about many different things, including people. It wasn't even sitting here thinking there was really nothing stopping him from indulging that curiosity.

The strangeness was that he was going to do it. That somewhere he found the nerve to take such a simple step, when until now he wouldn't have dared.

Until last night, you mean. Until Kayley took you places you didn't even know existed.

He knew it was true. After the night spent in her arms, feeling her warmth, her caring, filling him even as he filled her body, he felt strong enough to do anything. She'd sent him soaring, and he hadn't landed yet. If he had that behind him, he felt as if he could do anything. Make a life, a good life, even with two big strikes against him, prison and Ruffle.

He found himself grinning at the nickname she'd insisted on using from the moment she'd heard it. There was power in words, she'd told him, so give him the name he deserves.

Cutter was on his feet the moment Trip stood up. He looked at the dog questioningly. "Want to go see your buddy Rafe?" Cutter didn't waste a second but headed for the back door. "I'll take that as a yes," Trip said, the grin still on his face as he followed. Damn, even his steps felt lighter, as if he truly was still soaring after that night with Kayley. As if some huge weight had been lifted.

He missed a step as he remembered that moment, in the middle of the night, when he'd had a dream where Ruffle had gotten not to him but to Kayley. He'd woken in a cold, terrified sweat, only to have her turn to him and hold him, and whisper into the dark, "You don't have to carry this alone anymore, Trip. Let me help."

She already had helped, so much, with everything. He'd assumed this part of the burden was his alone. What he'd done, the stains on his life, his record, were his fault, and his to bear. And yet Kayley hadn't just offered to share the load. It seemed, if the way he was feeling now was any measure, that she had succeeded. And he wouldn't have thought that possible.

It was a brisk April morning, with the usual battle between winter and spring ongoing. Although the daffodils were the clear evidence spring would, as it always did, win in the end. Cutter had obviously understood what he'd said before, because once they were outside, the dog headed straight for the big outbuilding where Rafe was staying.

"Hey, dog."

He heard the deep, gruff voice coming from inside the building, through the small, human-sized door to the left of what looked like an extra-large, roll-up garage door. Cutter trotted in. But Trip hesitated just outside, the old uncertainty suppressed but apparently not quite vanquished.

"Come on in," the gruff voice said.

Trip made a mental note never to try and sneak up on

the guy, although he'd been pretty sure of that already. He stepped inside, then stood gaping. Whatever equipment Foxworth had in the main building, it couldn't match this. The most obvious was the helicopter that took up a lot of the open floor space. He didn't know much about them, had never been this close to one, and he found it both fascinating and somehow intimidating. Rafe obviously found it familiar, since he was apparently working on it, with some tools laid out on the concrete floor beside him, and a compartment on the side of the helicopter open.

But the open space held much more. There was a long workbench against the back wall with storage beneath, and several tall cabinets beside it. Locked cabinets, he noticed. What appeared to be a sizeable power generator in the far corner, behind a large, dark blue SUV. A small trailer and a four-wheel ATV took up what space there was between the vehicle and the helicopter.

In the near corner, just past a small refrigerator and a counter that held a microwave and what looked like a camp stove, was a door that opened into another space. He guessed that must be where Rafe was sleeping, and wondered why, given he could have had the luxurious by comparison quarters Trip was using. Maybe in the military he'd been used to more Spartan surroundings.

Like you were inside?

The comparison seemed odd even in his mind. No way he could be likened to this man, who had served honorably and well.

While you were—

He broke off the old refrain as Rafe glanced over at him. "Sleep well?"

"Not really," Trip muttered. Since when he had slept, that nightmare had hit. Then, with a smile he couldn't stop, he added, "Not that I minded."

"Since Kayley stayed."

Trip grimaced. He should have guessed nothing would get past this guy. "You noticed, huh?"

"Been expecting it."

Trip's brow furrowed. "Why?"

"Way you look at her. Way she looks at you." Then he nodded at Cutter. "Most of all because of him."

Trip drew back slightly. "What?"

"He's got a lot of skills. Knowing when people are supposed to be together is one of them."

He figured he was probably gaping, but couldn't help it. This tough, gruff guy believing in such fancy as a Morse code bark was one thing. This was something else entirely.

"Yeah," Rafe said wryly, "I get it. It's ridiculous. But it's also a fact that he's linked up a dozen or so people. Foxworth people, and probably a half a dozen of our clients on top of that."

Trip was too distracted by the bizarre idea the guy was presenting to do more than stare at him. "So, you're saying he's a...a matchmaker or something?"

Rafe didn't answer the question directly. "That thing he does, making sure you and Kayley end up sitting together..."

Again Trip's brow furrowed. "Yeah, it's happened a few times. At first I thought he just got in the way or wanted his spot on the couch, but then I wondered if he was a herding breed—" He stopped, because Rafe was giving him a knowing smile. "Wait, you're saying that was intentional? To...put us together?"

And again Rafe countered with another question, as if determined that Trip get there himself. "Anything else he's done that made you end up together when you didn't expect it?"

Last night. That trick when she was going to leave.

He gave a sharp shake of his head. "That's—" He stopped himself from saying *crazy*, but barely.

"Yeah. I know. But it also is what it is. A perfect track record is hard to ignore."

Before he thought, the words were out. "What about you?"

The man's expression changed, as if he'd retreated behind a mask. "He's a smart dog. He recognizes a lost cause when he sees one."

Trip felt a pang of sympathy. Which was what was really crazy, given their relative situations. Last night had changed more than just his outlook, it seemed. As if to put the seal on the end of that line of inquiry, Rafe put down the wrench he'd been working with and wiped his hands off on a rag he then dropped atop the toolbox.

"Come on," he said. "I need to get something from upstairs."

Since the only upstairs was on the headquarters building, Trip guessed he meant there. They headed back, Cutter ambling alongside, occasionally stopping to sniff something intently. Acting like an ordinary dog, and certainly not one intent on making new couples of people Foxworth and its people came across.

He'd dismiss it as silly, but…last night.

"Thought anything about what you want to do when we get this situation cleared up?"

He liked the man's confidence that they would do just that, although he was still a little boggled that he had this kind of help. "Not much," he admitted. "When I got out, I only had one goal."

"To thank Kayley."

"Yes. And after she told me what Foxworth had done, to thank you, too."

"That was Quinn. He'll go to the mat for someone he believes in." Rafe's mouth quirked. "I'm living proof of that. But what would you like to do when this is over?"

Trip appreciated the assumption it would some day be over. He pulled open the back door, letting Cutter trot past them into the warmth of inside, before he answered. "I...don't know. I don't think I'm going to have many options, given my history."

"The world isn't kind to people who make mistakes."

Rafe pulled off his jacket, and Trip did the same as he let out a compressed, sour chuckle. "And those who make a string of them like I did..."

"Brett would agree with you on that."

"The cop?" Trip asked, startled.

"He says some people should stay locked up forever. And that some people actually prefer the regimentation. The outside is too overwhelming. But that most want out, and after they've paid for their crime should be let out."

"I figured most cops would like to just throw away the key."

"Like anything, some. Not most. Brett and Hayley have been talking about that a bit lately. Started with you, in fact."

He blinked. "What?"

"When she heard the locket story, she started thinking about it." Rafe's mouth curved slightly. "Because that's what Hayley does, think about how to make people's lives better."

As Rafe headed upstairs, Trip wondered if Hayley had tried that with him, and how far she'd gotten. When he came back, he had something in his hand, which he held out to Trip. When he saw it was a phone, he gave the man a puzzled look.

"It's a Foxworth phone," Rafe explained. "Ch—" He

stopped, then said, "Quinn's sister had them specially designed. They function just like a regular phone, but with this." He indicated a red button on the top edge of the phone. "In an emergency, that will hook you up to the Foxworth in-house, private system. It'll signal all of us, and you'll be talking to whoever's handy."

Still not taking the proffered phone, Trip looked at him, and had the sudden thought that this man with the cool, steady gaze would take Ruffle down as fast as Quinn had. "Seems like right now you're the one who's always handy. Living here, I mean."

Rafe shrugged. "I'm getting a lot done."

"Like working on that helicopter. Do you fly it?"

The man let out a faint laugh. "Hardly. I don't even like flying in it."

Trip couldn't imagine the guy being afraid of much of anything. "Why?"

"Ever hear the phrase 'Two rubber bands and a Jesus nut'? That's what holds a helicopter together. While its innate opposing forces try to tear it apart."

"Why a Jesus nut?"

"Because that's what you say if it fails," Rafe told him dryly. "Take the phone." He did, hesitantly, wondering how long it was going to take him to figure it out; phones had come a ways. "Our main number's already in the contact list, if it's not an emergency," Rafe went on. "And Kayley's."

Trip blinked. "Kayley?"

He looked back at Rafe, whose casual words belied the knowledge in his eyes. "She's part of this case, after all."

"Oh. Yeah." *Well, that was brilliant.*

While Rafe made coffee, Trip spent a few minutes messing with the phone, hoping he didn't screw it up, and pausing to look at Kayley's name and number. After Rafe slid a mug of steaming brew across the counter to him—with a warning that he made it as strong as that lube oil he'd been using on the helicopter—he leaned back against the kitchen counter, his weight mostly on his undamaged leg, Trip noted. The limp had been slightly more noticeable this morning, so it must be bothering him.

Then he met Trip's gaze over the rim of the mug before saying, "What's your worst nightmare about your future right now?"

Trip was surprised at the question, but he didn't really have to think about it, because it was right there all the time. "That I'll screw up again. That I won't be able to find work because nobody's willing to take a chance on an ex-con, and I'll end up heading down that same path again."

"You really think you will?"

"I swore I wouldn't. But a lot of people have made that vow. Then they get desperate, and…" He ended with a shrug, and shifted his gaze to stare down into the darkness of the coffee in the mug. "Now I just don't want to go backward."

"Kayley said you had a friend inside."

"Robber? Yeah." He winced as he realized what he'd said. "His name's really Robert. Robert Goodwin. He's not a bad guy. He just got desperate, like I said. His kid needed special care he couldn't afford. So he robbed a convenience store. Somebody got hurt, not by him but by accident when something fell over, but…"

He let it fade away, certain Rafe didn't want to hear about it.

"You worried about when he gets out? What he'll do?"

"Yeah," he admitted. "He's a good guy, and he really helped me stay sane in there."

Rafe studied him for a long moment. "You think he's a better man than you?"

Trip met his gaze, sensing somehow this was the most important question yet. So he answered it honestly, despite how it made him look.

"Yes," he said. "He landed there trying to help his kid. I landed there because I—" he thought again of Cutter's expression when people didn't catch on fast enough for him "—was a...dope."

I would never fall for a dope.

Kayley's words rang in his head, and suddenly he felt steadier.

"What if you could help him? And others like him, and like you? Interested?"

"I...of course I would be. But what could I do?"

"Leave that to Foxworth," Rafe said, and pulled out his own phone.

Chapter Twenty-Nine

"And then he just said 'Leave it to Foxworth,'" Trip said. "What's that supposed to mean?"

Kayley smiled at him over the boxes of Chinese food she'd picked up on her way over. "They're the operation that took down a sitting governor who also happened to be a murderer. I would imagine they could do just about anything."

She actually knew a little more than that, since she'd talked to Hayley this afternoon after she'd finished her work for the day, but she'd been asked to keep it mum, and so she would. Because if this worked out…well, she didn't dare think about that. She'd get her hopes way up, and the crash that might come if it didn't work out would be ugly.

Trip ate another of the luscious shrimp, and tossed one to Cutter. Rafe had mentioned the dog loved them, but not to give him too much. Kayley had picked up enough food for three and invited him to stay. Rafe had given her the strangest look before saying, "Neither of you has to worry about including me. I'm pretty self-sufficient."

She wasn't sure if it was the expression on his face or the quiet words that had made her heart ache a little for the man who was spearheading the effort to help Trip.

"I looked the foundation up," Trip said, with a nod to

the phone that was on the table beside him. "With the phone he gave me. After I figured it out," he added with a grimace. "They've changed a bit."

"I use mine every day and sometimes can't keep up. Somebody needs to teach those people that just because you can doesn't mean you should."

"And if it ain't broke?" he asked, the frown gone now.

"Exactly."

He went on then. "I read some of the testimonials about Foxworth. Not just the ones on their own site, but from people all over. People who had to go against someone more powerful, or the government. Big issues, but small ones, too. Small to everyone except the person who has to deal with it. They really do fight for the little guy, don't they?"

"If you're in the right, they do. And they usually win." She smiled at him. "And now they're going to battle for you."

He put down his fork and gave a slow shake of his head, as if he was still having trouble processing this. "All because of that locket."

"Yes."

He held her gaze and almost in the tone of a confessional said, "It was an impulse decision, Kayley. I wasn't thinking about what was right, or anything like that."

"Sometimes I think our impulse decisions reveal who we are more than anything else."

His gaze shifted then, warmed. "Like your decision to open your door—and your home—to me, when most people would have slammed it in my face."

"That wasn't an impulse. That was a given."

For a long, silent moment, he just looked at her. Then, softly, he said, "So is this." And kissed her.

They made it to the bed this time. Kayley had wondered if anything could ever top their first night together, but Trip seemed determined to prove that beyond doubt. He hadn't forgotten a single thing about what she liked, what caresses drove her mad, and he discovered a couple of new ones she had never known herself. He made her wait this time as he stroked, kissed, and teased with his tongue, until she was practically begging him. And when he finally slid inside her, filling the empty place that had been aching for him, she cried out his name at the sweet, tight fullness of it.

She roused early in the morning to find him already awake, staring at the ceiling.

"Trip?"

He turned his head. He smiled at her, but even in the faint light of the room, she could see it wasn't a happy sort of smile. She reached out and flicked on the bedside lamp.

"What is it?" she asked.

"I… It's just that…" He stopped, then said with a sigh, "I don't ever want you to regret this. Doing this. With me."

Kayley felt a knot tighten up in her stomach. Would he ever get past this, this feeling of…worthlessness? "How could I regret something that makes me feel the way you make me feel?"

"What if I screw up, if I go wrong again?"

"You won't."

"You can't know that."

"But I can. Because you've never had so many people on your side before. Ready to help. You won't let them down." She gave him the best smile she could manage. "Or Cutter. Not after he vouched for you."

"It's you I don't want to let down."

"You won't."

He took in a deep, audible breath. "Ruffle's a…he's

cold as ice, Kayley. I've seen what he's done to others that have crossed him."

"But he's in prison. And you didn't cross him, not really."

"But he thinks I did. And he's not exactly the most flexible guy in his thinking. Once he's zeroed in on someone…"

"Foxworth will keep you safe. Don't forget who Rafe used to be, an expert sniper."

"Me? It's you I'm worried about."

She felt a flood of what she couldn't deny was pleasure at that. "He likely doesn't even know I exist."

"But he could. Some of the gang saw Debra, and they could have—"

A quiet, polite woof came from the doorway. It made Kayley smile. "Well, good morning, Your Cleverness."

Trip went suddenly very still. She glanced back at him, and saw that he was eyeing the dog warily. "What?" she asked.

"Just something Rafe told me about…his cleverness," he said.

"I'm sure there's no end to it," she said as she raised up on one elbow. Cutter came over and sat, looking up at her with that steady, amber-flecked gaze. "Is there, sweetie?" she asked, stroking his soft fur.

She wondered what Rafe had said that had made such an impact, but she put it aside for the moment, given the subject of the discussion clearly needed to go outside. And then she got lost in her own musings as they got up, wondering what the Foxworth man thought about her spending the night here the last two nights.

"Maybe I shouldn't presume to stay here," she said as they watched Cutter trot out into the meadow, apparently immune to the morning chill as he paused here and there to sniff. "I mean, this is their property and—"

"Rafe said he'd been expecting it."

She blinked, turned to look at him. "He said that about…us?"

He nodded. "That's what he told me. He said that is one of his—" he gestured at Cutter "—other talents."

"What is?"

He took a deep breath, but didn't answer right away. She saw his jaw muscles jump. Finally, he spoke one word. "Matchmaking."

He explained then what Rafe had said, including about the dog's track record. When he'd finished, Kayley was torn between an urge to laugh and the need to give the dog the biggest hug in the world.

"Hayley always said he was the reason they were together, and the others, but I didn't take it literally. I always just thought she meant that the cases he found brought people together."

"Rafe said that nudging thing he does, making you sit where you didn't intend to sit, is the first sign."

She did laugh then. "Well, he is a herding breed, after all."

He was staring at her now. "You don't think that's crazy?"

"I think silly humans need all the help they can get."

Chapter Thirty

Trip was sitting at the counter, messing with the Foxworth phone, when Kayley's cell phone rang. He looked up as she pulled it out of its pocket on the outside of her purse and looked at it. And smiled.

"Yes, of course I'll take the call," she said when she answered, but then, to his surprise, she held the phone out to him. "It's for you."

His brow furrowed. "What?"

"It's Robber. I gave them my cell number when I made the request, just in case."

For a moment he just stared at her, but then he took the phone. He said hello tentatively, but then heard Robber's voice.

"Hey, Three."

He sounded a little off, so Trip quickly asked, "You okay?"

"Yeah. Just…tired of this."

"I know, buddy."

"I guess you and your lady are doing okay, since you're right there with her?"

Your lady…

He wasn't about to deny it, not with Kayley sitting right here. But even as he thought it, she got up and took

Cutter outside, giving him privacy. And that, he thought, was very like Kayley, to think of that.

"I...she's amazing."

"I knew that the first time I saw her when she came to visit you."

"I don't doubt that," Trip said wryly. "I'm the one who was slow on the uptake."

"Seems you figured it out now."

"Now I just need to not mess it up."

"Always the big challenge, isn't it?"

Robber definitely sounded down. "What's wrong? You sound like hell."

"It's just that time."

"Crap." He looked down at the phone to confirm the date. He'd forgotten. "I'm sorry, man."

"I just need to know something's going right for someone," Robber said.

"It is," he said. "Better than I had any right to expect."

"Good to hear."

They talked for a bit longer, trading updates. When the call ended, Trip sat there for a while, his brow furrowed, tapping at the counter with his thumb. When the back door opened he looked up, in time to see Cutter trotting in and Kayley closing the door behind them.

"Is he okay?" were her first words. "I don't know him, but he sounded a little stressed."

Trip couldn't stop himself. He slid off the stool and went to her, pulling her into his arms and just holding her.

"If that isn't you to a T, Kayley McSwain. You don't even know the guy, but you can tell he's stressed out."

She hugged him back, and rested her head on his shoulder as if it comforted her. That was still a new feeling for him, that he could actually comfort someone.

"So, he is stressed?"

"Yeah. This week…it's the anniversary of his son's death."

She straightened, looked up at him. "How awful! No wonder he's wrecked."

"Yeah. I usually made sure he was too busy to think about it much, but…"

Her arms tightened around him. "You're a good friend, Trip."

"Maybe." He let out a compressed breath. "I just hate to think of him spending this day in there, with nobody to distract him."

"Won't someone else?"

"Nobody else knows."

She drew back, looking up at him. "You're the only one he told?" He nodded. "I rest my case," she said softly.

He lowered his gaze, unable to quite meet those lovely blue eyes. He couldn't even begin to describe what it felt like, having this woman on his side, fighting with him and for him.

"Let's go see him," she said suddenly, and his head came up sharply.

"What?"

"Let's go, and you can distract him like you always did. Is there something we can bring him, that he likes and can't get? If we leave now we can be there in—"

"Kayley, hold on. I…they won't let me see him. Ex-cons don't make the visitors' list."

She frowned. "Well, I've already been through the process. Maybe they'll let me transfer it over to him. Then I could go see him, and he'd know you wanted to, and—"

He pulled her back into his arms, and hugged her so tightly he thought it must almost hurt, but he couldn't help it. "It's a wonderful idea, Kayley, and I love you for it, but I don't know if they'd allow that."

She lifted her head and simply looked at him, with a wide-eyed expression. His brow furrowed slightly. Then, as if for the first time, he realized what he'd said.

I love you...

She was looking at him as if she was hoping he meant it as more than just *thanks for the idea.*

He went very still. He had no right. Not when his life was still chaos. Especially now when it was in danger from Ruffle. And when—hopefully—it someday wasn't? Maybe not even then. Kayley deserved better. No matter how much he wanted it to be him, she deserved better. Deserved someone who didn't come with all his baggage. Yet here she was, planning a trip to a state prison to visit a guy she didn't know, just because he was a friend of his.

He didn't speak, didn't dare try. The moment passed. And Kayley moved on. "What about a video call? Maybe they'd allow that? Let me call them. Maybe Officer Moreland could make that happen as he did with the phone calls."

He'd do more than that for you, if you gave him a chance. And you'd be better off.

Damn, he was losing it. Sitting here thinking Kayley would be better off with a corrections officer than him. A decent one, true, but still. But wasn't it the truth? He didn't know. He only knew it made him sick inside.

She'd already started to dial when she stopped, saying, "Oh, wait. We should probably run this by Rafe first, if Moreland can get it okayed."

He couldn't believe her. She was offering to go back there, alone, just to ease the pain of some prisoner who was a stranger to her? Not to mention thinking of an aspect he hadn't.

"No," he said. "What if he does have a connection there, who sees you and gets word to Ruffle?"

"Then he'll be confused, because before I came to see you, and now I'm coming to see a different guy. He'll think I'm one of those groupie types and dismiss me."

He stared at her. "No one," he said carefully, "in their right mind would think that of you."

"You saying Ruffle's in his right mind?"

He shook his head, exasperated now. "You have an answer for everything, don't you?"

"No. But Rafe might," she said, and headed for the back door. Cutter was at her heels, but the dog stopped at the doorway and looked back at him, clearly waiting as Kayley went on ahead. When Trip didn't move right away, he made a low sound, half whine, half growl, that ended on an up note. And when he had the thought that it sounded like *well?* Trip knew he was losing it completely.

"Yeah, yeah, dog," he muttered. "I'm coming."

And as they crossed the open space between the main building and the outbuilding, all he could think was that ten days ago the most complicated thing he had to think about was how to convince his mouth that beef stew fabrication was actually edible.

When he got there, where Rafe had clearly been working this time on the generator in the back corner, Kayley was already halfway through her rapid-fire explanation. He kept quiet while she finished. Then Rafe looked at him.

"This is the friend you told me about?" He nodded. "Let me call Brett. He's got some contacts in the system."

I'll bet he does, given how many he's probably put in that system.

But he remembered the man's non-condemning gaze, and his willingness to listen, and even help.

When he saw Rafe was looking at him, waiting, he was puzzled. Trip realized he was waiting for his go-ahead, but he couldn't speak for a moment. As if he'd read his expression, Rafe said quietly, "This goes how you want it, Trip. We make recommendations, or tell you if we think something's a mistake, but unless it's going to lead to disaster, the decisions are yours."

The decisions are yours.

Did the man have any idea what that felt like to him? What it was like to have autonomy back after so long? Meeting that steady look, he had the feeling the man understood completely.

His throat was too tight to speak, so he only nodded. And Rafe pulled out his phone. The phone with the red button to connect to Foxworth, the organization he couldn't even have imagined before, but now had on his side.

Thanks to Kayley.

Chapter Thirty-One

Kayley tapped the key to end the video call. They were upstairs in the Foxworth meeting room, where he'd never set foot before. Trip was very glad that it had worked out, because the smile Robber had just given her was much steadier than it had been when they'd started. Brett Dunbar's call, backed up by his fame from the governor case, had tipped the scale, and the video call had been approved in time to make it on that ugly anniversary. She had managed to get him talking about his little boy, listening and encouraging, knowing it was probably something he couldn't talk about much there, now that Trip was gone.

And he'd ended it with words that had made Trip's gut tighten. "He's a good man, Kayley. Maybe not quite good enough for you, but I'm not sure any man would be."

She'd given him her best smile then, and said, "I'm going to want you to say that in person in a few weeks." He'd told her it was still countable in months, but she'd insisted weeks had to sound better, and the end closer.

"That was a really kind thing to do," Rafe said.

"I think he sounded better at the end there," she said.

"He did," Trip agreed. He hadn't been allowed to take part in the call, but he'd been able to listen from across the room. And was even more in awe at Kayley's compassion and thoughtfulness. At the same time, that niggled at him, as part of his mind wanted to declare that was the only reason she was helping him.

He fought it back, because he knew it was the old Trip trying to screw with him. He was determined to quash that voice forever. Because there was no way in hell Kayley McSwain would have slept with him just because she felt sorry for him.

Trip studied his hands for a moment before looking up and meeting that intimidating gaze. "He's the one you should be helping. He deserves it more."

"I've got Liam looking into his case." Rafe smiled then. "We're pretty efficient. We can help more than one person at a time. And Foxworth has an added asset we didn't have back then with you, in case legal help's needed."

"What's that?"

"Gavin de Marco."

He blinked. He flashed back suddenly, to Ruffle declaring if he ever got in serious trouble, he'd just hire Gavin de Marco, the best damned defense attorney in the country, maybe the world.

"I...thought he dropped off the planet," he said, remembering how the man had vanished, walked away from what had to be one of the most lucrative careers ever built.

"For a while. But he's back, and he works with us now."

Every time he thought he had a handle on the scope and power of Foxworth, something new came along to show him he had no idea.

KAYLEY HAD BEEN a little worried that Trip might find being essentially stuck here at the Foxworth headquarters reminded him too much of what he'd just left behind.

Yet he didn't seem at all restless. In fact, this Saturday
morning he seemed more relaxed than she'd ever seen
him as they stood out in the meadow, which produced
more daffodils for Cutter to romp through every day, as
if they could force spring to arrive by sheer numbers.

Of course, the fact that they were spending every night
and sometimes part of the day as well making love might
have something to do with that, she admitted to herself,
feeling her cheeks heat even at the thought, since it amazingly got better and better every time as they learned
each other. She'd now explored every inch of that lean,
strong body, from that thick, rebellious hair that somehow looked styled even when she knew it hadn't been to
feet she was astonished to find were ticklish.

"Oh, now I've got you!" she'd exclaimed with a laugh.

And that had been when he'd looked her straight in
the eyes and said with quiet intensity, "Yes. You do."

It was as close as he'd come to acknowledging what
had grown between them. And every time she remembered it, her pulse gave a little leap of happiness. She even
regretted that Monday she had that seminar to do. She'd
much rather spend the day with him again.

She watched him endlessly throwing a ball for the apparently indefatigable Cutter. She was enjoying the scene,
not just for the happy dog, but for being able to simply
watch the way Trip moved. Which put her in mind of
other moves, and that quickly, her pulse had kicked up
again. But later, as they sat over the lunch they'd made
of leftovers, he nearly stopped it when he looked at her
and asked, "Why did you believe I didn't want to be what
I'd become?"

"I just knew. I could tell you weren't happy with
your life."

"But stupid me, I thought I was happy enough. Happy as I could be. Back then, when I was…with Debra."

The words came out before she could stop them. "Maybe it was my wishful thinking. Because I wanted you to be with me."

He went still. "Then? Kayley, I was on the fast track to where I ended up, and you were…you."

She'd done it now, so she couldn't back down. "Yes. I was afraid of you at first, because I knew the kind of guy she went for. But after that first time you had to wait for her, and we talked, I wasn't afraid anymore."

He studied her for a moment before he said, "I used to think about that. Those talks. After we left, and Debra would be yammering away about some petty thing, I'd still be thinking about our conversations."

He couldn't have said anything that pleased her more. Well, maybe one thing, but a declaration of love wasn't something she was allowing herself to even consider. Not in the midst of all this. But his words did make her say, very carefully, "I know you cared about her, but that didn't sound like…" She trailed away, wishing she hadn't said it.

"Like I loved her? That's because I didn't, not really." His mouth quirked wryly. "But then, she didn't love me, either." She let out a long breath, relieved. "Do you think I haven't realized that? That I was just a…an adventure for her?"

"I worried about it, a bit."

He reached out and took her hand. "Even then you worried about me."

"Yes."

He seemed to hesitate, then lowered his gaze to their hands. "I was in no danger of falling in love with her. I swore that off long ago. Swore I would never really fall in love."

She felt a chill ripple through her. He was warning her that he didn't love her, either. She should have known, should never have expected— Her careening thoughts stopped as his fingers tightened around hers, as if he'd felt her tension. And he gave her the reason she realized she should have guessed all along.

"I swore that because I was afraid if I did and I lost her, I'd turn like my father did."

That quickly her emotions shifted. She squeezed his hand back and said, "You wouldn't. He hurt you too much. You'd never forget that."

He let out a rough breath. "He wasn't always that way."

"I know. He just couldn't handle the grief. But it's part of life." She winced. "Easy for me to say. But I'm sorry it…ruined him. And your relationship with him."

His eyes went slightly unfocused, as if he were re-membering. And his voice was soft when he told her, "He named me, did I ever tell you? Trip for triple, because I made them three. Complete, he used to say."

And he'd gone from that to beating and abusing. No wonder Trip was wary. "You'd never be like him," she said firmly.

He looked up at her then. "You sound so sure."

"Do you think we only learn from our parents' good examples? We learn from the bad ones, too, probably even more thoroughly."

One corner of his mouth curved in that crooked smile she liked so much. "I didn't think your parents were ever bad examples."

"Well," she said thoughtfully, "my mom does tend to bake obsessively, and my dad does get tunnel vision now and then." She paused for effect. "Of course, his tunnel vision is usually focused on the cookies she's always baking, so it works out okay."

He laughed, making her effort worth it. "They sound… great."

"They are." She took a breath and went on. "They'd like you."

"The ex-con their daughter's sleeping with? I doubt it."

Something in his voice jabbed at her even more than the old, tired designation. Some undertone of…all she could think of was her own word, *wishful*. As if he were hoping she could prove him wrong. Well, she'd give it her best shot.

"No," she said. "The man who gave a little girl back her most precious possession. The man who worries about the friend he left behind. The man whose first thought after getting out of misery was to come and thank their daughter for doing what any friend should have done given the same circumstances. The man who lost far too early what I'm lucky enough to still have, loving parents. The man who endured abuse no son should, but who took it because he was afraid of losing his father, too. *That's* who they'd like."

He was staring at her now. And in that moment, looking into those suspiciously bright green eyes, she dared to hope she'd gotten through.

Chapter Thirty-Two

Trip supposed he shouldn't have been surprised, given what he now knew about Foxworth and their influence, and the fact that Detective Dunbar was clearly considered one of the team, even if it was unofficial, when the man showed up late Saturday afternoon. He was announced by one of Cutter's distinctive barks before he and Kayley even heard the car approaching. The same odd bark Trip had heard the first time the man arrived.

"Didn't want you thinking I'd forgotten about you," Dunbar said after giving Cutter a cheerful greeting the dog returned in kind, then giving Kayley a warm smile.

"I get the feeling you don't forget much," Trip said. "But it is Saturday."

Dunbar shrugged. "Got an update." Then, to Trip's surprise, he gave Cutter an order—or maybe a request—that the dog promptly obeyed. "Go tell Rafe I'm here, buddy."

The dog immediately took off through the door Dunbar had held open for him.

"Your eye's looking a lot better," the detective said when he came into the room.

Trip nodded. The bruising, thanks to Kayley's attention and warm compresses, was almost gone now. If the average person didn't know, they might not even notice.

Dunbar noticed.

As Trip had suspected, Rafe had been aware of the new arrival and was already on the way, so he and Cutter were back in barely a minute.

"Liam's coming," Rafe said as he came in. "He's in town, so he should be here—" Cutter let out another one of his singsong barks and headed for the door "—right about now."

"Let me guess," Trip said dryly as he watched the dog bat open the door and race through. "That's his special bark."

"Yep," Rafe said, and the usually taciturn man was smiling. "His and Ria's."

Trip heard the sound of tires on the gravel drive, and a moment later Liam Burnett was coming back through the door, Cutter dancing around him happily. The Texan smiled in greeting, pausing for a moment to focus on Trip and Kayley, then shifted to Rafe with a raised eyebrow. Rafe gave a little eye roll, and Liam grinned and looked back at them, then down at Cutter.

"Nice work, dawg," he drawled.

It didn't take much to interpret that, and Trip didn't dare look at Kayley, not after he'd told her about Cutter's supposed other skill. Besides, he wanted to hear what Dunbar had to say.

First was that Ruffle's cousin was still holding down the fort, which wasn't really a surprise. Second was that they seemed to have moved, and Dunbar's contacts in the city weren't sure where. Their old hangout, the one Trip had told the detective about, had been the vacant quarters of a former shipping business near the port of Seattle, but now it had been sold and scheduled for demolition.

It was the third item that hit Trip like a punch to the gut.

"It's not confirmed, just a possible as of now, but the

PD down in Tacoma thinks they may have spotted the cousin a couple of times in the last month. The gang unit compared the latest photos available, and it's their best guess. Still only a guess, though."

"Where?" Trip asked, his pulse starting to pick up.

"In the area of the rail yards."

"The warehouse," he said instantly. At Dunbar's suddenly intent look, he went on. "Ruffle always believed in a backup plan. He knew of an abandoned warehouse down there, near the railroad tracks, and always had it in mind as a bolt-hole if they needed one."

"Do you know where it is?" Liam asked.

"All I know is it was between the tracks and the first arm of Commencement Bay."

"That narrows it way down," Rafe said. "Liam?"

"On it," Liam said, standing up. "I'll check for warehouses for sale, or in foreclosure, or otherwise empty. And since you said Ruffle—" the Texan grinned at the nickname "—uses the web to search out potential victims, I'll check for any sudden increase in internet hookups or traffic in the area."

"He uses the dark web, too," Trip warned.

Liam's grin widened. "Brother, I learned on the dark web."

And then he was headed upstairs, two steps at a time. Trip tried to smile at the admission, was glad about the energy and determination, but all the while his stomach was churning. Because what would have been a two-hour journey at minimum, or a trip with a ferry wait and ride to slow him, was now down to a simple hour's drive.

Ruffle's surrogate, his apparently loyal cousin, was now much closer.

To Kayley.

And no matter how reasonable the thought that it

might not have been Boyd Ruff at all, and that even if it was they had no way of knowing who or where Kayley was, let alone what she was to him, he couldn't completely quash the steady drumbeat of worry.

He tried to put it out of his mind, but Kayley seemed to sense it. She seemed to know every time it crept into his mind, because the moment it did, she was assuring him everything would be okay. Even Rafe seemed to notice, because later, when they ordered a pizza, he stuck around for it.

Or maybe he just likes pizza.

Liam came down, claimed two slices, and went right back upstairs to work. But Rafe joined them at the table, although Trip had the feeling he wasn't completely comfortable.

"How did you and Quinn connect?" Kayley asked Rafe, as if this were just some casual dinner with a friend.

Rafe pondered that as if it were a much tougher question than it should have been. But then, if somebody asked him simply how he was doing, it wouldn't be an easy response, either. *Better than ever, but I'm terrified* didn't seem like a reasonable answer.

"I've known him since we were kids," Rafe finally said.

That surprised him. "Neighbors?" he asked.

"My aunt lived next door to the Foxworths."

He suddenly remembered Jimmy Swanson, a classmate who had lived next door. Remembered how he'd come to him and awkwardly expressed his sympathy after Mom had died. But Trip had been in no mood or shape to hear it. He'd always felt bad about how he'd turned him away.

And belatedly he remembered what Kayley had told him about how Quinn's parents had died. Wondered if

Rafe had approached Quinn as Jimmy had him. If he had, he'd probably gotten a better response.

"How old was Quinn when his parents were killed?" Kayley asked.

"Ten."

She sucked in an audible breath, as Trip winced and lowered his eyes. He'd ruined his life because his mother got sick when he was sixteen, died when he was nineteen, and Quinn Foxworth built this after losing both parents at ten?

And yet again, Kayley read him easily. "But Quinn had his sister, and other family, didn't he?"

"Yes," Rafe said. "His uncle. Who tried, but as Quinn says, he wasn't a kid kind of a guy."

"Hayley told me Charlie mostly raised him."

Something in Rafe's eyes shifted then. He was no Kayley when it came to reading subtleties, but to him it looked like a combination of pain and a sort of longing he would never have thought the seemingly unshakable man capable of.

"Yes," Rafe answer finally. "She was only fourteen when it happened, but she never, ever failed him."

"And now she runs the business end of Foxworth?" Kayley said with a wide smile. "She must be brilliant."

There was a second of silence that seemed somehow tense before Rafe said flatly, "Charlaine Foxworth is the most amazing woman I've ever met."

Even he could see the stiffness there. But Rafe ended it abruptly, getting up, disposing of the meal's debris, thanking them rather stiffly before saying good-night.

"Wow," Kayley said. "There's some history there."

"Even I got that," Trip said.

Then, abruptly and without explanation, Kayley said, "You had no one to help, Trip. No other family, no one to step up for you, no one to protect you from what your father became. And you took it, and took it, for his sake."

He met her gaze then, saw the intensity in it. "Always defending me, aren't you?" he said softly.

"Has anyone else, really, since your mother died?"

He took a long breath. "Not like you have."

That night he made love to her fiercely. He knew he was at the edge of his control, and it took every bit of the tiny bit of sanity having her naked beneath him left him not to snap and go wild.

And then Kayley broke their kiss and stretched around to nip at his ear, in a way she'd discovered sent more heat rippling through him, something he'd never known himself. As she did it, she whispered, "Stop holding back."

That control broke. He drove hard, and deep, burying himself in her sweet warmth, loving the way she clutched at him as if even this wasn't deep enough, as if she wanted to hold him there forever. And when she cried out his name, her body clenching around him as fiercely as he had driven into her, he exploded, pouring himself into her until he knew there was nothing left that wasn't hers.

Chapter Thirty-Three

Kayley thought this must be the best Sunday she'd ever had. They'd spent a long, lazy morning in bed—although *lazy* wasn't perhaps the best word for it, considering how they'd spent much of that time.

After a leisurely breakfast of leftover pizza—minus a couple of bits tossed to the ever-polite and, when it came to food, discreet Cutter—they went out with the dog, enjoying simply standing in each other's arms as they watched him romp through the meadow speckled with the bright yellow of the daffodils.

Kayley let her head rest against his chest, remembering how many times when she'd awakened in his arms, she would simply watch him sleep, just for the sheer tranquility it gave her. Because she remembered how edgy he'd been at first, how his sleep had been broken and restless, and seeing how relaxed he was now was a gift.

She didn't think it was just the sex that had done it; he was feeling more certain. As if it was finally sinking in that he was truly free. And the sight of him sleeping peacefully gave her more pleasure than any sight ever had.

That evening she reluctantly left. She had to do her final prep for the seminar, something she'd put off as long as she possibly could. Trip had understood, saying he didn't want her to risk something that could really help her build her business.

All the way home, when she'd intended to be mentally rehearsing her talk on remote working in human resources yet again, instead she'd gotten lost in wondering what would happen when this was all over, when he was safe from Ruffle's threat. She knew what she wanted, but she wasn't sure he wanted the same. He'd just gotten out. Did he even know what he wanted? Was she just the first bit of caring he'd come across upon his release?

By the time she pulled into her garage, she was laughing out loud at herself. If she'd still been with him and that thought struck, all she would have had to do was look at him, at the way he met and held her glance, and she'd be utterly reassured. But now, less than fifteen minutes out of his presence, she was flooded with doubts.

Resolutely she shoved the doubts that threatened into the dark corner of her mind where they belonged, focused on the task at hand, and used the promise of heading back to him as soon as the seminar was over as the thought that eased her into sleep that night.

TRIP WOKE UP early Monday morning, reached for Kayley, then spent a few frustrated minutes wondering how he'd gotten so used to her being there so quickly. A week today since that first night they'd slept together, and she was already…indispensable. He rolled over onto his back and lay there for a while, aching for her. When he finally got up, his shower was a chilly one. It helped a little, but he knew it would only take one stray thought or one of those vivid memories to set him off again.

He pulled on his jeans and let Cutter out, thinking crazily that he didn't mind at all taking care of the dog. Not that he took much taking care of, and he had a unique way of making what needed to be done quite clear.

Like sitting next to Kayley?

He was smiling about that when the dog came back in, and he put fresh kibble in the bowl. But Cutter had other ideas, one of those that he made clear when he went over and sat in front of the fridge. Trip laughed, dug out the bag of baby carrots and started tossing them to the dog.

"Your appetizer, huh?" he said when the dog stopped at three and trotted over for the more expected breakfast.

There was one lonely slice of now two-day-old pizza in the fridge. Well, not quite two days, he told himself, since it was morning. Day and a half, then. That didn't sound so bad. And it tasted okay, and would hold him. Maybe even until Kayley was done. She'd said she'd head straight here after the networking lunch that followed the seminar. Had even suggested they go for a drive, just to get him out of the house, as it were. If they cleared it with Rafe, of course.

Since he was about to go mad just sitting here, knowing progress was probably being made but not doing a damned thing himself, he'd agreed. He'd feel better if he knew Boyd was busy elsewhere, but… He grimaced at the realization that if Ruffle's cousin was busy elsewhere, it meant some other person, likely more than one, was being hurt or damaged. And he once more had to fight down the rising revulsion at what he'd allowed his life to become.

He was sitting at the kitchen counter, watching the clock tick down towards noon, wondering what on earth he was going to do, how he could ever have anything to offer Kayley in the way of a future, when an odd sound, a combination of buzz and ding, snapped him out of the painful reverie. It took him a moment to realize it was the phone Rafe had given him, which he'd left on the coffee table in front of the fireplace. He walked over and saw the red light was flashing.

He picked up the phone and pressed it, and Rafe was instantly there. "You've got a call from your buddy at OCC. I'll transfer it over."

He'd forgotten that Rafe had said Foxworth was on Robber's call list now. And a moment later he heard the familiar voice.

"Hey, Three. That Foxworth Foundation is something. I've never had anybody get added to my list that fast. Who are they?"

"They are something, and I'll explain later," Trip said. "How you doing?"

"Okay, now. Had a little thing Thursday. Why I'm calling."

"A thing?" That sounded ominous. "What happened?"

"Touchy."

"What about him?" Trip asked sourly, remembering all too well the inmate with the little-man complex who couldn't control his temper. The guy who seemed to try and get anyone close to release in trouble. The one who had leered at Kayley when she'd visited, and later tried to provoke him into a fight right before his release date, the fight that had given him the black eye and that would likely have botched up everything for him if he'd given in and struck back. "He finally get himself jumped or something?"

"Worse. He tried for Moreland. Damned toothbrush shiv."

Trip felt a jab of concern; he knew the damage those makeshift weapons could do. "Is he okay?" He knew some would laugh at him, worried about a guy whose job had been to keep him locked up. But Moreland had been an honest one, never unfair or harsh. And he'd helped Kayley get on Robber's call list. And probably Foxworth, and hence himself, as well.

"Yeah. I was there, so I yanked Touchy off him before he did any damage. But he got me, a little."

Trip swore. "You really okay?"

"Yeah. Just a couple of stitches, but it got infected, so they made me stay in bed in the medic unit for a while. That's why I couldn't call until now."

"What the hell set him off?"

"With Touchy, who knows? We call him that for a reason, right? But that's not the point, buddy. The point is, they pulled his ass right out of here. And you know where he likely ended up, for assaulting a CO."

"Probably back in max," he said, knowing that the Department of Corrections didn't cut any slack for inmates stupid enough to attack one of their own. And then it hit him, what Robber was getting at. Touchy could well end up under the same roof as Ruffle. "Damn," he muttered.

"Yeah. If I were you, I'd grab that girl of yours and get the hell out of Dodge."

Trip fought off the chill that tried to invade. "If I start running, I might never be able to stop. And I can't— won't—yank Kayley out of her life because of the mess I made of mine."

"But—"

"Listen, Robber, I've got these Foxworth people on my side now—"

"Hey, they obviously have pull, but Oliver Ruff is an entirely different thing. Some foundation isn't going to be able to deal with what he can do, even from inside."

Trip smothered the panic that was trying to build; Robber couldn't do anything more than he was already doing, warning him, and it wouldn't be fair to pay him back by letting him hear how freaked he was getting.

"Don't be so sure. Remember our former governor?"

"You mean the murderer who's probably just down the cell block from your old boss?" His friend sounded puzzled, clearly wondering what that had to do with anything.

"That's the one. And the operation that helped put him there was the Foxworth Foundation."

"Whoa. And now they're helping you? How'd that happen?"

"Kayley," he said simply.

Robber let out a long, low whistle. "I swear, buddy, if you don't wrap that woman up for good, I'm coming after her as soon as I get out of here."

"She's the best thing that's ever happened to me." And suddenly, because he was too much of a coward to say it to her, he said it to Robber instead. "I love her."

"I got that," Robber said, sounding like he was smiling. "Keep her safe, Three."

"With my life," he vowed, and he meant it more than he'd meant anything in his life.

Chapter Thirty-Four

When Rafe got there, Trip was pacing, feeling like he was about to fly into a thousand pieces. Even Cutter was on edge; the dog had been at his heels even though he'd only been walking the same path over and over.

He'd used the red button the instant the call with Robber had ended, and Rafe had answered as quickly. He'd also picked up on the urgency in Trip's voice, and told him to hold on because he was on his way over. He'd never been so glad to see the man's steely gray gaze. Rafe listened to it all, and without a word pulled out his phone and made a call. Trip heard him concisely relay what he'd just told him.

When the call ended, Rafe looked back at Trip. "Brett's checking on where Anthony Fossey, aka Touchy, went. He'll get back to us ASAP."

Trip nodded, thankful more than he could say that these amazing people were on his side. "If I know Ruffle, and I do, he's got a network well established. He pays a lot for information. Even inside he'll have something worked out. And if that's where Touchy went, he knows about Kayley." He drew in a shuddering breath as he glanced at the time on the phone. "I need to check on her, but she should still be doing her presentation."

"Call the venue," Rafe said. "Find out if all's going as planned."

Trip nodded, thankful somebody's brain was firing on all cylinders. Apparently when it came to Kayley, he couldn't think straight in more ways than one. As he made the call, Rafe made another one, but he didn't even try to listen, he was so focused on reaching someone at the small hotel who knew about the seminar in one of their meeting rooms.

When the woman in charge finally came on the line and assured him everything was proceeding on schedule—she'd even listened to the first part of Kayley's talk and was impressed—he started to breathe again.

"She's okay," he said when he saw Rafe looking at him as the call ended. "She's winding up right now. Then she has a Q and A, the lady said maybe ten minutes or so, although maybe more since there's a lot of interest. Then there's a lunch for all the attendees."

"Text her in ten minutes. She's probably got her phone muted during her presentation anyway."

Trip rammed his fingers through his hair. "Yeah. Thanks." He gave Rafe a sideways look. "I'm glad somebody's thinking straight."

The other man's gaze was steady. "You love her. Makes it tough." Trip drew back slightly. Had the man been listening to his call with Robber, when he'd admitted it for the first time? Rafe shrugged. "When even I can see it, it's pretty obvious. Besides, there's him," he added with a nod at Cutter, who had come over to sit at Trip's feet.

Trip looked down at the dog, who shifted to lean against his leg. Instinctively he reached down to stroke the dark fur of his head. And immediately felt a little calmer, a little less anxious. Rafe went on in a business-like tone that was almost as reassuring as Cutter was.

"Liam's on his way. He says Teague's on a plane home, so it's just us, but we'll deal if this turns into anything. How much does he know about Kayley?"

He managed to say it evenly. "He saw her a few times, when she visited me. He knows her name. And she's listed on flyers for that seminar, and on the website for it. With a photo of her."

"I'll go get her, and have Liam head there now. He's closer."

"I'm going," Trip said flatly. Rafe studied him for a moment. Trip didn't know what decided him, but he nodded.

"All right. I'll grab some gear and meet you two out front." Trip blinked, looked at Cutter. "He's an operational part of the team. And he knows you and Kayley are the mission." The man's mouth quirked with a rare sign of amusement. "He won't be left behind anyway, trust me."

He pulled on the best socks he had, the only shoes he had, a T-shirt, and then the heaviest outer shirt. He'd noticed the chill when he'd let Cutter out. He grabbed his jacket, and had taken two steps toward the door when Cutter barked. He looked back to see the dog sitting beside the kitchen counter. His brow furrowed, wondering what the dog was doing, but as he looked he noticed he'd forgotten the Foxworth phone.

He went over and picked it up. The instant it was in his hand, Cutter dashed for the front door. As if that had been the reason for the act. Which was crazy, no matter how smart Rafe said the dog was; how could the animal possibly know that object on the counter needed to go with them?

When he stepped outside, he saw the big, dark blue

SUV from the other building already sitting out front. The back was open, and Cutter took off at a run and leaped inside. Trip closed the hatch and climbed into the front passenger seat, and they were rolling. A glance at the clock on the dash told him the ten minutes wouldn't be up for another three minutes—it was barely ten since Robber had called—but he typed out the text to Kayley anyway.

"Tell her to wait there for us," Rafe said, and Trip nodded.

"I don't want to scare her, so I'll just say there's news."

"ETA about twelve twenty."

He nodded again and input it. Tapped a finger on his knee as he watched the time tick down. Sent the text a split second after that tenth minute ended. Then sat there still tapping that finger, waiting.

He felt Rafe's look, and gave a wry shake of his head. "I went into burgs and shakedowns less nervous than this."

"The only one at stake then was you. And I get the impression you didn't care all that much. Then."

Trip winced inwardly as that hit home. He nodded toward the back of the vehicle and Cutter. "I thought he was supposed to be the intuitive one."

To his surprise, Rafe smiled. "Maybe I've learned a little, hanging out with him."

Trip remembered the maneuver with the phone now in his hand, and decided he could believe it. He—

An answering text chimed. He read it swiftly. I'll wait for you.

He breathed easily again. "She's all right. She'll wait there for us." Rafe only nodded.

And then she sent one more word.

Always.

His breath slammed to a halt in his throat. And that, weirdly, seemed to make his eyes water. He sat there staring at that single word, wondering how somebody could feel so damn many things at once.

And then Rafe got a call, routed through the car's system. He recognized Dunbar's voice in the moment before Rafe said, "Go ahead, Brett."

"Fossey's there." Trip felt a chill sweep over him. "They moved him immediately, and he was there before midnight the same night. Spent a couple of days in solitary, but was transitioned to gen pop by the weekend. I'm trying to find out if he and your guy made contact, either directly or by grapevine. Nothing yet, but I wouldn't want to bet he hasn't. Prison networks and wheeling and dealing are pretty efficient."

He barely heard the rest of it, as Rafe thanked the man and disconnected. And as if he'd understood, Cutter gave a low half whine, half growl from the back. Trip didn't think he was mistaken that they picked up some speed.

"Seven minutes," Rafe said.

Trip clenched his jaw and held on.

KAYLEY SHOOK HANDS with the seminar moderator and thanked him again for the way he'd really gotten the discussion going. He in turn complimented her nicely for her presentation, saying he'd learned some things himself. He'd been about to say something else when the text from Trip had come in, saying there was some news and to wait there. He and Rafe were on the way.

"Boyfriend?" the moderator asked.

She looked up at him, a little startled, then smiled. "Does it show?"

"Oh, yeah." He gave an exaggerated sigh. "The good ones are always taken."

She laughed, thanked him for the compliment, then gathered up her purse and laptop case. She'd put together an instructional video she'd played during her presentation, showing each step of how she did her work, and even a sample interview call that had resulted in an advantageous job offer for a client. It had worked well, she thought as she walked out toward her car to put the laptop in so she didn't have to deal with it when Trip got here.

Boyfriend?

Oh, he was more than that. Much more. And now she dared to hope that they both wanted the future they could build together. It would take time. He needed to get used to being free, and she had to give him that time. She knew there was always a chance some of what had leaped to life between them could be due to that heady new freedom, but she didn't think it was enough to matter. Not when it had been there long before. And she—

"Whoa!" she yelped as someone bumped into her, hard, as she pulled her car door open. She started to apologize, assuming it was her fault because she'd been so lost in her thoughts of Trip and where they would go from here.

"Kayley?" the person—a man she saw now—asked.

"Yes?" He must be someone from the seminar, if he knew her name. Although she didn't recall anyone who'd been in her session dressed like this, or with the tattoo than ran up the side of this guy's neck.

And then the man who had collided with her moved, with startling swiftness. He yanked her arm behind her fiercely. In the same instant his other hand came up and sealed her mouth. She tried to scream, even knowing it was useless. Her eyes scanned what she could see of the parking lot. Empty. She couldn't see much because of how tightly he was holding her mouth and head. And he was strong. Very strong. When he spoke, in a hissing sort of whisper, his voice held more menace than she'd ever heard.

"Don't fight, woman. It's not you we want."

Not you we want.

Her stomach clenched as a chill swept through her. Trip. They were after Trip. And they were going to try to use her to get to him.

Chapter Thirty-Five

"She said she'd wait," Trip murmured as they pulled into the parking lot. *Always.*

"We'll find her," Rafe said. "She—"

He broke off as Cutter erupted into furious barking. He slowed the car, while Trip looked around, hoping to see Kayley waving them down from somewhere close. He saw a few people standing over by the main doors of the place, but no Kayley. He scanned the parking lot, and didn't see anyone there, either. Cutter kept barking.

"You need to learn to say left or right, dog," Rafe muttered, barely audible with the cacophony from the wayback.

Trip wasn't sure what that was about, but when the man started to turn the wheel to the left, the barking continued, even louder.

"Right it is then," Rafe said, and pulled the wheel the other way. The barking eased, although low growls continued.

Distracted, Trip turned in the seat to look back at the dog. He was on his feet, staring out the side window of the SUV. Had he interpreted that right, that Cutter had in essence told Rafe which way to go? He shifted his gaze back to the man behind the wheel.

As if he'd sensed the shift, Rafe said with a grimace, "Don't ask. I've learned to just go with it."

"A dog giving you directions?"

"No. *That* dog giving me directions."

"I know he's really smart, but—" The rest of those words died unspoken. Because he'd just spotted a familiar small green SUV. "There's her car at the end of the row," he said. How had Cutter known it was down here, and not the other row they'd almost gone down?

"Told you," Rafe said, this time with a wry half smile.

Trip looked back at the dog. "Thanks, buddy." Cutter threw him a brief glance, but the low-pitched growls never stopped. And the sound of them made the hair stand up on the back of his neck.

Then they rolled up behind Kayley's car. Cutter's growls got louder, but Trip barely registered it. Because now, from here, he could see the driver's door of the car standing open. He could see the strap of the case he'd seen her load her laptop into dangling over the edge of the driver's seat.

And on the ground were Kayley's keys. Even from here he recognized the thistle key chain.

He jumped out of the SUV and ran. Skidding to a stop, he stared down at the silver thistle. And all Trip could think was that, despite all he'd been through, he'd never felt this cold in his life. Cold unto numbness. Because there was no doubting what had happened here.

He was vaguely aware of Rafe speaking, a beeping sound, and Cutter snarling now. And then the dog was there beside him, sniffing madly at the ground. That snapped him out of the daze, and he looked up in time to see Rafe grabbing something out of the back of the big SUV, wrestling with his jacket for a second, then spinning around with an agility that belied the occasional limp Trip had seen.

Cutter looked over his shoulder, practically trembling with eagerness. This was not the dog Trip had come to know. This was something else altogether.

Rafe snapped out, "Go."

The dog took off, nose to the ground, Rafe right beside him. Tracking, Trip realized. Instinctively he grabbed up the keys and shut the car door, using his shoulder because of some vague idea of fingerprints. Then he followed at a run until he was even with man and dog. Brilliant, uncannily clever dog.

They traversed the parking lot quickly, until they reached the street. And then Cutter slowed, sniffing in a very orderly pattern, tail up, ears forward intently, back and forth along about a ten-foot distance along the curb. And then, with an almost pitiful whine, the dog sat.

"Okay, dog, got it," Rafe said. Then he looked at Trip. "Trail ends here."

Trip looked at Cutter. There was no mistaking the inference. "They put her in a car." Rafe nodded. His gaze was narrow, his jaw tight. He was angry, Trip realized.

Good. Because I'm way past that.

He heard Rafe talking on the phone again, he guessed to Liam, giving him a search area. Trip wasn't sure what good that would do when they didn't know what kind of vehicle it had been, and this was a much more populated area than sleepy little Redwood Cove. But then Rafe was headed back to the hotel and, close behind, Trip watched with amazement as, the moment the man dropped the Foxworth name, they were on their way to look at security video.

It was a good thing he'd skipped anything more than that leftover pizza this morning, because the video made him nauseous. The images of Kayley being grabbed by a hulking, aggressive man who towered over her, and then half dragged, half carried to the panel van parked exactly where Cutter had signaled the trail ended were burned into his mind, probably forever.

"Is that him?" Rafe asked.

He couldn't speak, could only nod. He'd hoped never to see Boyd Ruff again. He stared at the time stamp in the corner because staring at her car in the image made it worse. Three minutes before they'd gotten here. A mere hundred and eighty seconds.

A lifetime.

He heard Rafe asking the security man to zero in on something, but he couldn't process it. His mind was locked onto a simple fact. He'd done this. This horrible video would play through his head for the rest of his life, because it was his fault. He'd brought this disaster down on her, brought the pure crap he'd made of his life into hers.

He belatedly tuned in to Rafe talking, now apparently to Liam. "—go to headquarters instead. You know what we need. Put Ty on it if you have to. I'll call Brett."

There was barely time for Liam to have answered, so obviously he wasn't questioning the rapid-fire orders. But then, anybody who'd question an order from this man deserved to have their sanity questioned in turn. Including him, he thought as Rafe ordered him back to the SUV, along with Cutter, who had somehow morphed into an entirely different kind of dog, alert and on guard, his entire demeanor shifted from wackily clever to all business. And it was only then that Trip noticed that Rafe had a handgun in a holster clipped to his belt. That was what he'd been doing with his jacket back at the SUV.

Crazily, all he could wonder was if snipers were as good with handguns as they were with rifles.

"We'll start a grid search until Liam comes up with something," Rafe said.

Trip didn't answer, just got in. Couldn't stop himself from looking back over at her car, as if somehow she would magically be there, safe and sound. She wasn't. If she was hurt, or worse—

His mind skittered away from the possibility, even as it multiplied the guilt he was feeling a hundredfold. He couldn't think about that. Boyd had taken her for a reason, and that reason was to get to him. Ruffle wanted him dead, and he'd do what it took to make that happen.

They started to crisscross the streets around the hotel, although Trip wasn't sure why, given five minutes had passed. Surely the van was long gone by now.

"He's probably going to contact you," Rafe said.

"I know." He already had the phone, the phone Kayley had texted to, in his hand. As they pulled to a stop at a light, Rafe glanced at him. Trip held his gaze. "He'll want a trade. He wants me."

"Yes."

"Then that's what we do."

"Trip—"

He cut the man off. Foolhardy, no doubt, under any other circumstances. But right now he didn't care. "We do whatever it takes to keep Kayley safe. All she's ever done is help me, and I won't let her pay the price for my stupidity."

"He wants you dead," Rafe said.

"Yes." Some tiny part of his mind was marveling at his utter lack of hesitation. But the rest of it, and his gut, knew only one thing. Even knowing it was a death sentence, he would do it. He would trade himself. For Kayley.

"Just so you know," Rafe said then, his voice strangely casual, "he's not getting what he wants. And Kayley's going home safe."

He wanted to believe. He knew Rafe was deadly serious, but he also knew Ruffle, and his people, and how cold-blooded they were.

He heard the sound of the in-car system activate. Rafe tapped the button above the rearview mirror.

"Northeast." Liam's voice came through the speaker, short and clipped, no trace of the drawl now. "Followed him as far as the old church on Bay View North, then ran out of cameras."

Rafe made a turn before he even answered. "Good. Not a big neighborhood beyond, so that narrows it down."

"It should be— Hang on, it's Ty."

Trip remembered something about their guy in St. Louis, supposedly even better at this than Liam. Which he found hard to believe. But then Liam was back, proving the point.

"He wants to know if they've made contact yet."

"No," Rafe answered. "But they will."

"Trip's phone is on?"

"It is."

"Have him call here," Liam said.

Rafe looked at Trip. "Dial it, not the private system."

At this point he was beyond questioning the workings and abilities of Foxworth. He called up the number, one of the two in the contact list. Felt his gut knot all over again at the sight of the other number, Kayley's. He dialed the first one.

Liam answered immediately. "Okay, just hang on, Trip, with the line open. Ty's getting a fix."

Rafe was driving with purpose now, clearly having a destination. Somewhere beyond an old church, in a small neighborhood. Where Kayley apparently was now. Being held, perhaps hurt, by one of Ruffle's men. Maybe even Boyd himself. Trip's jaw clenched violently at the images that formed in his head.

Funny, he'd felt as if his life were beginning anew the day he'd walked out of that place just two weeks ago. And now it was going to end, and while he didn't want that, he couldn't help thinking that if he was going to die, it couldn't be for a better reason than to keep the one person who had ever stood by him safe. Maybe it might even make up a little for some of the things he'd done.

"All right," Liam's voice rang out of the upper speaker, "he's got the lock on it. You can hang it up now."

Trip did so, then looked at Rafe. "What does that mean?"

"It means when they call you, because it's our phone, Ty will be able to backtrack the call. So your job is to keep the guy talking as long as possible. On speaker, because you're driving. Fake static interference, or you can't hear him, or you're stupid, whatever you have to do. Just keep the connection open as long as you can."

"Not sure I have to fake stupid," Trip said bitterly.

"We'll deal with your self-perceptions later," Rafe said, and with certainty added, "Or Kayley will."

"I can be there in twenty," Liam's voice said. "Fifteen if I break a few speed laws."

"I think we may need you there, to coordinate with Ty on the tracking. Stay live with us. And find me a spot."

"Copy that," Liam said, although he sounded a little disappointed. "When you get the call, I can— Hold on, D-squared is calling."

Trip's brow was furrowed, wondering both what "find me a spot" meant, and who on earth "D-squared" was. He looked at Rafe, who answered the obvious with a faintly amused grimace. "Detective Dunbar. Liam tends to nickname everything."

Trip clung to the ease and certainty in the man's demeanor as they drove on. They made a turn onto a small road that started uphill. Did that mean they were getting closer?

Then Liam was back. "One of his contacts thinks he knows who really ratted out Ruffle on the murder. Another prisoner there, bargaining for early parole. He's working on getting the name."

"Good to know," Rafe said, and again Trip noted the man's ease. It seemed the closer they got to chaos, the calmer the man got.

They'd barely gone another minute when it happened. The phone he was holding rang and simultaneously vibrated, sending a shock through him out of proportion to the stimulus. Because he knew what it was. Despite the strange phone number, he knew.

And he knew Kayley's life depended on how he handled this.

Chapter Thirty-Six

"It's not her phone," Trip said, although he knew they had to have gotten this number from it.

"Probably a burner. Liam?"

"Copy. Radio silence."

"Answer now?" Trip asked.

Rafe nodded. "Ty can't start until the connection's open. Speaker," he reminded him.

Trip tapped the speaker icon and answered, a little surprised that his voice was fairly steady.

"Mr. Callen." The raspy voice was familiar. Boyd Ruff. Kayley was in the hands of the most brutal of Ruffle's remaining gang, who also happened to be a blood relative. And he felt a kick of anger that this man had Kayley in his clutches. He almost answered with the man's name, but stopped himself.

Stall. You've got to stall.

He knew the man had a healthy ego, just like his cousin. *So poke it.* "Depends," he said instead, the anger allowing him to play it almost flippantly. "Who's asking?"

"You should show a little respect to the person who has your pretty little friend."

"I've got a couple of pretty friends. You're going to have to narrow it down."

He gave Rafe a sideways glance, in time to see a nod of approval.

"You always did have a smart mouth."

He waited as long as he thought he could get away with before saying, "Am I supposed to know who you are? Because your voice clearly wasn't important enough for me to remember."

That did it. "You think I'm playing here, Callen? Because I'm not. I've got your lady friend here, and if you don't cooperate, she's the one who's going to be very sorry."

He fought down a chill. Grabbed for some of the bravado he'd once had, dealing with Ruffle's crew, and then later inside. "Gotta know who you are before I decide to believe you."

Boyd let out a crude suggestion.

"Sorry, can't. I'm driving." It was strange, how talking as he once had felt so strange. As if he really had become a different person in just a couple of weeks.

Kayley. She's why. And you're going to save her, no matter what it takes. Even your life.

"Then you'd better drive toward me, asshole. Or your lady's going to be screaming soon. Because I plan to sample her thoroughly before I end it."

He wanted to scream himself. Let loose a string of promises of what he would do to Boyd if he so much as breathed on Kayley. And it took every bit of control he had not to do it.

"Well, we still have a couple of little problems. I don't know who you are, and I don't know who you supposedly have. How am I supposed to decide to come to you without knowing that, Mr....?"

Boyd swore again. "Ruff, and you damned well know

it. And I've got your friend Miss McSwain. The one who so nicely visited you when you were locked up."

There was only one way they could have known that. So it had been Touchy. Just as he thought it, he heard a couple of clicks from the speaker above them. He looked at Rafe, who mouthed *got it*, but also made a gesture to indicate he should keep talking. Which made sense, because they didn't want Boyd to know they'd pinpointed where he was. Rafe took out his own phone to call Liam directly.

Trip went back to Boyd. "I'm supposed to just believe you've got her?"

As if he'd been waiting for the question, Boyd sent a photo, time-stamped just before the call had begun. His stomach rebelled again. Kayley, looking a bit bedraggled but glaring at the camera, or more likely the man behind it. *Stay angry, honey. It'll be over soon, and you'll be safe.*

"Then I guess I need to know where you are." The man rattled off some directions. Trip gave Rafe a startled look when he pulled off to the side and halted the car, although he didn't turn it off. He pointed at the phone and mimed writing.

"Hold on, man, I haven't been here in a long time. I'm going to have to pull over and write this down." He watched as Rafe got out, leaving the driver's door open, and headed for the back of the SUV. Remembering what that had resulted in before, Trip wasn't surprised to see more weaponry. This time it was a long, intimidating-looking rifle with the most serious mounted scope he'd ever seen outside of a movie.

He snapped back to the call as Boyd swore again. Then the man said, "Make it fast. She's got a smart mouth herself, and I'm about to slap it shut."

Trip continued to stall, saying he had to find a spot, then something to write with, since he was out of it with current tech and didn't know how to just make notes on the phone. He had the fleeting thought that maybe it was good he had that to fall back on, being out of touch for so long.

Never thought I'd say that.

He did make some notes on the back of his hand with a pen he found in the glove box. But all the while he kept track of Rafe, who had clearly geared up for lethal force if necessary. And was now back talking to Liam while, oddly, looking at what appeared to be a compass.

"—the yellow building," Boyd said.

"Yellow?" Trip echoed as Rafe finished by letting Cutter out of the back of the SUV. "How fitting."

"You want this to end for her right now?"

He tried to gauge how far he could push Boyd. The man had always been more talk than action, which was why Ruffle had put him in charge of just that. But no member of the crew couldn't be brutal if necessary. Even Boyd. And the fact that he was still in charge hinted he'd probably picked up in the action department.

If it was just himself, he'd go further, prodding, poking. But it wasn't. It was Kayley, so he had no choice.

"Okay, okay, just getting all this down. Turn left at the abandoned church, up to the end of the road, yellow building on the left."

"You've got ten minutes."

"Hey, wait, I'm further away than that, and I don't know that road, and—"

"All right, twenty. Any later and you'll be here to pick up her sexy little body."

He heard a click, and the phone flashed. The call had

ended. Duration less than four minutes. Four minutes to determine the rest of his life. Which could end very, very soon.

"Here's the plan," Rafe said, glancing at his watch as he leaned into the SUV. "Keep that red channel live on the phone, so I can monitor things. In twelve minutes, you drive on up there. Give Cutter and me time to get to high ground." Trip frowned. He wasn't going to be there? "Make him bring her out. When you see Cutter, you don't know him. Do what you have to to get Kayley clear. But remember we need the cousin alive."

Trip gaped as the man turned and, followed by the now-all-business Cutter, walked into the trees beside the road, heading as he'd said, up. Do what he could? He'd die to get her clear, but then what?

The duo had vanished now, hidden by the thick evergreens. Trip sucked in a deep breath. He had to trust them, didn't he? Trust that this was somehow going to work out? Trust. He had so little of that left, and Kayley had most of it. But he couldn't believe Rafe would ever let Kayley get hurt and—

It hit him belatedly.

High ground.

Sniper.

Suddenly he understood, and could breathe again.

He walked around and got into the driver's seat. Studied the controls of the unfamiliar vehicle. Hoped he remembered the basics of how to drive. Then he watched the clock. Spent the time willing Kayley to be all right and, thinking he might not come out of this, whispering an apology to his mom, who on her deathbed had ordered him to go on and live his best life.

"I didn't do it, Mom," he whispered into the silence.

"But I would have, starting two weeks ago. I hope that's enough for you to forgive me."

And in exactly twelve minutes, he put the SUV in gear, pulled back onto the narrow road, and started toward Kayley.

Chapter Thirty-Seven

Kayley kept her chin up, and stared at the man looking out the big, half-open slider window. She guessed the bright yellow structure must have been a repair shop of some kind once, judging by the workbenches and cabinets, but it looked long abandoned now.

Inside, her heart was hammering and her stomach churning. She couldn't speak; he'd gagged her the moment she'd called his cousin Ruffle. Well, after he'd backhanded her across the face, making her upper lip swell and her cheek throb. Which she actually didn't mind, because it kept her brain divided between that pain and the pain of her wrists, where she was straining against the zip tie he'd used to bind her hands behind her before he'd then used a second tie to fasten her to a pipe that ran along the floor of the building. So she was effectively trapped, even with the door just a couple of feet away.

She knew her wrists were bleeding, but she kept trying, had some faint idea it might make them slippery enough to slide free. Boyd was sitting on the workbench beneath the window. He had one leg dangling, swinging it casually, as if he were just passing the time without a care in the world. And he played with the butt of the gun tucked into his waistband a little too familiarly.

He'd told her if she behaved herself, she could walk

away from this. She didn't believe him. She'd seen him. If he'd planned to let her go, he'd have worn a ski mask or something so she couldn't identify him. No, he planned to kill both her and Trip. Trip, who'd just gotten his life back, and now this. He'd done nothing but pay for his mistakes, from the moment he'd refused to help Ruffle beat up that old man, and had given Emily's locket back. Her heart ached for him, above and beyond her fear for herself. And if she had any lingering doubts about how she felt about him, they were vanquished now.

She heard the sound of a vehicle approaching. Her head came up. Boyd's did, too.

"Well, well, looks like your boy really decided you're worth dying for," Boyd said as he slid off the bench. When he opened the door, she saw the front end of a large, dark blue SUV as it slowed to a halt just feet away. And she saw Trip in the driver's seat.

Worth dying for...

Every muscle she had squeezed tight at the thought. But then her brain kicked in. She knew that car. She'd seen it parked next to the helicopter at Foxworth. Her heart picked up the pace at the realization he wasn't alone. This wasn't going to be as simple as Ruffle's cousin thought it was going to be.

Her captor stepped out and slammed the door shut behind him, cutting off her view. She worked even harder at the tie, trying to ignore how much worse the pain was getting. If she could just get up on her knees, she might be able to see out the window. But then she froze because she heard Trip's voice. She'd been afraid she might never again.

"Looking scummy as always, Boyd." Odd, he sounded almost...arrogant. Something the Trip who had shown up on her doorstep two weeks ago hadn't been at all.

Boyd called him an obscene string of names, and ended by saying, "I never did believe you were really one of us."

"You're smarter than I thought you were."

For a moment Kayley wondered why Trip was insulting him, then realized it was to keep him on edge. Maybe he was hoping he'd get angry enough to make a mistake. She closed her eyes and prayed he'd noticed the weapon.

"You're the stupid one. Turning on my cousin like that."

"I didn't, not that he'd care once he made up that tiny mind of his." Boyd swore again, but Trip went on. "He needs to look closer to home. His new home, that is. The guy who rolled on him is under the same roof." Was that true? Had Foxworth found that out? "Now, get Kayley."

"You don't give the orders, Callen."

"I do if you want to tell Ruffle you've got me." He said it almost cockily, but then warmed her by adding, "And she'd better not be hurt, because if she is, you're going down."

Boyd let out another curse at the nickname, and Kayley almost smiled at how much even his cousin hated it. But then Boyd ended it with, "You make one wrong move and I'll grab you by that stupid hair of yours and slit your damned throat."

"You're not getting anywhere close until I see Kayley. I see her alive and well, and you walk away with the prize."

Belatedly it struck Kayley that what she was hearing was the Trip he'd had to become, to survive both in the world he'd been in, and the prison where he'd paid the price for that choice. That was the last thought she had time for, because Boyd suddenly yanked open the door he'd slammed shut. He stepped inside, and for a moment, past him, Kayley saw Trip's face. His expression was so full of relief at the sight of her that she realized he'd been afraid she might already be dead.

Boyd cut the zip tie that held her to the pipe, then dragged her roughly toward the door. She wobbled as she tried to get her feet under her. Winced as Boyd wrenched her arm, probably intentionally as he yanked her up straight. And then they were outside.

"All right, pretty boy, here she is," Boyd snapped. "Now, you're going to come over here all nice and po- lite, so I don't have to shoot you both."

Trip didn't answer. His head moved. He was look- ing toward the trees. Boyd's gaze followed. Kayley saw movement, but down low. And then a dog trotted out of the underbrush, casually, stopping to sniff here and there. Cutter. Looking as unthreatening as he possibly could.

"Guess your neighbors don't believe in leashes," Trip said, but he was looking right at her. Her mind started racing. Neighbors? Out here? They were pretending he was just a neighbor dog? But if Cutter was here, Rafe was here. Out of sight, hiding? But why— It hit her sud- denly and hard. Who Rafe was, and had been.

And Cutter kept coming, just an ordinary dog wander- ing, seemingly uninterested in them at all. Then, rather blandly, Trip added to Boyd in a mocking tone, "Unless you've gotten lonesome and wanted a doggie to snuggle up to at night."

Kayley was certain now this was an act for Boyd's benefit. Playing to his temper, keeping him off balance. And it worked; Boyd spun back and swore once again. Took a step toward Trip. In the process let go of her ach- ing arm.

"Cutter, now!"

The shout came from the trees. Cutter erupted into

motion. In a split second he went from ambling family dog to furious whirlwind. Snarling, he burst into a run toward Boyd. The man instinctively recoiled at the sight of the bared fangs. Trip launched. Boyd reached for the gun in the waistband of his jeans. Cutter got to him first, his jaws locking on Boyd's wrist. The man screamed. Trip was there, not waiting but scooping Kayley up into his arms. Boyd kicked at the dog. Trip spun, kept going, until they were safely behind the Foxworth vehicle. Boyd grabbed the gun with his free left hand. Fired a wild shot she wasn't sure he'd meant to. Cutter's snarls became fiercer. And then there was another, much louder shot. The window right behind Boyd shattered, pieces flying, enveloping him in an avalanche of broken glass. The man went to his knees, covering his head with his free arm.

"Next one's through your ear," came a voice from the trees.

A moment later Rafe was striding out, rifle still at the ready. Boyd looked from the dog whose jaws were still clamped on his arm to the approaching man. He caved. He dropped the gun, and practically blubbered, "Get him off me, get him off me!"

"Maybe," Rafe said. He went and kicked the gun Boyd had dropped out of reach. Then he walked over to them as the man on the ground continued to wail and beg, while Cutter hung on. Trip had pulled the gag off of her, and was cupping her face tenderly. "Kayley, you all right?" Rafe asked. Trip couldn't seem to speak now that it was over. But he took the knife Rafe pulled out of his pocket and handed to him, and cut her free.

"I will be," she managed to say despite the dryness of her mouth. "I've had some awful Mondays before, but this one's the topper."

Her slightly wobbly attempt at humor made Rafe smile, but Trip just held her tighter.

Rafe went to the rear of the SUV and came back with a case bearing a red cross on the lid. "For her wrists," Rafe said to Trip, who nodded. Then he looked over his shoulder; Boyd was practically in tears now. "Cutter, guard."

The dog released the man's arm, but the snarling didn't stop. As Rafe headed toward them, he stayed on his feet, his hackles up, his teeth bared. Boyd shuddered visibly and curled up on the ground, instinctively protecting his most vulnerable parts from the dog who had ambled in so calmly, then in an instant become a ferocious beast.

Trip was holding her against him, and she soaked up his warmth and his strength. Then he was apologizing, over and over, for bringing this down on her. She hushed him with a kiss, albeit a light one, because her mouth was hurting. Once Trip realized this, and pulled back enough to see her swollen cheek, her bloody wrists, his gaze shifted to Boyd and went dark.

Then Rafe crouched beside the cowed man. Kayley stopped Trip from going himself with a hand on his arm, knowing the last thing he needed now was to end up arrested for killing that vermin.

They could hear Rafe clearly from here, and Kayley thought she'd never heard anything scarier, except maybe Cutter's attack growl. Kayley wondered what it was in the human psyche that made an animal attack one of the most frightening things imaginable.

"You've got a choice, Ruff. You're going down for kidnapping, assault, extortion, and who knows what else. Unless you decide to do something stupid and die right here and now."

"Just k-keep the dog off me."

"Maybe," Rafe said again. "Callen didn't turn on your

cousin to get sent to minimum security. He earned it by returning some stolen property. A locket your cousin didn't want anyway. He should remember that, so tell him. We'll arrange the call. And tell him somebody else from your crew did roll. Guy named Max, who might just be in the same cell block, who's looking for an earlier shot at parole."

Boyd was staring at him now, and even from here Kayley could see he knew who Rafe was talking about.

"The price for that info, and for you staying alive to leave this nice, quiet place where it would be easier to just bury you, is you convincing your cousin of the truth. You write him a nice and polite message—" Kayley saw the man wince as Rafe quoted the exact words he'd used on Trip "—and we'll see he gets it. If he believes you and backs off Trip Callen and you or any of his crew never so much as breathe the same air as Kayley McSwain again, you'll live until you do yourself in with some other stupid move." Rafe's voice went so cold Kayley thought she could feel the chill from here, three feet away. "If you don't convince him, then you'll be dead long before you ever see a prison cell. I'll see to that personally."

Kayley shivered; it was hard to believe this was the same man she'd come to know. Even though she understood it was in part an act, there was a genuine threat in his manner and his voice, backed up with the obvious ability to carry it out, and she could see by the fear in Boyd's face that he believed it.

Trip's arms tightened around her. "I wouldn't want him mad at me," he whispered to her. "Or Cutter, for that matter."

She hugged him back as she watched Rafe pay Boyd back a little by using a similar zip tie to fasten his hands tightly behind him. Then she heard a tiny whine, and noticed Cutter was shifting his paws restlessly.

Even as she saw it, Rafe told the dog, "Stand down, buddy. Good job."

Instantly the dog's entire demeanor changed, and he became the Cutter she knew again. He turned to look at them, and Rafe smiled slightly as he said, "Go. I know you're worried."

The dog spun around and darted at them, head and tail up, no trace of the fierce warrior showing now. There was something in those amber-flecked dark eyes she could only call happiness. She dropped down to greet the dog, and heedless of her wrists threw her arms around him. Trip crouched beside her, bracing her as he stroked the dog's dark head.

"Thanks, buddy. I'll never underestimate you again," he whispered, sounding a little shaky. Just as she felt.

Because it was over. The nightmare was finally over.

Chapter Thirty-Eight

Trip looked at the man sitting across from him in the main room at Foxworth headquarters. The detective had arrived at the scene at the yellow building on Monday and pretty much taken charge. And Trip had actually smiled when he'd heard the man murmur, "Yellow. How appropriate." Who'd have ever thought he'd have something in common with a cop?

There had been a massive amount of paperwork and interviewing to be done. Just the thought of talking to so many LEOs made him nervous, but he'd been treated with respect by them all. One of them, the deputy who had been the first uniform to arrive, had looked at him assessingly, and Trip had braced himself for what he'd thought was inevitable. But instead he'd gotten only a nod.

"Dunbar says you're good," was all he'd said, and Trip knew it was a measure of the respect the man held among his colleagues.

By now, Friday, Trip's face muscles were actually getting used to smiling. Because he'd spent a lot of that time with Kayley. She had wanted him to come back to her place, but Rafe had recommended he stay here until they were sure Ruffle had shifted his focus, and he wasn't about to cross the man after all he and Foxworth had done. Or risk Kayley on the chance Ruffle clung to his stupid idea.

Rafe walked in from the kitchen and handed Brett a steaming mug. It was raining again, fairly hard, attested to by the man's wet hair. Even Cutter hadn't been inclined to stay outside long. But then, the dog had been lolling about ever since the day he'd handled Boyd, much less animated than he had been.

"He knows his job's almost done," Rafe had said wryly when Trip mentioned it.

"Almost?"

Rafe had shrugged. "You'll see."

But now he sat down, and simply waited.

"Kayley?" Brett asked.

"She should be here any second," Trip said. "She had a video appointment with a client this morning."

He didn't mention that up until then she'd been here, and had left him very pleasantly exhausted after an impossibly sweet night of intimacy to add to his hoard of most treasured memories. A hoard that was growing every moment he spent with her. And he refused, for now at least, to let the fact creep in that he still had nothing to offer her, and no idea what he was going to do with the rest of his life. Right now he was too busy loving her and celebrating that he still had the rest of his life.

"We'll wait, then. She should hear this—"

Brett stopped when Cutter abruptly got to his feet, his ears cocked toward the door. The dog let out a happy bark and trotted that way.

"Guess she's here," Trip said, and got up to follow him.

Cutter had opened the door for her, and she bent to pet the dog before straightening to greet Trip. Despite the fact that it had been barely two hours, he wanted to pull her into a fierce hug and never let go. He settled for pushing back the hood of her coat and letting his hands cup her face. Then he helped her get the wet garment off and hung it on the rack inside the door.

The two other men stood as she came in, without comment, but as a matter of course. She smiled at them, then took the seat Trip urged her toward, closest to the warmth of the fire after she'd been out in the wet chill. As she sat, Trip saw Cutter staring at him, as if he were ready to act if necessary. Trip gave the dog a crooked grin.

"Don't bother," he told the dog, and sat down where Cutter had always herded him to before, right next to Kayley. With a satisfied whuff the dog trotted over to his bed before the fire and resumed his lolling. Trip couldn't miss Rafe and Brett exchanging amused glances, but he didn't care. Kayley was here, beside him, and right now that was all that mattered. Except for whatever news the detective had come to give them.

"Cut to the chase?" Brett suggested.

"Please," Trip said, heartfelt.

"Ruffle is in solitary, after an attack on another inmate early this morning."

"Max?" Trip asked, sitting up straighter.

"Yes. Apparently this was the first chance he'd had at him. And he was heard to accuse him of being a traitor. To him, personally."

"It worked!" Kayley exclaimed.

"It appears so." Brett's mouth quirked. "And it seems Ruffle has been a big enough pain in the backside that the staff was almost happy about a fight that would normally annoy them."

Trip couldn't help smiling at that.

"Also, word on the street is that the hit on you is recalled. Ruff knows Foxworth is with you now, so I don't think they'll try again. And he knows how rough his life will get inside if he goes after you again, as a witness. I think you're both safe now."

Trip let out a long, relieved breath and tightened his arm around Kayley. She smiled widely up at him, and he smiled back. But it faltered a little when Brett spoke again, as if in warning.

"There's a long process ahead for you, both of you. Boyd Ruff's trial, your testimony. The defense will go after you, and your record, hard, Trip."

He'd known that. Expected it. Dreaded it. But he'd get through it, as long as he had Kayley. Again he fought down the doubts about the future. He only said, "I know they will."

Brett nodded, smiling himself now. "After the way you charged Ruff to get to Kayley, I think you'll stand up to it okay."

"That was thanks to Cutter, and Rafe," he said, insisting on the truth. And as if Brett knew that, he nodded approvingly.

"He'll have Foxworth help," Rafe said.

"All you need," Brett said, and the three simple words pounded home to Trip just how lucky he'd been. And he owed it all—hell, he owed everything—to Kayley.

They spent the weekend together back under her roof, Trip just reveling in the lifting of that heavy, life-threatening load and being with her. But he gradually started to feel the pressure of a new load, and by Sunday afternoon it was no longer just hovering. It had landed. Heavily. It was the simple fact that something very basic still hadn't changed. He had nothing to offer Kayley.

"Trip?"

She sat down beside him on her couch, the couch he'd slept on that first night. She didn't need Cutter at this point to urge her into that spot; she always took it. Which made Trip ache inside, now that he was finally facing the reality of his life. They had one more thing to do today—another meeting with the Foxworths, who had returned from St. Louis yesterday—and then it was truly over. And he'd be face-to-face with the bleakness of his future.

"What's wrong?"

"Nothing."

"Don't fib. You look worried. You shouldn't. It's over. You're safe. We're both safe now."

"I…yes."

"Then what's bothering you?"

He drew in a breath, long and painful. "Us," he said, all he could get out.

She drew back sharply. "What's wrong with us? I love you and—" She broke off suddenly. He saw color rise in her cheeks. "You've never said it," she whispered. "Does that mean you don't—"

"I don't have any right to say it," he said, knowing he sounded almost desperate. "Kayley, I still have nothing to offer you, no kind of life. I have no job, and not much hope of finding someone who will hire me. I…" He stopped because she was shaking her head.

"But do you? Love me, I mean?"

"Of course I do! You have to know that. But—"

"I'll know it when you say it."

She wanted the words. She deserved the words. He'd thought he was doing the right thing by holding it back, because he had nothing to give, but he couldn't bear her distress.

"I love you, Kayley McSwain. More than anyone, or anything. More than I thought myself capable of."

The smile she gave him then blew everything else right out of his mind. "All right, then," she said, as if all was settled.

"But—"

She put a finger to his lips. "But nothing. We'll work it out, Trip. We beat Ruffle at his game. We helped put Boyd in jail. This is nothing."

When she put it that way, it sounded reasonable. But that had all been with Foxworth help, which was ending today, after what he supposed would be a final summation, or however Foxworth dealt with the end of the cases they handled. But Kayley wanted to hear none of that, and pointed out it was almost time to leave.

When they stood on the doorstep of the Foxworth home, Trip was caught off guard when he heard Cutter's happy bark from inside. He'd gotten so used to the dog being where he'd been, at their headquarters, he hadn't really thought about him being back home with his owners now. Although he wasn't quite sure who owned who anymore. And he had the feeling Hayley, who answered the door with a smile as delighted as the dog had sounded, knew it and didn't care.

He'd seen Rafe's car, the deceptively nondescript silver coupe that purred like a big cat, betraying the man's mechanical expertise, so he wasn't surprised when he saw him inside. He was talking with another man, who Trip supposed owned the other, much sleeker black vehicle in the driveway.

That other man turned to look at them. He appeared lean, yet moved in that way Trip had learned inside meant not to underestimate his strength. His dark hair was thick and a bit long, and his eyes dark, so dark they almost appeared black. But above all he had presence, that kind of charisma that was almost a tangible, physical thing. This was the guy who owned the room the moment he walked in.

Trip's eyes widened as he suddenly recognized the

man he'd seen news photos and videos of, and that Ruffle had once joked about hiring.

Gavin de Marco.

Rafe hadn't been kidding before when he'd said the world-famous attorney worked with Foxworth now. Even Kayley was impressed, he could tell.

And the man was good. If Trip hadn't spent enough time inside to be aware of physical maneuvering, he might not have realized so quickly that he'd been isolated and ended up face-to-face with the man. And questioned. What might have passed for casual, getting-to-know-you talk about any and everything from anyone else seemed like a questioning from this guy. And while he'd vowed no more lies, ever, Trip doubted he would have been able to lie anyway, not to this man.

He felt relieved when it apparently ended. They walked over to where Rafe was talking to Quinn.

"Charlie knows that," Quinn was saying. "What she doesn't understand is why—" The Foxworth boss stopped midsentence when he saw them. Trip noticed Rafe seemed almost relieved.

"I'll leave you to it," Rafe said rather gruffly, and walked away.

Quinn seemed to suppress a grimace, but then looked at de Marco, who nodded slightly. He'd been assessed, Trip was certain. For what, he had no idea. A little late for Foxworth to be worried about whether they should have helped him in the first place.

"Hayley?" Quinn called to his wife, who was over with Kayley near the kitchen. "Ready?"

"Absolutely," she said cheerfully. "The comedy team of Kayley and Hayley will be right there."

Trip couldn't help smiling at that. When Quinn gestured him down a short hallway, he went, curious now as to how exactly this would go. Maybe they wanted a statement from him, or a recommendation or review or something. Not that his would be worth much. But he'd be more than willing to give it; they'd flat-out saved his life, and more importantly kept Kayley safe.

Quinn opened a door into a spacious room that was clearly a home office, with a large, two-person-facing desk, shelves and filing cabinets, and a couple of extra chairs. De Marco took a position leaning against the desk, as Quinn gestured them into the guest chairs and took one of the desk chairs. Hayley stayed on her feet, looking a little keyed up. Cutter had followed them, and took up a position beside the two-person desk, which Trip had a suspicion was his usual position when his people were in here.

"All yours," Quinn said to his wife.

Hayley grabbed the desk chair he presumed was hers, pulled it forward, and sat, right in front of Trip.

"You," she said rather fervently, "are the answer to a problem I've had for a while."

Trip blinked. "I am?" He didn't really care what it was. If he could help her, he would. After what they'd done, he owed them anything they wanted, short of murder. Maybe.

"I've been working on this idea for a long time—ever since I met Emily, in fact—but the pieces just wouldn't come together."

"Emily…" he murmured. The locket girl. So this was…specific to him?

"Yes. She mentioned, that first time we met, how she always hoped she'd be able to thank you."

"She did." And beautifully. His throat tightened a little at the memory.

"I know." Hayley smiled. "Emily and I have talked

about how hard it is for people who really are good people but make a mistake that lands them with a prison record."

"Or several mistakes," he said sourly.

"Yes," Hayley said, and for some reason he liked that she didn't deny that. "But with understandable reasons. Abuse, as you had, or desperation, as your friend Robert had."

He smiled slightly, remembering his talk with Robber the day after it had all gone down, thanking him for the warning that had in essence saved both him and Kayley. And felt a kernel of warmth blossom inside as he remembered Kayley's vehement promise that they would help him when he got out. He wasn't sure how much help he himself could be, but having Kayley in your corner would help anyone.

"What I've wanted to do," Hayley went on, "is set up an operation to help people like you, and your friend. First I needed a location, which I couldn't quite decide on. But we recently acquired a building in the next town over that I think will work nicely."

"Oh!" Kayley exclaimed. "The whistleblower case! You mentioned you'd ended up with a building out of that."

Hayley grinned. "We did." She looked back at Trip, who was still feeling a bit lost. "I know there are government agencies that supposedly help, but they're limited in what they can do, and sadly, in efficiency."

Ain't that the truth, Trip thought.

But he said nothing as Hayley finished firmly, "We're not."

"If you want me to…make suggestions, I'd be happy to. Don't know how much they'd be worth, but—"

"I don't want suggestions," Hayley said. "I want you to run it."

Trip stared at her. He couldn't have heard that right. But she barreled on.

"You're the last piece, Trip. I hadn't yet found anyone I trust to run it, and I didn't have the time or the knowledge to do it myself. But I trust you. It's a perfect fit. You'll be taken seriously by those referred to us because of your past, and you'll have Foxworth behind you, so you'll start with a certain amount of respect."

"It won't be a regular kind of job," Quinn put in. "The hours may be crazy, as needed. You'll have to use the instincts you learned in prison to vet the people coming in—although we'll get you some help with that—and you'll have to be very aware of not upsetting the surrounding community."

"You can't really...want me." He could hear the disbelief in his own voice.

"Hush," Kayley said, sounding utterly delighted. Then, to Hayley, she said, "You need a website, and brochures, with his bio on everything. His history will resonate with people coming back to the world, and the locket story will convert anybody who doubts he's for real, now that he's who he never had the chance to be."

"Exactly what I was thinking," Hayley said, her smile even wider.

"You or I better write it," Kayley went on. "The guys won't pull the right heartstrings."

Hayley looked as if she was ready to start right now. "Maybe we should do it together."

Trip was shifting his stunned gaze from woman to woman, speechless. He glanced at Quinn, who was grinning. Even de Marco had a smile playing around his lips, and he guessed the man usually didn't betray much.

"You're serious?" he said when he could remember how to speak. "You're all serious?"

"I wouldn't agree to the exorbitant salary she wants to pay you if I wasn't serious," Quinn drawled, picking up a couple of stapled pages and handing them to him.

It was an employment contract, with Foxworth. And Quinn had obviously been joking, but the salary was indeed exorbitant, to his eyes. He sat there, staring unseeingly at the pages in his hand. It didn't seem possible. He couldn't believe it. Wasn't sure he should. His head was almost spinning. He couldn't even think.

And then Cutter was there, resting his head on his knee. Remembering the comfort the dog had always given, he put a hand on the dark fur. Felt it again, that soothing. Kayley took his other hand and held it tightly. Suddenly his world righted itself, and he realized what this really was.

He looked up into Kayley's loving blue eyes. And saw the future he'd never expected to have.

Not just a future, but someone to share it with.

Someone he loved more than he could express.

"Welcome home, Trip," she whispered. "At last, truly welcome home."

He swallowed hard. "I was home the moment you opened that door and I saw your eyes again. I love you, Kayley."

"I know," she said, a tiny bit of impishness in her smile.

And Cutter made a small, throaty sound that somehow sounded like satisfaction. Or maybe it was *about time!*

At this point, Trip would have believed anything.

Epilogue

Trip looked up as the door to his office opened. One of the volunteers, a kid working for school credit, stuck his head in.

"Somebody else here asking for you," he said.

Trip got up. He'd already had the pleasant surprise of Mrs. Larson stopping by. The teacher who had shared that bus ride with him, had given him the lift to Kayley's place, had been smiling as if she'd always known it would all work out for him.

He walked out into the main room of Fresh Start Northwest. He wasn't worried. Foxworth had installed state-of-the-art security, and he had a little training under his belt now, but they'd never had an issue in the four months since they'd officially opened. It had been a slow start, but they were building a reputation solid enough that, paired with the Foxworth name and backing, they were convincing local employers to take chances on people they might not ordinarily. That Foxworth put their money where their mouth was meant a lot around here.

He saw the man the moment he stepped into the waiting area. And by the time the newcomer looked up and saw him, Trip was grinning.

"Been waiting for you," he said.

Robber smiled back widely. As he should, out three

months early, earned by pulling Touchy off the day he'd gone after Moreland.

They practically collided, and Trip figured a bear hug was in order, he was so glad to see the guy who'd helped him survive. Robber—no, Robert now, he reminded himself—apparently felt the same and pounded him on the back in greeting.

"I hear Ruff and the real turncoat are seps now," Robert said, referring to the practice of keeping two codefendant inmates housed in the same prison in separate units, because one had ratted out the other.

"We call him Ruffle around here," Trip said with a grin, and was rewarded with a laugh.

"You," his old friend said, looking around, "really run this place?"

"Hard to believe, huh? I've got help, though."

"Any of that help have a pair of pretty blue eyes?"

His grin widened. "You mean my wife? She does have a set of skills uniquely suited to the mission," he said. It was true, and Kayley had been helping.

"Listen to you, talking like some CEO or something." Robert looked around. "I guess that's what you are."

"I've even got an office. With coffee. Come on in."

They went in, but Robert stopped and took a step back to look at the door. Trip guessed what he was staring at by the way his brow furrowed. He shifted his gaze back to Trip.

"I did it legally when we got married," he said quietly.

"Good for you," Robert said, just as quietly. "He doesn't deserve to have you as a namesake."

Trip knew in that moment that the idea he'd had, and broached to the Foxworths, was a good one. For everyone concerned.

"Come in and sit down," he said. "I need to talk to you about the fact that I need more help here."

"More help?"

"Yeah. I need somebody like you."

His old fellow inmate's eyes widened. And Trip thought seeing that dawning of hope in someone's eyes, and knowing he'd done it, made it all worth it. He'd explained to Kayley's parents on the day they'd told them they were engaged that if he put it completely behind him, it would have been for nothing. That he had to remember the lessons he'd learned. They'd understood, as they seemed to understand it all. Especially the appeal he'd humbly made to them later. They were everything she'd promised they were, and they welcomed him more than he thought he had any right to expect. And gave their full assent to his request.

Ready to make the job offer to his old friend, he was smiling again as he pulled the door closed behind them.

The door with the nameplate that read Trip McSwain.

* * * * *

LET'S TALK

Romance

For exclusive extracts, competitions
and special offers, find us online:

- facebook.com/millsandboon
- @MillsandBoon
- @MillsandBoonUK

Get in touch on 01413 063232

For all the latest titles coming soon, visit
millsandboon.co.uk/nextmonth

MILLS & BOON
A ROMANCE FOR EVERY READER

- **FREE** delivery direct to your door

- **EXCLUSIVE** offers every month

- **SAVE** up to 25% on pre-paid subscriptions

SUBSCRIBE AND SAVE

millsandboon.co.uk/Subscribe

JOIN US ON SOCIAL MEDIA!

Stay up to date with our latest releases, author news and gossip, special offers and discounts, and all the behind-the-scenes action from Mills & Boon...

 @millsandboon

 @millsandboonuk

 facebook.com/millsandboon

 @millsandboonuk

It might just be true love...

GET YOUR ROMANCE FIX!

Get the latest romance news, exclusive author interviews, story extracts and much more!

blog.millsandboon.co.uk

MILLS & BOON

MODERN

Power and Passion

Prepare to be swept off your feet by sophisticated, sexy and seductive heroes, in some of the world's most glamourous and romantic locations, where power and passion collide.

MILLS & BOON
MEDICAL
Pulse-Racing Passion

Set your pulse racing with dedicated,
delectable doctors in the high-pressure
world of medicine, where emotions run
high and passion, comfort and love are the
best medicine.

MILLS & BOON
True Love

Romance from the Heart

Celebrate true love with tender stories of heartfelt romance, from the rush of falling in love to the joy a new baby can bring, and a focus on the emotional heart of a relationship.